CROSSING LINES

A NOVEL

BY

WARREN DRIGGS

Published by
Paradise Rim Books
Salt Lake City, UT

ISBN: 978-0-9987795-8-4 (Paperback)
eISBN: 978-0-9987795-9-1 (eBook)

Book Design by GKS Creative, Nashville

Library of Congress Information is on file with the Publisher.

Also by Warren Driggs

A Tortoise in the Road
Mormon Boy
Swimming in Deep Water
Old Scratch

PROLOGUE

IT WAS A HANDWRINGING PREDICAMENT when Katherine got pregnant in high school. Then again, maybe she didn't get pregnant after all. It could have gone either way, you know—the plot between her philandering egg and her boyfriend's promiscuous sperm could have just as easily been foiled, or at least thickened in a cruel twist of fate.

Katherine, who sometimes went by Kate, had wheat-colored hair, long legs, and high cheekbones. She knew she was pretty, gorgeous actually, but was dogged by insecurities like most girls in her Dixie High School class of 1980. There was that dainty little bump on her nose (that her parents claimed they couldn't see) and she insisted she was too flat. She wanted breasts like the ones her friend Sandra pompously lugged around. But Sandra tended to be pudgy and always sat with her tippy toes on the floor so her thighs wouldn't be squished flat by the seat, and Katherine didn't want that.

Katherine was popular at school, pretty as she was, but she wasn't obnoxious about it like other girls in the in-crowd. Take her friends Sandra and Lisa, for example. They treated the school hallways like fashion-show runways and whenever they stood still it was hard to escape the suspicion that they were posing. The girls were competitive with each other but at least Katherine had voted for Janet when she'd run for Student Body Secretary. Sandra had even come up with Janet's campaign slogan: *Don't Whistle Dixie—Vote for Janet!* But she and Lisa had voted for the other girl and then disguised their relief when Janet lost. "I can't believe it, Janet. Everybody I know voted for you. Gol, Michelle isn't even that popular."

The teenage girls attended the same church every Sunday where the drumbeat of chastity thumped, and thumped. This preoccupation with sex, and specifically its brazen wickedness, was stressed well beyond anything that happened to be mentioned in the Sermon on the Mount. Sex was taboo, the ultimate no-no, but surely not the discussion of it, for it was awkwardly discussed in church from the first fledgling sign of a hormone.

The girls now sat on folding metal chairs in their weekly Sunday school class, a lovely picture of Jesus on the wall. Jesus was tall and ruggedly handsome with blue eyes, gleaming white teeth, and blond highlights in his brown wavy locks—the sort of action movie star you might see on a poster near the theatre marquee. The girls looked down, inspecting their nails and picking lint from their modest dresses as their Sunday school teacher reminded them, again, that their bodies were temples and must be kept clean until they were married. Katherine squirmed on her chair. How awkward was this, listening to their dowdy teacher trying to talk about sex? This was a conversation to be having at their gym lockers or at the mall. And what could this woman have known about sex anyway when she was nearly fifty? Katherine wondered if she even did it anymore. Highly doubtful.

"I think Sandra and Eric are doing it," Katherine whispered to Janet as they left the class following a stark reminder that if they lost their virginity they'd be like a stick of chewed gum. "I came right out and asked her and she's all, like, 'Well, Eric's really pushy about it.' And I'm all, like, 'so are you?' And she's all quiet about it."

"Well," said Janet, "all I can say is Eric's a complete jerk for forcing her into it."

"Maybe she doesn't think it's that bad," said Katherine.

"Are you being serious right now? Of course she does. It's one of the worst sins you can commit. Everybody knows that." Janet was a stickler about these things and refused to soil her temple until she had officially declared her I Do's.

"What about you and Keith?" asked Janet.

Katherine had been dating Keith Murphy for six months, a boy who would have eagerly smeared dirt all over his temple from head to toe. He was average looking, at best, and it was something of a surprise that Katherine fell for him in the first place when she could have commanded the pick of the litter. (He *was* the captain of the football team, however, so at least there was that.) His stringy brown hair hung long in the back, mullet style, and his teeth were small squares, leaving extra space between each tooth as if there hadn't been enough of them to go around. Katherine's friends whispered that he looked like a carved pumpkin. Others said he could floss with a belt.

"I'm telling you it's not worth it," said Janet even though she had no idea if it was worth it or not. She was an ordinary looking girl who'd been christened with an underbite which caused her lower jaw to stick out like a slightly opened drawer and because the boys didn't drool over her with eager intent she demanded that Katherine share her unblemished commitment to virginity. "You have to draw your line and stick to it. You draw that danged line in stone and never cross it. That's what I do." Janet had, in fact, drawn her line with impeccable righteousness but unfortunately, despite her private longing, no boy had seen fit to approach it.

"I know it's not worth it," said Katherine. "And Keith doesn't want to rush me."

This was simply not true. He desperately wanted to rush her, for this had been his top priority guided entirely by the radar of his loins.

"All I know is that guys only want one thing and I just don't want you to get hurt."

One night a few weeks before high school graduation, Katherine crept in past her strict curfew. Her blouse was untucked and her hair stuck up like the whiskered seeds of a dandelion as she tip-toed down the hall to the bedroom she shared with her younger sisters. She was holding her breath as she passed the gallery of family photos hung in cheap oak frames along one entire wall of the hallway. A few of the photos were crooked as if they'd been bumped by a shoulder or a thrown ball, even though her mother had helplessly insisted no balls were allowed in the house. Her father had been seated in the center of each family photo with her mother at his side while the children in their Sunday best stood orbiting his head like a crown.

She had nearly made it to her room when the lamp on her parent's bedside table turned on.

"Katherine? Katherine honey, is that you?"

"Yeah, sorry," she whispered as she poked her head into her parent's bedroom. "I didn't want to wake you up."

"You know we can't sleep when you're out. What time is it anyway?" her mother asked as she squinted at the clock on the nightstand. "Why, it's nearly midnight! Where on earth have you been young lady? You know your father needs his sleep."

"Um, nowhere. Keith and I were just talking."

Her mother had pulled the bedsheet up to her chin in a fit of modesty. "I'll not have you out this late. And I don't like that Murphy boy. I'm sorry, but I just don't." Her face was covered with cold cream and a hairnet trapped her sponge curlers. She looked dreadful. "You shouldn't be dating boys who aren't active in the church. It's not right. He has different values than you do."

"But Mom, no he doesn't. He has normal values just like us."

"Listen to your mother," said her father from the other side of the bed. "He doesn't have your upbringing and I don't want you spending time with him. Have I made myself clear?" This was a direct commandment from her authoritative father and she had neither the nerve nor the necessary disrespect to outwardly disobey him.

Katherine was the oldest daughter of Dale and Jackie Coombs, stalwart members of their Mormon community in St. George, a small desert town in southern Utah where The Church was as prominent as the red sandstone cliffs that surround it. Simply put, the church ran the show. Dale was an insurance claims adjuster (and appeared to have the ideal temperament for it) and Jackie was a full-time homemaker, a virtual necessity because they had eight children.

Dale loved his children but seldom showed them affection (and it was awkward when he tried—and he did try), and he was rarely sentimental, unless he became choked up over a passage of scripture. He wore a crew cut, his posture was erect, and he'd rarely been seen with his shirt untucked.

Dale was also the bishop of their local Mormon congregation and lorded over his neighborhood flock with righteous fealty, constantly on the prowl to stamp out sin. His stern countenance made him look older than he actually was and the deep furrows in his forehead made it hard to imagine he had ever been young or carefree. Dale was not known for his nuance—there was right and there was wrong. He was gruff, patriarchal, and sexist to a fault. Of course, he didn't consider his sexism to be a fault at all because the world was spinning in the wrong direction, what with all this focus on equality. It was time to batten down the hatches and return to the days when people generally knew their place.

Katherine's mother, Jackie, who was commonly known around the conservative neighborhood as Sister Dale Coombs, was plump, having labored through a combined twenty-four trimesters since she was nineteen years old. It was unclear whether she enjoyed being referred to as Sister Dale Coombs instead of, say, Jackie Coombs, because no one thought to ask her. But, as it turned out, her entire given name had been erased and replaced by her husband's. The Coombs's wanted even more children but the Good Lord had seen fit to award them just the eight.

Katherine had been horrified as an adolescent when she'd put two and two together. Her parents had done it *eight times?* That her parents would actually do such a thing (and eight times no less) was both appalling and unimaginable. Surely any sexual thoughts her parents may have once had had long since expired. At least Katherine hoped so. Therefore, she'd about *died* when her mom awkwardly broached the subject of birds and bees shortly after Katherine had her first period. She'd sat with one child-bearing hip on the edge of Katherine's bed and said something about how boys were like little factories and sometimes needed to blow off some steam. "I'm sorry to be so frank," she'd said.

Katherine learned more about sex from her girlfriends who doled out The Facts between bites of French fries. "You can't get pregnant if you do it when you're having your period," said Sandra. "Eww, that's disgusting," said Janet while the rest of them privately contemplated just how disgusting it might be. "Did you guys see Brad when he got hit in the balls during the Snow Canyon game? I bet it kills when that happens," said Sandra. "Brad's so cute, I'd kiss them better," said Lisa, shocked at her own audacity. The others looked at her wide-eyed. *"Li-sa!"* Sandra dipped a fry in ketchup. "My big sister said it hurts the first time."

Katherine had resisted, she had, but her line had been too thinly drawn by the time she and Keith found themselves in the backseat of his mother's burgundy station wagon following the high school graduation dance. Keith's powder-blue tuxedo was an inside-out wad on the floorboard and his cummerbund was tangled around his shins.

"No, Keith, we can't," she whispered.

"I know, I know. I won't really put it in—maybe just barely."

The line had now been blown to smithereens, right there on the rear vinyl seat. Maybe they could do it, a little bit, just this once.

It was over as quickly as it started.

1

KATHERINE

I COULDN'T BELIEVE I'D JUST HAD SEX. I mean, it's not like I'd *planned* it—it just sort of happened. Besides, I wasn't going to be a nun forever. I tried to figure out how I felt about it on the ride home. I knew it was wrong, dead wrong, but I didn't get hit with a bolt of lightning or anything. I scooted over as close as I could to Keith on the bench seat of his mom's station wagon. Whenever I moved, it felt like I'd sprung a leak onto the vinyl seat. It sort of smelled and I worried my parents would smell it, too. Ugh, my parents. Hopefully, they'd be asleep, but my dad was a piece of work. He'd probably be waiting up for me like the Sex Police.

We parked in front of my house. It was almost two o'clock in the morning and I knew I was dead if my parents were awake. They always threw a fit about my curfew, even if I was only a few minutes late, like I'd been out on a crime spree or something. And yet the closest I'd come to committing an actual crime was when we toilet papered Sandra's house during a sleepover. I was not the criminal type.

"You can just let me out here in front," I said to Keith.

"Are you sure? I can walk you to the front door if you want."

"No, it's okay."

He asked me if everything was all right.

"Um, yeah, I'm good," I said. "Are you okay about it?"

"Yeah, for sure."

What I really wanted him to say was that he still loved me just as much, or maybe even more. My dad always said boys were only after one thing and when they got it, well then Adios Amiga ma'am. Of course, that's my dad for you, always trying to put a positive spin on things.

"Sorry I'm so uptight about it," I said. "I just want us to do the right thing."

He leaned over and kissed me but it seemed like he mostly did it to be nice, because he hadn't kissed me that same way *before* we did it, I can tell you that. I got out, closed the car door as quietly as I could, and walked down our gravel driveway. It doesn't seem as crunchy in the day but at night it makes a racket. My steps were so loud I thought I'd wake up the whole neighborhood. I passed my little brother's rusty red Radio Flyer on the lawn that was filled with about an inch of dirty water and a layer of decaying leaves. I opened the screen door as slowly as I could because I knew it squeaked. My dad had plenty of WD-40 but I think he left it squeaky on purpose because it was like a curfew alarm. Squeak. Violation!

I stepped into the dark living room and paused, listening. All was quiet, even our dog, Enos, could not be rustled awake so late at night. I didn't see my dad at first because my eyes hadn't adjusted to the dark. I'd hoped to make it to my room and get in bed so I could pretend I'd been there all along. But there he was, sitting on the sofa in the dark wearing only his sacred Mormon undergarments. They are like old fashioned one-piece long johns that come to your knees. I assumed I'd have to start wearing them once I turned twenty-one just like my mom and all the other adult women I knew. That meant I'd have to throw away my sleeveless shirts, dresses, and most of the shorts I wore. None of those clothes had been too skanky, of course, but they wouldn't cover my new sacred underwear.

I'd been told this special underwear protects us from danger and evil so we weren't supposed to remove them except to bathe. Some people claim they're magic underwear—that you won't get stabbed or burned to death if you're wearing them, but I'm not sure I believe it. What, the knife is just going to bend when it hits the cotton? And what if you get stabbed in the neck or somewhere that isn't covered by the underwear? I don't think those people who claimed they were magic had thought it all the way through.

"Where have you been, young lady?" I could tell he was mad—why else would he be waiting there in the dark at two o'clock in the morning?

"Oh, hi, Dad. You scared me. Sorry it's so late. We all went out after the dance and I didn't realize it was so late."

"Were you with that Murphy boy again?"

"Yeah, I went to the dance with him. Mom knows."

"You're spending too much time with him and I don't want you to think you can come and go anytime you want. As long as you're living under my roof you'll live by my rules."

"But, Dad, I'm not even in high school anymore. I'm almost eighteen and none of the other girls have—"

"I don't care about the other girls. I'm the bishop and I won't have my own daughter out all night doing heaven knows what with some boy who doesn't go to church and doesn't share our values."

"But, Dad, he does too share our values."

Just as I said this I felt another gob of Keith's values leak into my underpants. Geez, how much of that stuff *was* there? I stood as far away from my dad as I could. See, he's the bishop and all the kids in the neighborhood are supposed to confess their sins to him. The adults, too. They probably lie though, especially kids like Brian Hansen who was having sex all over the place.

"We'll talk more about this in the morning."

I had a restless night given all that had happened. For starters, I'd never seen a full grown penis before. There had been a boy in our neighborhood named Lyle who showed me his "thing" when we were about seven. Mind you, I hadn't asked to see it. This debut showing hadn't been as traumatizing as it might have been—as it *should* have been—because he tried to show his "thing" to just about anyone. He and his family moved away shortly after that and I presume he's still trying to show it to anyone who'll look at it. And, of course, I was also trying to process how I felt about losing my virginity—an inevitability but one I was not prepared for.

The next morning was Sunday and my mom and dad had come into my room to wake me up for church. They told my little sister Kristy, the annoying one, to leave so we could be alone. My mom sat at the foot of the bed and stared at my sheets with the sailboat print. I saw it register on her face that she'd mistakenly switched up the sheets with one of my little brothers' beds. Personally, I didn't care if my sheets had sailboats or princesses. Besides, this was no time to fret about sheet gender.

My dad stood over me, glaring. Here comes another lecture on staying out late—in those early morning hours when only Satan is still awake. I had it memorized but I didn't want to act like it because my dad was still mad and it felt like my lost virginity was plastered all over my face, plain as day.

"Katherine honey," my mom began, "boys at your age are nearly grown men."

"Uh-huh."

"And, you see, they have certain urges."

"Uh-huh." I would've rather been discussing my latest bowel movement.

"I don't want to embarrass you but you're old enough now to know these things. No good can come about in the middle of the night."

"Jackie," my dad interrupted as he held up his hand, "let me handle this." He obviously didn't like the way my mom was pussy-footing around. "That Murphy boy wants one thing and one thing only and he's probably not getting proper encouragement at home."

"But, Dad, you're not being—"

"Don't you 'but' me. I know what's going on with the youth these days. They don't realize how important it is to stay morally clean. But let me tell you something young lady, it *is* important. Now, is there anything you'd like to tell me?"

"Dale!" my mom interrupted, petrified that we were on the verge of a frank discussion about s-e-x and wanted to head it off at the pass. "I'm sorry, but I don't think this is the proper place and time."

My dad ignored her and stared me down. "Well, is there?"

"No, Dad! Gol. Keith and I are just dating. That's all."

"Well, I better not find out that he's trying to take advantage of you."

"Dad! He's not, okay? Gol. Give me some credit for once."

He gave me the Dad Stare for a few more seconds and then said: "It's time to get up. Church starts in an hour."

I decided I wouldn't breathe a word of my sin to anyone. Only God would know, and I hoped He'd consider the fact that I'd waited as long as I had. Which hadn't been easy, by the way.

I had to share a bathroom with just about everyone. Kimberly and Kristy were already in there, hogging it like they always did. It was worse on Sunday mornings too because everyone was trying to get ready for church at the same time. My baby sister, Karolyn, was howling in the background and my three brothers, Kenny, Korbin, and Kelly, were arguing over whether they had to wear a sport coat. Geez, weren't the clip-on ties dressy enough? They complained about the same thing every Sunday morning. "And Korbin," my dad said, "no bandanas or any of that other nonsense. Now get going." This warning was necessary because Korbin always wore a uniform, or part of a uniform.

You've probably noticed all the "K's." After my parents named me Katherine, they thought it'd be fun to keep it up with the K's all the way through. Personally, I thought it was sort of dumb, but that's my parents for you.

I'd have to say we were middle-class, or maybe a notch below that. My dad was an insurance adjuster and my mom stayed home all day. Plus there were all us kids to feed so you could do the math. Our house wasn't that big to begin with and that was even before Grandma Coombs moved in with us bringing her collections of S&H green stamps and small commemorative spoons. There were jars of Mentholatum and all the old coupons she'd saved. Even the kitchen had to make room for all the ketchup packets she'd swiped over the years. I figured this was a short term problem because my grandma was in her eighties and probably wouldn't make it much longer, especially given all her "spells." I didn't even know what a goiter was but I assumed it must have been a life-threatening ailment, and I didn't know anyone else with water on the knees. Then there was Enos, the aging dachshund we rescued from the animal shelter. His name became Enos after Kenny said he looked like a penis and my parents freaked out when Kelly started telling everyone our dog's name was Penis. No, my dad had said, "Kenny said *Enos*."

Anyway, I finally wedged into the bathroom that morning just in time for Kristy to annoy me.

"How's Kee-eeth?" she said in that irritating sing-song way after my parents left to do battle over the sport coats.

"Shut up," I said.

"Yeah, shut up," Kimberly told Kristy.

"Why don't *you* shut up?"

Kimberly looked at me and rolled her eyes to show she understood how it was to have a boyfriend. This was a hoot because Kimberly was just as annoying as Kristy.

We were running late for church (we were always running late) when we all crammed into the family station wagon with the faux wood siding, an embarrassing jalopy I wouldn't drive even if you paid me. My dad wore his shiny dark polyester suit over his white short-sleeved dress shirt. His too-wide tie was pinned to his shirt with a tie clasp. This was his Sunday uniform and he never deviated from it. He also wore it to work Monday through Friday. So Saturday was the only day he dressed down. And by dressing down, I mean he wore clothes you'd see at the local IFA—clothes a farmer who wasn't hip would wear. Meanwhile, my siblings were in the back seats touching and breathing on each other "on purpose!" Let's just say there wasn't a lot of Christian spirit packed in there.

"I called this spot."

"I was here first.

"Move your fat butt."

"Make me."

"You're dead meat when we get out."

"Mom, Kristy touched me!"

"Did not."

"Did too."

My dad flipped out by the time we got to Bluff Street, which was only about a block from our house. "Knock it off back there!"

"But he started it."

"You heard your father," my mom said. Her role was to preserve the peace, at least when my dad was around. I think she was more afraid of him than we were, which is saying a lot. My mom was the peacemaker and had learned over the years to talk to my dad in a soothing voice when he'd get wound up—sort of the way you'd talk to a toddler with a butcher knife in his hand.

We went to church every Sunday because we had to keep it holy. That meant no movies, shopping, swimming, or anything remotely fun. (Unless you'd count my little brothers climbing around the perimeter of the living room without touching the floor during their annoying Hot Lava Phase—from sofa to piano bench to end table to window sill.) The reason for this restriction was because God created the world in six days and needed to rest on the seventh day. I probably would have rather worked another day because church was three-hours long. Yeah, three hours.

Sunday school was boring, as always. The lesson this time was a reminder that we couldn't smoke or drink. Those are also big no-no's in our church—not nearly as wicked as premarital sex, but still pretty darned wicked. Throw coffee in there, too, which is on the list of banned substances. I assumed our Sunday school teacher knew nothing about smoking, drinking, or coffee either. Of course, I was no one to talk but I once took a few sips of coffee when I was over at Sandra's house. I thought it was nasty but I pretended it really hit the spot because I didn't want to look like a complete nerd.

"Sister Harding is such a prude," whispered Janet about our teacher. I guess it takes one to know one because Janet might have been the biggest prude I knew, although she once went through a short swearing phase to get in good with Sandra. That phase lasted about a week and then she went back to saying edgy things like "H-E-Double-Toothpick" which was about as spicy as she got.

"You okay?" she whispered again when I didn't respond.

"Yeah, why?" I was a bit distracted because it felt like I was holding a home-made poster advertising the milestone of my lost virginity.

"I don't know, you just seem sorta quiet."

Keith wasn't at church that day because, according to my dad, he had no morals. He finally called that afternoon and we met up that night for The Talk. This talk lasted about three minutes, max, and then Keith showed why my dad had probably been right all along. He basically said the damage had already been done so we might as well keep doing it. Very romantic. I told him we ought to wait, maybe not do it every time, you know.

"And what if I got pregnant?"

I thought I detected him flinch—a reality startle. Then he acted like he knew all about it even though his sole expertise on the subject came from the school maturation program where he and his eleven-year-old friends had tried not to giggle at all the penis and vagina talk.

I was no pregnancy expert either but at least I'd *thought* about it. In fact, I swear I felt my eggs getting thoroughly fertilized at that very moment. But, then again, it wouldn't happen on the very first time, right? Nevertheless, it was still enough to scare me into a renewed state of virginity because my dad would have killed Keith and me both, in one shot.

My virginity fast didn't last long because Keith had urgently purchased a supply of condoms at Erickson's Drug Store. He said he'd bought a *Sports Illustrated* to dilute the scandalous purchase because he'd been too chicken to march up to the checkout counter with just the condoms. So he'd plopped the condoms down on the conveyor belt as if they'd been a casual afterthought. "Oh, and I might as well get these, too."

It was the next night after his big purchase when he said, "Hey, um, I got us some rubbers so we don't need to worry about it anymore." I mean, you could just feel the romance in the air.

We went through the supply in a week. I could tell he hadn't practiced with one, which is understandable I suppose because he obviously didn't want to *waste* one. He'd finally ripped it open with his teeth and then rolled it up his You Know What the same way my grandma used to roll nylon stockings up her legs.

Don't get me wrong; I liked it, too. And since we'd already done it I hoped God would be lenient and punish me just once for The Sin. Then again, I had to acknowledge that each time we did it represented a fresh infraction. Repentance only works if you say you're sincerely sorry and then never repeat the sin again, otherwise your repentance is fake in God's eyes and it backfires.

I didn't tell a soul, not even Sandra who'd also done it with her boyfriend. I knew all about her sexual escapades because she'd eagerly told me about them. Actually, she pretended she didn't want me to know, but then made sure I did. And then there was Keith who bragged to his football buddies that we'd been doing it like clockwork ever since graduation night. I was embarrassed whenever I saw one of his friends because I figured they'd all pictured us doing it.

I still couldn't shake the fear that I might be pregnant even though we used condoms almost every time. Waiting for my period was the worst. I started to panic when I was three days late but I didn't tell anyone, not even Keith. After a week, I went to Erickson's Drugstore for my own awkward purchase: a home pregnancy test. I just about fainted on the spot when I saw Sister Ferguson in the store. I grabbed a can of Aqua Net hairspray and then roamed the aisle pretending to be torn over conditioners until she finally left. I then walked boldly to the checkout counter and paid for my contraband.

I hid the pregnancy kit in my purse until I got home and then locked myself in the bathroom. I sat on the shag-carpeted toilet seat, opened the box, and read the instructions about three times. I then took the strip out and put it on the sink next to the toilet. I needed a cup to pee in and I thought about using the one my little sisters used to rinse out their mouths after brushing their teeth because that's probably what they would've done to me. I didn't want to go back to the kitchen where my mom would have put me to work setting the table or stirring the ground beef for the Sloppy Joes. I finally found a Dixie cup in the cabinet under the sink, next to the plunger. I peed into the cup and then used the little dropper thing that comes with the kit to put three drops of pee onto the strip.

The instructions said to wait three to five minutes but I peeked after two. Still nothing. If there were two pink bands my life would be over. It didn't actually say that in the instructions but it might as well have. Please, just one pink band. Please, I beg you! I prayed hard, but then figured God would probably ignore me because I'd spit in His eye. But I did it anyway, just to be on the safe side.

I closed my eyes and waited two more minutes and looked again. Two bright pink bands.

I was pregnant.

2

KATE

SOMETIMES I GO BY KATE just to be a bit rebellious. I suppose there's nothing inherently rebellious about the name Kate, which seems like a perfectly reasonable nickname for Katherine, but even though it still starts with a K my parents didn't like it very much. I'm not sure why.

Anyway, the morning after my high school graduation I woke up to my mom's hand on my shoulder. She was sitting on the edge of my bed and my dad was looming over her. I knew it was because they'd somehow figured out that I'd had sex the night before, how I don't know. My mom was saying something about how boys were like little factories and have these urges, and that no good can come about in the middle of the night because that's when Satan pulled his shenanigans. Then my dad interrupted her and asked me, point blank, if there was anything I needed to confess. Ugh, it was so humiliating and I thought I was going to die.

I didn't argue about going to church that day. In fact, I acted like I really wanted to sit for three freaking hours in church because I didn't want to arouse any suspicion that I was now officially wayward. I even waited patiently for my turn to use the community bathroom I shared with my sisters. When I think back on it, *that's* what should have aroused suspicion right there because I wasn't very patient with my little sisters, I'll admit that.

We used to divvy up the three bathrooms in our house but then my grandma moved in with us and got her own. We probably could have shared with her but I took a big fat pass on that one. I didn't want to be brushing my teeth next to her dentures floating in a cup. Her face looked like a prune and when she removed her teeth her cheeks were sucked into her mouth. She also had a lot of bowel issues so I figured out of sight, out of mind.

I loved my grandma but she was old and crotchety, especially toward my mom. She thought my dad could do no wrong and my mom could do no right. She even blamed my mom when *she* was the one who'd tried to back our station wagon out of the garage and dented the driver-side door. The entire time that my dad was out in the driveway crouched down near the side of the car trying to suck the dent out with a toilet plunger, my grandma was standing there in her house dress and slippers with her hands on her hips, happily blaming my mom for the dent because my mom hadn't forewarned her that it was a tight squeeze.

The Sunday school lesson that week was on not smoking and drinking, which was chicken feed compared to having premarital sex. If having premarital sex was a 9.5 on a scale of 1-10, which it surely was, then I'd say drinking booze and coffee was about a 6.

As the weeks passed, I was petrified that I might be pregnant. I didn't think I was because we'd only done it, like, maybe twice without a condom. But you never know. I'd heard all kinds of stories about how you barely needed to do it, so I was worried. I'd even heard rumors that the stuff might leak into the jackpot through your jeans.

I didn't know what I was going to do with my life now that I'd graduated from high school. My parents hadn't gone to college and didn't expect me to go either because I was a girl. They didn't exactly say it like that (well, actually they did), but there was no way they were going to pay for it. I figured I'd get a girl-job as a secretary or receptionist until I got married. Girls got married early in my town to get a jump on having kids. In fact, my entire Sunday school class would probably be married by the time we were twenty-one-years old—even Laura B. who wore headgear until she was eighteen. You hit twenty-five and the rumors start to fly that you just might be a lesbian (which would be in the 9 range on the scale).

So, yeah, college probably wasn't in the cards, but the gender rip-off didn't end there. It trickled down to about everything. Girls weren't honored with special religious privileges in our church like the boys were. We didn't get to play on the ward basketball team or go on all the scout trips like the boys did either. They told us we were extra special because we were girls and had our own game. But the ante to get into *that* game was small—you only had to be a girl.

I was always taught that God was a male, so boys got a break right out of the chute, being God's budding clones and all. I never heard squat about a female Creator which seemed rather unfair and pretty small-minded to restrict God's gender like that. So you can add heresy to my list of sins because I imagined a genderless God. It made me feel better about myself.

I wasn't a feminist, at least not back then. I knew my role and, to be honest, it was second-class. Now, the church didn't come right out and say I was second-class. Well, actually, come to think of it, it did. My number one role in life was to be worthy of my future husband and to support him. I was groomed to be ladylike and submissive. It started with Eve in the Garden of Eden because she had the audacity to do what she wanted and basically wound up cursing all of mankind in the process. Women got the short stick from the get-go and it's been that way ever since as far as I can see. Consider the Biblical superstars—they're all male. Oh, you've got that selfish brat Eve I suppose, and there's Mary Magdalene, but even then there's the suggestion that poor Mary may have been a hooker. Men ruled the roost, they just did, and we were supposed to go along with it lest we be accused of being too bitchy.

When I reflect back, I realize that the men in my life had taken my power and all without asking. They'd just taken it as if it was their inalienable right. They justified it by reminding we womenfolk that they were simply following God's orders. But now I see it. And I also see that I was complicit in this blatant theft because I had let them—I'd practically rolled out the red carpet. Hey, I'm just a girl so order me around as you please! I recently heard another woman complain about the injustice and her friend told her if she didn't want to be treated like a rug, then she ought to get off the floor. Sounds about right.

Anyway, because I was just a girl, I got a job waiting tables at The Gable House instead of cramming for a college entrance exam. The Gable House was the nicest restaurant in town. I got the job because the creepy manager thought I'd look good in the waitress uniform—an Old English dress with a corset and a push-up bra. I didn't care what the pervert thought as long as I was making good tips. And mostly I was, but I got stiffed a few times. Take the time a couple was driving through town on their way to Las Vegas and brought their own bottle of wine to the restaurant. This caused a mad panic because, believe it or not, none of us knew the whereabouts of a corkscrew. We finally got the bottle open back in the kitchen but bits of cork were floating in it like little pieces of driftwood from a shipwreck. And, like a dummy, I thought you were supposed to pour it all the way to the top of the glass, like a Diet Coke. How was I supposed to know? So that was bad enough, but then the manager hauled two portable partitions over and wrapped them around the table-for-two in the middle of the dining room. The couple asked him what on earth he was doing. He told them he didn't want to offend the other patrons with all the liquor. Sayonara to that tip.

My relationship with Keith changed after we had sex. I wouldn't say it was worse, it was just different. In a way it was more physical and in a way it wasn't. For example, we used to spend hours making out to the long version of "American Pie" but as soon as we started going all the way, Keith was unzipping his pants before the Chevy made it halfway to the levy. So there you go—bye, bye, Miss American Pie. Skedaddled with my virginity.

I think I was determined to love him more than ever—that he needed to be my one and only because of that line we'd crossed. I assumed we'd get married, of course, and I wanted to be married in the temple. But if we didn't stop fooling around we wouldn't be allowed to get married there. See, in our church you could still get married in a regular Mormon ward house if you were a misbehaving non-virgin but you couldn't get married in the *temple*, which is strictly off-limits to sinners. Your local bishop asks you a series of personal, probing questions and will only sign the required permission slip authorizing your entry if he's satisfied that you're worthy. No one is allowed entry into the temple without the properly signed slip. Even Jesus would require one (but, in his case, airtight ID verification might do). You could always lie and deny you'd had sex, but if your bishop catches even a whiff of blown virginity he won't sign the permission slip.

Keith didn't seem to care much about getting the temple permit; he just bought more condoms.

"I think we need to slow it down," I said.

"Why?"

"*Why?* Don't you want to get married in the temple?"

"Yeah, but what's the big deal as long as we get married some day?"

"But if we don't get married in the temple, everyone will know it's because we had sex. It'd be embarrassing and my parents would kill me."

"Then just don't tell them. It's not like they're going to find out."

So I didn't tell anyone, not even Sandra, my big-busted friend who was having sex with her boyfriend every second. Keith, on the other hand, was too proud to keep it to himself. I later found out he'd told all his buddies, including one blabbermouth who assured me I didn't need to worry because Keith told him we'd been "usin' rubbers." This gave me no small comfort.

I thought about confessing because it'd been drilled into our heads since birth that we needed to confess our sins—that it was actually a *blessing* to do such a thing—to rid ourselves of the overwhelming weight of sin. But do you know who I'd be confessing my deep, dark secrets to? My dad. Yeah, my freaking *dad*. That's because my dad was the neighborhood bishop and he's the one who took everyone's confessions. Um, say, Dad, you got a second?

To tell you the truth, I was a lot more worried about getting pregnant than going to hell. I could worry about hell later.

My periods were as regular as clockwork, so I started to freak out when I was late. I kept doing the math in my head. Yep, I was definitely late. I felt sluggish and bloated like I normally did before my period, but this time I figured it was a fetus in there, growing like a weed—hands, fingers, toes, vital organs. After five days of fretting I could take it no longer so I borrowed a friend's car and drove to Erickson's Drugstore to buy a home pregnancy kit. I saw our neighbor, Sister Ferguson, in the store and quickly stashed the pregnancy test kit on a shelf in the hair products section and grabbed a can of hairspray instead because I knew she was nosy and would have tattled on me.

I was almost home when I started. I usually hated my period, no shocker there, but not that time. No one in history has ever bled with more relief. I pulled into the parking lot of a 7-11 and threw the bag with the unused pregnancy test kit into the public trash.

I wasn't pregnant.

3

KATHERINE

I SAT ON THE CARPETED TOILET SEAT and stared at the home pregnancy test strip. Maybe there'd been a mistake. I set it to the side and closed my eyes for a full minute and then looked at it again. Still two pink bands, big as life. I reread the instructions, the part about how reliable the test was, and found it was only 97% accurate. I decided that wasn't very accurate at all. Besides, there was a warning on the label which said the results could be wrong if the test wasn't properly performed.

The box came with a spare strip, but the instructions said it was best to wait a day before retesting, and preferably do it in the morning so the pee could sit around in your bladder all night. Well-marinated pee must be more reliable for some reason. I only knew there was still a chance my life wouldn't be going straight down the tubes.

That evening, all ten of us in my family were sitting around our kitchen table like it was the Last Supper. Speaking of that famous meal, most of the walls in our house were adorned with religious art because if Jesus wasn't in it, it probably wasn't worth hanging. Our kitchen table was so old it might have been the one they actually used back then and it was so scratched my mom no longer bothered with a tablecloth. A small "K" had been carved into the table with a butter knife but the culprit remained on the lam because we didn't have assigned seats and because everyone's name started with a K.

There was the usual collection of mismatched water glasses and silverware on the table. I mean, nothing matched—there were even a few plastic Scooby Doo cups sprinkled in. A baking sheet filled with Tater Tots sat in the middle of the table next to a bowl of string beans that'd been mixed with a can of Cream of Mushroom soup. Kenny complained that's all we ever ate so sometimes my mom would sprinkle broken potato chips over the string beans and Cream of Mushroom to add some pizazz. She might also throw in a can of chipped beef. In the meantime, my dad just sat there with his arms folded waiting to be served.

My mom limped over to the table to sit, the last one to do so, as always. She'd had polio as a child which caused her to slightly drag one leg. I never interviewed the doctor or anything but there'd been no reason to disbelieve her. After all, it would've been a terrible practical joke to be faking it all this time. As for my dad, he didn't seem to let my mom's polio bother him much.

"Take off the cape for dinner," my dad told Korbin.

"How was your day, Katherine?" my mom asked.

"Huh?"

"Your day. How was it?"

"Oh, it was okay, I guess."

"Is everything all right? You seem upset."

"No, I'm good," I said. "I mean, yeah, everything's okay."

"She's probably daydreaming about Keith," said Kristy, pronouncing his name like Kee-eeth with that annoying little singsong of hers. I swear she's mental.

"Shut up, I said."

"Why don't *you* shut up."

Korbin picked his nose and tried to secretly wipe the booger under the table.

"Ew, you're disgusting," said Kimberly.

"I'm not disgusting, you are," said Korbin.

"You're both disgusting," said Kenny.

"At least my face isn't disgusting."

"At least I'm not a retard."

Down came my dad's fist on the table causing the tater tots to bounce. "Stop it! All of you!"

"But she started—"

"I said stop it, and I meant it!"

This just made Karolyn cry even louder from her highchair in the corner and Kelly, who's head rose just above the table top, shrunk down another inch. Grandma Coombs hardly seemed to notice the strife. She just sat there gumming her string beans while my brothers were trying to stab the tater tots rolling around on the baking sheet with their forks. And then she farted. Kenny about spit out a tater tot and Korbin had milk coming from his nose because this was the funniest thing that had ever happened at the dinner table. Well, funny and utterly gross at the same time. My dad gave us the eye, basically daring us to laugh. Meanwhile, grandma keeps gumming the string beans like it was the most natural thing in the world, which I suppose it was, while the rest of us waited for the smell, trying to decide if we wanted it to stink or not.

You know how when you're a kid you think everyone over fifty is old? Well, my grandma really was old. She must've been born in eighteen something-something and couldn't even hear her own fart. If life is a conveyor belt that we're plopped onto at birth, my grandma was about ready to fall off the other end. Her skin was the sickly color of Vaseline and her neck sagged like a wet dish towel. If she bumped into anything at all she'd get a bruise, so her arms and legs looked like they belonged to an aging leper. She still cared about her hair though, I can tell you that, and she insisted on going to the salon once a week. Maybe her hair was the only thing she could control so she always had it "done up pretty" in the arresting style of a gray-bluish helmet. No one was allowed within five feet of her when she'd come home from the salon because she worried someone might bump it.

Kenny was finally brave enough to break the silence. "I saw Keith after school. He was hanging out with some girls from Snow Canyon. I waved but I guess he didn't see me."

I'd heard the same thing from Janet and when I'd confronted Keith about it he'd said it was no big deal, which sort of made me think it was probably a big deal. But sitting at the kitchen table that night all I could think about was that unused test strip I'd hidden in the bathroom cabinet behind the spare rolls of toilet paper.

I wanted to wait for my potent morning pee but I couldn't resist. So, after dinner I locked myself in the bathroom again and peed directly onto the strip. I didn't want to mess with the middle man. I didn't want to mess with the dropper. I waited exactly three minutes. I was still sitting on the toilet seat when I held the strip up for inspection.

Two pink bands. I was still as pregnant as they come.

Keith didn't call that night like he said he would. I figured he was probably working with his dad at the plumbing store. Then I thought about Keith's parents and realized I'd never even met them. All I knew about them was that they drank coffee and didn't go to church. I knew that didn't mean they were bad, necessarily, but I had to wonder if they could be good grandparents when they couldn't even keep the basic commandments.

Then I thought about my own parents. They were going to lose it. What had I been *thinking!* I was a good girl. I wasn't like Melanie Dalton, a girl in my Geometry class who probably didn't even know who the father was. It didn't seem fair because a lot of girls were doing the same thing and didn't get pregnant. I swear I was like Mother Teresa compared to some of them.

If I had only obeyed the commandments none of this would have happened. And now Satan was probably laughing his guts out. Well, at least someone thought it was funny.

I couldn't sleep. Mostly I thought about my parents and how I would break the happy news. I practically wanted to barf. There I was, tossing and turning all night long while Keith was probably having a nice peaceful dream about going to school in his underpants. I'd wake up with bags under my eyes from loss of sleep and he'd probably wake up with a boner, just like my little brothers always did. They'd stroll to the bathroom every morning with their little tighty-whitey teepees pointing the way, yawning and rubbing the sleep out of their eyes like this was normal behavior.

The weight of being pregnant outweighed the guilt of having sinned. But both were heavy, heavier than anything I'd had to deal with up to that point in my life, and I could think of nothing else.

I finally decided to tell Janet. She was a goodie-two-shoes but she *was* my best friend. I knew she'd be disappointed in me because Janet bragged about her virginity like she had to battle for it every day, beating boys in heat away with a stick. We were sitting in her car, an old beater with a missing rear-side window which had been replaced with a black plastic garbage bag held in place with duct tape. She was talking about a boy she hoped would ask her out, a boy who wasn't too popular in high school but would probably become a surgeon.

"So, yeah, I'm sorta into him because he's going to BYU in the fall and is really smart. He's not too bad—"

"I think I'm pregnant."

"—looking but . . . wait, *what?* But I thought . . ."

"I know. We weren't going to, it's just that . . ."

"Are you sure?"

"I'm late so I took one of those home pregnancy tests."

"You can't tell from just one," she said helpfully. "Maybe it's wrong."

"I did the test twice."

She tried to rally. "I still bet they're wrong sometimes."

"What am I going to do?"

"What did Keith say?"

"I haven't told him yet," I said. "I just found out Monday."

I knew Janet would hate Keith over this. I also knew this would fortify her devotion to the church in a scared straight sort of way. And, finally, I knew she'd be thanking her lucky stars it hadn't been her in this predicament. I can't blame her for that because that's what I would've been thinking if the shoe had been on the other foot.

"What about your parents?"

"They don't know either." Then I started bawling. It came on all at once with snot and bubbles too, a shoulder-racking sob.

Janet tried to be reassuring but didn't offer any concrete solutions. After all, what could she say? I told you so? You should have listened to the church leaders? Neither one of us mentioned the abortion option. An *abortion?* That might have been an option for some but not for me. I'd already committed one second-degree felony with God and I didn't want a first degree on my record.

Janet leaned over and hugged me, promising to be there for me, whatever that meant. What I *wanted* it to mean was that she'd take over when I had to tell my parents, or when I started to show, or when it came time to push.

Then I had my little chat with Keith. He'd come over later that night to show off his new pick-up truck. Actually, it was a hand-me-down from his dad as a high school graduation gift. A faded *Murphy's Plumbing* was stenciled on the side of the door.

"Check out my new stereo. I installed it myself," he said with more pride than should've been called for. I mean, I could see the wires.

"Yeah, that's great."

"And do you like my new gun rack?"

A *gun rack?* Who did he think he was dating? Annie Oakley? Maybe I was being too hard on him for being so happy and gay. After all, he didn't know what was about to hit him.

We drove a few blocks and parked on a secluded road down by the Santa Clara River. That was a favorite make-out spot and for the life of me I don't know why. I mean, it wasn't a pretty place at all. Twenty feet away from this popular romance zone was the skeleton of an old washing machine, or maybe it was a dryer, probably a Maytag, rusting away in a clump of sagebrush. Keith turned the truck off and shoved an eight-track into the tape deck. I could tell it'd all been pre-planned, *The Best of Bread*, because he knew anything from Deep Purple would set an improper mood. Boys are so obvious.

He was just settling in for a make-out session when I told him I was pregnant.

I didn't see his face because I was looking down at my lap, but I can only imagine what it looked like. I also imagined his testicles spontaneously retracting in fear.

"Seriously?"

"I wouldn't lie about that."

"So, like, are you sure?"

"Yeah, I'm sure. I should have started my period by now, so I took one of those home pregnancy tests and it came back positive."

He stared at me. I knew what was going through his mind. P-A-N-I-C. "But . . . so . . . like . . . are you sure?"

"What are we going to do?" I started bawling again, even though I told myself I wouldn't.

"But we used rubbers every time."

"Keith, I'm pregnant, okay? I didn't try."

"I just can't believe it because of the rubbers and all so I was just thinking . . . I don't know . . . maybe . . ."

"Maybe what?"

"Maybe it's not mine?"

I couldn't believe it. Of all the things I hoped he'd say, or wouldn't say. "How could you even say that?"

"Well, if you say it is then I guess it is. I'm not saying it isn't. It's just that—"

"It is, okay?"

"So what are you going to do?"

"What am *I* going to do?"

"Hey, you don't need to get all mad. It's not my fault."

"Really? Then whose fault is it?"

"Nobody's I guess."

"So what are we going to do?"

"I don't know," he said. "What do you think we should do?" He probably hoped I'd already come up with an airtight plan that would make this mess go away, or at least be kept to myself.

"I guess we should get married."

"But . . ." He just sat there in the cab of his new truck, cocked slightly to his right so that he was sitting on his wallet that was probably squishing the condom he'd hoped to use that night.

"What else would we do?" I asked.

We sat there in the dark cab, looking straight ahead at nothing, processing this life-changing dilemma and coming up empty.

"If you don't want to get married, then I guess I'll just have the baby by myself."

"No, yeah, for sure. I guess that's what we should do. It's just that . . ."

"It's just that what?"

"It's just that my parents are going to flip out. I wasn't, like, you know, planning to get married and all that. At least not right now. I wanted to see if I could walk-on at SUU and maybe get a football scholarship."

"My parents will be mad, too, especially my dad. But I don't think we have a choice."

"Well, maybe you could, you know, get an abortion?"

"There's no way I could do that."

"But wouldn't it be . . ."

Yeah, it was messy and our entire collective wisdom on the subject could have fit onto a fortune cookie. Keith asked a few more times if I was absolutely sure I was pregnant. "Sometimes those tests are wrong," he said, as if he would know.

This might sound like I think I'm some kind of saint, but I felt sorry for him. Yep, that's me all right, Saint Katherine. I reached over and held his hand and scooted closer to him, putting my head on his shoulder. He kissed me, which I thought was nice, but it lingered. Then he started to unbutton my shirt.

I pulled back. "What are you doing?"

"What?"

"Do you think we're going to have sex? As in *now?*"

"Well, yeah, sort of."

"Come on, Keith," I said, still with a bit of tear snot on my upper lip. "We can't just keep doing it like nothing's changed."

"Why not? Now that you're pregnant I won't even need to wear a rubber."

Can you believe it? Who was this guy?

"Hey, sorry, okay? You don't need to make such a big deal about it."

He drove me home and dropped me off in front. I walked up the crunchy gravel driveway without caring how much noise it made. Wake up the whole neighborhood for all I care. I was well within my curfew anyway. Besides, how ridiculous was it that I, a pregnant mother-to-be, still had a stupid curfew? So, yeah, it bugged me that my parents treated me like a child, but

I also had to reluctantly acknowledge that becoming upset over being treated like a child was childish in itself.

I decided not to tell my parents for a while. So I put it off, hoping there had been a mistake because you never know about these things. Two weeks later Aunt Flo still hadn't paid a visit. In the meantime, the stress was tangible. It was oppressive, weighing down on me like the heavy lead shield the dentist puts over your chest when he x-rays your teeth. And all the stress was causing me to breakout. Pregnancy and acne, the perfect high school graduation combo gift.

I waited another month (and two more home pregnancy kits down the drain) before I finally told my parents. I'd kept stalling, waiting until they were in a good mood, but my mom was on one, like it was her time of the year, and my dad was ornery about the Larsen's broken-down Winnebago permanently parked in front of their house across the street (blocking the dazzling view of a large concrete mermaid prominently stuck in the middle of their half-dead cactus garden). So there really wasn't a very good time.

"We haven't seen much of Keith lately," my mom said as I sat over breakfast and tried not to barf from the smell of the eggs. She had a laundry basket on one hip and the baby on her other hip. "Are you still seeing him?"

That's a laugh, I thought.

"Uh-huh," I said.

We heard a crash from the other room—a tipped over lamp as it turned out. She turned her head and yelled *"Kenneth Dale Coombs!"* to prevent a homicide because Kenny was chasing Korbin around the house, threatening to kill him for barging into his room when he was talking to a girl on the phone, and

Korbin with his cape and cowboy hat was tipping over chairs, lamps, whatever, to block his warpath. Actually, Korbin was big for his age and rather heavy—"hefty" my mom said, so he could hold his own against his big brother if he really wanted to. In the meantime, my youngest brother Kelly, who generated whispers over his budding sexuality, was bugging my mom for more fabric to complete his latest creation on her noisy sewing machine. When he gave up, he retreated to his room and his tuba. This tuba was regulation sized and it dwarfed him. Poor Kelly would practically disappear behind it when it rested on his lap. The rest of us tried to be good sports about it but the house was small and there was no place to hide from the noise. Honestly, it didn't sound right when he'd blow on it and we never heard anything that resembled an actual song. My dad wasn't very patient with it which required my mom to politely scold him. "Please, Dale, it's all he has."

I didn't know *when* I'd get a chance to talk to my parents in private. Honestly, there was always something—Kimberly tearing the house apart looking for her retainer that she lost about once a week, or whining because I wouldn't let her wear my new plaid top (that I'd paid for with my own money), or Korbin begging to camp out in the backyard with a homemade bonfire, or Kristy asking where the Elmer's glue was so she could paste one more leaf onto her photosynthesis poster, or Karolyn crying from colic, or Kenny just being Kenny.

The chaos was enhanced by illness. Someone always had the croup, or pink eye, languishing in misery on the sofa while waiting for my parents to learn about the invention of the aspirin. There was usually at least one mixing bowl on the floor next to one of the kids' beds. We weren't pill poppers in my house growing up. You had to be in mortal danger before they'd dole out a pill. And it had to be dire before they'd take us to the doctor, like you had to have the measles that wouldn't go away. My parents believed fevers, rashes, and stomach bugs "passed," and they usually did, eventually, which just gave my parents additional proof that modern medicine was largely overrated.

Anyway, my pregnancy wasn't just going to pass. It was only going to get worse if history was any indication, so I had to tell them. It was like that feeling you get when you have to vomit, so you lie down on the sofa all day hoping it'll go away, but it doesn't. You finally get the courage to just stand up, dodge the mixing bowl, and run for the toilet because you know it's coming, sooner or later, so you might as well get it over with.

The next night I tapped on my parent's bedroom door after they'd put all the troops to bed.

"Come in," my mom said too quickly. I think she wanted to make it perfectly clear there was nothing going on in there, thank the Lord. I would have been scarred for life and no amount of therapy could have saved me.

I opened the door and closed it behind me. They were in bed with the light off.

"Can I talk to you guys for a minute?"

"It's awfully late," my dad said.

"Of course you can," my mom said. She reached over and turned on the lamp, then patted her side of the bed. "Here, sit down and let's talk."

I'd thought about what to say a million times, of course, but I couldn't figure out how to make "I had sex with the immoral boy you told me not to see and now I'm pregnant" come out well.

I looked at my parents and started to cry.

"What is it, Katherine?" They looked at each other with a concerned look.

"I'm pregnant."

They looked at each other again. I'm sure it was the last thing in the world they expected me to say and they were in shock. "But . . . how . . . when did . . . who . . .?"

"I know I shouldn't have. And we only did it once." I was crying pretty hard now. "I was late so I took a test and now . . ."

Silence. Eye of the hurricane. Comprehension trying to catch up. My mom then reached out her hand to me. She had the saddest look I'd ever seen. My dad, on the other hand, totally freaked out.

"You're pregnant? Is it that Keith kid? I thought I'd made myself clear that you weren't to see him! And now you're *pregnant?*" The eye had cleared passed and now we were on the backside of the eye wall.

"Dale, please, you'll wake the kids."

"Wake the kids? You think I care about that now? Maybe they *ought* to wake up! Maybe they ought to come in here and see what happens when you disobey the commandments!" Big long pause that felt like a year. "You are supposed to set an *example* to your sisters and now look what you've done! This is completely unacceptable!"

"Dale, please."

"Don't you please me! My own daughter is sleeping around with some . . . some . . . kid who cares nothing about you or what you stand for?"

"Dad, you don't know him."

"Don't know him? I don't *want* to know him!"

"But, Dad, we want to get married now."

"Oh, you're damned *right* you will!"

"Katherine honey, are you sure you're pregnant?" This was a familiar theme. It must be catchy for people who don't know what else to say.

"Yeah, I'm sure. But we only did it once." I wanted to drive that point home, even if it wasn't true.

My dad had stood from the bed and now faced me. If anyone else could have seen a silent movie clip of the scene they would have known the older gentleman with the crew cut standing in the baggy long-john underwear was terribly upset about something. "How *could* you?" he waited. "How could you bring this shame to our family?" He waited again. "What are we supposed to tell the neighbors in the ward? Huh? How do you expect me to be the bishop and stand up in church when I can't even keep my own daughter in line? We raised you in the church! We raised you to be better than this! And now you expect us to just *accept* it? You expect us to be *happy* for you?"

"Dale, honey, please." She touched his arm.

"No, Dad. I just . . ."

"You just what?" He stared at me, which was worse than the rant. Parents get upset with their kids, I get that, but this was different—there was almost a loathing quality to his look. "We'll talk about this in the morning. I think you've said enough for one night."

My dad's anger made me less sorry for some reason. I can't explain it. If his objective was to shame me, he did an excellent job. But it would have been more painful if he'd put his arms around me in his disappointment and said he loved me. I would have felt much worse with that.

I stood and opened their door then closed it softly behind me. I felt sick to my stomach. I was relieved to have gotten it over with, so there was that, but in the aftermath of a hurricane there is destruction. I suppose my dad had been partially right that I needed to be the example setter as the oldest. But that came with a lot of pressure and sometimes it felt like I couldn't just be a regular kid because all the other kids looked up to me, so whenever I screwed up my parents flipped out more than if my younger siblings had done the same thing, which didn't seem fair. There were times I would've preferred hiding out somewhere in the middle of the pack.

I could hear my parents' voices from the other room even though I couldn't make out what they were saying (but I had a pretty good inkling). I lay on my bed and looked through my bedroom window at the crescent moon smiling down from the sky, but to me that night it felt more like a smirk.

Thirty minutes later my bedroom door opened and my mom came in wearing her bathrobe. She sat on my bed and took my hand. It looked like she'd aged ten years in the past half hour.

"Katherine," she whispered, "you've made a mistake but Heavenly Father still loves you, and so do we."

She leaned down and kissed me on the forehead.

4

KATE

I CAN'T TELL YOU HOW RELIEVED I was when I started my period. What if I'd been pregnant? What would I have done? All I can say is it would have been awful. My parents would have fainted, face down, and when they came to they would have sent me to one of those wilderness camps for wayward teens, the ones where half the kids die of thirst.

I was glad I hadn't told anyone. I decided I'd tell Keith, however, just so he'd know we'd dodged the bullet and needed to cool it for a while. But there was no way I was going to tell Janet who would have judged me, or Sandra who would have been thrilled to know I was no longer morally superior to her. And my parents? I would've rather died. I *might* have confessed to the bishop but since he was my dad there was no way.

I do have a confession to make though. The church always said you'd feel cheap and dirty if you prematurely cracked the virginity code but I didn't feel all that bad about it. I mean, it wasn't *that* big of a deal. People do it all the time, you know. But not Mormon kids, at least not as much, or at least they must hide it better. I concluded that, while it was indeed a terrible sin, I hadn't hurt anyone and I hadn't broken any laws (at least not man-made laws). Maybe I was a devil child—a devil child masquerading as a stick of stale, twice-chewed gum.

So, yeah, I dodged the bullet and there was no big mystery to it—sometimes the egg is fertilized and sometimes it isn't. Well, actually that is a bit mysterious when you think about it. If the mystery had gone the other way I would've had to marry Keith within seconds and hardly anyone would have come to our wedding. Those who did would've had to pretend they didn't know it was shotgun-style. They would've stared at my tummy in silence and agonized about my eternal salvation. Come to think of it, I doubt my parents would have even given me a wedding. They probably would've saved the showy thousand-dollar budget and sent me off to a Justice of the Peace across state lines. My mom would've had to sneak me a few used pots and pans and some of her old Tupperware with warped lids.

The night before I started my blessed period, we'd all been sitting around the kitchen table. Enos was sprawled out below the table waiting for one of my brothers to drop him a scrap. He appeared to enjoy lying under the table farting. And his breath was another thing altogether. But we tolerated Enos and his various stenches because no one had the heart to return him to the animal shelter. Grandma bragged that he liked to sit on her lap to get warm but we all knew Enos took comfort with his snout in *anyone's* crotch. Anyway, we were busy stabbing the tater tots on the baking sheet in the middle of the table when my mom asked about Keith. She had no idea that the daughter sitting across from her was freaking out over that immoral boy's sperm paddling hopefully toward a big payday. Then Kenny said something about seeing Keith hanging out with girls from Snow Canyon High. I was fretting so much about being with child that I didn't have the brainpower to focus on what he was saying.

That night Keith came by so I could admire his new (but old) pickup truck.

"You've got a new truck."

"Well, actually it's my dad's old one but it runs great," he said, nodding with pride as he gently petted the hood. "He gave it to me for graduation."

We drove out to a gravel parking lot overlooking the Santa Clara River. This was our town's Lovers Lane. Boys thought it was such a romantic place, sitting there next to the noisy freeway. I don't know about you, but nothing makes me quite so frisky as a bunch of semi's rushing by. Keith had installed an eight-track under the dash and mounted the speaker above the pickup's rear window on the passenger side. He'd duct-taped the stereo wires around the doorframe so it wasn't a custom job. I didn't want to burst his bubble, so I didn't mention that I'd smacked the speaker with my head when I climbed into the cab and would probably wind up with a knot on my forehead.

He leaned back, all content, getting ready for some romance. The music that was supposed to get me all revved up began blasting behind my right ear. *Baby I'm a want you, baby I'm a need you . . .* I'll say this about Keith; he really had a knack with the ladies.

I thought he ought to know about my pregnancy scare because it might entice us both to push the re-set button before barreling ahead with more sex, or potential marriage, or whatever. Having premarital sex might not be a big deal to some people but I'd been taught it was The Sin Next To Murder, which is a pretty big deal when you think about it—worse than lying, cheating, or drug trafficking. It was even worse than armed robbery. Treason? Way down the list. So, yeah, it was a big deal to me. I always figured I'd only do it with one person in my entire life—my husband—and I needed to get it right. Call me a prude, but that's the truth.

"Keith, I don't know if I should tell you this, but I thought I was pregnant."

"You thought you were *pregnant?* But we used rubbers."

"Not the first time."

"But . . ."

"Don't worry, I'm not. I just started my period. But I thought I was."

He leaned his head back and let out a breath. "Man, that would've sucked. We need to be careful from now on."

"Maybe that was a good wakeup call and we shouldn't do it anymore."

I could almost hear the horrified thoughts ricocheting around his head. *Wah? Not do it anymore?* This was an unthinkable nightmare. "Why not?"

"You know why not. It's not right, and I feel guilty about it. Don't you?"

"A little, I guess. But more kids are doing it than you think—it's just that girls don't talk about it like guys do."

"Guys talk about it? Like what guys?"

"I don't know. Just some guys."

"You haven't told anybody, have you?"

"Of course not."

I slid closer to him and we listened to the music. *If a picture paints a thousand words then why can't I paint you . . .* I was so relieved about not being pregnant that I may have given him the wrong impression, because no sooner was I smelling his Juicy Fruit breath than he was unbuttoning my blouse.

I pulled back. "Wait, Keith, maybe we shouldn't do this."

"It's okay, I have a rubber," he said as he cocked his hip and reached for his wallet.

"But I'm on my period, remember?"

He was visibly disappointed as I saw him silently evaluating the pros and cons. Personally, I thought the cons outweighed the pros and it wasn't even a close call. I'm sorry to be so graphic but, ugh, the mess. I thought I owed him something for his vast unfulfilled hope—like it'd been my fault for having a period and I needed to make it up to him. How stupid, right?

"Well, you could . . . you know . . ." he said as he looked down at his pants. "But only if you want to."

Yeah, like I'd get a big kick out of putting that ugly thing in my mouth. Kids around school were saying "If It's Oral, It's Moral" and you just know it was a boy who'd come up with that one. I didn't know how moral it was but I didn't want him to feel bad, so I unzipped his pants. He wiggled and shimmied as I pulled them down to his knees.

A few days later, Sandra came into The Fairway Grill, a greasy spoon on the main drag in town where I waited tables for lunch traffic. (I worked at the classier Gables House restaurant, the one with the free-flowing-wine, only on weekends.) Kids ditched school to hang out at The Fairway Grill and sneak cups of coffee. In our Mormon town, coffee was as wicked as the hard stuff so it was pretty edgy to sneak a swig or two. Now, drinking coffee wasn't The Sin Next To Murder, but it was still forbidden. By the way, the church doesn't formally rank sins once you get past #1 Murder and #2 Premarital Sex, but there's an informal ranking. For example, drinking coffee was probably worse than, say, shoplifting, but not as bad as grand theft auto. And everything on the list was significantly worse than the crime of removing the tag from your mattress which doesn't even make it on the Mormon list of no-no's. Anyway, the high school kids with no moral rudders would belly up to the counter at The Fairway Grill and put five heaping teaspoons of sugar into each cup and hope to be seen by the in-crowd.

It was slow in the grill that afternoon so I sat down in the booth next to Sandra as she stirred in the teaspoons of sugar like a seasoned pro. The front of my light-blue uniform had a few drops of smeared condiments and I'd tried to dab at the stains with a wet napkin but the resulting water spots made me look like a wet nurse. Even with the low flats I had to wear, I was still taller than Sandra, and I think it bugged her. She might have been incrementally taller if she had smaller breasts because, while she was awfully proud of them, she was also self-conscious of their enormity and tended to hunch over and pull her shoulders inward.

"How's Keith?" Sandra asked as she blew on her coffee, just as sophisticated as can be. Knowing Sandra and how competitive she was with me, I should have known it was a trick question.

"Good. He's at work today over at his dad's plumbing store."

"That's what he told you, huh?" This was clearly why she'd come by the grill to see me—to rub it in.

"Yeah, why?"

"Well, I just saw him hanging out over at Wirthlin Park.

"Really? Was he with Rob and Eric?"

"Uh, *no,* he was with some really cute girl from Snow Canyon. I think she's a sophomore."

"Just them? How do you know?"

"Because I just saw them. When he saw me, he tried to hide behind that truck he's been driving. What a douchebag."

"Oh."

Keith was at the park with another girl? And he'd lied about going to his dad's work?

"Sorry to give you the news," said Sandra, who was no sorrier than fly to the moon. "Are you guys, like, serious?"

"Um, sort of."

"Well, I think he's a jerk. He hit on me the other day but I just ignored him. I don't get what you see in him. He's not even that cute. He's got that ugly long hair in back and his teeth are all, like, separated. You're way better looking than him."

Sandra then started talking about going to college at UNLV that fall. Las Vegas is only an hour and a half drive from our town of St. George. As she yammered on about UNLV, I thought about Keith and that girl from Snow Canyon High. For some reason I was more upset with her, a girl I didn't even know, than I was with Keith. Explain that one.

"Why don't you come with me?" she asked.

"Huh?"

"Why don't you come with me to UNLV?"

"Seriously?"

"I know some girls down there and they say it's way cool. It'd be fun if you went."

I finished my shift, robot style. Keith was cheating on me? He didn't call that night or the next day either. When I finally saw him, he acted like everything was normal.

"Are you going out with any other girls?"

"Whaddya mean?"

"You know what I mean. Are you, or aren't you? It's a simple question."

"I don't know."

"You don't *know?*"

"Okay, yeah, I might have gone out with a few other girls, but it's no big deal. It's not like I'm sleeping with them or anything."

It felt like I'd been run over by one of those semi's.

"Hey, it's no big deal."

"Not a big deal? Are you being serious right now? I gave up my virginity to you! I could have been pregnant! I thought we were going to get married!"

"Well, yeah, but we aren't married yet. Gol, you act like I murdered somebody."

I decided I needed to dump him. I couldn't be in a relationship with someone who sneaked off with cute Snow Canyon girls. As soon as I made up my mind that we weren't going to celebrate our golden wedding anniversary together, he got uglier. I don't mean to be petty, but his teeth looked like an uneven picket fence that was missing every other slat. And that stringy long hair in the back was just gross. This is who I gave my cherry to? And I almost barfed when I thought about what I'd done to him in the cab of his stupid pickup truck.

I began to seriously think about UNLV and wanted to talk to my parents about it, alone, without interruptions. But how was I supposed to have a serious talk with my parents while being serenaded by a chorus of musical arm-pit farts, or Korbin running around with a bath towel pinned around his neck pretending to be Superman, or nearly burning down the house while trying to light katydids on fire in his bedroom? Honestly, there was always *something*. Take Kelly who was always trying to rally an audience to see his musical reproduction of *Bye Bye Birdie* or *The Music Man* in the living room (he'd sewn the costumes). Either that or he'd be in his room with his tuba, screeching out sounds that never resembled the sound a tuba was supposed to make. Then there was Kristy who set up a lemonade stand in front of our house EVERY SINGLE DAY. The poor neighbors thought it was cute, at first, but then drove an entire block out of their way so they wouldn't have to pass her. And don't forget Kimberly who was taking Spanish in the ninth grade and thought she was bilingual. She walked around the house all day saying dónde está la biblioteca until my dad finally told her to knock it off or move to Tijuana. I'm sure the neighbors also heard about the time Kenny burned a hole in the palm of Larry Wilcox's hand using the sun and a magnifying glass. It looked like poor Larry had pried himself off the cross. Larry thought it was funny because he was as dumb as Kenny, but his parents were not amused.

A few days later, after my parents had gone to their bedroom for the night, I tapped on their door. I didn't dare barge in without warning because I would've killed myself if I'd caught them trying to make me another sibling. Literally killed myself.

"Come in," my mom said too quickly. I think she would have killed herself, too.

My parents were in bed with the light off.

"Can I talk to you guys for a minute?"

"It's awfully late," my dad said.

My mom reached over and turned on the lamp, then scooted over and patted her side of the bed.

"What is it, Honey?"

I figured they'd say college was dumb—that a degree wouldn't help me change a dirty diaper or make a pot of Cream of Wheat for all the kids I was supposed to have.

"A lot of my friends are going to UNLV for college and it sounds like a really good idea. I was thinking about going into nursing or something like that. I don't think it costs that much and I'd for sure help pay," I said all this as quickly as I could before my dad could put the kibosh on it.

"But we haven't even talked about college," my mom said.

"I know, but I need to apply within the next few weeks to get in this fall."

"We thought you'd just keep working at the restaurants until you got married," my dad said. "That's good money for a girl. Why waste all that money on a college degree you'll never use?"

"But, Dad, I've lived here my whole life and think it'd be good if I lived somewhere else for a while. I could always come back if I didn't like it. It's not that far."

"Well, we can't afford to send you away to some high-falutin college just so those liberals can cram all that crap down your throat. Because that's what they do—they brainwash."

"Lots of kids go to college, Dad."

"I'm not saying college doesn't have its place, but you'll probably be a homemaker like your mother here and it makes no sense to spend a fortune on college."

Maybe I should have been more upset than I was—knowing that my parents would have been all for it if I'd been a boy. Never mind the fact that I got a 31 on my ACT, which was a lot higher than my brother. But I don't think my mom even knew what the ACT was. And my dad, who might have known, who *should* have known, only wanted to know how my seminary class was going. (Seminary is our religious class in high school.) I didn't expect them to form a conga line to celebrate my ACT score but it would've been nice if they'd at least wondered out loud if maybe I was worthy of college.

"I could take out a student loan. That's what Sandra's going to do."

"What about Dixie State here in St. George?" my mom asked. "Wouldn't that be a lot cheaper?"

"Maybe. But I'd rather go away. I just want to see what it's like."

"We can't afford it," my dad said. "So you'd have to pay for it yourself. But it's late. We can talk more about this some other time."

I stood and opened their door then gently closed it behind me. I lay in bed listening to my parents' voices from the other room. I couldn't make out the words but I figured my dad, who hadn't gone to a single day of college, was lecturing my mom on how stupid it was, especially for a girl.

My bedroom door opened a few minutes later and my mom came in wearing her bathrobe and sat on my bed.

"Your father is just concerned that you'll forget who you are if you go away to college, but we'll figure something out if that's what you really want."

Then she leaned down and kissed me on the forehead.

5

KATHERINE

OUR SHOTGUN WEDDING three years ago was hardly the wedding I'd dreamed of. I always thought I'd go downtown to Bridal 'n More with my mom and closest girlfriends to try on modest wedding dresses. There'd be Martinelli on ice and we'd sip from fancy champagne flutes while a complete stranger in the changing room used clips and pins to temporarily pull everything together before I'd come out and stand on a pedestal while they all gushed over which dress was "me." Instead, I wore the same dress I'd worn to junior prom even though it was tight around the middle. It wasn't white, of course, because I was impure.

We only sent out a few invitations. My aunts and uncles were there and that's about it from my side. I overheard my mom tell a neighbor it would be a small get-together for family only. The neighbor knew I was pregnant but, for my mom's sake, pretended she knew it'd been in the planning stages for months. I cannot say how this neighbor knew I was pregnant but I'm pretty sure she didn't learn the scandalous news from my parents. They didn't breathe a word—not to my siblings, not to their friends, and not to me. In fact, I don't think my parents even talked to *each other* about it. My mom emphasized to this neighbor who'd expertly pretended not to know *why* I was getting married that everyone in the family was thrilled about the forthcoming union. You see, in our town we had to pretend that everything was just peachy because we belonged to the true church and had to prove it by always being happy and joyful, even if it was fake. And it was fake as often as not. That's why my mom only cried in her bedroom with the door closed.

The wedding took place in my aunt and uncle's backyard which had a little gazebo. They'd strung some Christmas lights around the patio and put out a few stackable plastic chairs. A card table held a tray of brownies next to the boom box and sign-in book. A very stylish ballpoint pen was stuck in a pen stand next to the open book. My uncle Reed was tasked with taking the photos because he'd recently won a fancy new camera in a drawing of some kind. I think he took more photos of his garden and the geraniums he'd just planted than of the bride and groom. The whole shebang cost less than a thousand dollars. "We can't condone this," my dad had said. "What message would it send to your sisters if we gave you some elaborate $3,000 wedding? That it's okay to do what you've done?"

And what exactly *had* I done? Had I murdered anyone? Had I vandalized the chapel? Had I even hurt anyone's feelings? I'd only done the thing God had wired me to do, the thing that every single adult in my life had done many times, including, of course, my parents. But I'd done it prematurely, at least according to my church and community, and my dad wouldn't let it die. So, yeah, Dad, I screwed up, okay? What did he expect me to do? Rewind my transgression? Retroactively surround my eggs with sperm retardant?

"I know how you feel about it, Dad. And I'm sorry, okay? What else do you want me to say?"

"Katherine honey," my mom had said, "I think what your father is trying to say is your sisters look up to you and when you—"

"You don't need to speak for me, Jackie. I am the patriarch in this home. There are consequences when we disobey God's commandments and I won't glamorize it with some big fancy wedding."

My dad avoided Keith and his family because it'd been their collective lack of moral values that'd led to this embarrassing backyard wedding in the first place. He cozied up to Keith briefly however in hopes that we'd take Enos with us to our new apartment but Keith said there was no way he was going to take that dog. He said it was a girl dog and he didn't like girl dogs, even though Enos was a male through and through. The proof of that was his relentless humping of just about anything, even inanimate objects like tree trunks and garden statues, so I figured Keith might relate to Enos in that way. But no.

So my dad didn't like Keith, at least initially. My mom, on the other hand, was one of those cheery Everything-Happens-For-A-Reason types. She didn't welcome Keith into the family like a normal son-in-law, for how could she, but she did say: "It'll all work out for the best. You'll see." She even fake-happily suggested Keith would fit right in because his name also started with a K. So at least there was that.

Keith's parents were just as bad. Their disapproval, however, hadn't been wrapped up in religion and sin like my parents. No, they believed against all reason that I'd intentionally entrapped Keith. Yeah, right, I'd intentionally gotten myself knocked-up at eighteen so I could be shamed in my community and immediately begin the servitude of motherhood, sharing my life with a boy I hardly knew—a boy who'd barely graduated from high school, had no money, and would never become the bishop. And I don't think they appreciated it when my dad told Keith he would marry me whether he wanted to or not. So the Coombs's and the Murphy's got all dolled up in their church clothes and smiled long enough for the I Do's and about three photos from Uncle Reed's new camera. Then they went home and told all their friends how weird the other family was.

I had always been slightly disappointed to hear my parents describe their own courtship because there wasn't much to it and they were both boring storytellers. They'd met at a church dance when they were in high school and never dated anyone else. In fact, my dad bragged about never having kissed anyone else and how he didn't even kiss my mom, not even a wicked peck on the cheek, until they were officially engaged. This story was meant to demonstrate sexual virtue in action but I thought it was rather extreme and I had always pledged not to go that route. My mom's mom was a hard-nosed dictator and my mom probably would have married just about anyone to get out from under her mother's overbearing thumb. I'll bet she was also eager to ditch her maiden name. I am speculating here, but Jackie Yankoff didn't have the right zing to it. Unfortunately, she'd simply traded her mother's thumb for my dad's.

Just like my mom, I'd begun to lose my identity the second we were married. For starters, I was no longer Katherine Coombs. I was now Katherine Murphy, or, even worse, I was Mrs. Keith Murphy. This was no surprise because I'd been trained to take my husband's name and honor him, even if I didn't particularly like him. This training started at birth when I'd been groomed to be submissive, pretty, and desirable enough to be claimed by a man. It was very different for my brothers who'd been groomed from birth to be tough, independent, manly men of the house. They were to be the selectors and not the selectees. They got trucks, balls, and microscopes at Christmas and us girls got dolls and aprons for our little play kitchens. The same year Korbin got a BB gun, microscope, and tool set (complete with an electric drill) I got a toy vacuum and clothes iron, which went nicely with my collection of mini spatulas and brooms.

Keith and I rented a cheap duplex on Bluff Street with a detached carport for Keith's truck (oh, trust me, he made that pretttty clear—it was *his* truck), cobbling together just enough hand-me-down furniture to partially fill it. The ugly brown-plaid sofa was one of those that converts into a bed and was hard as stone. Keith insisted on a waterbed which were all the rage at the time. Me, I thought it was dumb. I mean, all the sloshing was ridiculous. It had a small leak too so we always had a beach towel nearby. Whenever Keith moved I thought there'd been a nearby tsunami and it'd wake me up. And getting in and out of the danged thing was a challenge. The small TV on our dresser was an old black and white job with rabbit ears wrapped in tinfoil. A macrame plant holder hung from a ceiling hook in the corner of the living room with a sickly-looking fern spilling out of it, a holdover from the previous renter, or maybe the renter before that. We kept it.

My low expectations were met. "You made your bed, and you'll have to sleep in it." It was my dad's favorite line. I should have embroidered it on a pillow and given it to him for Father's Day. I swear, sometimes I think he *wanted* our marriage to be bad to prove a point. I'm not sure what the point was, and I'm not even sure that's what he wanted, but he didn't appear to root for us. He hardly even spoke to Keith, other than to remind him how perilous our salvation would be unless we repented for our sin, post haste. Oh, and to get some free plumbing advice every now and then.

So, yeah, it wasn't all Shangri-La, that's for sure, but it wasn't *that* bad. At least I was no longer living under the roof of The Bishop and no longer had a curfew. I could shower whenever I wanted without my annoying little sisters banging on the bathroom door for me to hurry and we never ran out of hot water.

Speaking of showers, I learned Keith was an every-other-day showerer, if that. He'd go through a bar of soap about once a year. Swimming counted as a bath, too. And I was surprised that he only brushed his teeth in the mornings because, according to Keith, he was just going to sleep so why bother? And then there was the matter of bathroom etiquette. I'd grown up with little brothers who couldn't hit the broadside of a barn when they peed but I got over it because I didn't need to clean it up. But with Keith, I swear it gushed out with more force, drilling into the bowl so hard I thought it might bore a hole in the porcelain. And I knew more force meant more mist—little shards of urine shrapnel flying everywhere. I was leery of going into the bathroom with bare feet.

I shouldn't pile on, but there was also his list of phobias which included doing dishes, laundry, and mice. We'd been living in the apartment for a week when a little bugger darted across the linoleum floor in the kitchen. He jumped up on a chair and started screaming. I didn't like it either but it wasn't like there was a cobra on the loose. He ordered me to do something quick. *Me* do something? "But I'm not used to them," he screamed in panic. "Shit, there it goes! Hurry! Get a broom or something!" This was my knight in shining armor, up on the kitchen chair shrieking about a mouse.

He probably wasn't crazy about some of the things I did either. In fact, I know he wasn't. "I don't get why you need so much hair stuff," he said. "I mean, I could understand it if you still had long hair, but not since you cut it short and it turned brown all of a sudden." I'd actually cut it to surprise Prince Charming with the new look but all he'd said was that it made me look "like a mom." Yep, the very look I'd been going for.

Now that we had the official marriage certificate from the Washington County clerk, we no longer had to sneak around to have sex and Keith assumed we didn't need any unnecessary foreplay either. So, one day it was the Sin Next To Murder and the next day we were outright *encouraged* to do it, like rabbits, because there were millions of little souls up in heaven who needed to come down to earth to get a physical body. That's what we Mormons believe and that's why we generously have so many kids. You're welcome.

"Hey," Keith would say, as he stood splashing pee into the toilet, "I think we have time for a quick poke if we hurry." Boy, he sure knew how to work the charm, standing there with dirt under his fingernails in his gray, untucked Murphy's Plumbing

Supply shirt with pit stains and jeans that could stand up by themselves. About the most romantic thing he ever said to me was, "That waitress uniform makes you look hot. Let's screw." When I told him I'd be late for work, he said, "Come on, it'll be so quick you'll hardly feel a thing." He whined when I told him I still needed to go despite the irresistible invitation, as if I had completely abandoned my wedding vows. "So now what am I supposed to do? Gol, I thought we were supposed to be married." I would usually go along out of wifely duty, sloshing around in that bed like we were wrestling in a rowboat adrift at sea. Fortunately, I wasn't prone to seasickness.

And I was pretty sure he loved the Raiders more than me. I'll level with you here; this football obsession was just weird. Here was a full grown adult male committed to a black and white jersey with the image of a pirate and crossed swords. Not only that, but he refused to ever let me wash it because he swore that would jinx the team. And this was to be my lifetime companion? When we were dating, I pretended to be on the edge of my seat over the stupid game. Oh, wow, the wide receiver got tackled by the linebacker! But I no longer had to pretend now that we were married. So, yes, I'll admit I might have misled him and he didn't get what he'd bargained for in a spouse, one who dressed up in the team colors and yelled obscenities at the refs on TV, a bowl of Cheetos on her lap. But did he honestly think I'd been *serious* when I'd said I hoped the Raiders would beat the Chiefs? If he was that dense then maybe that's on him.

Keith worked at his dad's plumbing supply store and I juggled my two waitressing jobs. We scrimped along as our little fetus hung onto the wall of my uterus for dear life. When my belly began to look like I'd swallowed his football helmet, Keith was good to remind me of it.

"So, like, are you going to eat all that?"

"Yeah, why?" I asked.

"I don't know. It's just that you're getting fatter than I thought you would." This did not magically zap my hunger, it just made me cry. My hormones were all out of whack and it felt like I was losing control of my life. I'd become pregnant against my wishes. I'd married against my wishes. I'd grown fat against my wishes. And all this happened because I hadn't followed the church's rules, which were also against my wishes. I felt small and powerless like I'd been sucked down the rabbit hole and swept away by the Mad Hatter. I even dreamed weird things, like delivering a litter of puppies. Another time it was a lime-green alien that came out of my belly button.

I realize this will make me sound like a brat, but most people thought I was better looking than Keith. They said I'd "married down" and I was arrogant enough to believe them. They said it to flatter me, but it actually depressed me and now I felt stuck. So, yes, it may sound egotistical, but I *was* better looking than Keith. I just was. I may have been smarter too, but let's just call that a draw. He trounced me, however, on the self-image scale. I thought I was too fat, or too flat, and I could never get my hair right, it was too curly and frizzy. But Mr. I'm Perfect thought he was amazing and I was jealous of his blind spots. His breasts were catching up to mine and his love handles were a heaping handful, on each side. His hairline was receding too, so he compensated for it by keeping his hair long in back. I'm sorry, but it looked like a bad toupee that needed to be scooted forward about two full inches.

"Maybe you should start going to the gym as soon as the baby's born," he said.

"Let's buy a gym membership together," I said. "That might be fun."

"Nah, I'll probably just keep workin' out on my own."

Yeah, right. He hadn't worked out since we got married and would've required mouth-to-mouth if he did a conventional sit-up. So, instead of working out, he just sat around Murphy's Plumbing Supply with his work buddies eating Doritos and complaining about how fat and stupid everybody else was.

My water broke when I was hauling a tray of cheeseburgers at The Fairway Grill. I didn't know *what* had happened. I hadn't twisted funny, or poked it, or done anything at all but suddenly my legs were wet and there's this puddle on the tile floor.

I called Keith at work and he picked me up in the truck. I was pleasantly surprised he didn't make me sit on a towel or a bucket. We sped to the hospital with him frantically narrating the entire way: "Don't change light, don't change, don't *change!*—I think I'll turn on Bluff. No, it'll be quicker to go straight down Sunset—Come on, Bozo, get out of the fast lane!—Hang on, I'm running this yellow!"

When we got to the hospital they lollygagged around like they had all day. Didn't they know I was in freaking *labor?* Would it have killed them to give me a shot or something? Hey, Doctor McDreamy, the lady in 203B is dilated to twenty-seven, think maybe we oughta do something? When the big moment finally came, Keith almost missed it because he'd gone down to the cafeteria for another snack after I'd yelled at him for mumbling something about it being gross.

Jacob was perfect. I thought he looked like me but Keith and his parents insisted he was a spitting image of their side of the family. I understand. Keith's co-worker, who had no filter whatsoever, said he thought Jacob looked like a small, elderly British man, a reference I didn't particularly appreciate. But now that I look back at his baby pictures, I must privately confess there may have been some resemblance.

I'm glad I loved little Jacob as much as I did because it was much harder than I thought it would be. The lack of sleep, my stretched-out body, and now the worry over another human being I was responsible for, a human being that was completely dependent on me. Was he hungry? Was he in pain? Was I doing it right? And if so, why did he cry so much? Did he feel warm? Did he have colic? Was his poop the right color? You know, all the thing moms take on. I was overwhelmed. I called my mom who was overwhelmed herself and couldn't give me much help, except for bland encouragement that it would get better.

My hormones didn't snap back the moment he was born like I thought they would. If anything, I was more emotional, crying for seemingly no reason. A woman at church helpfully informed me I was going through a bout of "garden variety" postpartum depression. Garden variety? Oh, okay. As if carrying a child for nine months and everything that came along with it was not enough. I also think I was going through a mourning process after Jacob was born. I didn't mourn for him—my mourning was more selfish. I mourned for the death of my pre-motherhood life. Never again would I be free and childless, responsible for no one but myself. That life was officially over and deserved some mourning. I would never not be a mother again.

By the time he was one year old, I was pregnant again. When we told people this second pregnancy had been a surprise, half of them asked us if we knew how babies were made. Ha ha, never heard *that one* before.

Most of my high school friends were getting married by then. You hit your mid-twenties in my town and you're an old maid. Either that or people think you're still in the closet. I told them all how amazing married life was, just like all the disenchanted married women had told me before I became Mrs. Keith Murphy. That's what we do—we tell each other how happy we are. It's designed to make us feel better. Maybe other communities are the same, I don't know, but around here it's a big no-no to confess unhappiness or anything amiss in our lives. We were the Chosen People after all, the lucky ones who'd been handpicked by God to be Mormons, so we all played along because no one wanted to sabotage our exclusive heritage with all that chosen-ness riding on the line.

One of those recently married girls was named Cathy. She'd become Mrs. James Blake after dating Jim for two months at Dixie State. They promptly began breeding at the recommended rate. She confessed to me they were so tired they'd squeeze their breeding into the slot between the Five-Day Forecast and the Eyewitness Sports. And if that isn't sexy, I don't know what is.

We shared the side-by-side duplex with Cathy and Jim and became friends because we went to the same church and babysat each other's kids. Jim was quiet and let Cathy do all the talking. This made sense because she never let him speak anyway, even if you directed a question directly to him. For example, if you asked him how his job was going, she would answer for him that it was going all right but his boss was a lunatic. I think he'd basically just given up trying to get a word in. Cathy was outspoken and had at least one opinion about everything. Having more than one opinion on the same topic allowed her to talk more. The original Chatty Cathy, I'm telling you.

Cathy came over to treat me to some of her opinions one Saturday morning with her darling little Emily in tow. This little girl was about the cutest kid I'd ever seen. And she hadn't learned to talk yet, thank goodness.

"You won't believe what happened yesterday," Cathy said. "But I'm sworn to secrecy so I can't tell you what it was."

"Okay."

"Fine, I'll tell you if you insist. But you have to promise you won't tell anyone else."

She then tells me about some lady in our neighborhood who'd been caught shoplifting a package of diaper wipes down at Walmart, like this ought to be front page news. This just in! I thought the shocking part of the story was why anyone would shoplift diaper wipes.

"Have you seen those cute aerobic outfits down at Target?" she asked. "Jim would kill me if he knew I bought one because we're trying to save money for a down payment on a house because renting is a waste of money. It's the worst thing you can do."

"Why?" I asked, only because I figured she was going to tell me anyway.

"It just is."

"We're renting," I said, "because we can't afford to buy."

"I'm with you. Buying a house is a waste of money because you'd go in debt. Debt is the worst thing you can do, by the way."

"But I thought you just said—"

"That's why we'll probably keep renting."

"Same with us," I said.

"But, yeah, you'd be nuts if you didn't buy a house soon."

"But I thought you just—"

"Hey, is Keith around this morning?"

"Uh-huh, we're pretty much here all day. Didn't you see him outside washing his truck? He's supposed to be watching Jacob splash around in the kiddie pool."

"Yeah, I saw him. By the way, it's not very smart to own a truck. Bad gas mileage."

"Uh-huh."

"Listen," she said, "why don't I leave Emily with Keith while we run down to Target for a few minutes. You'd be crazy not to buy one of those aerobic outfits."

"Keith won't be happy if I buy another outfit."

"Just tell him you've had it for a long time. He'll never know."

Cathy returned a few minutes later with Emily, her adorable fifteen-month-old daughter. She informed Keith that as long as he was babysitting Jacob, he would also watch Emily while she and I ran a quick errand. Keith shot me a look which I pretended not to see. Cathy then plunked her daughter into the two inches of water in the blue plastic kiddie pool next to Jacob which sat on the strip of grass between our two driveways.

"We'll be back soon," Cathy told Keith. "I just changed her, but if she has a stinky diaper you can just use one of Jacob's."

As we got into Cathy's new minivan, the one they financed over seven years even though debt was the worst thing you can do, I gave Keith a little shrug to let him know I basically had no choice.

Keith had been waiting all morning for a call from his buddy to confirm a tee time and the phone rang in our house a few minutes after we drove away. He left the garden hose running next to the bucket of soapy water and ran into the house to take the call. He swore he was only inside for one minute, two tops, and I have no reason to doubt him.

Jacob was splashing in the shallow pool when Keith came back out, but fifteen-month-old Emily was lying face down in the two inches of water. He fell to his knees on the edge of the inflatable pool which caused the water to drain over his legs and onto the grass. Emily wasn't breathing. He shook her and then held her slippery body to his chest and patted her back like he was burping her. The neighbors said they heard Keith screaming from inside their houses as he knelt on the soaked grass with Emily's tiny body in his arms.

6

KATE

AFTER TONS OF COAXING AND POUTING, my parents finally agreed to let me go to UNLV but I'd have to pay for it because we were the poorest family in the neighborhood. At least I think we were. We weren't poor like those African children you've seen with flies in their eyes, all ribs and despair, but we had to drink powdered milk and you've got to be pretty poor to do that. And I remember that most of our purchases were of the layaway variety.

I'd saved up $1,200 which I applied to the tuition and got a student loan for the remainder. Sandra honked for me in her VW bug and we were off to college, straight-laced me and my quasi-bad girlfriend who sometimes drank coffee. As we were getting ready to drive away, my parents gave me (for the umpteenth time) the *Remember Who You Are* speech. I made a note to myself that when I had kids I wasn't going to treat them like axe murderers. But, in fairness, I *was* going to Vegas.

The *Remember Who You Are* speech is basically designed to guilt you into keeping the commandments. And "keeping the commandments" essentially meant no drinking, smoking, or premarital sex. Sandra obviously hadn't been given the same speech, which may be understandable because her parents drank coffee. She yanked the leash off her neck before we had even hit the freeway onramp and the entire drive was spent prepping for how much fun we were going to have. Not a word about actual school, studying, or possible majors. When we arrived in Vegas she acted like she'd never even heard of the commandments, jumping straight from the St. George puddle to the Las Vegas pond with a squealing cannonball. All I did was stick my big toe in, at first, and even then it felt wrong, like I'd turned my back on Jesus and the one and only true church.

I figured I'd start fresh in Vegas and began going exclusively by Kate. I like my given name but Kate just seemed more college-ish than Katherine, don't ask me why.

We shared our dorm room at Tonopah Hall with two other girls from San Jose, California. The first thing I asked them was if they went to Disneyland very often. They looked at me like I was from Mars. Then I asked them what they were. "What we *are?*" "Yeah, like what religion are you guys." They looked at each other and then back at me like I was a religious alien. You see, that would have been a perfectly reasonable question in my town and everyone would have known what I was talking about. Sandra tried to rescue me by suggesting we go somewhere for coffee.

I couldn't believe how much drinking and sex was going on. I thought I'd moved to the suburbs of Sodom or Gomorrah. I'd never even had a sip of alcohol and I was pretty naive when it came to sex. Okay, I wasn't a virgin anymore, thanks to that cheating Keith Murphy, but I was the Flying Nun compared to some of those girls. Speaking of Keith Murphy, part of me hoped he'd get that girl from Snow Canyon pregnant for good. Maybe even have triplets so he wouldn't have time to watch his stupid football games.

My freshman year was an adjustment, let's just say that. I was embarrassed to be a conservative Mormon girl from a podunk little town in Utah. I'll admit that. Maybe that's why I went overboard a few times to prove I wasn't a prude, which made me feel like a complete traitor. Remember in the Bible when Peter denied knowing Jesus three separate times? Well, that's how I felt when my sorority sisters made fun of Mormons and I went along with the laughs. I did it more than three times, too. When they'd ask if I was really a Mormon, I'd usually say something like, "Well, yeah, sort of." Sort of? *Sort of?* I was freaking born and bred—as hardcore as it gets. The Coombs family coat of arms should have featured a Fabio-looking Jesus caressing a Book of Mormon, and my photo should have been on the cover of the hymn book.

Everyone was anxious to see me drink, like it was their mission to bring me up to speed on vice. Even Sandra got into the act, urging me to go slow when what she *really* wanted was for me to get wasted. I suspect she wanted company in her heresy. It probably assuaged her own guilt to know she wasn't the only handpicked Chosen Person to fly off the rails.

When I look back over my life to that point, I realize I'd always done what everyone else wanted me to do. Go to church? Check. Be straight-laced? Check. Please my parents? Check. Please my old friends? Check. Please my new friends? Check.

Believe this? Check. Believe that? Check. Yes, I had become a diligent checker-offer.

I'd been tamed, convinced that I should enjoy my little cage and never leave it. I had rarely strayed from my parents' wishes, the pleaser that I am, doing all the "should's" to everyone's satisfaction. But now I'd committed a few unexpected "shouldn't's" that no one saw coming, especially not me. And I'd committed them despite the *Cliff Speech* I'd frequently been given—you know that old standby meant to discourage you from going along with the crowd. "Would you jump off a cliff if your friends told you to?" Uh, no. "Good girl, then do what is right and don't follow the crowd." And yet, that's exactly what I'd done my entire life—I had followed the crowd. But, of course, my parents would've reminded me there were crowds and then there were crowds and I was supposed to follow the *correct* one. Which, surprise surprise, happened to be their crowd.

The church was like those bumpers you see at a bowling alley. You might not always roll a strike but you won't roll a gutter ball because the bumpers won't let you. Well, now the bumpers were down and I was free to roll gutter balls to my heart's content. I realize there is value in a good bumper and it wasn't complete horseshit to have been taught that sex and booze were evil, but I think the evilness was overblown to scare me back into my cage where they thought I belonged.

So, for the first time in my life I was surrounded by a different crowd in college and the pressure to drink kept building. I finally decided I might as well get it over with so the girls poured me a glass of cheap whiskey. The only time I'd seen anyone drink whiskey was in a Bonanza saloon. I lifted the glass and took a whiff. I thought it smelled like something you'd put on a sore, or something you'd use to clean a paint brush. It was so nasty I could only take a few swigs but I acted like I was practically guzzling it because I didn't want to disappoint them, or be a loser. Geez you guys, that really hits the spot!

Now that I had sinned, my string of unblemished virtue broken, I figured I might as well go all in. After all, if I was going to hell for drinking that whiskey I figured I might as well have myself a nice little sinning binge. It's the same way I felt after doing it with Keith Murphy the first time. Hey, as long as you're eternally doomed you might as well have some fun before you face the music, right?

I started drinking a little more each time and it didn't kill me. In fact, it was fun (even though the taste was awful, and anybody who says otherwise is a liar). There were a few times I drank way too much and got so sick I wanted to die. No, seriously, I wanted to die, barfing all over the place. And there was the time Sandra passed out at a frat party. There she was, my Sunday school cohort, sprawled out on a ratty old sofa in the Sigma Chi house, dead to the world at two o'clock in the morning. While she was out cold, a few guys took a magic marker and drew a penis and a pair of hairy balls on her forehead. Sandra didn't think it was funny when she eventually came to, but when the ink finally disappeared after a few embarrassing days of walking around campus with a faded penis on her forehead, the drinking started right back up again.

There were times I wished I'd just gone to the local college in my hometown. How my life would have turned out differently! If I'd stayed home I probably would've followed a different crowd because there was basically only one. My trail would have been well blazed and my parents and extended family would have been pleased. I also would've had better grades if I hadn't been up all night partying, the bumpers would have seen to that. I wouldn't have had to clean up Sandra's barf and I wouldn't have had to hide in a broom closet with a beer in my hand either, wishing I had run like the other kids when the cops came. On the other hand, I probably would've had stretch marks and been lactating by the time I was a sophomore in college.

My parents had always preached that I'd get burned if I played with fire and yet I'd hardly been singed as far as I could see. The break from religious orthodoxy was refreshing. Notwithstanding the occasional gutter ball, I was doing just fine without the church's hands all over me like that two-timing Keith Murphy's used to be. What eventually happened to me—the near rape, murder, and life of vice—would have been Exhibit A for why you don't go down that road in the first place. See, that's exactly what happens, they'd say. Sure it's sad but you can't say she wasn't warned. She got what she had coming to her.

I called my parents every Sunday and the conversation went about the same each week.

"Dale!" my mom would yell into the distance, "it's Katherine calling long distance. Pick up!" and a few seconds later my dad would pick up another extension.

"How's your school work going?"

Bad. "Good."

"Learning anything useful?" my dad would ask.

"Yeah, I think so." Like how to do Jell-O shots and tap a keg.

"Did you go to church today?"

No. "Yes."

"How's the bishop in your student ward?"

No clue. "He's fine."

"Are you confessing to him as often as you should?"

No chance. "When I really need to, yeah."

"Well, we know darned good and well that there are bad influences down there," my mom would say. "Just remember who you are and what you stand for."

"Yeah, Mom, I know."

"And don't forget that the way you dress can influence a boy to take advantage of you."

I was reminded of the "Modesty Checks" I endured as a young teenager at church. Our young women's teacher would have each of us stand in front of the Sunday school class and raise our hands above our head to see if any mid-rift showed. Or they'd have us bend over to ensure that boys, those lecherous twelve-year-old pigs, couldn't see up our skirts or down our bony cleavages. If a boy tried to go too far, we were taught it was largely our fault, the budding temptresses that we were. You see, boys couldn't help themselves so it wasn't really their fault. We girls were the ones who'd likely brought it on, reaching for a book on the third shelf and unwittingly exposing an inch of our tummy.

I found a job waiting tables at a rundown café off the strip. The Lucky Traveler's travelers appeared to have no luck at all and a refreshing lack of ambition for anything other than gambling. You could tell who the regulars were by the way people ignored them when they came in. They ate dry pork chops and chicken fried steak while ruefully lamenting having hit the sixteen only to have the dealer bust. They'd convinced themselves against all reason that they'd been *this* close to living on Easy Street and how none of it was their fault because the casinos were rigged. Why these Einstein's kept feeding the beast if they thought it was rigged, I'll never know.

Ricky Waters was one of those unlucky gamblers, I just didn't know it at the time. He looked like George Clooney, in George Clooney's dreams. He was so handsome he looked fake. His hair was dark, his eyes were blue, and his teeth were white. His skin was a shade darker than mine—like a lightly stained mahogany board—which set off his blue eyes and white teeth. He looked quite different than the Lucky Traveler's other patrons, I'll just say that. With a single glance you could tell more about the regular clientele than you probably wanted to know. Most of them would shuffle in with plastic-mesh baseball caps and T-shirts stretched across their bellies, or polyester leisure suits with sleeves that hung to their knuckles. But then there was Ricky Waters. He was Mr. Suave with a capital S and I couldn't figure out why he hung out at a crummy place like the Lucky Traveler.

"So why are *you* working here?" Ricky asked after I put a tuna melt and fries in front of him. "A girl like you belongs over at the Flamingo, or Desert Inn."

I could have asked him the same thing but instead I said it paid the bills, or something about that original.

"Listen," he said in that sexy movie star way of his, "I've got a big deal coming in, but for now this is all I've got for a tip." He dropped a marijuana joint on top of the bill. "But I'll make it up to you next time."

"Uh, sure, no problem."

I had never seen a marijuana joint in my life. Drugs! Crime! Yikes! It was hand-rolled and twisted at each end like a skinny

Tootsie Roll. I couldn't even figure out which end you were supposed to light. I was almost afraid to touch the danged thing and had no idea what it would cost, or what would happen if I actually smoked it. I figured I'd probably be a heroin addict within a week, a heroin addict with a wicked case of lung cancer. Anyway, I didn't dare throw it away for some reason and hid it in the bottom of my underwear drawer when I got home.

I got a pit in my stomach when Ricky returned to the Lucky Traveler the next day. It was the good kind of pit, the kind that flutters, but I pretended I had no pit at all—just going about my business, ho hum, like drop-dead gorgeous men talked to me and gave me illegal drugs every day of the week. He was sitting in Annette's station that day and every time I looked over at him I got busted. He finally waved me over.

"Sorry if I'm staring at you," he said, "but you're the most beautiful woman I've ever seen."

Was he *serious?* Okay, I knew I wasn't *the* most beautiful woman he'd ever seen. I'm not that dumb. But still, he hadn't said that to Annette, who I thought was pretty cute. At least I don't think he had.

Quick, I thought, say something casual and amusing! But in the moment all I could come up with was, "Gol, thanks. We have new uniforms." Lame, I know, but in my defense I was nervous and he was so handsome it threw me off.

"Can I get your phone number?"

"Sorry, but I don't even know you."

"I'm Ricky, Ricky Waters," he said and held out his hand. I wanted to lick it.

I wiped my hand on my apron and stuck it out. "I'm Kate." My hand was ice cold and clammy which was just my luck.

"So, can I have your number now that you know me?"

I gave it to him. What else was I supposed to do? I didn't want to be *rude.* I bet every woman in Nevada would've done the exact same thing. In fact, they probably would've confirmed it in a handwritten letter on scented stationery, notarized and sent by certified mail.

He called me the next day and asked me out for that weekend. I didn't have any plans but I said I did because I didn't want him to think I was a loser. He asked me out again for a time when I actually *did* have plans, but I said I didn't and then promptly canceled my trip back to St. George for the weekend where Janet had been trying to line me up with a returned missionary who, I'm sorry to say, may have had a terrific personality but was no looker.

Ricky was such a gentleman, at first, and didn't try anything fancy. Looking back, I think it was his go-to strategy—pretending a physical relationship was too important to be rushed. He said he wanted to get to know me on a deeper level first. I fell for it, too, because I wanted to. Pathetic. In fact, by the time he finally made his move, I was practically egging him on. Straight out of the ol' Ricky playbook.

He tasted like cigarettes, which sort of grossed me out. But he *was* gorgeous with a lean stomach and strip of hair trailing down from his belly button like a fuse. And unlike Keith who was clumsy and quick, Ricky was all about me. There wasn't a mad rush in the cab of the pickup truck, banging my knee on the gear shift and bonking my head on the stereo speaker. Oh, Ricky knew what he was doing all right.

I only lived in the dorm rooms for a semester and then moved to a dumpy apartment on the west side of town, about a mile from the strip. I shared the apartment with Sandra and another girl named Deborah. Sandra had already sown most of her oats, planting and harvesting them in record time, and was now talking about moving back to St. George to give Gary Young a try. Gary had just returned from his two-year mission and had ants in his pants. Sandra would probably move back home and pretend to be a virgin, settling for a bit of light petting until they got married a few months later when poor Gary could finally crank up his rusty little factory.

My other roommate, Deborah, had been born sowing oats. I swear she could have gone pro. She dressed like a hooker and wore so much make-up it looked like she applied it with a paint brush and roller. A line of hickeys dotted her neck like a chain of islands and she made no effort to hide them. She was the kind of girl mothers looked at, shook their heads, and praised the Good Lord she wasn't their daughter. Deborah also worked as a waitress but always had enough money to buy skanky clothes and quarts of makeup. When she showed up in a new sports car, I figured her parents must have been loaded. Sandra said Deborah was rich because she was Jewish. Huh? I didn't even know what she was talking about.

I was naïve, I'll admit that. And maybe I was overly sensitive about my upbringing, but it bugged me when people who knew nothing about Mormons would make insensitive or naïve comments of their own, leering at us like we were kooky polygamists. Take Deborah for example. When she found out I was from Utah, she asked, "What is about you guys anyway?"

"What do you mean?"

"You just have some weird food stuff." Here she was, Queen Jew, calling *my* food stuff weird. That's the sort of thing I'm talking about. Or how about when Catholics and Evangelicals tease us because we happen to believe in angels?

Anyway, Deborah and I were alone in the apartment late one morning. I was sitting at the kitchen table doing my bills and she was sitting on the sofa with a bowl of mac and cheese on her lap. Her feet were perched up on the coffee table and there were cotton balls wedged between each toe. The room smelled of nail polish. I had loaned Ricky $1,000 because he was in a short-term bind. He'd sworn to me that he'd pay me back right away because he was working on a big deal and would be coming into a lot of money very soon. How was I supposed to know that "very soon" meant, like, never? You must remember that I didn't know the *real* Ricky back then. After I paid my bills I barely had enough left over to eat.

"Hey, Deborah, how do you do it?"

"Do what?" she asked as she sat blowing on a spoonful of mac and cheese.

"I'm busting my butt at the restaurant and I'm always broke."

"I don't know," she said. She was scraping the mac and cheese off the spoon with her teeth because it was still too hot. "I guess I'm just good at budgeting."

"But you spend way more than I do. Do your parents send you money or something?"

"That's a laugh. My parents hardly know I'm alive."

"So what's the secret? You couldn't make that much waiting tables."

"I don't," she said.

"Okay then, so what *do* you do? You have a second job or something?"

"It's nothing. It's no big deal."

For some reason this seemed like a big deal to me. I was living on Top Ramen. "Come on, Deborah. What's your secret?"

"Promise you won't tell? Not even Sandra?"

"Tell what?" I asked as I slid my checkbook to the side and leaned toward her in a conspiratorial way.

"Okay, but you need to promise you won't tell anybody."

"Yeah, okay."

"I work two nights a week at a club."

"At a club? What do you mean? What club?"

"Sugar & Spice."

"Sugar & Spice?" I knew I'd heard of it and it took me a minute to place it. "Hold it. Isn't that that sleazy strip club place over by Circus Circus?"

"Yeah."

"So, what, you wait tables there, too?"

"I'm a dancer."

"Like in a show?" I asked.

"It's a strip club, Kate. I'm a dancer. You know? Like on the pole?"

She was casually telling me this as she ate her mac and cheese, the way she might describe how many scoops of laundry detergent she used when doing darks.

"You're a *stripper?*"

"Yeah. And you promised not to tell anyone."

"So . . . like . . . you get *naked?*"

"Hey, I make about $600 bucks a night. You should try it."

"But what if your parents found out?" I still couldn't believe she was a stripper. I knew they had them, somewhere, but this was someone I actually *knew*. I would've been less surprised if she'd told me she was the mother of ten and her husband was the freaking governor.

"Like I said, my parents hardly know I'm alive. My mom lives in a trailer park somewhere and had something like eight kids. She has no clue what I do and probably wouldn't care anyway. And I've never even met my real dad."

This confession made me like her more for some reason. Maybe it's because I felt sorry for her. I mean, it sounded like her mom just spat her from the womb between boyfriends. At least I knew all my siblings.

"Gol, Deborah, I'm sorry."

"Hey, it is what it is. But you should think about it—the club I mean. I know the owner guy and I bet he'd hire you in a second."

7

KATHERINE

CATHY AND I WERE JUST GETTING BACK into her minivan after our Target shopping spree when we saw a fire truck go by, and then an ambulance. You know how it is when they speed past and you feel sorry for whoever had the heart attack, or whoever is watching their house burn down? Well, that was the momentary feeling I had but it didn't linger because Chatty Cathy was yammering on about how smart I was to buy that new aerobics outfit we couldn't afford.

The yammering continued as we rounded the curve in our neighborhood and saw a fire truck in front of our duplex. The yammering abruptly stopped. We were confused. There were no flames or smoke so why was a fire truck there? The neighbors were standing on their front lawns and porches staring at our empty front yard. The garden hose was still running onto the driveway next to the bucket of soapy water. We jumped out of the car and ran across the driveway to our side of the duplex, passing the nearly empty kiddie pool and reaching the front door just as Keith was coming out. He was holding Jacob who was still wearing his soaking wet diaper.

I'll never forget the look on his face. Vacant. Stunned. Numb. Like the look of a soldier stumbling back from the gory front lines—processing the un-processible somewhere in the nooks of his brain.

"Where is she!" Cathy screamed. "Where's Emily!"

Keith looked at her with a dull, empty expression. He must have heard her but there was no focus in the look.

"Where *is* she!"

"In there," he said and stepped to the side so Cathy could get past him.

The wail from inside our duplex a few seconds later was animalistic. I can think of no other way to describe it. It was the most awful thing I've ever heard.

"Keith!" I screamed.

"I was . . . the phone rang . . . I was just gone for a minute . . ."

"Oh no, no, no, no, Keith, please, no."

I ran inside. Emily was lying on a stretcher in our cramped living room. She was so tiny. It looked like she was on a giant changing table and they were about to remove her waterlogged diaper. Cathy was on her knees next to the stretcher, hands covering her face. *No! No! No! No!* A paramedic was kneeling next to her. He put his arm around her but she pulled away, jumped up, and then collapsed onto the stretcher next to her daughter like a puppet whose strings have suddenly been cut.

"I'm so sorry." It was Keith, in barely a whisper. "I tried . . . but I couldn't . . ."

Cathy turned around from the stretcher and lunged at him like a wild animal, beating him on his chest with her fists. *Why!*

Why! Why! Keith didn't resist her, he just stood there in a state of shock, still holding Jacob off to the side on his hip. His brown T-shirt and pants were wet from having held the two children in their soaking diapers. I felt sorry for him—pity really. I knew his life, our lives, would never be the same again, for these are the tragic moments that forever mark time. Like B.C. and A.D., all future events in our lives would be timed, framed, and measured by this day. A fireman tried to pull Cathy away, but she turned on him next, then limply fell into his arms and sobbed.

The next ten minutes are a blur. I remember taking Jacob from Keith who numbly handed him over. I remember Cathy prying Emily away from the paramedic and rocking her, shushing, shushing, shushing, reassuring her lifeless little girl that it would be all right. I remember seeing Keith standing out in the front yard facing the street, his back to us. He was just standing there like a statue, his arms hanging helplessly to his sides. I remember Jim sitting on the step of our porch, his head down and hugging his knees, slightly rocking, like a passenger waiting for the plane to crash. I remember the gurney being wheeled out with a blanket covering Emily's body but not her face. It looked like she was merely sleeping, so precious and small. I remember no one was in a hurry—there had almost been a reverence to it all. I never saw the kiddie pool again and have no idea what happened to it. Maybe Keith threw it out.

I spent a lot of time over at Cathy and Jim's the next few days but I doubt they even knew I was there. They were just surviving. Friends and relatives swarmed all over their half of the duplex but carefully avoided our half. Not one of them checked in on us. Not one. I doubt they considered Keith to be a monster because they knew it could've happened on anyone's watch, but they were uncomfortable. You could just tell. So while the Blake's were surrounded with love and compassion, Keith spent his time alone in our bedroom, flogging himself. No one asked how *he* was holding up. No one brought *him* a casserole. He'd tried to call Cathy and Jim to apologize, again, but Jim made it pretty clear that he'd already done plenty. I'm not saying they owed him a casserole, of course not, but still.

I went to the funeral alone. It was heart wrenching and they weren't even trying to make it sad. If anything, they were trying to make it happy, like Emily was in a better place and all of that. And the more they tried to make it happy the sadder it became, because everyone knew, deep down, that you couldn't dress up this sort of tragedy with a pep talk that no one could actually rely on. Oh, they pretended to rely on it—on the promise that Emily was better off where she was up in heaven—that in some perverse way this was a *good* thing in the big scheme of things. But that was a stretch because no one wanted Emily in heaven.

They had a viewing in a room off the chapel before the funeral service began. Friends and relatives formed a line and walked through to witness Emily in the small casket, dabbing the corners of their eyes with wads of Kleenex. The casket was surrounded by standing sprays of pink roses, carnations, lilies, and mums. On her chest was a small light-blue bunny Emily used to hold in a headlock all day long. She couldn't go to sleep without it and now it would be buried with her. Cathy and Jim stood at the end of the line next to the casket to receive the well-wishers like the bride and groom in a wedding line. After seeing the dead child and her bunny, the guests (is that what they were, guests?) milled about in clusters whispering. Like most of them, I didn't want to look at her, but at the same time

I did. I'd only been to a few viewings in the my life but they were old people who looked waxy and fake, their hair made up in their favorite, blue-tinted bouffant. They looked dead. But not little Emily whose skin was perfect, whose body was perfect. It was a macabre event in a way—gawking over this innocent dead child.

Keith wanted to go to the funeral but he didn't think he should because Jim and Cathy might not have wanted him there, which was probably true. But then when he didn't go they said he was insensitive for not caring enough to go. *Gol, Keith Murphy didn't even go to the freaking funeral? Can you believe it?* When we went to the grocery store, people saw him out of the corners of their eyes and switched aisles. If they didn't have time to make the ol' switcheroo, they pretended to study the ingredients listed on the bottle of ketchup they weren't going to buy.

Then the police got involved. I hadn't even considered the fact that Keith might face criminal charges. *Criminal* charges? Did we need a lawyer now? They took a statement from Keith in our living room. I got the sense that the officers wanted to be there about as much as we wanted them there. After Keith tearfully completed his statement, the officers hugged him. They later called to inform Keith there would be no formal charges.

Now that our lives were ruined, I needed it to be Keith's fault. And it was, I suppose, but it's hard to stay mad at someone who is already heartbroken. It's also hard to know how you'd react if you were responsible for such an awful thing. In fact, I presume it's rather impossible, but Keith never tried to justify what had happened, or to lessen his culpability in the deal. Me, I think I might have been more defensive if you want to know the honest truth.

"Maybe we should move," he said.

"But I love it here."

"Me too, but we can't be their next-door neighbors. They won't even look at me. They hate me."

"They're devastated, Keith. They lost their daughter while you were supposed to be watching her, in case you've forgotten."

"It's my fault, okay? You don't think I know that? I was washing the truck while you were off running around with Cathy and I had to watch the kids. So, yeah, it's my fault."

"You *had* to watch them? So now you're going to blame *me* because you had to watch your son for a few minutes? Are you being serious right now?"

"That's not what I'm saying, Katherine. It was my fault and I'm sorry."

We had to move. It was just too awkward. I'm not blaming the Blakes. They were distraught and simply trying to survive. I could even understand on some level why they'd begun to avoid me, too. After all, I was married to the man who'd taken the phone call. But what did they want me to do? Did they want me to divorce him and take his truck? And then I realized I was making it all about me and they probably hadn't sat around plotting ways to make me suffer as if they had nothing else to think about.

Moving presented a big problem because we were dead broke. My first thought was to move in with my parents, but even though my Grandma Coombs had since passed away, her downstairs space had been swallowed up by Kenny and Korbin before she'd even been buried. I call dibs on grandma's room!

Let's just say I didn't see evidence of a gaping hole in their hearts with her passing. As for me, my grandma's legacy consisted of her poverty stories, her old-person smell, and the dent on the side of the station wagon that still bore the circled imprint of the toilet plunger.

Keith's parents, Vaughn and Dottie, had extra space and let us move in with them. Oh joy. I appreciated their offer, I did, but moving in with the in-laws hadn't been on my bucket list. I think Vaughn felt guilty because he'd recently been forced to cut Keith's pay at Murphy's Plumbing Supply. (Keith had lobbied hard for Murphy and Sons, but his dad was a stickler.)

Our new living arrangement started off on the wrong foot. "What," Vaughn said that first day, "the Mormons don't like you anymore?" Ever since he quit the church, Vaughn had made a living out of nitpicking about us Mormons. It appeared to give him great joy.

"Dad, that's not fair," Keith said. "Jim and Cathy are just upset."

"But I thought they were supposed to turn the other cheek."

"Our friends are members of the church and they've been really good to us," I said.

"Yeah, Dad, they've been good to us." Did Keith really believe that? Probably not, but I liked how he stood up to his dad which was something he didn't do very often.

I liked him even more when he didn't flip out like I did when Jim and Cathy sued him. Yeah, the Blake's sued Keith for a million dollars.

8

KATE

I COULDN'T BELIEVE MY ROOMMATE was a stripper—an actual full-blown *stripper*. I wanted to tell Sandra but I'd promised not to, so I hoped she'd find out some other way because I wanted to gossip about it. Maybe the secretary at Sugar & Spice would call and leave a message on our answering machine that Deborah's stripper shift had been canceled or something.

In the meantime, I was gaga over the handsome and mysterious Ricky Waters. I only saw him at the restaurant or my apartment because he said his upscale condo was being remodeled and was a mess. How was I supposed to know he lived in a sleazy motel off the strip and was behind on the rent there, too? Looking back, should I have interrogated him? Should I have hired a private detective to do some snooping? Maybe make him take a polygraph? Is that what it comes down to these days? I'm a trusting person and I trusted him.

"He's too old for you," Sandra said. "And there's just something fishy about him."

I can see how she might have thought that, but I also knew Sandra hated the fact that Ricky was so handsome. She would have preferred I dated someone ugly, especially since she'd hit a dry patch and her only prospect at the time was the returned missionary back in St. George who was a total nerd. His idea of a date night was to read the scriptures together and then splurge on root beer floats.

"You just don't know him like I do," I said.

"Is he dating anyone else?"

Probably. "No."

"Are you sure?"

Um, not really. "Of course I'm sure."

I was an idiot for falling for that "you're the most beautiful woman I've ever seen" crap. I know that. But I didn't want to give Sandra the satisfaction of being right about Ricky (or really anything, for that matter), so I was doubly determined to make it work.

"It just seems strange that he has such fancy clothes and a BMW when he doesn't even have a regular job."

Sandra was right about that—it was strange. Very strange in fact. But I rationalized it away because I wanted to. Besides, maybe he really was a big-time businessman. How was I supposed to know? I was a naïve and trusting girl who didn't know squat about high finance. I didn't even own a credit card.

"He's really smart," I said. "He'll probably make a fortune off all his business deals."

Ricky was smart all right, at least smart enough to realize what a sucker I was. Instead of paying me back the $1,000 he'd already borrowed, he doubled down.

"Kate, I really hate to ask you again, but could you loan me another $1,000? I only need it for a few weeks. I've got some big money coming in but they keep delaying it. I'll pay you interest if you want."

"Gol, I'm super tight right now," I said. "Like, how long?"

"Maybe two weeks. Three tops."

"Could you repay both loans by then?"

"Easily. I'm totally embarrassed about all this. I mean, a measly thousand bucks? I could take it from some other investments but the money's tied up and I'd have to pay capital gains."

Oh, right, capital gains. Like I knew what capital gains were. Who did he think I was? Mrs. H. R. Block? I gave him another thousand because he was so handsome. Then he said he was falling in love with me and I would've given him a kidney. When he surprised me with a $200 necklace a few days later, I would've also thrown in my gall bladder.

Three weeks passed and still no money from Ricky. I knew he'd eventually repay me, and hopefully before our silver anniversary, but I was desperate. My rent was due and so was another tuition payment.

Deborah was in the kitchen of our apartment whipping up a protein shake in the blender. She didn't cook much, none of us did—microwaved Hot Pockets or a protein shake was about as culinary as we got. Besides, even if I were a master chef, there are only so many recipes that call for Top Ramen.

"So, hey, Deborah," I said when she turned off the blender. "I'm kind of short on my share of the rent this month. Any chance you could cover me? I promise I'll pay you back next month."

She hit the start button on the blender for about ten more seconds and I thought she hadn't heard me. "Can't you get it from your parents or something?" she shouted over the blender's racket before turning it off.

"Well, I—" and then she hit the start button again.

When the blender finally stopped for good I told her I'd already called my parents who'd turned me down. This was a lie. I hadn't called them because I knew what they would've said.

She glugged the thick green sludge into a glass then held the pitcher up and licked the spout to get the drips. She took her own sweet time, leaving me hanging without responding. She then lit a cigarette and leaned back against the kitchen counter. We had a No Smoking policy at the apartment but this was no time to get technical with her. I decided I'd give her a mild reprimand about the smoking if she turned me down.

"Listen," she said as she leaned her head back and exhaled a contrail of smoke, practically daring me to call her on it, "why don't you come with me to an audition. You'd make, like, $1,000 in two nights. You'd be good."

"You mean at the stripper place?"

"Yeah, it's not a big deal. Lots of girls at UNLV do it and they aren't sluts or anything."

I didn't know the precise definition of "slut" but I figured "stripper" had to be a potential synonym, at the very least.

"What exactly would I have to do?"

Did this question imply that I would seriously consider actually doing it? Helllooo? I was the total antonym of stripper, or at least I thought I was.

"It's like they have these auditions every Wednesday, okay? And about ten girls show up and the owner just asks you to dance and stuff. Then he tells you if you can come back for amateur night. It's not that hard. The girls aren't even that cute."

"Amateur night?"

"Yeah, the new girls dance for two or three minutes each, okay? Then the audience votes for who they like. If they like you, then you get invited back to be a regular. That's when you really start raking in the money."

"All I have to do is dance?"

"Well, you gotta take your top off—but it's not like you have to get totally naked or anything."

"How many people would see me?"

"I don't know, maybe thirty or so. But it's pretty dark and you're only up there for a few minutes."

"Dance? Like how?"

"Just on the pole and stuff."

"On the *pole?* I wouldn't even know how to do that."

Here I was getting worked up over how to dance on a pole when what I *should've* been worked up about was taking off my freaking shirt in front of a bunch of pervs. I was about an 8.5 on the modesty scale. I hardly dared take my shirt off after gym class to shower, and even then I'd wedge myself into my open locker as far as I could, using it as a shield. And yet my concern was over my pole dancing skills? It was like being asked to jump into a pool of bloodthirsty sharks but declining because I didn't want to get my hair wet.

"It's not that hard," she said. "I didn't even practice the first time. Besides, they don't really care how good of a dancer you are. I mean, come on, it's not about that."

"I'm not saying I'd do it or anything, but you're saying that *if* I went and met this guy, and *if* he hired me, I'd make $500 for one night?"

"Probably. Something like that." She took another drag, put her head back, and blew another contrail. She then tapped off the ash into the kitchen sink like it was a convenient ashtray.

"There's no way," I said. "I mean, what if somebody I knew saw me?"

"I wouldn't worry about that."

"But what if they did?"

"Some girls wear hats and stuff, but I'm telling you the chances you'd know somebody are, like, zero."

"Do you have to sign anything?"

"No, you pretty much just go whenever you want to."

I'll admit, it sounded like a fairly easy way to make a quick buck. Easy, that is, if you'd call getting naked in public "easy."

"How long are you going to keep doing it?"

"I don't know," she said. "Probably until I graduate." This meant she'd be doing it well into her nineties because she hardly ever went to school. She'd be in the Guinness record book for Oldest Collegiate Stripper.

"I don't think I'd dare," I said. "I'm going out with Ricky tomorrow night anyway."

"I'll tell the owner about you just in case. We're pretty tight."

"Thanks," I said. "And hey, I just want you to know that I don't think you're bad or anything."

"Yeah, whatever, but I hope you'll do it with me sometime because it's kind of fun if you know what I mean."

It didn't sound kind of fun to me, if you know what I mean. This was not exactly my definition of Girls Night Out. I wasn't even comfortable going to one of those Chippendales shows I saw on the billboards all over town. You'd think I'd check that off the list first.

The next night, Ricky took me to a nice restaurant where a glass of wine was fifteen dollars (and the glass wasn't filled to the brim either) and he paid with cash. He wore a new blue-gray sport coat and looked more dashing than ever. There went my spleen! I was running out of dispensable organs at this rate. We were having a nice time until he "forewarned" me that he might not be able to pay me back for another few weeks, "maybe even a month, just to be on the safe side."

When I got home the next night after another shift at the Lucky Traveler, I went into my bathroom and locked the door. I stood in front of the mirror and tried to be all sexy while I took off my clothes like a real live stripper. I rolled up my panties to make them as skimpy as possible then put one hand on my hip, thrust it to the side, then raised my other arm up in the air like I'd seen models do. I turned and stuck my butt out and wiggled it because I figured they did that too. Maybe I was doing it the wrong way because it wasn't sexy, at all. I looked totally ridiculous and felt like a complete idiot.

There was no way I could actually do this. For starters, my boobs were too small. Then I thought to myself, is *that* why you're antsy about the whole thing, because your stupid boobs are too small? Seriously? Isn't it something like, uh, news flash, it's against the freaking *commandments?* Then I thought about the money and how broke I was. Five hundred dollars in less than five minutes? And Deborah said it would be super dark.

I decided I needed another rehearsal. Not because I was going to do it, but *if* I did I needed a little practice. It made absolutely no sense to be rusty. I was alone in the apartment the next afternoon and went into the bedroom I shared with Sandra. I stripped down to my bra and panties and stared at myself in the full-length mirror nailed to the back of the closet door. Not too bad, I thought. I put on a pair of Sandra's highest heels (only a hooker would wear such ghastly things) and slid a Blondie cassette into the boom box. I found the "Call me" track, then bent over and let my hair fall down. I shook my head and tossed it back so I'd look even sexier.

I grabbed the bathroom door frame with both hands, pretending it was a pole, and gyrated my hips as my hands slid down the door frame. I'm lucky I didn't get a sliver. After that, I grabbed the door knob with both hands and leaned back, arching at the waist and throwing my head back just as sexy as can be. Then I took off my bra and started whipping it around my head like I was about to rope a calf, pretending there were thirty guys hootin' and hollerin'. *Call me, call me any, anytime, call me. Call me . . .*

The music was loud and I didn't hear Sandra come bombing into the room, so focused was I on being sexy.

"What in the hell are you *doing?*"

"Oh shit, you scared me." I immediately stopped trying to be so sexy and lassoing the calf with my bra. "I'm not doing anything—just sort of messing around."

"Sort of messing around? You're wearing high heels and making love to that door. Are you drunk or something? Geez, you look like a freaking stripper."

Well, apparently I'd nailed the look. "I know—it's stupid. But Ricky said he likes it when I do stuff like this, so yeah, it's kinda dumb, huh?"

"Ya think?" She collapsed on the bed with a sigh and kicked off her shoes. "Mind if I turn off this music? I've got a headache."

I tried to kick her high heels into the closet when she rolled over to the boom box on the nightstand but one of them got stuck on my foot. So there I was, standing like a half-naked stork with the remaining high heel twisted around my ankle.

Sandra lay on the bed, absorbed in thought. "Listen," she said, "I've been meaning to talk to you about something. It's Deborah. I'm worried about her. I think she might be on drugs or something, you know what I mean?"

"Yeah, sort of," I said as I nonchalantly tried to shake the high heel off my foot.

"Where's she getting all her money? And what's the deal with all the make-up?"

"Beats me," I said.

"Maybe she's a drug dealer."

"I doubt it. Her parents must be sending her money or something."

"Well, I think I'm going to talk to her," Sandra said.

"I'll do it," I said. "I need to talk to her about that cute leather jacket she borrowed anyway."

"Okay, but if she's a drug dealer she'll probably deny it."

The next day, I drove by Sugar & Spice on my way to work. It looked like a dump to me—a gray cinder block box with no windows squatting in the middle of the lousy part of town. A sign sat atop a pole in the asphalt parking lot between the potholes. It was the kind of sign that had those removable black letters. It read: SUGAR & SPIC. The "E" must've blown off in a windstorm. Either that or the owner was racist. There were only two cars in the parking lot that afternoon; both of them pimped out Lincolns.

I might have dared go inside but it looked like one of those abandoned warehouses where the bad guys take people to tie them up and torture them. I drove by again later that night and the parking lot was full. A neon sign on the cinder block wall read *Beer and Liquor.* It was written in cursive between two martini glasses that seemed to be festively dancing in the air. Another neon sign advertised *Live Dancing.* I got a pit in my stomach—the bad kind of pit this time.

Ricky was sitting at our kitchen table smoking a cigarette when I got home. I was annoyed because I'd already complained to him about Deborah's smoking in the apartment and worried we'd be evicted. Plus it smells gross, it just does. He took one more drag, then blew out the smoke and watched it. He dropped the cigarette into a nearly empty glass of water with a tiny hiss.

"I can't believe it," he said, shaking his head. Apparently, the guy who owed him the money was still dragging his feet. I braced for another loan request because I'd become his very own little ATM. Instead, he suggested we go out for a drink, wondering out loud if I'd be willing to pick up the tab from my tip money.

"I'm tired tonight, Ricky. Mind if we just stay here?"

"Oh, yeah, sure. I just thought maybe you'd want to go out."

He stood and started rifling through my cupboards looking for something to drink. He didn't find any booze, but he did find the box of Tagalongs I bought from my little sister's Girl Scout troop that I'd been saving for some binge eating while wallowing over my poverty.

"Hey," I asked him, "have you ever been to a strip club?"

"Um, I think I went once," he said as he munched on my Tagalongs. "A buddy dragged me to one but it was a long time ago."

I'd read somewhere that when people lie they glance up at the ceiling. Well, Ricky was studying the kitchen ceiling like he was on a tour of the Sistine Chapel.

"Why, you wanna go to one?" he asked, suddenly all perked up. "I could probably find one and take you." Yeah, I'll bet he could.

"No," I said. "I was just wondering what they're like inside."

"Well, I don't know that much about them." Liar liar. "But I could probably ask around to find a good one." Pants on fire.

"Are the girls totally naked?"

"Um, I'm not really sure about that." The thought crossed my mind that I ought to be on the lookout for a fire extinguisher because a gigantic bonfire was about to break out in his pants.

"What do you think of the girls who work at places like that?"

"I don't know. I guess some of them are pretty skanky. Why?"

"I was just wondering."

"I know they make a shit load of money though—like about $1,000 a night."

I wondered if my $1,000 loans were helping to finance his vast knowledge of these places he pretended to know nothing about. I wondered if it might be a good idea to sneak into Sugar & Spice to do some surveillance on him.

Ricky left and I sat down to eat the last three Tagalongs he had somehow missed. A song by Linda Ronstadt was playing on the radio. . . . *Woah-woah is me. Poor, poor pitiful me.* I had to figure out a way to make more money, that's all there was to it. . . . *I met a man out in Hollywood. Now, I ain't naming names but he worked me over good* . . . I chewed the last Tagalong, feeling sorry for myself and taking time to enjoy my last remaining edible luxury. . . . *Lord, have mercy on me. Woah-woah, is me. Poor, poor pitiful me.*

A few days later I told Deborah I'd go to an audition just to see what it was like. I emphasized this would be strictly for observational purposes only and I made her pinky swear she wouldn't tell a soul.

9

KATHERINE

"I THOUGHT THE MORMONS didn't believe in suing people," Keith's dad said.

"It's not because they're Mormon, Vaughn," I said.

"Yeah, Dad," said Keith. "You can't blame the church for everything."

I was upset that Cathy and Jim were suing Keith but I knew it didn't have anything to do with the church. Mormon's occasionally sue people too, you know. Did Vaughn think his constant needling would inspire us to dump the church? Even if I didn't believe it was true (which I did), I would stick with it for no reason other than to prove him wrong.

"Well, don't ask me to throw out the coffee maker now that you're living here."

"Come on, Dad."

Vaughn lifted his empty glass of lemonade and my mother-in-law, Dottie, hopped right to it, immediately taking his glass into the kitchen. I heard her crack open an ice tray and then the clinking of cubes in the glass. Vaughn smiled at me the way you would when you're showing off how well you've trained your dog. Dottie was back two minutes later with a fresh refill. Vaughn took it without even a nod of acknowledgment.

"Just don't send the missionaries my way, okay?"

Vaughn was heavy-set but pretended he wasn't. He usually wore cargo pants and a T-shirt a size too small. I could not ignore the possibility that Keith would morph into his dad one day. He was already on pace.

I was more upset at Jim and Cathy than Keith was. I know people grieve differently but they were so *angry*. Heartbroken I could obviously see, but mad enough to badmouth us all over town and then sue? Keith made a mistake—a huge, devastating, tragic mistake and their loss was unimaginable, but it'd been an accident and suing us wasn't going to undue their heartache. What did they plan to do with the money anyway? Go on a Caribbean cruise? Buy a new Cadillac? Remodel the rumpus room?

A few years earlier, Keith had taken me to play golf and I'd hit the ball so far off target that it hit a guy in the other fairway smack dab in the head. He dropped like a sack of flour and I thought for sure I'd killed him. Fortunately, he only wound up with a goose egg and a whopper of a headache. I swear I felt worse than he did. And I felt that way for months. Now, I'm not equating that guy's goose egg with Emily's tragedy of course, but in a small way I could relate to how Keith must have felt. A very small way. If he could only take it back—if he could only rewind those few seconds that made all the difference. Keith's behavior that day was careless but it wasn't commensurate with the consequences in its wake.

Anyway, Keith had been at work when a guy showed up asking for him. "Does a Keith Murphy work here?"

"Yep, that's me. Now, what can I do you for?"

"Here, these papers are for you. You've been served. Good luck." He turned and left the plumbing supply store with a smirk on his face.

The lawsuit claimed one million dollars in damages. They might as well have sued for ten bazillion because we only had insurance up to $100,000 and we'd be on the hook for the rest. Good luck collecting that! We could barely afford the two boxes of Tagalongs I'd bought from my little sister's Girl Scout troop and our savings account had about $350 in it. The complaint accused Keith of "wanton and careless disregard" for their child's safety. I'd never heard of wanton so I looked it up in the dictionary and it means a "deliberately cruel or violent action." Deliberate? Cruel? Violent? It had been an *accident.* Did they think their suffering would magically go away if we robbed a bank and paid them a million dollars? Would it even reduce their suffering? Perhaps, a bit, but I doubt it.

The lawsuit got our old neighborhood all riled up. Some thought Jim and Cathy were sue-happy, trying to make a buck off the tragedy, while others said they would've sued Keith's socks off, too. Oh, it'd been wanton all right.

Jim and Cathy were mad when they found out we were upset about the lawsuit. "Oh, so now the Murphy's, of all people, act like *victims?*" Cathy had told a mutual friend. "Gimme a break. We're the ones who lost our daughter."

Actually, we didn't feel like victims, we felt like punching bags. Jim and Cathy kept emphasizing to anyone who'd listen that it wasn't about the money. Well, you could've fooled me because if it wasn't about the money then what *was* it about? They sure as heck weren't suing for all that wanton-ness to get their daughter back.

Emily's death changed Keith. Rather than becoming bitter and defensive, he became humble and grateful for what he had. The arrogance, the cockiness, the certainty of his specialness, was gone. All that gross male entitlement went up in smoke. It's hard to explain, but that's when I fell in love with my husband for the first time.

We were lying in bed and it was dark. There was no more sloshing, thank goodness, because we'd left the waterbed back at the duplex for some other lucky tenant. I'm a side-sleeper and I stared at Keith's profile as he lay on his back looking up at the ceiling. I knew he wasn't sleeping because he wasn't snoring and his mouth wasn't hanging open like it usually was (and his eyes happened to be open).

"I know how much you've been through, Keith. I know it's been hard."

"I can't even imagine what they must be going through. If we lost Jacob . . . I don't think I could survive it."

After a few more quiet moments, he said, "You know, it's weird, but I think God was trying to tell me something."

"What do you mean?"

He rolled over to face me. "Maybe things happen for a reason. Maybe I needed to get straight with God."

I wanted to cry. I couldn't allow myself to think that God allowed this to happen for my marriage. How selfish and mean would *that* have been? And I certainly wasn't convinced that little Emily had to die for Keith to find God because there are less tragic ways. But, then again, God works in mysterious ways and if He knows when every sparrow falls, He must've known about this and the rippling effect it was destined to have, because everything we do has a rippling effect. Sometimes the ripples are good, sometimes they're bad, and sometimes they're tragic.

"I think God does things to teach us lessons," I said. "In fact, sometimes I wonder if He made me get pregnant for a reason, too."

Don't get me wrong, I wasn't going all Mother Mary here, blaming God for my out of wedlock pregnancy, but I did wonder. I know plenty of people would say God had nothing to do with it, that it'd been a sperm and egg doing what they were designed to do—magical in a way but not supernatural. And maybe they'd be right but I was trying to make sense of the randomness of pregnancy (among other things) and I choose to believe God is in charge of these things.

"You really believe that?" Keith asked.

"Remember how upset we were when we found out I was pregnant?"

"Yeah, I thought your dad was going to kill me."

"But he didn't, and now look how lucky we are to have Jacob. Maybe God knew what He was doing."

That night, for the first time in our married life, we knelt to pray next to the bed with a real mattress in Keith's parent's guestroom. Keith was our spokesman and wasn't too smooth about it either. He didn't jazz it up with a bunch of Thees, Thous, and Halloweds. He must've assumed God already knew he was only the assistant manager of a plumbing supply store and not Robert Frost. I'd bet God doesn't fixate on the actual words anyway, what with all the different languages and dialects out there. I bet He just looks directly at the person's heart. Keith thanked Him for Jacob and asked to keep him safe. I thought he was about ready to wrap things up, but there was a long pause and he started to cry. Soon his whole body was shaking. I put my arm around his shoulder, the two of us kneeling by the side of the bed in the dark until Keith was finally able to finish: "And please bless Jim and Cathy the most."

A small part of me resented his maturity, you know what I mean? I was still mad at the Blakes for suing us and Keith's maturity made me feel like a self-absorbed brat. Personally, I would have asked for more personalized blessings.

A few days later, the Blakes agreed to accept our insurance company's settlement offer of $100,000 and the case was over. Keith thanked God for that, too, in his prayers that became a nightly tradition.

We started fresh in our new neighborhood with our new-found faith and devotion to God. Keith was even more committed than I was, which was something I never saw coming in a million years. He'd gone and done a one-eighty.

We got a surprise too. I was pregnant again.

10

KATE

DEBORAH AND I DROVE over to Sugar & Spice on a rainy, windy afternoon in Vegas. This was a monsoon-like pelting and the windshield wipers could barely keep up, flapping back and forth as fast as they could. The inside of her car smelled like an ashtray but I couldn't roll down the window to get some fresh air because of the rain. A pine-tree air freshener hung from the rearview mirror but it had to be a decade old. I kicked an empty Burger King sack out of the way to make room for my feet. The console overflowed with cigarette packages, hair clips, pens, and sunglasses. A few moldy french fries were wedged in the seat.

"So what's this guy's name?" I asked.

"I think its Wayne or Walter, or something like that," she said, "but he goes by Crock."

"Crock?"

"Yeah, and he's actually a pretty nice guy. Treats the girls fair as long as they keep the rules."

"What are the rules?"

"I don't know, just stuff like you're not supposed to let any of the guys touch you or have sex with you. You know, just the basic stuff."

Oh, I see, just the basic stuff. The common workplace challenges. Hey, Kate, try not to let Bob in accounting have sex with you.

"Have any guys tried to touch you?" I asked.

"Couple times. But I just tell them to stop and they usually do. They have bouncers, too, so it doesn't get out of control."

This was not the pep talk I needed. I thought it was supposed to be dark inside and I'd be binocular-distance away. And now I'd be so close that they could actually *touch* me?

But now we were in the car and on our way. I could have demanded she turn around and take me back to the apartment where I could fix myself a hearty meal of Hamburger Helper. But I didn't because the momentum was toward Sugar & Spice and the audition. The inertia toward the strip club was the default and Deborah was driving, so it wasn't entirely my fault. I'd gone back and forth about whether to wear a button-up shirt or a pullover, practicing with each one to decide which was sexier. What a laugh. There's absolutely nothing sexy about watching yourself get naked, even if you do it to Barry White. I finally chose the shirt with buttons because I could drag that part out longer. And I wore shoes with a medium-sized heel because I didn't want to sprain an ankle.

We parked next to the same pimped Lincoln I'd seen there before, stalling a few moments in the car because of the rain before bravely stepping out into the parking lot. I held an umbrella out in front of us as we ran across the lot, plowing through the windy downpour like the prow of a ship. Deborah was gripping a cup of coffee sloshing around in its snug little cardboard jacket. She always had *something* to drink in her hand, and it was usually something that was against the commandments.

"So it's Crock?" I shouted over the wind and rain.

"Yeah, like in crocodile," she shouted back.

The heavy wooden door to the place was locked and Deborah knocked. I don't think it was a secret-code knock, but it might have been for all I know. While we were waiting for someone to open it, Deborah said, "Oh yeah, and act like you know who Dean Martin is."

"Who?"

Just then the door was opened by a giant bald man with a web of jagged scars on his cheek which made his face look like a treasure hunting map. I later learned he'd been in a drunken brawl and got knifed in the face. He was still drunk when they'd brought him into the ER and wouldn't hold still while they were trying to stitch him up. The doctor finally threatened to sew his head to the table if he didn't stop wiggling. Sure enough, the guy kept jerking his head from side to side, so the doctor sewed both of his earlobes to the operating table while the nurses held him down. It sounded like a scene from Gulliver's Travels to me. The doctor told the nurse not to cut the thread until he was at least twenty miles away. And this was the crowd I was getting involved with?

Deborah told Gulliver we were there to see Crock and he let us in. The place was dimly lit and smelled like Deborah's car. I've just never been a big fan of stale cigarette smoke. When my eyes adjusted to the light, I saw a bar to the right with a million liquor bottles stacked in front of a large mirror. A collection of sofas and loveseats were positioned around the perimeter of the room and small dining tables and chairs were in the middle. There was an ATM conveniently located in the corner. I noticed an elevated stage, maybe two or three feet high, at the far end of the room.

"Who's the guy I'm supposed to know?" I whispered to Deborah as Gulliver led us past the empty tables. "Was it Don Martin?"

"No, it's Dean. Dean Martin."

"And who's he?"

"Not sure," she whispered back. "I think he's some old singer who's supposed to be famous. Crock's real proud because he was a customer once."

We were led down a dark corridor to an office where Crock sat behind a large aluminum desk, hunched over an accounting ledger. He held a cigarette that was burning precariously close to his nicotine-stained fingers and it occurred to me that I ought to warn him. He was middle-aged, a bit overweight, and slightly disheveled—the look of a guy who misses a belt loop every now and then.

There were no windows in the room which was lit by sputtering overhead fluorescent-tubes. The walls were covered with cheap mahogany paneling and cardboard boxes were stacked against two of those walls. A framed business license for Sugar & Spice was the only thing hanging on a wall. There was a photo of a woman and three young children on the credenza behind the desk. It was propped up next to a bowling trophy with a little golden man atop who would forevermore be stuck in his mid-bowling pose.

Crock had a pockmarked face and I had immediate sympathy for him because I figured he'd had acne as a kid, the kind a dab of makeup wouldn't hide. Maybe not even a whole tube. They probably called him Zit Face in high school, so he'd already suffered plenty. And his two front teeth had to be fake because there was a small gap between his gums and the top of the teeth and they were too big—so big that his upper lip didn't completely cover them. I'm sorry to say it, but he looked like a beaver.

"Yeah?" he asked without looking up.

"Hi, Crock," Deborah said. "This is the girl I was telling you about."

He looked up. "It's Deanna, right?"

"Actually, it's Deborah." I'm sure she felt pretty stupid because she was supposed to be tight with the owner. So I felt sorry for her, too.

"Yeah, Deborah, of course, sure. So, what's your name?" he asked me as he pointed his two front teeth in my direction.

"I'm Kate."

He stabbed his cigarette into a purple ceramic ashtray that looked like it'd been made with Play-Doh—probably his kid's third-grade art project.

"You know how to dance?"

"Sort of, I guess."

"You ever danced at a place like this before?"

"No."

"You ever *been* in a place like this?"

"Um, not really."

"But she's told you what we do here, right?" he asked as he stole a look at Deborah.

"Well, sort of. She just said that you dance and maybe take your top off."

"No, you always take your top off," he said, and looked again at Deborah.

"How old are you?" he asked me.

"I'm twenty-one."

"You sure about that?"

"Uh-huh."

"You got a boyfriend?"

"Yeah."

"Does he know about this?"

"Um, not really."

"Listen, Kate. You seem like a pretty good kid. But I don't want your boyfriend coming around here and causing trouble. You understand?"

"Yeah. He wouldn't."

Crock stared at me for, like, five seconds straight. He was sizing me up—trying to decipher if I might cause him trouble.

"Okay, let's see what you've got." He stood and squeezed past us. We followed him down the hallway to the main sitting area where he sat at a table near the stage.

"Sorry," he said, "but our tech guy isn't here so I don't have any music right now." He motioned toward the stage. "Just step up there and dance for a few minutes. Feel free to use the pole while you're at it."

I hadn't noticed the tether-ball pole in the center of the stage. I looked at Deborah who nodded. I gulped and made the lonely walk, stepping up a few feet onto the scuffed platform that was covered with scratches and gouge marks. *Just think about the money. Just think about the money. Just think about the money.* I grabbed the pole with one hand and spun around it. Then I grabbed it with both hands and slid down like I'd practiced with the bathroom door jamb. The pole was cold and coated with lotion and makeup.

"Okay, take your shirt off." It was so matter of fact, neither a stern command nor a polite request. He didn't sound too excited either, I'll just say that, like he'd seen it a million times before. Ho-hum here come more boobs I've gotta look at it.

"Like now?"

"Whenever you're ready," he said and checked his watch.

I looked at Deborah and then at Gulliver who was standing over by the bar with a rag in his hand. I was tempted to ask him to leave, or at least turn his head but then I realized he'd seen it a million times, too. After all, wasn't that the whole point—doing it in front of other people? I unbuttoned my shirt, trying to be all sexy about it. Crock probably thought I had Parkinson's disease with the way I was shaking and it didn't come off the least bit sexy, if you ask me. Hey, let's see you do it. Besides, it was awkward doing it acapella.

I took off my shirt and let it fall to the floor. What now? Was I now supposed to say something? Maybe pretend to moan or giggle? Or perhaps do a little twirling? I cannot tell you in a million years how weird this was.

When I was a child, my parents took me to visit my cousins who lived in Enterprise. My Uncle Bert owned a cattle auction up there and between chores we'd sit around as the prized cattle was paraded in front of the men who wore sweat-stained cowboy hats, plaid shirts, and boots with dried manure on them. They critiqued the meat without regard to the cows' feelings. Well, that's what I felt like as I stood on that stage. An ordinary side of beef.

"Take your bra off," Crock said, again so matter of factly.

I reached behind my back and undid the clasp, holding the bra in-place with my other arm before taking another breath and then lowering it. I didn't drop it to the floor because it felt safer to hang onto it.

I couldn't believe what I'd just done. Here I was standing up on a stage at a strip club in front of two strange men without my shirt on. And I'd done it voluntarily! I was having an out of body experience. Anyone who says it's liberating is full of crap.

"Okay, now take off your shorts. You can leave your panties on."

Well, *that* was awfully big of him. I undid the button and unzipped my shorts, letting them fall to my ankles. I stepped out of them and stood there. For some reason I'd been less embarrassed to take off my shorts than my shirt. I don't know why.

Now, of course I knew I'd be mortified to take my clothes off in front of strange men, and you can bet your life I was, but I was even more embarrassed to take them off in front of Deborah. That surprised me. Maybe it's because I knew she'd be inspecting every flaw. Men wouldn't do that—they'd just stare at my boobs—they wouldn't examine the three extra pounds on my thighs. Well I'll be darned, Darrell, you're absolutely right, she actually is a bit knock-kneed now that you mention it.

"Sorry, they're kinda small." I know it wasn't the sexiest thing to say, but it just came out.

"No, you're a beautiful girl," Crock said. He wasn't creepy about it though. In fact, so far at least, he hadn't made a single leering comment or look. Dare I say he was *professional?* "I know this is uncomfortable, but you'll get used to it. Go ahead and put your clothes back on if you want."

If I want? If I *want?* Nah, I'd prefer to leave them off while we sit around and chat about the weather for a while, that is if you're okay with it. Or we could play a quick game of gin rummy and chat about the Oscars if you prefer. I turned around and dressed quickly.

"Okay, you're welcome to come back Saturday night. But, listen, I don't want you coming back unless you want to. Understand?"

"Yeah."

"We've got a lot of steady customers and I run a nice place. Dean Martin's even been here a few times. Our customers don't really care if you're a good dancer, but they expect you to take your clothes off like you want to."

"K," I said, like I would ever want to.

It was still pouring rain as we raced back to the car.

"Be careful with the seat. I don't want it to get wet," she said as she reached into the pile of dirty clothes in the back seat and handed me a crumpled UNLV sweatshirt. "Here, use this."

"I can't believe what I just did," I said as we pulled out of the parking lot. Boy, was that the truth. The entire reason I'd done it was to make some quick money and yet it occurred to me then that I hadn't been paid a dime. I'd done all that for freaking *free*. But I was so relieved to have it over with that I was almost in a silly mood. It might be similar to the exhilaration you must feel when the parachute actually opens like it's supposed to and you land safely without so much as a twisted ankle. Don't get me wrong, I was still grossed out by the whole dingy process and I couldn't understand why a guy would get all turned on by seeing a drunk girl get naked—a drunk girl who didn't like you at all and only got naked because she had to. You'd think they'd be embarrassed and ashamed of themselves. In fact, everyone involved in the transaction ought to feel the same way.

"That's how I felt the first time," Deborah said as she cracked the window open an inch and lit up another cigarette. "But you get used to it."

"I'm not sure I could do it for real."

"Sure you could. You just did. It's basically the same thing. I just keep thinking about the money."

"Do you think that Crock guy thought I'd be okay at it?" I'd take any feedback at this point.

"Yeah, I'm sure he thought you'd be good."

"Really? Or are you just saying that?"

"No really, I think he liked you. Come on, Kate, what guy wouldn't?"

"Yeah, but my boobs are too small."

"So what?" said the girl with great tits. "Besides, some guys like them smaller."

That was simply a ridiculous statement and whatever credibility Deborah may have once had flew out the car window and into the rain with that comment. Guys like small boobs, my foot.

"I don't know," I said. "I need to think about it for a while."

"Hey, it's just shits and giggles on amateur night. Even if you only did it once, it's like five hundred bucks."

So I'd crossed another line and this one was a biggee—I had officially auditioned as a stripper. This would not have been merely improbable a year earlier, it would have been inconceivable. No, make that two weeks earlier. But, then again, I wasn't a *real* stripper, and the guys weren't allowed to touch me or anything. Besides, it's not like I was totally nude and I'd probably only do it once. I wasn't hurting anyone and no one would find out about it either. Who knows, I might even donate some of the money to charity to atone for my completely victim-less sin. No, not a sin, more like an indiscretion. Yep, I'd practically talked myself into believing I'd be doing a *good* thing. Maybe not "good" as in volunteering at the soup kitchen, but "good" as in "not as bad as it sounds."

11

KATHERINE

LIVING IN THE SAME HOUSE with my father-in-law was awful. I couldn't understand why he continually made fun of my beliefs. Maybe it made him feel intellectually superior, even though neither one of us listened to NPR or had been to a single day of college. Or maybe it was salve on some wound the church had inflicted in the past, I don't know. But just because I believed in God and angels didn't make me a crackpot. Vaughn believed in some pretty bizarre things, too. For example, he believed the Raiders were more likely to win the football game if he wore his lucky socks. Now, you tell me which is more ridiculous.

Vaughn had also been raised Mormon so he had the inside scoop on all the tender spots to poke, which only made it worse.

"So, Katherine, what do you think about polygamy?"

"I try not to think about it, Vaughn. It doesn't concern me."

"But what about Brigham Young? Doesn't it bother you that he had eighty wives?"

"Not really. That was a long time ago. You know we don't believe in polygamy anymore." Besides, Mr. Know It All, Brigham Young only had fifty-five wives. I didn't say that, of course, because his point was well taken whether Brigham had eighty or only fifty-five, so I would've just been nitpicking. My point is that I clearly knew more about it than he did.

"Pretty strange if you ask me."

"Vaughn, I really don't want to talk about this, okay?"

"Would you rather talk about the secret golden tablets?"

"I believe in God and Jesus, just like everybody else."

"But everybody else doesn't have the magic gold tablets."

"I believe the church is true. Keith and I both do and I'm sorry if that offends you."

"Oh, it doesn't offend me. It just amuses me."

"Come on, Dad." Keith said.

Vaughn was sitting in his Lazy Boy in the living room like he was the King of Siam, bossing poor Dottie around left and right. "You two can stay here," he said, "but you'd probably be able to afford your own place if you didn't pay all that tithing."

"Dad, please."

"Hey, I'm just saying maybe you could afford the rent if you didn't give away so much money to the church. Course, what do I know?"

Not much.

"Vaughn, let it go," said Dottie. "You kids are welcome to stay here as long as you like." She looked at me. "Don't listen to him."

That night I broke into tears again. I was a pregnant mess anyway and my emotions were on edge, so the last thing I needed was Vaughn making fun of me. "I don't know what's up with your dad."

"I know," said Keith. "I'm sorry. Try not to take it personally—it's just the way he is sometimes."

"I'm six months pregnant. What does he want? Does he want to throw us out now?"

"Of course not. He's just that way. Don't listen to him."

A week later, Keith and I were over at my parent's house. Jacob was playing with my little brother Korbin who wore a doctor's lab coat, scarf, and cowboy hat. He had a row of four horizontal dots in the middle of his forehead from the time he got stuck by a fork a few years earlier. He'd been extra annoying and Kenny had thrown a fork at him from the other side of the kitchen. I'll never forget that salad fork twirling through the air and sticking in the middle of Korbin's forehead like a pocketknife in a tree trunk. Thunk. I kid you not. Nobody said a thing at first because we were all in shock. I mean, there's this fork hanging limply from Korbin's forehead. It hung there for a moment—one Mississippi, two Mississippi—before dropping innocently to his lap. He didn't cry, at least not at first. He must have been stunned like the rest of us. And then he started screaming like he'd been stabbed with a fork in the middle of his forehead. That's when Kenny claimed it hadn't been his fault because the fork had accidentally slipped out of his hand. My initial instinct was to feel more sorry for Kenny than Korbin because I knew my dad was going to flip out. Which is understandable I suppose.

So, anyway, we were over at my mom's house in the kitchen and Korbin was playing Legos with our little Jacob in the family room off the kitchen. I was a bit nervous because Jacob was trying to eat them. He'd put anything in his mouth. Other moms told me that was a good thing for him to stick things from off the floor into his mouth because he was being exposed to germs that way. They told me this as if it was the most sensible thing in the world.

"Your dad and I have something to tell you," my mom said.

"What is it? Is something wrong?"

"Oh, no, nothing's wrong."

"Then what is it?"

"Your new baby isn't even born yet," my mom said, "but it'll have a new aunt or uncle within a few months!"

"What do you mean?"

"Well, it looks like your new baby will only be a few months older than its aunt or uncle," my mom said with a giggle.

I didn't know what the heck she was talking about.

"Just tell her, Jackie," my dad said.

"Don't you see?" asked my mom. "You're going to have another little brother or sister!" She waited for me to jump up and down. "Because I'm pregnant, too!"

"You're *pregnant?*"

"Yes! Isn't that fun?"

"But I thought you were . . ."

"Too old? Apparently not! Omigosh, I've been so excited to tell you. I didn't want to take the spotlight off you and your new baby, but I couldn't stand it any longer. We'll be pregnant together! Maybe we can have a joint baby shower, and we can trade off babysitting. It'll be so fun!"

My parents didn't believe in birth control. They believed God would link up the sperm and egg when He had the fancy to do so. That's all there was to it. So no, I guess it wasn't all *that* surprising. The more surprising thing (at least to me) was the overwhelming evidence that my parents were still doing it at their age. Nobody wants to think about their parents having sex, at any age.

Anyway, it caught me off guard. I loved my mom and would never intentionally hurt her feelings but, come on, *another one?* I was farther along with my second child than my own mother? It was hard to hide my . . . my . . . my what? Embarrassment for her? For me? For our whole family? Once the initial shock wore off I completely overreacted with phony joy, but my mom wasn't stupid. She saw.

If I'm being totally honest, I was also upset because this would give my father-in-law additional ammunition. He'd never pulled a punch about us Mormons and our breeding habits. And now this? A mother and daughter joint baby shower? Keith was an only child and Dottie told me she'd always wanted to have more children but Vaughn had been unwilling. I know for a fact Keith would have loved to have a sibling or two but it was not meant to be. In fact, he often said one of the things he was attracted to was my big family and the chaos.

I was in Vaughn and Dottie's spare bathroom a few days later, the one Keith and I had been using. It had an adjoining shower and bathtub. I drew a bath and undressed while the tub filled. I removed a towel from the hook across from the tub when something caught my eye. There was a small gap in the sheetrock around the hook, about the size of a cashew. The hole was hidden when the towel was on the hook. It then occurred to me that Vaughn's workroom where he kept his tools was on the other side of the wall.

I covered myself with the towel and stood to the side of the hole to dress. It was Vaughn's poker night and he was out, so I walked into his workroom and turned on the light. It creeped me out to go in there because there was a deer's head with its antlers hanging on the wall. Vaughn had placed a New York Yankees baseball cap on the deer's head which just added to the shame. The deer's glassy eyes stared me down like I'd been the jerk who'd shot it and then cut its head off.

The only thing on the wall that separated Vaughn's workroom from the bathroom I'd been using was a cheaply framed photo of pudgy Vaughn and his equally pudgy golf buddies. It hung on the middle of the wall, but too low—just above waist high. I lifted the photo from its nail. Behind it was a small hole a few inches from the nail. I bent down slightly and put my eye to the hole and nearly vomited.

I had a perfect view of the bathtub and shower.

12

KATE

RICKY HINTED THAT HE'D PROBABLY PROPOSE. Or maybe I just read too much into it when he said: "Who knows, maybe we'll get married someday." He repaid me $500 of the $2,000 he owed and also bought me a pair of tall leather boots. I loved those boots so much that I barely hesitated when he asked to re-borrow the $500.

I only had a year left to earn my degree in fashion merchandising. I think my parents were proud of me, at least according to my sister. "Mom and dad brag about you all the time," Kristy told me. I'd hoped that was true, but the only thing I'd ever heard from them on the subject was when my mom said my degree might help me dress my kids better. You know, the fashion part.

I was dead broke and needed tuition money. My parents didn't have enough to chip in. Besides, what would I've said when they wondered where all the money went? Would I tell them the truth? Would I tell them I'd squandered it on the guy

I was having pre-marital sex with on a daily basis? If so, they would've totally freaked out and disinherited me on the spot. Yikes, there goes my twenty dollars! So, I decided to earn it the old-fashioned way—the way women have been earning it, tax-free, since, like, forever.

I'd like to believe it wasn't a conscious choice, like a decision I'd earnestly deliberated over after drawing a line down the center of a yellow legal pad with columns for the Pros and Cons. I'd like to believe it just happened without my conscious approval, something that had happened *to* me, as if it hadn't really been in my control. But when I think back on it, I have to admit it didn't "just happen." Then again, in my defense, it wasn't *A* decision, as in just one. It was a series of them, meaningful in hindsight but each one seemingly small at the time. A harmless fib here and a little white lie there. It was casual, at first, and then it started cascading—one lie to cover an earlier one. It was a lot of work just to remember my lies and when I'd forget, I'd just make up another one. It had been fairly easy to justify them, too. After all, how else was I supposed to pay for college and rent? I surely didn't want to impose on my parents. So, yeah, I guess I'd made my own bed.

Deborah was having a cigarette on the small deck overlooking the parking lot of our apartment.

"Um, Deborah, so what would I wear?"

"You're doing it?"

"I might. I'm still thinking about it."

"I just wear cut-offs and a tank top."

"Just cut-off jeans?"

"Yeah, the ones I wear are pretty short."

Ya think? I'd seen them and they hardly had a crotch at all, it was pretty much just the seam.

"What about shoes?"

"Just wear high heels. They're hard to dance in, but you'll get better tips."

"Are you going Saturday night?"

"Yeah," she said, "I told Crock I'd be there. They do the amateur night first and then us regulars go on."

I detected some pride. Oh no, she was no mere amateur, she was a *regular* and they were counting on her!

"Well, Ricky's going to be out of town. So, if I went, and I'm not saying I will for sure, but if I did, what time would it start?"

"About eight."

I spent two more days justifying my decision before telling Deborah I'd go, but just to watch. She told me that was stupid because as long as I was going, I ought to make some money. "It's all in cash, too, so you don't have to pay any taxes on it."

Did she honestly think *that's* what was holding me back? Like I was obsessing about the marginal tax rate for strippers? Phew, all cash.

"Fine. Maybe I'll do it, but you have to swear you won't tell anybody. Ricky would be mad and my parents would have a heart attack. Seriously, they'd drop over dead. And Sandra would put in a collect call to my bishop."

"What's a bishop?"

"Never mind, it's a long story. Just promise me you won't tell a soul.

"Yeah, whatever."

"No, come on, I'm serious. You have to swear."

Deborah didn't know my parents like I did. Their final deathbed plea would've been to have me repent. They'd put it in their Last Will & Testament, in bold type, on page one, so no one would miss it: Katherine doesn't get diddly squat until she undergoes an ecclesiastical enema.

"Fine, I won't tell anybody," said Deborah. "Promise."

"So, like, what do you do?"

"Follow me." She led me into her bedroom and locked the door. Now, I'm not the neatest, cleanest, most organized person on earth. My clothes aren't hung neatly on hangars in a color-coordinated way and I don't fold my underwear or socks into tidy little balls in dresser drawers labeled "Underwear" or "Socks" to remind me where they are. But Deborah's room looked like, well, it looked like the inside of her car. This was no compliment. Old cardboard pizza boxes, the crust of a piece of toast on a dirty dish surrounded by crumbs, an unwashed glass with the dried film of a protein shake, and clothes piled everywhere. Her bed was unmade and you had the impression her sheets hadn't been washed in weeks.

"First you need some good music," she said as she rummaged through a stack of cassette tapes. "Here, this one's good. It's that 'Girls, Girls, Girls' one by Mötley Crüe." She then dug through a mound of clothes on the floor in the corner of the room and found a thong. I turned my gaze when she stripped to put it on right in front of me, like it was nothing. I knew I was a fellow girl but still. Next came the denim cut-offs with the quarter-inch crotch. She slid the cassette into the boom box and away she went, gyrating just like they do in the movies. She was wearing a white tube top and took it off, but not the same way my brothers whip off their T-shirts when they play shirts and skins in basketball. No, she *slithered* out of it then turned around and bent over. I thought her butt was going to hit the ceiling fan. After twirling around an imaginary pole in the middle of the bedroom, she turned off the music.

"There. See, it's easy," she said, just as casually as if she'd just demonstrated the proper way to bake a potato. She wasn't even winded.

A few days later, Deborah, Sandra, and I were all in the apartment together. "Hey," Sandra said, "I'm driving back to St. George Saturday afternoon because Randall's giving a talk in church on Sunday to report on his mission. Wanna go home with me for the weekend?"

I stole a glance at Deborah. "Um, sorry I can't. Ricky and I made plans for Saturday night."

"But I thought you said he was going to Reno this weekend—to visit his mom or something."

"Oh, yeah, he decided not to go." Ricky actually was going to Reno to visit his mom like he did every two weeks (at least that's where he *said* he was going). He was self-absorbed and narcissistic, but he was good to his mom, I'll give him that.

I felt bad lying to Sandra but what choice did I have? Was I supposed to tell her I couldn't go to church with her because I'd be too busy stripping to Mötley Crüe? She would have been mortified and I didn't want to upset her. So it justified another lie, naturally, to protect her from being too upset.

I cut three more inches off a pair of denim cut-offs and pulled at the hems to fray them a bit. I then went to the mall and bought a cheap black wig along with a three-pack of the skimpiest underwear I'd ever seen. I debated going with a pattern, like maybe leopard or something but eventually decided to go basic (that is if basic meant an inch of off-white fabric). I know you get used to them, and they don't show panty lines, but it felt like I was flossing my crack the first time I put them on. I mean, they covered virtually nothing and it bugged me that with so little fabric they could get away with charging twice the cost of a sensible pair of panties. I'd decided to wear the same button-up top I'd worn to the audition and borrowed a pair of Deborah's high heels. The strap on one was hanging on by a thread and was missing the loop thingee that kept it down, so the extra inch of plastic strap stood at attention from the buckle. I figured nobody would be looking at my ankles.

The wig itched like crazy and didn't fully cover my long blond hair, but it disguised me well enough. It would've been humiliating, obviously, if someone had recognized me but at least there'd be the tit for tat. "So, tell me, Bishop Jensen, what exactly are *you* doing here?" I caked on the make-up like I was frosting a cupcake and stepped back from the mirror. I didn't even look like me. I looked more like a slutty raccoon. A slutty raccoon with an ugly, itchy wig.

Deborah was sitting at the kitchen counter filing her nails when I teetered in from the bedroom in the heels. A red Dixie cup with two inches of straight vodka was nearby. She looked like a hooker, too.

"Holy shit!" she said, looking me up and down. "You look great."

"Do you think this is okay?"

"Perfect. You'll be a big hit. And check out those legs!"

I tugged at my shorts to pull them down as far as they'd go, which wasn't much. "Are they too short?" I asked her. "Tell me the truth. I feel half naked."

"They're good. Trust me."

"What about the wig? Do I look like me?"

"I'd never recognize you in a million years. Here, have a seat," she said and then got up and poured an inch of vodka into another red cup. "You're gonna need this."

"Seriously? Ew, I can't drink that stuff straight. I don't know how you do it."

"You get used to it."

It was dark as we drove to Sugar & Spice in Deborah's filthy car but I still slouched down in the seat. This time the parking lot was almost full and men smoking cigarettes were leaning their backs against the cinder block building. They ogled us as we walked past and I thought of those cartoon characters whose tongues hang down to the ground and their eyes pop out of their heads connected to mini-Slinkys. Then there were other men loitering about who didn't even bother to look at us, like workers in a slaughterhouse who'd lost their appetite for the meat. I caught the funky scent of marijuana.

It was dim and smoky inside. Deborah grabbed my elbow and pulled me to the bar. "Pour us two, will ya Dennis? This is Kate, by the way. She's new." Dennis looked at me. "You'll do all right," he said. Deborah slammed her drink and waited while I sipped mine, one disgusting sip at a time. It was so nasty I couldn't just *drink* it. Why not just chug a pint of Turpentine while you're at it? I hadn't eaten all day because I was nervous and wanted to be skinny, so the alcohol hit me fast.

I looked around and was surprised to see so many women there with their boyfriends or husbands. What a charming date night! Shall we go to dinner and the symphony tonight, Dear? Nah, let's just hit that sleazy strip club again.

We walked down the hall to Crock's office and found him deep in thought, his elbows resting on the desk and his hands making a teepee under his chin. "Hi, Crock, it's Deborah." I think she wanted to remind him of her name right off the bat. "I just wanted to let you know she came. Remember Kate?"

"Okay," Crock said, barely looking up. "Just give your tape to Rob, unless you don't care what you dance to." I hadn't expected a three-day new-employee orientation with breakout sessions but this seemed like a rather casual employment arrangement, especially given my job description. I'm sure you go through more training your first day at McDonalds.

"Who's Rob?" I asked as we left the office.

"He's the DJ. Come on, I'll introduce you."

I'd seen tattoos, of course I had, but never like this. Surely this Rob guy would come down with ink poisoning. And the pain! How do you hold still? We're talking dragons, flags, barbed wire, names, dates, roses—you name it. His ear lobes had those gauges and it reminded me of photos I'd seen of African tribal women in National Geographic. The look may have its fanbase, but I wasn't a member. I mean, how did that ever become a thing? And what on earth happens when you take them out? There had been a time in my life, even a year earlier, when I would have judged him as an immoral sinner simply because of his tats and gauges, someone who would steal my purse and quite possibly even rape me. When I told him I didn't have a tape, he said, "No worries, I'll pick something short for you."

The other dancers weren't very friendly and most of them looked higher than a kite. They weren't especially cute either which surprised me, and you could tell most of them didn't own a gym membership. I hate to be mean, but I swear half of them looked more like lunchroom ladies than exotic dancers. I knew this was amateur night but it wasn't karaoke for crying out loud. They were imposters, and so was I. Their collective lack of beauty, however, gave me some confidence (*some*, I must emphasize) because in this subjective line of work, many of these girls were objectively unworthy.

DJ Rob blew into the mic. "Welcome to Amateur Night," he said. "We've got a great lineup for you tonight. Let's give it up for Roxy!" A middle-aged couple near the stage clapped and then suddenly stopped when they realized they were the only ones clapping. I can only assume they weren't her parents. At least I *hope* they weren't her parents. The music began and Roxy walked onto the stage, fleshy and drunk. Was she doing this on a dare? Did she lose a bet? Or did she honestly think she was sexy and could make a career of this? Then again, maybe she just needed to make a tuition payment, too. I scanned the audience which wasn't paying much attention, thank the Lord above.

Roxy danced around the maypole to "Pour Some Sugar On Me," her industrial-sized bra clasping her wondrous breasts that had to be triple Ds, all natural. She only removed it for the last stanza. There were a few boos and Roxy told the hecklers to fuck off as she left the stage, her voice thick with booze. The hecklers just laughed.

"Next, please give a warm welcome to Kate." I was horrified because, like a complete idiot, I'd forgotten to give him an alias. Why not just announce my phone, address, and social security number. The song "Abracadabra" started playing and my out-of-body experience began as I walked onto the stage. I had to concentrate because I'm more of a tennis-shoe girl and the high heels were hard to walk in. I tried not to look into the crowd which was buffered by a haze of cigarette smoke. I once heard that a good strategy to overcome your fear of public speaking was to pretend everyone in the crowd was naked. Ha!

I wanted to get it over with, so after one quick drag down the pole (I went with the two-hand option and stuck my butt out like Deborah had shown me), I unbuttoned my shirt and heard a few whistles.

Before I knew it, my shirt and black lacy bra were off. It was happening so fast! I went back to the pole and did a few one-hand twirls. And then the music stopped and it was over. Three minutes. Three minutes of complete humiliation. I grabbed my shirt and bra and held them to my chest. People were throwing wads of money at me. I suppose I should've been happy, but I wasn't. I picked up the wads with one hand, pressing my shirt and bra to my chest with the other, and teetered off the stage as quickly as I dared.

Once I got to the safety of the dark corridor, I realized I'd forgotten to take off my shorts. I also realized I was holding more money than I made in an entire shift at the Lucky Traveler. I ducked into a corner and put my bra and shirt back on.

Deborah found me in the back hallway. "See, that wasn't so bad." She took a drag and blew cigarette smoke out the corner of her mouth so it wouldn't hit me in the face. "It goes quick, huh?"

"I freaking can't believe I just did that."

"Come on, I'll buy you another drink."

I gulped this one down. I didn't want to be sober. We sat at a table and watched the other girls pandering for money in the most humiliating way, pretending they were super-models when they looked more like regular Walmart shoppers instead. I tried to decide if they had super-duper self-esteem that allowed them to do such a demeaning thing, or perhaps no self-esteem at all. Perhaps they wondered the same thing about me, I don't know.

". . . so whaddya say? Should we bring her back up?" DJ Rob was saying into the microphone to some cheers. "Where is she? Where's Kate? Let's bring her back up!"

I felt Deborah pushing me toward the stage. "You won! Come on, go!"

A few people were clapping like I'd won an achievement award and I realized I would have to do it all over again. I was sick to my stomach. I honestly thought I would vomit. I don't know how I got there but suddenly I was back up on the stage and the same song was playing.

I was taking a twirl on the pole when the plastic strap on my high heel broke. I stumbled and the crowd laughed. I tried to put it back on but it wouldn't work without the stupid strap, so I took the other heel off and the crowd laughed again. I slid down the oily pole and then removed my shirt and bra. Some guys were standing next to the stage waving bills at me. I edged closer to them and they hollered for me to take off my shorts. I vaguely remember unbuttoning them and letting them fall to the stage. A man reached toward me and I backed up. I then realized he wanted to give me some money so I drifted closer and he reached up and shoved a twenty under my panties, at my hip. Another guy did the same thing, then another.

I picked up my clothes and held them in front of my chest and bent down to collect more crumpled money before the music had even stopped. I was humiliated, completely and to the fucking core. I didn't count it right then, but later figured I'd earned $390 for my indignity. It wasn't as much as had been advertised, but still it was more than I earned in five shifts at the Lucky Traveler.

Crock pulled me aside before I left that night. I was still wearing my black wig. In fact, I'd pulled it down so low that you could hardly see my forehead. He smiled tightly to hide his two front teeth, but it was no use. They were simply too big. He delivered the happy news that I was invited back the next weekend, in part because his best girl, someone named Trixie (of course her name was Trixie), had broken her leg in a skiing accident, or something like that. It felt like the time I'd tried out for the Jr. High School play. I wasn't very good but, as a booby prize, Miss Phillips made me the understudy for the lead in *The Unsinkable Molly Brown*. When Lindsey came down with mono a few days before the grand opening, I was thrust into the lead. Dread. Excitement. Panic. And I'd been fully clothed.

So, yeah, now I was a budding regular who'd be given at least four dances instead of just the two. Oh joy. Dean Martin might even show up. I could hardly wait.

I cried myself to sleep.

I'd strung together enough money for fall semester's tuition but my heart wasn't in it, so I decided to take the semester off. I told myself I'd save some money and return the following spring.

Ricky fully supported this postponement because, according to him, college was for losers who didn't have enough moxie to go it alone. And surely he ought to know. He also didn't want my money going anywhere else.

I was homesick on one hand and yet glad to be out of St. George on the other. The longer I'd been away the more I could see how sheltered and naïve I'd been, how I'd been like a blindered horse and wasn't supposed to see anything but the well-beaten path directly in front of me. The thought of returning to the bubble was claustrophobic when it hadn't felt that way before because now I knew it was indeed a bubble. A safe and friendly bubble to be sure, but still a bubble. Even though I was reluctant to go home, I always made the weekly long-distance phone call to my parents. Fortunately, they didn't have FaceTime way back then or I would've had to hide the occasional cigarette and wine glass.

"So, how's your school going?" my mom asked.

Bad. "Good." I couldn't bear to tell them I hadn't enrolled that semester. "But I'm taking a lighter load this time because it's been tough getting all the classes I need."

"Are you going to church?"

No. "Yes."

"Are you reading your scriptures?"

Of course not. "Of course."

I had become a chronic, full-time liar. I lied to my parents, I lied to my old friends because I didn't want them to judge me, and I lied to my new friends about my background because I didn't want them to think I was a religious weirdo. I was pathological, lying every which way. I would've been summa cum laude if they offered a degree in lying. I even lied about things

I didn't need to lie about. For example, why would I tell my mom I went for a jog when I hadn't? I mean, who cares? My mom didn't like people who jogged and went to aerobics classes anyway (and she hated Jane Fonda because my dad said she was a communist who singlehandedly cost us the Vietnam war). She thought people who exercised were too worldly and consumed with vanity. So, yeah, lying to her about going to church might have made sense, but not that.

Everyone lies about *something*. Even the most honest person on earth disguises the truth when it suits her. Maybe it's telling a friend she looks good when she doesn't, or denying a secret crush. In my case, I lied to my parents to spare them from my heresy. At least that's what I told myself, as if my lying was semi-virtuous. But wouldn't the truth have been more loving, more authentic? It was *my* life after all. If they couldn't accept me then whose fault would that have been? But what made all this honesty and truth so tricky was my own ingrained belief that they were right—that my childhood cocoon was the safest place for me to be. And that belief probably wasn't far off track, especially when I compared the comfort of that cocoon to a strip club.

"Did we tell you Kenny's going to Dixie State for a semester before he serves his mission? He prayed about it and decided that'd be a good idea, so long as it doesn't interfere with his mission."

Kenny and the rest of my brothers had been told they'd serve a two-year mission from the time they squeezed out of the womb, practically from the time they crowned. In fact, just about every boy from my high school had gone—the jocks from the football team, the nerds from stage crew, the brainiacs, the most popular, and the most invisible. It was the natural progression of things in my hometown. If you didn't go, people thought you were selfish, unrighteous, or just plain gay. It was hardly a surprise, therefore, when the answer to Kenny's prayer over whether he should go on a mission was answered in the affirmative.

"Yeah, you told me," I said. "I'm excited for him."

So I wasn't a bit surprised that Kenny would go on a mission but I *was* surprised he was going to college because he wasn't the sharpest kid, and that was even before his so-called "brain injury." About five years earlier he'd tripped over his own eighth-grade science project, a paper mâché volcano with dried baking soda running down the side, and smacked his head on the side of a desk on his way down. I was there and saw it happen. At first I thought it was hilarious, but then I felt bad for laughing when I saw he'd been knocked out cold. Everyone freaked out. Trauma around our house was always exciting, especially if it was safely inflicted on one of my younger brothers. Anyway, he had a gash on his head and wore an elaborate turban for two weeks until everyone quit noticing it. He'd been the toast of the town, extravagantly turbaned as he was, but after a few weeks his audience of sympathizers swiftly consisted of no one. Even my mom had moved on to Karolyn's possible tonsilitis.

To his credit, Kenny *had* been given a partial scholarship to Dixie State. This had definitely not been an academic scholarship, however. He was a wrestler in high school and a pretty good one at that. My dad couldn't have been more proud of the Dixie High Rebels' 155 lb. state champ. I was slightly embarrassed for him, however, because of the way he strutted around in his earmuff headgear with the dangling chin strap and that silly orange singlet he wore, cupping his genitals like the onesie Karolyn wore until she was nearly two years old. I mean, you could *see* the outline of the danged thing in that orange onesie. Was this something we were just supposed to *ignore*? The singlet was orange with black trim because those were the school colors and Kenny had been on display in front of the entire student body frantically groping, grabbing, and twisting together with another singlet-wearing boy in a sweaty, violent tangle. And yet Kenny was a self-described homophobe, an irony that was presumably lost on him. I thought it was good, for his sake, that he spent so much time in a room with a padded floor and walls.

My dad thought Kenny's wrestling was worthy of admiration and went to all his matches. It was always Kenny this and Kenny that, especially when he was gearing up to be the state champ. But I don't recall him going to Kelly's tuba recitals or Kimberley's dance concert. And I don't remember a word from him when I made homecoming queen.

"We were thinking maybe Kenny could go down and visit you for a few days," my mom said. "Maybe you could take him around your college campus there in Las Vegas so he'll know what college is like. He could even go to some of your classes."

"I don't know," I scrambled. "They're pretty strict around here. It'd probably be better if he just walked around the campus at Dixie State. Besides, I don't know where he'd stay."

"Well, your dad and I wanted to surprise you and come down for the weekend. We'd love to finally meet your roommates and that boy you've been dating."

There was no way I could allow that. Simply no way. "I was actually thinking about coming up to St. George this weekend,"

I said. This was a lie, naturally, but I needed to head them off at the pass.

"Are you sure? Because we'd love to meet Richard. Your dad is especially anxious to talk to him. You know your dad."

My dad and Ricky? Oh boy. Knowing my dad, he'd probably combine the Dad Interview with the Bishop Interview to be sure Ricky was worthy. So, tell me, Richard, are you living the principles of the gospel? Uh-huh, I see. Moving on then, are you having any problems with masturbation? How about heavy petting?

"Shoot," I said to my mom. "Ricky is traveling on business for the next week or two. But, yeah, for sure you need to meet him sometime. He's really great."

"There's something else we want to tell you," my mom said.

"What is it? Is everything okay?"

"Well, we wanted to tell you in person, but I guess I can just tell you over the phone."

"Tell me what?"

"You're going to have another baby brother or sister!"

I was speechless. My mom was pregnant? It took a second or two for this news to register and I literally looked for a chair to sit down on. "Really? Wow. I thought you and dad were done having babies."

"We thought you'd be happy."

"Oh, sorry. I am. It's just that I wasn't expecting, you know, that . . ."

"Neither were we! But everyone here is so excited, even Kenny. I think he was embarrassed when we had Karolyn for some reason. And now Karolyn will have a little one to play with. It'll be good for her to have someone to baby."

I needed a drink, stat. It's not like I was addicted or anything because I still hated the taste, and how can you be addicted if you hate the taste? My mom was going to have her ninth baby when my own eggs were probably on the verge of getting a tad stale. So, yes, a stiff drink was definitely in order, regardless of the taste.

I had easily convinced myself I didn't have a drinking problem. It was this same talent that allowed me to convince myself that I wasn't a real stripper either; one who danced on poles in G strings for crumpled wads of money from lecherous pigs. No, I was Katherine Coombs from St. George, Utah. I was raised to shun R-rated movies, the perils of coffee, and the worldly ways of promiscuity. I was raised to be a master evaluator of sin and to obediently shut it down the moment I caught a whiff of it. I needed to believe *that* Katherine was still alive and well.

But when I pulled my wig down low and caked on the extra layers of makeup, I knew I was fading into someone, something, else.

13

KATHERINE

I COULDN'T BELIEVE MY FATHER-IN-LAW had been spying on me. And that's exactly what he'd been doing, I was sure of it. Why else would there be a hole in the wall? I pictured him in his cargo shorts and flip flops crouched down with his eye pressed up against the other side of the wall as I undressed. I pictured him breathing into the wall with one palm pressed against it and the other one down his shorts. It literally made me sick to my stomach.

Then I started to wonder if it was somehow my fault—if I'd been unknowingly complicit in some way. Had I not been modest enough? Had I somehow egged him on? I'd been taught that men had a tough time controlling themselves so we women had to take responsibility for them. Now, no one came right out and said it in those exact words, but that was the undisputed gist. If you don't want men to sexually harass and assault you, then stop wearing such a tight sweater. But, no, it hadn't been my fault! This had nothing to do with me. How could it possibly have been one ounce my fault that he did this? I wasn't the perpetrator. I hadn't aided and abetted. I was the *victim*.

I'm a conservative woman who isn't up to speed on feminism, but I'm not stupid and I'm not a doormat. I like men, I do, but I grow weary of them giving me unrequested shoulder massages, or telling me how good I look, or telling me how cute I am when I get angry. It's annoying, and creepy. I decided I needed to stand up for myself and not just let it slide like women have been doing for centuries. Men need to be held responsible when they treat us like their pets.

"We're moving," I told Keith that night. "Tomorrow."

"Whoa! What's going on? What's the big rush?"

"It's your dad, Keith. He's disgusting."

"Listen, I know he can be hard on the whole religion thing but don't take it so personally. He's just trying to get a rise out of you. Besides, they're letting us stay here for free."

"Keith, your dad is a pervert."

"Come on, my dad's not a pervert. What are you talking about?"

"Did you know he's been spying on me when I'm naked?"

"What? Are you serious? How? My dad wouldn't do that. He might be a jerk sometimes, but he's not a pervert. Come on, Katherine, he's practically fifty."

"You obviously don't know your dad. He drilled a hole in our bathroom wall so he can watch me *shower!* I'm so grossed out I can't even talk about it."

"What are you *talking* about? You're overreacting."

"Oh, so now I'm overreacting. Your dad is spying on me in the shower and I'm the one who's overreacting. Got it."

"Katherine, calm down. He's not spying on you. Be serious."

"You don't believe me? You think I'm making this up? Come here and I'll show you. It's sick."

I grabbed Keith's arm and pulled him out of our bedroom, down the hall, and into the bathroom. I lifted the towel from the hook. "There you go."

"What? What are you talking about?"

"What am I talking about? Look for yourself! Can't you see it?"

"See what?"

"The hole. Look, there's a hole right there," I said and pointed to the small coma shaped space next to the towel hook.

"So what? That's just where they made the hole a little too big for the hook," Keith said. "Come on, Katherine. You're blowing this thing totally out of proportion. You're just overly emotional being pregnant and all. We'll move soon enough, okay? But we don't need to move tomorrow."

"Do you know what's on the other side of this wall? Do you? It's his freaking tool room. Come here if you don't believe me."

Keith followed me out of the bathroom and into the tool room. I turned on the light and walked over to the framed golf photo and lifted it off its nail. "See for yourself if you don't believe me." I then crouched down and looked through the small hole in the wall to demonstrate to Keith the way you're supposed to look through a small hole in a wall.

Keith looked next. He stood, then bent down and looked again. I think he was trying to make sense of it. "Okay," he said, "but we don't know what this hole's doing here. Look, it's just a few inches below where the nail is. It's probably just where he hammered the first nail and then decided it was too low for the photo so he pounded in the nail a few inches higher."

"Come on, Keith. Don't do this. That's bigger than a nail hole."

"Not that much bigger."

"Oh, come on! It's twice as big as the nail and you know it. And what's it doing so low on the wall? Nobody hangs a picture this low."

"Calm down. I'm sure there's a reasonable explanation for this so let's not jump to conclusions. Besides, why would he want to spy on you anyway? You're seven months pregnant."

I stared at my husband. I knew Keith was fairly dense, and I had reason to believe he loved me, but saying something like that, at a time like that, was just plain mean and insensitive.

"How could you . . ."

"Wait, I didn't mean it like that. I'm sorry, that came out wrong because any guy would want to see you naked, even if you were pregnant."

I stared at him. Was he for real? Did this caveman admission reflect the view of all mankind? I chose to believe Keith was just an idiot and wasn't trying to hurt me. When he realized he was just making it worse, quite a bit worse I might add, he said: "It's just that I can't believe he'd do something like this."

We stood there with that creepy looking deer head staring at us with contempt. If only it could talk I bet it would have ratted Vaughn out, especially after what he'd done to it. I figured anybody who would cut off a deer's head and hang it on a wall had serious issues anyway. Put a baseball cap on its head and now you really need to get some therapy.

"Are you going to confront him or do you want me to?" I asked. "Because this is the sickest thing I've ever seen in my life."

"Let's just think about it for a while."

"What's there to think about?"

"I just don't want to accuse my dad of something like this unless we're sure he really did it. That's all I'm saying."

"Great, I'll tell you what; let's wait for him to come home tonight and then I'll make a big announcement that I'm going to go take a nice long bath. Yeah, let's do that and I'll give him a good show." I put my head down and shook it. "It's sick, Keith. It's sick and I can never use that bathroom again."

"I know you're upset, but let's just wait and decide how best to handle this."

"I don't want to wait. For all we know he might be sexually abusing Jacob. That's what sex perverts do."

"Oh, come on Katherine. He's not sexually abusing anybody. Be serious."

"*Me* be serious?"

"Even if he did it, and I'm sure he didn't, but even if he did, I don't want my mom to find out about it."

"Why not? I'd sure want to know if you ever did something this sick."

"You didn't see him."

True.

"And you didn't hear anything."

Also true. But the shower was on and I didn't have my freaking ear pressed to the wall expecting to hear my father-in-law *panting*.

"So, why don't we just give him the benefit of the doubt?"

In a way, I felt sorry for Keith who was forced to overrule basic logic to preserve a shred of respect for his dad. I might have been defensive, too, because this was not something anyone with an ounce of decency would comfortably acknowledge—that your own flesh and blood was capable of such a disgusting thing.

We were all together the next evening on Vaughn's and Dottie's backyard patio listening to Vaughn tell us how magnificent the new fish pond in the corner of the yard looked (which, to be honest, looked like a homemade fish pond in the corner of the yard). I wore the frumpiest, loosest clothes I could find, basically an extra-large poncho. I couldn't even look at Vaughn, but I could tell he was looking at me from the corner of my eye. That alone creeped me out. He then hoisted himself from his lawn chair and squeezed me on the shoulder as he stepped past me to point out how expertly he'd stacked the flagstone border around the fishpond. That obviously creeped me out, too. And then do you know what he said to me? He said, and I quote: "You're really starting to show." I about barfed. I jumped up from the lawn chair and ran through the open sliding-glass patio doors and into the house.

As I was running in, I heard him say, "What the hell's eating her? All I said was she's starting to show."

I was in our bedroom crying, face down on the floral bedspread, when there was a tap on the door. It was Dottie, my mother-in-law, who quietly closed the door and sat on the edge of the bed. She put her hand on mine.

"Katherine, what's the matter?"

"I'm sorry, Dottie. You've been so good to let us stay here but I can't do it anymore. I just can't live in the same house with him."

"Oh, my goodness, I'm so sorry. Marriage can be tough. There are ups and downs but you'll get through this, whatever it is. You'll see."

"You don't understand. It's—"

"Oh, I understand more than you think," she said. "Keith has always been headstrong and stubborn, but he loves you.

Now, I know he's not perfect, but he's a good father and a good husband. When you're pregnant you get extra emotional. It's the hormones. Just try to be patient with him." She stroked my hand. "Would you like me to talk to him? Would that help?"

"It's not Keith," I said.

"Then what on earth is the matter?"

"It's Vaughn."

"Vaughn?"

"He's been spying on me when I've been taking showers."

I can't imagine what must have been going through her mind in those few seconds as she was trying to process the unthinkable. The shock, the incomprehension, the denial.

"What in the world are you talking about?"

I let loose with all the juicy details, even the ones that weren't necessarily factual, I'll admit. But, really, there was only one legitimate suspect. Dottie sat, stunned. I think she was probably sick to her stomach, too, but then she rallied and must have decided it wasn't documented truth because she didn't want it to be. Dottie was a good person and I doubt she would have blamed me for her husband's demented behavior, even though the spurned spouse does it all the time—blames the other woman (or the man, on occasion).

She left me stricken in the bedroom and a few minutes later Keith came in. He was upset.

"Did you just tell my mom?"

I didn't respond. I was lying face down on the bed with my head turned away from him to a wall where a drawing of Keith as an adolescent boy was hanging in a cheap frame. It was the kind of drawing you have commissioned at the county fair—

the kind where the head is ten times larger than the little body drawn beneath it.

"I thought we were going to think about this," he said.

"Why Keith? Why should I have to protect him? I haven't done anything wrong."

"But we agreed we wouldn't say anything."

"No, Keith, that's what *you* said."

We heard the sound of muffled voices and footsteps receding down the hall and into the guest bathroom Keith and I had been using. Then we heard them move out to the hall again and into Vaughn's tool room. The deer probably hadn't seen this much action since it'd been beheaded. A few moments later there was a knock on our bedroom door. It opened before we had a chance to answer.

If I thought Vaughn had come to apologize for his sick voyeurism, or commit to therapy for the sexual deviant, I was dead wrong.

"Who in the hell do you think I am?" he shouted. "You think I was *spying* on you? And you go around telling everybody that I'm some kind of *pervert?* The hell I am!" He slammed his fist down on the dresser and a picture frame tipped over. His tight shirt had become untucked in his fury and rode up his torso to expose his fat belly which looked like escaping cream filling. "This story you've concocted is absolute *bullshit!* You hear me? It's *bullshit!* You think I want to look at my son's wife? Don't flatter yourself! That hole has been there forever and if you had cared to look you would've seen other holes in the wall, too. It's where my tool rack used to be. That hole is one of four that held my shelf. You'd have seen that had you cared to look, but you just went ahead and accused me with no basis. And the crack in the bathroom by the towel was put there by the guy who installed the hook. I had nothing to do with it!"

"Dad, calm down."

"I won't calm down! And I won't have someone living in my house who accuses me of this shit. If that's what you think about me, then get the hell out of my house!"

Dottie stood slightly behind her husband, cowering because he was so angry. I think she had suspicions of her own, despite the loud defense. In fact, they were probably more than mere suspicions because she knew darned well that the golf photo was a recent one taken shortly after we moved in. And it was hung awfully low—lined up perfectly with the towel rack hole. How could she have casually dismissed all of that?

Keith gave me the silent treatment for the rest of the evening. That wasn't his usual style when we fought, it was mine. But this was an unusual situation.

"Why are you mad at *me?*" I asked.

"You know why."

I sneaked into the tool room the next morning for another private inspection after Vaughn and Keith left for work and Dottie was tethered to the phone cord in the kitchen, gossiping with a neighbor about another neighbor who was a gossip. I tried to avoid the unsympathetic gaze of the deer but his eyes were the kind that seem to follow you wherever to go. I leaned in close to look at the wall.

There were four holes spaced evenly apart and the paint was possibly faded where a tool shelf *might* have been. So, yeah, his story was possible, but I still had my doubts.

Vaughn was there to help us when we moved to our new apartment, working extra hard with the boxes and sticks of furniture which we'd had in storage. The storage rental probably cost more than our used furniture. We couldn't afford a moving van—Keith shuttled back and forth with the stuff in his truck instead. We were out in Vaughn's driveway next to the pickup truck with the last load of pots and pans when he pulled me aside. "You know you can stay, but I understand you want to have your own place."

"I think it's best we leave."

"Katherine, listen to me." He made a move to put his hands on my shoulders to get my full attention and then must've thought better of it. "I want you to know that I never spied on you. I didn't know you could see through that hole. I swear on my life that I never looked and I'm sorry this has upset you so much."

Was he telling the truth? Perhaps. But I didn't think so. I didn't *think* so.

"Thanks, Dad," Keith interrupted, "but we think it's time we had our own place anyway."

"Well, I'm just sorry about the whole thing."

"It's no big deal," Keith said, even though it was a very big deal, at least to me.

I've thought about it for some time now but I don't obsess over it. In fact, Vaughn and I get along pretty well. I have concluded that he was telling the truth. On the other hand, there remains that tiny inkling.

St. George summers are hot, like 110 degrees hot, and our new apartment (which was very old) had a swamp cooler that only worked sparingly. It had been mounted on the roof above the hallway. So, yeah, the hallway was cool but that's about it.

I was thirty-eight weeks along, splayed out on the bed with no covers, face up, sweating like a pig. It wasn't pretty. But Keith, bless his heart, heard somewhere that sex was the best way to induce labor. This was undoubtedly another theory cooked up by the guys down at the factory.

I wasn't in the mood, as you can imagine, but Keith was persistent. He was determined to plant his seed, even though the one he'd planted thirty-eight weeks earlier was still clogging the way. I wondered if his eyesight was out of whack because I'm here to tell you that I looked about as sexy as a sweaty walrus. I'd basically thrown in the towel by then and lived off donuts and Twinkies, knowing full well it would make my post-pregnancy recovery that much harder but not caring enough to forego any Hostess product. I'd only been shaving from the knees down, too, and then only every other week. So, I say okay, fine, I'll do my wifely duty if you insist because that is the sort of wife I am. And whaddya know. Seven hours of pushing later, my OB said "we" just needed one more big push. So we pushed and our little Jenna slid into the world.

Exactly two months later, my mom delivered little Jenna's Aunt Kylie who was officially sixty days younger than her niece.

14

KATE

I WENT BACK TO SUGAR & SPICE even though it'd been awful the first time around. Why did I go back if it'd been so awful? That's a good question. Why *did* I go back? Was it simply because I was broke? I think that's too easy, and it isn't the whole truth anyway because poor people don't automatically migrate to careers as bank robbers, or strippers.

I think part of it was based on my belief that as long as I'd fallen from grace it made no sense to wallow in poverty on my trek to hell. Naïve and sad, I know, but that was also the logic I used after taking my first drink. As long as I'd broken that commandment, snapping it in half with that first swig of whiskey, I might as well go all in. Same thing with losing my virginity to Keith Murphy. At least I knew what to expect at Sugar & Spice the second time around. And I'd been drinking more which made it incrementally easier. I said incrementally—I couldn't just waltz onto a stage stone-cold sober and take off my clothes. I wasn't an exhibitionist.

I told the DJ that I wanted to go by Kandy, with a K. Maybe I should've picked a less obvious stripper name but at least it wasn't Katherine. *Let's give a warm welcome to Katherine Coombs, the Pride of St. George, Utah!*

I bleached my hair which made me look even more like a stripper. But, trust me, that isn't why I did it. I would've colored it lime green if it would've kept me anonymous. My friends said my new hair color looked great but they probably trashed me behind my back. "Wow, she looks like a freaking stripper." They would have preferred that all other women be no better than average looking. I probably would've had more girlfriends if I'd been twenty-five pounds overweight with three-inch roots.

I know how it works. I didn't like Melissa Eckersley in high school because she was too pretty (and it didn't help that she knew it). I even helped spread an untrue rumor that she never showered in gym and had nasty B.O. And when she was debating whether or not to get braces, I said I thought they'd look good with her smile when what I really wanted was for her to show up at school in headgear.

I recognized some of the girls at Sugar & Spice when I went back the second time and they weren't the friendliest bunch.

"So what'd you say your name was?"

"It's Kate, but I'm going by Kandy here. What about you? Do you go by your real name?"

"You're a nosy bitch aren't ya?"

"Sorry, I was just trying to be nice."

The regulars didn't want me around because more competition was bad for business. I understand, even though I've never considered myself to be a capitalist. Then again, maybe it was simply a new-girl-initiation thing, I don't know.

The following night, Ricky said we needed to talk—that he wanted to get something off his chest. I hoped he wasn't about to tell me he got lost and just happened to swing by Sugar & Spice and saw me twirling on the pole. He might have been able to concoct some possible excuse for being there because he was even a better liar than I was, but why was *I* there? And why, pray tell, had I gone and forgotten to take my clothes?

Ricky chose a crummy one-star Chinese restaurant off the strip to lay it on the line.

"So what's the occasion?" I asked once we were settled into the booth scanning the laminated menu. I'd been on edge for weeks because it felt like I was walking around with one of those sandwich boards announcing I was a genuine stripper. *Come see me strip! Only ten bucks!*

"Listen, Kate," he started, "we need to talk." He set the menu to the side and rested his forearms on the paper placemat that helpfully advised us we were living in the year of the rat. "I think it's time we were honest with each other."

"Okay." Here goes nothing, I thought. Apparently the wig, makeup, and name change hadn't been enough.

"I feel bad that you have to earn all this extra money to keep loaning it to me."

"It's okay, I don't mind it's just—"

"I really want to pay you back. Honest. I'm not using you and I hope you believe me."

"Of course."

"So, whew," he said and put his hands through his luscious hair. Why he wasn't on a shampoo commercial, I'll never know. "I haven't been totally honest with you about my work. See, I started out in business but then I started gambling. And that's pretty much what I do now."

"You gamble in business?"

"No, I just gamble. I'm a professional gambler, and lately the house has been lucky."

"Is that what you wanted to talk about?"

"Pretty much, yeah."

I was relieved this had been the reason for our little honesty chat. It felt like I'd been granted a stay of execution because, duh, I already assumed that's what he did. Anybody with half a brain could've figured it out.

"The thing is, I have some businesses but they aren't very big and they don't do so well. I finance them through gambling."

"But—"

"No," he held up a hand, "let me finish." He looked down at the table. "See, I need you to know that I don't own a condo that's being remodeled, either. I actually live in a shitty little motel."

I've never understood this obsession with gambling. I mean, I *kind of* get it, I guess, because people say there's an adrenaline rush with each roll of the dice. I can even understand how someone might become addicted to the thrill of it. Why else would they continue rolling the dice to the point of ruin?

I looked across the table where he sat exposed, this handsome, proud man who'd just confessed that he didn't even have a job and lived in a shitty little motel. It must have been hard for him to come clean and I felt sorry for him. I was also relieved, slightly euphoric even, to know that my own dirty little secret was still safe.

I actually didn't care if Ricky had a lot of money. I was used to a life of scrimping. I'd been raised without money and had even been trained to believe it was the root of all evil. Camels through eyes of needles and that sort of thing. I have noticed, however, that that sort of preaching appeals mostly to poor people because it makes them feel better about themselves. Even though it might appeal to poor people, I think it's aimed at rich people who the preachers hope will fear enough for their salvation that they'll give their money to the church. Of course, I never had to worry about that because I was always broke. I wasn't Kate Rockefeller. I bought most of my clothes from JCPenney and only on rare occasions would I splurge for a new top at the Nordstrom discount rack.

"Why didn't you tell me, Ricky? I don't care if you own a fancy condo. That's not what I care about."

"I don't know. I was just embarrassed."

"Don't be."

"And I was afraid if you knew the truth, you wouldn't stay with me. I'm sorry."

I leaned over and kissed him. "I love you Ricky Waters, and I'd do anything for you."

I knew his confession should have sparked a reciprocal disclosure but I kept my mouth shut and let him think he was the only liar. Pretty messed up, huh? Another thing that was messed up was the fact that I knew going forward that poor Ricky now owed me the benefit of an undisclosed fib of my own. If there ever came a time to unburden my secret, I'd remind him that he'd been dishonest with me first. Pathetic, I know.

Ricky's humble little confession didn't inspire me to come clean with my parents, either. They didn't need to know that I was a big hit at Sugar & Spice or that I'd dropped out of school. Why bother them with that? Besides, I was just taking a little breather—a temporary sabbatical which would allow me to save money. So, how about that, Mom and Dad? Your daughter is earning her own tuition money by dropping out of school to strip. Not a perfect solution, but overall pretty sensible, right? Entrepreneurial even.

In just three nights I'd earned over $1,300 at Sugar & Spice. I was making more money than my dad. Deborah told me the money would get even better once I learned the ropes. But, seriously, how much rope learning was involved here? You basically get drunk, take off your clothes, try not to trip on your heels, twirl around a tether-ball pole, and reach down to pick up the money. A monkey could do it.

I kept reminding myself that I didn't *need* to do it—I only did it when I wanted to, having completely forgotten that I didn't want to do it at all.

Then there was Ricky. I've tried to understand why he had such a pull on me. He was gorgeous, of course, so that was part of it. A big part, actually. But there was more. He was broken and I thought I could fix him. Why I thought such a thing when I was also breaking is a mystery. That's why I decided to take a few more shifts when he approached me for another bridge loan of $1,000.

15

KATHERINE

THERE WAS SOMETHING DIFFERENT about Kylie, my new little sister. My parents tried to overlook her small ears, flat nose, and the single crease in her tiny palm. When my Aunt Eloise mentioned the slight upward slant to her eyes, my mom got defensive. "Shame on you for suggesting this little blessing from God isn't perfect." But, come on, they had to know, deep down.

I spent a lot of time over at my mom's house with my own new baby, Jenna, who looked normal—the way babies are supposed to look. When friends and neighbors saw Kylie for the first time, they overdid it. They said things like: "Oh, she's so beautiful! And look how tiny she is. I think she looks just like Karolyn with the shape of her little head. And look at all that hair!" But when they walked away, I bet they said, "Ugh, that was so awkward. I didn't know what to say. Obviously, they know she has Down's, right?"

The sad comparison between my daughter and my youngest sister was inevitable. It wouldn't be mean-spirited or unkind.

In fact, it would probably be loving and sympathetic, a compassionate acknowledgement of the cross my parents had to bear. It would also be permanent and the comparison would trail the two girls for the rest of their lives. They would forever be linked but they wouldn't be on the same soccer teams or gossip about boys at sleepovers and they wouldn't gush over the latest teen idol or obsess about clothing fads. They just wouldn't.

The look in my mom's eyes was heartbreaking but she adamantly insisted, maybe too adamantly, that this was a blessing and not a curse—that she was actually *glad* in some perverse way that Kylie had Down syndrome. Maybe I would've done the same thing and looked at all the positives I had yet to see but might have been hidden out there somewhere.

My dad's emotions were tangled. He might not go so far as to call it a blessing, but he was loathe to blame God for anything. Things were heavenly produced whether they were good or bad. But why had God foisted this challenge on him? He'd done everything the church had required. He'd never missed a church meeting or a tithing payment. He read the scriptures and prayed every day. Yet God had still seen fit to send him Kylie along with the obligation to care for her for the rest of his life. There went their retirement in a motorhome, booking those trailer parks from Cheyenne to Niagara Falls. Gone was the dream of an empty nest. And, make no mistake, it'd been God who'd directed it because He's present in all things. There are no chromosomal mistakes—biological errors aren't really errors at all. However, even though my parents didn't believe God made mistakes, they wanted Him to fix this particular one.

My dad was still the bishop, so he had the power to give special healing prayers. For the prayers to work, however, you must have faith. You could pray until the cows came home and it wouldn't do much good unless you had faith that the prayers were hitting their target. To bolster the impact of prayer, it helps to get into the right frame of mind by fasting before the blessing. Now, I suppose the more meals you skip the better but the rule of thumb in our church was two meals. I'm not sure who came up with that arbitrary two-meal rule, but we believed it must've been inspired by church leaders, presumably after they'd fasted for two meals. Going without food and water was designed to humble everyone up and make them focus on the power of prayer, at least that's my understanding.

I wasn't a big fan of fasting. This was not meant to be an indictment on fasting per se but, personally, I found it was easier to concentrate on the prayer if you weren't so focused on your hunger. But maybe that's just me.

My family fasted all the time when I was growing up. Whenever someone was sick or dying my dad would declare a fast. I hated it as a kid and wasn't crazy about the concept as an adult either, but at least I tried to be a better sport about it. I just didn't understand why God couldn't simply fix the problem at hand without requiring us to be hungry in the meantime. Let's say your kids really want to go to Disneyland. Do good parents agree to take them, but only on the condition that the poor kids suffer from regular hunger pains first? Or let's say your daughter has a broken leg. Do you require her to make dietary sacrifices before taking her to the doctor? But, alas, that's the way it was. And seems we all wanted Kylie to be normal, we agreed to fast with a good attitude. Everyone that is except Kelly.

"How come Karolyn gets to eat? It's not fair."

"Thop being mean," said Karolyn who had a slight speech impediment that wouldn't allow her to say s's.

"It's because Karolyn is only five years old and doesn't understand." This was my mom's explanation to seven-year-old Kelly who presumably should have grasped the obvious concept.

"But I'm starving," he said.

"Yeah, that's not fair," said my nine-year-old brother, Korbin. "If Kelly gets to eat, then so do I."

The family was on the verge of religious mutiny. I know my younger brothers loved their baby sister and didn't want her to have downward simdrum, but they were starving.

"Stop it, both of you," my mom said. "This is for Kylie."

"Yeah, thop it, huh mom."

"What's so wrong about Kylie anyway?"

"Yeah, what's so wrong with her? Gol."

"There's nothing wrong with her," my mom said. "She's perfect."

"Then how come we can't eat?"

"The doctors said she might not be as big and strong as you two when she grows up. That's why we need to pray for her."

"Oh."

"And you two are old enough now to say your prayers, so that's why we decided you shouldn't eat either."

"Krithy can't eat either, huh mom. Only me."

"That's right. The others are old enough to know better."

I could tell they didn't have a clue what my mom was talking about. And, to be perfectly honest, I didn't think she explained it very well. But giving her the benefit of the doubt, they'd put her on the spot in a tricky situation. Even though Korbin and Kelly didn't want to jinx the blessing, I saw them sneak a slice of bread and take it to their room. I didn't have the energy to bust them. Besides, I figured God was going to do what He was going to do with this situation regardless of what these innocent boys did and whether or not they ate a slice of bread probably wasn't going to sway Him much. At least I hoped not, for Kylie's sake.

Our neighbor, Mel Patterson, came over to help my dad with the blessing (only adult males were allowed to give blessings). Mel was the janitor of our church meetinghouse and was one of the nicest men I ever knew. He was as round and soft as a donut and I remember he was always whistling the theme song from the *Andy Griffith Show* while he mopped and vacuumed. He even whistled while cleaning up after Dave West puked all over the foyer following sacrament meeting one Sunday, and that's the sort of janitor you want.

Anyway, after church one Sunday, we all congregated in my parent's living room. We had to scoot the coffee table out of the way and push the sofa back so it pinned the curtains against the window to make room. Then we put a kitchen chair in the middle of the room where my mom sat with Kylie on her lap. My dad and Mel then put their hands on top of Kylie's head that was roughly the size of a coconut, with about as much fuzz, and began to pray while the rest of us stood in a circle around them silently praying along. I noticed Korbin was wearing a sheriff's badge pinned to his shirt, a bandana, and galoshes. My dad must not have seen it or he would have made him lose it because this was a solemn event and a sheriff's badge didn't really fit, to say nothing of the galoshes.

My dad basically commanded Kylie to lose the extra chromosome. He didn't use those exact words but that was the gist of it. He hedged his bet, however, by saying she should stick with the standard twenty-three pairs, but only if God agreed. This made sense because you can't hogtie God like that and expect to get away with it. Besides, He's probably going to do what He's going to do. But then I wondered why we even bothered with the blessing in the first place if God wanted Kylie to have the extra chromosome. And He'd just barely given the chromosome allotment to her a month or two earlier so He might not have been inclined to change His mind so quickly. But I suppose it never hurts to ask.

When the prayer ended, we all opened our eyes to see if Kylie looked any different. We weren't expecting immediate results because we knew the healing blessing might take time to kick in. But we also knew that if we had enough faith we could move mountains. It says so right in the Bible. And this seemed like a much smaller ask than moving a mountain.

As Keith and I were packing up Jacob and Jenna and all their paraphernalia for the drive home, my little sister, Kristy, asked if she could talk to me in private. We walked down the hall to my parent's bedroom and closed the door for privacy. Kristy said she worried the blessing wouldn't work and it'd be her fault because she'd kept her eyes open and spied on everybody during the prayer. I tried to reassure her that God wouldn't penalize Kylie for that infraction, small as it was. In fact, I told her I didn't think God would penalize Kylie for anything Kristy had done, no matter how bad it'd been. I think this made her feel better, but there was still that fear in her eyes that she'd gone and undone the whole thing—all that fasting and nothing to show for it.

For the record, I didn't blame God (and certainly not Kristy) for Kylie's continued chromosomal irregularity. And even though the blessing appeared to be a bust, no one's faith wavered, including my own.

The head cheerleader at my high school was named Theresa Lowe. During a timeout at a basketball game, one of the boy cheerleaders threw her up into the air for a back flip which they had rehearsed a thousand times, only this time he couldn't quite catch her and she landed awkwardly on her neck. I didn't actually see it happen because Janet wanted me to admire her new corduroys and I'd turned my head a moment before the muffled crack on the gymnasium's hardwood floor. Several of the boys around us laughed but then fell silent. Students and faculty rushed in to help but probably made it worse because I'd always heard you aren't supposed to move someone if you suspect a spinal cord injury. The EMT's put her on a gurney and wheeled her out of the gym as students gawked, hands covering their mouths with looks of shock as they tried to process the enormity of Theresa's fate. And then there was the question about whether they should continue with the basketball game. It was decided that the game must go on (we *were* playing our rival). I realize there was nothing the coaches and referees could have done at that point, but it didn't feel right. The gym's energy had been zapped and the students were subdued as Theresa was receiving the awful news three miles away that she was now paralyzed.

Theresa was a member of our church (nearly all the kids were) and you want to talk blessings? You want to talk prayer? Well, the entire community was on their knees for a solid week. And the sheer number of healing blessings she received in the following days was a testament to their faith, if not their desperation. Theresa remained a quad but the general consensus was that God had stepped in to save the day because she could have died with a broken neck like that. We all thanked God in prayer for having been there for her.

I sat in Jenna's room the night of Kylie's blessing, rocking her to sleep in the worn upholstered rocking chair. An empty bottle was wedged into the cushion, presumably forgotten from a midnight feeding. I'd spent many hours in that chair breastfeeding, shushing, and reading books where the animals were always dressed in uniforms—bears as policemen, dogs as firemen, and seals as butlers. The room smelled of baby powder, Desitin, and the faint hint of dirty diapers from the pail by the changing table. There were bite marks on the rail of the crib, souvenirs from Jacob in the days before he learned to climb out. I marveled at the number of stuffed animals in the room. How they had accumulated! A teddy bear with a red stocking cap was within arm's length and I picked it up. A small crusty remnant of spit-up was on the bear's small paw. A five-foot-tall giraffe presided over the room from the corner and a Cinderella nightlight cast a warm glow as I rocked.

I looked down at Jenna's hands. So innocent, so perfect with one less chromosome than her aunt even though not a single blessing had been given on her behalf. Was it fate? Or was it all by grand design? Surely this chromosomal discrepancy wasn't the result of Jenna's or Kylie's exceptional behavior because they were only a few months old and hadn't done anything good, or bad. Was God directing all this joy and sorrow, all this happiness and pain? Or, in Kylie's case, was it just unholy luck?

16

KATE

I WASN'T THERE for my little sister Kylie's birth. My parents told me to focus on my schoolwork instead. Yeah, all that schoolwork was a killer. I wanted to confess that I'd temporarily dropped out, or at least I thought I should, to decant myself, but then I chickened out. My intentions were usually pretty good but my follow through was only so-so.

The next weekend, when Kylie was about a week old, I borrowed Deborah's car and drove home to St. George to see my little sister for the first time. No one had bothered to tell me she had Down syndrome. Maybe they hoped she'd outgrow it before I saw her. Or maybe by telling me it would have solidified the diagnosis. Anyway, they pretended she was just as normal as can be.

"Where is she?" I asked as I came in the front door. "Where's my new little sister!"

"Gol, what happened to your hair?" asked Korbin who was dressed this time as a WWII soldier with cowboy boots. "It looks white."

"How come you smell like smoke?" asked Kelly.

"Yeah," said Karolyn, "you thmell like thmoke."

I was a fairly regular smoker by then but I didn't want to end up with a hole in my throat, trying to talk out of my thorax and dragging an oxygen tank around, so I kept it to no more than half a pack a day. But this day was different and I'd smoked about five cigarettes on the drive up to steady my nerves. I'd rolled down the windows and let the wind rip through the car as I chewed on one Cert after another. Apparently it hadn't been enough but at least it aired out Deborah's smelly car.

"So, where's Kylie?" I asked.

"She's downed," said Kelly.

"No she isn't," said Korbin. "So shut up and quit being stupid."

"I'm not stupid."

"Yes you are, Stupid."

"Am not."

"Are too."

"I think he's thupid, too," said Karolyn.

"Hey, it's okay you guys," I said.

I walked down the hall to my parents' bedroom as my little brothers trailed behind me calling each other stupid. I passed the gallery of family photos in the hallway, each of us frozen in time. None of us could have known what the future held when the photos had been taken—not the good, not the bad, not the unintended, and not the irreversible. I would later look at those photos and marvel at how far I had come because an updated chronological snapshot would have shown me in a thong and heels. Some may have said how far I'd fallen, not how far I'd come. But I couldn't have arrived to where I am now without experiencing everything I did.

My mom was propped up in bed feeding Kylie with a bottle. She must have been plain empty by the time this baby came along because she'd gone straight to Similac.

"Can I hold her?"

My mom handed the pink bundle to me. As the oldest, I'd been changing diapers and burping babies for ten years so I knew what I was doing. I peeled away the blanket and looked at my infant sister, and then at my mom.

How could my mom have thought I wouldn't notice? Was this something we were just going to ignore? Kylie looked like Velma Oldroyd in our ward, a girl we called That One Mongoloid Girl Down The Street because we didn't want to be rude and call her a retard. And it only made it worse that they'd named her Velma.

"See, she's normal, huh?" said Korbin to bring me into the vast family conspiracy. "Don't listen to Kelly—he's stupid."

I looked at Kylie again and then back up at my mom. "Is she . . . okay? I just . . . it's just that she looks a little bit . . ."

"She's perfectly healthy, but the doctor said we won't know for a while."

"We won't know what?"

"Well, one doctor thinks she might have Down syndrome, but I don't really trust him. We just don't know for sure."

"You mean, she's *retarded?*" I know you're not supposed to say that word anymore—it just slipped out—and I felt bad for saying it.

"Of course not," my mom said and then burst into tears. "I'm sorry we didn't tell you." She stopped crying and suddenly became defiant to chase the bad away. "We still don't know for sure. She's our special angel, that's all we know."

I think she hoped I'd say something reassuring, something like, "I don't think she looks that different," or "The doctors are crazy because she looks totally normal to me." Instead I just stared down into the face of our new special angel. I was so happy, and yet so sad. I decided right then that I loved this little girl more than anyone else in the world and would always have her back.

"She's beautiful, Mom," I said and bent down to kiss her tiny forehead. A tear dropped from my chin to Kylie's cheek and I wiped it with my thumb. "She really is."

I decided to spend the night at my parent's house rather than drive back to Las Vegas that night. I knew I was welcome, of course I was, but I'm fairly sure my parents worried that I'd infect my younger siblings with my worldly ways. Let's just say my dad didn't roll out the fatted calf to celebrate the return of his Prodigal Daughter, and I didn't see my mom break out the good china either. But, in fairness, she never broke it out and I wondered what she was saving it for. It was like my Aunt Eloise who covered her new living room sofa with plastic and never removed it.

"What have you done with your hair?" my dad asked. "I don't think it sends the right message."

"What message? I'm not trying to send any messages, Dad. Lots of girls have bleached hair."

"Maybe girls in Las Vegas do, but not girls around here. To be honest young lady, it looks like you're a girl on the street."

"Dale!" my mom said. "Is that necessary?"

"And it smells like you've been smoking," he said.

"I don't smell it, Dale," my mom lied to preserve the peace.

I thought about blaming it on the casino I'd stopped at to use the restroom on the drive up, but that was just pathetic. So I did the next most pathetic thing—I acted like I didn't know what he was talking about. "What smoke?" I asked as I took in a few whiffs of surrounding air. Sniff. Sniff. "I don't smell anything."

My dad had no positive proof so he switched tactics. "I've been thinking," he said. "Maybe it's time you came home and finished up school here. There are things that go on in Las Vegas that would shock you. Besides, you probably won't meet many good LDS boys down there."

"Dad, there are a lot of nice guys out there who aren't Mormon. Ricky's a great guy."

"He might be for all I know, but you'd never marry him because he couldn't take you to the temple."

There went my dad again, telling me what I'd never do. Advice is one thing, I get that, especially if it's solicited. But my dad rarely gave advice—he lectured. And it was always unsolicited.

"There are worse things than not getting married in the temple," I said.

Now, if you're reading this you're probably thinking, well duh, of course there are worse things. But you don't know my dad.

"There are worse things?" my dad asked. "And what exactly is that supposed to mean, young lady? You don't want a temple marriage?"

"No, Dad, I'm just saying that's not the most important thing in the world."

"And it's exactly that kind of talk that concerns me. Listen to yourself. I think it's time you moved back to St. George to get your head screwed on straight. Besides, your mother needs your help with the kids."

I'd gone from being a sheltered girl who'd never tasted coffee because of its blatant wickedness to hanging out with strippers in record time, a meteoric transition that didn't give me time to fully process what was happening to me. I don't use that as an excuse, but I was less prepared for adulthood and all that came with it than most young women who grow up without obsessing over reading scriptures and the Second Coming of Jesus.

You might not believe me given all my topless gallivanting in Vegas, but I still believed in the church. Just not quite as much. My parents saw my belief getting watered down and it scared the crap out of them. They weren't blind, you know, so it was time to circle the wagons lest I wander too far from camp and get hauled off by the wicked guys.

A big part of me was proud for having had the courage to break out of my cage. I suppose it hadn't been *that* courageous, and I wasn't particularly proud to be a stripper, but I was finally making my own way and it was liberating. I was afraid, however, to publicly declare my escape—afraid to let people know I was a free bird. I feared if they knew I'd escaped they would send out the cavalry of saintly saints with their heavenly nets to scoop me up and gently place me back into my cage. They would say they were re-caging me out of love, of course, because they cared about me and didn't want me to go to hell. They would be so frantically *congenial* in their dire judgment over my salvation and would emphasize they were only doing what was best for me. But all this loving concern over my freedom was suffocating. It felt like I was being raped by a gang of Care Bears.

The next day my dad announced that we'd all fast for Kylie and he'd give her a healing blessing. My dad was big on giving blessings and gave them for a variety of reasons, but mostly to cure illnesses. You probably wouldn't get a blessing for a routine ailment like, say, athlete's foot, although I suppose you could. But they would be tailor-made for something as significant as Down syndrome (even though I doubt anyone with Down syndrome has ever been cured by a blessing). Anyway, my dad liked giving them. First of all, I think he sincerely believed they actually worked despite the dismal track record and, secondly, I think it was a power trip—the righteous leader altruistically agreeing to be God's spokesman for the unfortunate, or the sinner. Stand back, he's about to perform his religious duty! I probably shouldn't be so hard on my dad but he was proud of his standing in the church. Too proud, in my opinion. I'll bet my mom would have approached the task with more humility if she had ever been allowed to speak for God in these matters of life and death.

I'm afraid to say I didn't think the blessing would work. This alone was not compelling evidence that I'd lost my faith, however, because I still believed in God. Only this time I didn't hold my breath waiting for a miracle cure. Nevertheless, I fasted and prayed along with the rest of the family just in case. Then I felt bad for not believing it would work so I prayed double to undo the effect of my faithlessness because the last thing I wanted was blood on my hands, dooming my little sister to a lifetime of Down's.

Our neighbor, Mel Patterson, came over to help my dad perform the blessing. He was the janitor at our ward meetinghouse and his wife was about the nicest person I knew. (She was pretty ditsy though. One day my mom locked herself out of our house and needed to get into our garage to open the door to our kitchen. Sister Patterson wanted to help so she brought over her own garage door clicker to save the day. She pointed and clicked at our garage door for five minutes.) Mel was nice, too. He always wore navy-blue coveralls and spent most of his free time tinkering and whistling in his garage.

Anyway, once the blessing began my dad begged God to heal Kylie. If I'd been God, I would have sat up and listened because my dad was laying it all on the line. He was so sincere and so sad, like it'd been his fault somehow that Kylie was imperfect and was now asking God from the bottom of his heart to fix her. When the blessing ended, we all stole looks at Kylie to see if it'd worked but she still looked about the same.

"Is she all better?" Kelly asked.

"Heavenly Father loves Kylie very much and He will take care of her."

"I know. So, is she better now?"

"We'll wait to see what Heavenly Father wants."

"Why doesn't Heavenly Father want her to be better?"

"He does, Kelly."

"Oh. Then why doesn't He fix her?"

"He might."

"Do you think she'll be better in the morning?"

"We don't know, Kelly."

"So can we eat now?"

I thought Kelly had made a fair point. Why *didn't* God fix her? It was His prerogative to do so and He never struck me as being unfair or whimsical. As the days wore on, no one said a word about the botched blessing. Of course, maybe it hadn't been botched at all—maybe God wanted her to be just the way she was and no amount of groveling was going to budge Him. As they say, the Lord answers all prayers, it's just that sometimes He answers no.

I think back to the time Theresa Lowe, a cheerleader at my high school, fell when a boy cheerleader threw her into the air and then forgot to catch her. She was made a quadriplegic and it was so sad. People prayed. Oh, they prayed all right. First they prayed to make the nerves regrow and when they didn't regrow, they prayed in thanks for God's great love in watching out for Theresa because she'd nearly died, but didn't. I was one of those two-prong prayers. When my first prayers weren't answered, I switched to the second prong, giving thanks to God for His watchful love. But when I reflect back on it, I'm not entirely sure what I was thinking. I mean, if God really loved her and was actually watching out for her, then why did the boy drop her? Why didn't God intervene? And if there had been a lesson to be learned by the dropping, why couldn't Theresa have just twisted an ankle? Was it really necessary that He make her a quad? It was the first kernel of doubt that maybe there wasn't a God after all. This kernel was quickly dismissed at the time because, obviously, there is a God, right? How could there not be. But what kind of a God is He?

I'd planned to return to Vegas the next day. For one thing, I was running out of things to wear. I'd only brought my most conservative clothes because I knew if I'd worn my collection of halter tops and daisy dukes there would've been a series of fainting spells, one after another.

"You look awfully thin," my mom said that night over a casserole. "I don't think you're getting enough to eat."

Korbin finally showed up smelling like Enos because he insisted on sleeping with our dog and his various stenches tended to rub off on Korbin and his collection of outfits. He sat at the table in camouflage pants, a chauffer's hat, and cape. I was impressed by his ability to mix and match. As long as it involved a uniform. I saw my dad shake his head.

"I'm fine, Mom."

"But you're so thin."

"Jackie, quit riding her about her weight," my dad said. "She looks fine." He then turned toward me. "Don't listen to your mother."

My mom just shrugged it off—like a woman who's come to expect that she's going to be criticized every now and then whether she deserves it or not.

I thought that was the end of that, but then my dad said my wardrobe was too "revealing" and that I was playing right into Satan's playbook.

"Dad, its fine. This is what everybody wears."

"Not here they don't."

I don't know how my mom did it. She loved my dad because she said she would when she was a teenage bride. That's about it as far as I could see. And now it seemed like she was stuck. Maybe I'm being too hard on my dad and maybe my mom didn't feel stuck at all. But she'd only been 18 years old when she'd pledged her life to him, in sickness and in health. What did she know about him back then? It couldn't have been much. And what did she know about herself? Geez, for that matter, what did she even know about sickness and health? Where was the escape clause when she changed, or when he did? I guess it was divorce, but that came with enough shame in our community to make it a pretty lousy escape clause.

Ricky was in the kitchen when I came home. I dropped my overnight bag on the floor with a thud.

"You look like you could use a drink," he said.

"I'm just tired," I said.

"So, is your sister really retarded?"

"She's not retarded, Ricky. She has Down syndrome, okay? I hate it when people say she's retarded."

"Sorry, I'm not trying to be a jerk about it. You're the one who said she was retarded or something."

"No, I said she had Down syndrome. Period."

"Whatever you say. I once knew a kid in elementary school who had it and I can't remember if they put him in a home or not."

"A home?"

"Yeah, you know, like a mental institution."

"Ricky, my little sister is not going to live in a mental institution."

Maybe I needed a drink after all.

The day after the healing blessing in St. George, my whole family had gone to church together. I'd gone along because I didn't want to hurt my mom's feelings and I didn't want to fight about it with my dad. All eleven of us walked in together, scooting sideways down the pew like the Von Trapp family. I guess I would've been Liesl, the oldest of the Von Trapp kids. She'd be singing about how she was sixteen going on seventeen in her story, but I'd still be a stripper in mine. The sermon that day was basically the same as it always was—a never-ending campaign to re-sell something everyone in the congregation had already bought.

Word had already spread within the ward about how the bishop's newest addition was retarded and I could feel people whispering from the pews, in reverent tones, of course.

I milled about in the foyer after the meeting and then retreated to the area just outside the front door where ward members informally congregated despite a stiff breeze that day. I couldn't decide if I wanted to talk to anyone, or not. The feeling must have been mutual because hardly anyone approached to talk to me either and those who did smothered me with kindness. I know I should give those who were brave enough to talk to me the benefit of the doubt and assume their kindness was genuine, but it felt obligatory to me. More like pity. So, yeah, most of them avoided me but you better believe they saw me because I stuck out like a hooker in a nunnery. The prodigal daughter returning from Sin City, stripper hair and all.

While I was waiting for my parents to round up the brood, I overheard a few women talking in hushed tones on the sidewalk near the parking lot. They were wearing their Sunday best and holding their Bibles and Book of Mormons to their chests. I edged closer.

". . . and that's why I say enough is enough, because that's what happens when you're older. Besides, she already has too many as it is."

There were times in my life that I'd been embarrassed by all the kids in my family. I can admit that. I'd overheard enough of the ridicule and it didn't feel good. I had silently taken it out on my parents for being so square. Like, come on Mom and Dad, stop it already. Don't you know we're the laughingstock of the whole neighborhood? But that afternoon when I heard that pious old fuddy-duddy at church gossiping about my family I felt proud to be a Coombs.

I could be critical of my parent's breeding habits but I didn't appreciate it when someone else was. Who did this woman think she was? Mother Mary? I looked over at my mom who was holding Kylie on one hip while trying to lasso Karolyn as she gripped the front of her homemade dress in a fist with her free hand against the breeze. She would have been crushed, absolutely crushed, to hear what these women had just said behind her back, and I had a rush of affection for her.

Maybe that's why I was so defensive when Ricky had so casually said that my little sister was retarded.

17

KATHERINE

SO I HAD ANOTHER BABY. If you're counting, that made three and I was only twenty-five-years old. I was on pace with my *mom*, practically dripping with kids. And don't think we didn't hear about it from Vaughn who suddenly became preoccupied with over-population for the first time in his life. How many more, he wondered incredulously, as if it was any of his business, which it obviously wasn't. This wasn't China.

I pledged to lose the baby fat but then I'd get pregnant again and it was no use. At this rate there was no way I'd be going to my ten-year high school reunion. I gained it all in my hips too, exactly where I didn't need it. I was starting to look like a ripe pear. Fortunately, the men in my life were good to remind me of my weight gain because, obviously, I was unaware of it. Take my dad, for example.

"Katherine," he said, "you look a little heavier to me."

"Dale!" my mom said. "Don't listen to your father, Katherine. You look beautiful."

"I'm just saying you should watch what you eat, that's all. Your metabolism changes when you get older."

I thought my mom was going to slug him in the nose, or maybe give him a kidney punch, that is if she had enough strength to penetrate his own swollen love handles. As for me, I just tried not to cry. He also said women are more prone to gain weight because they don't work, so it's much harder for them to burn off the calories. Believe it or not, that comment actually helped because it was so ridiculous it tainted everything else he said.

My hair was also getting bigger. I'm slightly mortified when I look back at the photos because this was my Crimping Phase. It was thick and shoulder length so I sort of looked like the Sphinx. I couldn't tell if Keith liked it or not. "You changed your hair," was all he said. Unfortunately, he didn't change his—he looked like he'd gone to a barbershop with a picture of Benjamin Franklin and asked them to copy it. He didn't update his wardrobe either, parading around in a golf shirt tucked into jeans with a braided belt and white New Balance sneakers.

I tried to help by buying him clothes for Christmas that were a bit more . . . stylish. But he was a stubborn advocate of the early-eighties look that was so becoming. And I suppose it was if you liked that particular look of a young father who'd been determined to look sixty. I probably shouldn't talk because when I look back on the photos from those days, I didn't look like I'd hopped off the page of the Macy's Spring Casual Collection either. But at least I tried.

Our gift giving began to dwindle once we started having kids. We went all out at Christmas the first year of our marriage, wrapping and hiding our thoughtful gifts to each other.

Clothes! Cards! Cologne! Anything from Radio Shack! I even learned how to crochet and slaved away at an afghan for Keith. I think he appreciated the effort, even though the original rectangular design wound up in the shape of a state like, say, Nebraska or one of the other ones that are boring to drive through. Within a few years we were just giving each other socks and the occasional kitchen accessory. It had finally dwindled to an unwrapped 4-pack of furnace filters and that's when I knew it was time to call a truce. Now if I want something in mid-June, I just buy it and say it was for Christmas. It relieves his guilt and I get what I want.

My three-year-old daughter Jenna and her three-year-old Aunt Kylie played together almost every day, and usually at our house to give my mom a break. Of course, Jenna didn't know Down syndrome from Adam. She didn't zero in on Kylie's small chin or the skin folds on the inner corner of her eyes. And Jenna didn't care that Kylie's tongue stuck out a bit because her mouth cavity was too small to fit a regulation-sized tongue. Jenna was bigger than Kylie too, so she had someone to boss around. So, at least for now, they were best friends.

My mom agreed to watch my kids for a few days, however, because Janet invited me and her friend named Carol to go on a girl's trip to Los Angeles. The plan was to get on a TV game show because she'd been obsessed with them since high school, especially The Price is Right.

Our husbands thought there was no end to their martyrdom. "I don't see why you need to go to California," Keith whined. "Can't you just stay here, maybe order in a pizza and play games or whatever? Hey, I'd baby-sit for a few hours."

This was rich because Keith had just returned from a three-night hunting trip with the boys. He hadn't even asked me if he could go; he'd told me. And did I flip out? Did I whine for two days? I did not. I even pretended to be excited for him when he returned with the exhilarating news that he'd bagged a six-point buck. That's what he said—he'd "bagged it." I'm obviously not a hunter but I think we all ought to agree you bag groceries, not two-hundred-pound wild forest creatures. My point is not to nitpick about hunting lingo, but rather to state that I don't put up a huge fuss when he takes his annual deer hunting trip, or when he's gone all day Saturday to play golf with his buddies. In fact, I doubt he's even aware of how these little getaways with the guys might affect me. This obliviousness was not criminal but neither should it come with a blue ribbon. I would have advised him to keep his mouth shut at this point but then he said it was no big deal for me to babysit the kids because I was used to it. He was right about that—I was used to it.

"Janet wants to get on a TV game show in Los Angeles," I'd said to Keith. "It sounds like fun. My mom said she'll watch the kids during the day and I'll only be gone a few days."

"So you'll just go and leave me alone with the kids?" Again, amnesia about deer hunting, golf, and everything else he does whenever he wants.

"Well, they are your kids."

"Yeah, but—"

I got everything ready before I left, basically leaving it all on a silver platter for him. I printed up the daily schedules, lined up a few babysitters, and set out what the kids would wear each day I'd be gone, including their jammies. I'd even pre-prepared several meals in labeled cartons in the fridge. And still Keith felt like a martyr.

Janet and Carol pulled into our driveway in Janet's minivan and honked for me. I was excited because I hadn't been on a vacation since our honeymoon. And what a doozie *that* had been—camping at Zion National Park for two days in my in-law's R.V. (which was a generous misnomer because it was actually a musty trailer they insisted on calling an R.V. because it had a port-o-potty). It rained every day and even Keith got sick of trying to have sex the whole time because there was nothing else to do.

"So what did Randy say about watching your kids?" I asked Janet when I climbed into the back seat.

"Oh my gosh, you would've thought I'd asked him to climb Mount Everest."

"Men are all the same," said Carol, who couldn't have known men very well. She was heavy-set, single, and at twenty-eight-years-old was approaching the Don't-Sell-Past date in our community. But we all pretended she had plenty of time.

"What did Keith say?" asked Janet.

"He wasn't crazy about it either," I said, "but I think it'll be good for him. These guys need to bond with their kids."

"I'm not sure I want to get married and have kids," said Carol.

"Why not?"

"I don't know," she said. "Men are just way too demanding."

Janet and I agreed, to make her feel better.

We hadn't driven more than twenty minutes when Carol wanted to stop at a convenience store to load up on road-trip snacks. I'm good with a few snacks but Carol really stocked up for the six hour drive. She bought at least one thing from every aisle. Doritos, Butterfingers, licorice, Jolly Ranchers, and even some Pop Tarts.

"I'll be so freaking nervous if we get on the show," I said once we were back on the road.

"Not me," said Carol as she crunched away on a handful of Doritos. "The Price is Right is my favorite show on earth. You just need to concentrate and not get carried away with all the noise and stuff."

"Okay, how much is a can of tomato soup?"

"Fifty cents!" shouted Carol.

"Large tube of Crest?"

"Ninety-nine cents?" said Janet.

"No, it'd be more like a dollar five," said Carol, who'd been studying for weeks. She had a stack of recipe cards with a picture of the item on the front and the retail cost on the back.

I suggested we split the prize money if one of us won.

"Sounds good to me," said Janet.

"Let's just wait and see," said Carol. She obviously didn't want to share the new Mustang; not with how much she'd been practicing. "Besides," she said, "it'd be way too hard to share a washer and dryer or something."

We drove through Las Vegas on our way to Los Angeles. I had a $15 gambling budget and was sticking to it. Technically, our church preaches that gambling is a sin because it . . . well, actually I'm not sure why. But it's wrong, I do know that. Even though we knew gambling was a sin of some variety, we stopped at the Golden Nugget anyway, figuring we'd all go to hell together. We gathered around the nickel slot machine and took turns blowing through our rolls of coins. Girls gone wild! Carol freaked out when two cherries in a row popped up. "Gol, Carol," said Janet, "you're really good at this!"

The woman two stools down from us with a bucket of nickels in her lap was smoking. Carol pulled a face and dramatically waved her hand in front of her nose. The woman noticed the scene Carol was making and took an extra-long drag and blew it our way.

A cocktail waitress trolled by with her push-up bra, fishnet stockings, and tray of sin juice. "Can I get you ladies anything?" We all shook our heads. "No thanks." The cocktail waitress walked away and we stared at her from behind.

"I'd never wear anything like that in a million years," said Carol. "You couldn't pay me enough." Now, I hate to be rude, but I didn't think she needed to worry about it because they don't make outfits like that in her size. They just don't.

"Las Vegas just makes me feel dirty," said Janet.

"Me too," said Carol. "These people get caught up in all this glitz and glamour and think it makes them happy," she continued as she pulled the lever again and held her breath. When she won fifty cents she shrieked with joy, "but it's impossible to be happy if you aren't living the commandments. Wickedness never was happiness, just like the prophet says."

We nodded along in agreement because that's one of our church sayings. How on earth could that cocktail waitress have been happy living a life of unbridled sin—dressed like a hooker with those fishnets and tutu? She'd obviously made her bed with the eat, drink, and be merry crowd, the very crowd that was walking on thin ice with God and was anathema to my upbringing.

We blew through our gambling budgets in twenty minutes and walked out from the dark, air-conditioned casino into the parking lot where it was 110 degrees. Carol automatically got into the front seat because she had declared early on that she got car sick whenever she had to ride in the backseat. I wasn't about to insist on a doctor's note, but did this so-called "condition" require her to ride shotgun the entire time? I could have claimed the same ailment but I'd already come to learn that Carol was pushy that way.

We passed a billboard for a strip club on our way out of town called Puss 'N Boots. An illustrated woman was bent at the waist wearing only a string bikini and pair of cowboy boots. She had about a twelve-inch waist and boobs that were way bigger than they were supposed to be.

"I feel sorry for those girls," said Janet, motioning to the billboard. "I mean, look at her. That's disgusting. I'd kill Randy if he ever went to a place like that."

I shook my head. "Can you imagine stripping naked in front of all those gross guys? Seriously, who would even *do* that?"

"Some girls just don't have any morals," said Janet. "I know I'd never do such a thing, that's for sure. You couldn't pay me enough."

"Same here," I said.

"Me too," said Carol.

It would have been highly unlikely for any of us to be in that position, almost impossible really, but we all wanted to be formally on the record, even Carol.

The next day, we waited in line on the sidewalk in front of the Hollywood studio for two hours behind a threesome dressed as a potato, carrot, and something that might have been a squash. The couple directly behind us was stuck in a pair of four-foot-square dice. There were pirates, hobos, and sailors. It was hot and the makeup was running. The guy under the Darth Vader suit must have been drenched.

Carol had sewn our Three Musketeer costumes. She'd told us several times that it'd taken her hours and hours to make them, and I believe her (although the number of hours it actually took increased with each retelling). An usher escorted us to the third row in a real live television studio. Lights! Camera! Action! Bob Barker came out to the stage about fifteen minutes before the cameras started rolling. He was dressed casually in in a golf shirt and stepped down into the audience to shake a few hands. I about *died* when he reached his hand out. "Bob Barker. Love the mustache. Thanks for coming."

"Omigosh! Bob Barker just shook my freaking hand!"

"I know," said Carol.

"And he said he liked my mustache!"

"I know," said Carol.

A few minutes later the show began and Bob appeared from behind the curtain in a suit and tie, obviously a quick changer. The applause signs came on for the studio audience and we enthusiastically obliged.

"Katherine Murphy! Come on down!" I almost peed my Musketeer pants. Was it the handshake? The mustache? Even though I'd called in to radio shows and filled out a bazillion raffle tickets over the years, I'd never won anything in my life, not even a loaf of banana bread at a church fundraiser.

Janet practically mauled me as I scooted sideways along the row and then ran down the aisle, high-fiving carrots, hobos, and pirates like a complete idiot. It was happening fast and it felt like I was having an out-of-body experience as I stood on the elevated stage looking over the audience. I wouldn't say I was nervous, per se, but it did flash through my mind to picture the audience members naked because I'd heard that's what you're supposed to do if you're nervous on stage in front of a crowd.

So there I was on national television wearing a Three Musketeer costume and a handlebar mustache, standing next to the Stunning Assistant whose legs practically went up to my throat. She wore a sexy sequin dress with high heels which looked even sexier than normal next to me and my costume. One elegant hand rested on her hip, teapot style, and the other, the spout, was lifted gracefully to a small table as if the Mona Lisa were displayed there instead of a box of Arm & Hammer and a can of SpaghettiOs.

I guessed the price of the SpaghettiOs and moved on to another round where I nailed the price of an aerosol can of Raid. I was stumped by the cost of a five-pound bag of C & H Sugar and looked into the audience where everyone was shouting different prices at me. Janet was jumping up and down like a pogo stick yelling "$1.69! $1.69! $1.69!" Carol was sitting next to her, shrugging her shoulders as if she hadn't the foggiest idea what a bag of sugar costs even though I bet it'd been on one of her recipe cards.

Try not to act stupid. Try not to act stupid. Try not to act stupid. But, yeah, I didn't take my own advice and when I made it to the Showcase Showdown, I got so carried away in the excitement that I flung my sombrero into the audience like a Frisbee.

They pulled back the curtain to find Stunning Assistant sitting at the wheel of a brand-new Sea Ray motorboat. She wore a scarf, large Jackie Kennedy sunglasses, and a swimsuit cover-up. Who wouldn't want to spend a day at the lake with her? She lightly brushed her long-manicured fingers along the edge of the boat like she was checking for dust.

"Don, tell us about these magnificent Showcase prizes!" Don, who no one could see, used his luxurious voice to describe the boat, water skis, and a seven-hundred-year supply of Coppertone.

It was a blur when I won. I remember hugging Bob Barker and his portable microphone smacking me in the chin and then turning around to hug someone else. Janet was suddenly on the stage and we bounced together in rhythm, chest to chest. I noticed Carol was still in her seat pretending to fuss with her costume.

We were led to an office in a building next door to the studio where I had to fill out a bunch of paperwork. Carol paced around the room, checking her watch about every thirty seconds and reminding us how heavy traffic was going to be. Meanwhile, Bob had fled the studio within two seconds of hearing ". . . and stop. We're off the air," presumably to beat the traffic. He didn't even say goodbye.

"I can't believe I won!" I said as we reached the car. "Keith is going to freak!"

Janet insisted that I ride in the front seat for change, the new celebrity that I was. Carol was quiet.

"I still can't believe it," I said as we left the parking lot.

"I was surprised," said Carol. "They usually give away a new car."

"But the boat is awesome!" I said. "It'll be so fun!"

"Yeah, but it'll probably be expensive to maintain," said Carol. "Plus, it's not good to be in the sun too much. But if you like it, I guess that's all that matters."

"I'm still in shock. I've never been lucky in my whole life!"

"They probably picked one of us because of the costumes," said Carol.

"Omigosh, Carol, thanks so much for making them. Did you guys think it was weird when I threw my hat?"

"Heck no!" said Janet. "I loved that part!"

"It got smashed," said Carol. "I was hoping to keep all the costumes. I probably spent fifty hours on them."

"I'm so happy for you, Katherine!" said Janet.

"Me too," said Carol, from the back seat. "But I might be getting car sick soon, just so you know."

18

KATE

WORK AT THE LUCKY TRAVELER had run its course. Hauling greasy food around for minimum wage didn't make a ton of sense, not when I was crushing it on the side. Ricky, the investment guru that he was, said working at the restaurant had become "financially imprudent." He astutely pointed out that I could make more by taking off my clothes in public. I could have reminded him that if he got a real job he could make more, too, which seemed like a financially prudent thing to do.

A friend of a friend knew the guy who hired cocktail waitresses at the Golden Nugget. This friend told me I'd make about $150 in tips per shift. Not too shabby, I thought. I sweated the job interview but I shouldn't have because the hiring guy asked me a total of three questions, and two of them were about my favorite things to do in Vegas. He had a creepy vibe about him, the vibe all girls can feel because we're not stupid. Very gross. Memo to men: If you think you're getting away with it when you leer at our tits, you're not. I think the manager at the Golden Nugget just wanted to see me in the fishnets and short skirts they make you wear. Honestly, the skirts were like little black tutus.

I trolled around the roulette tables, blackjack dealers, and one arm bandits four nights a week in those fishnets and tutu, carrying trays of watered-down drinks to pot-bellied gamblers who tried to flirt with me in their sexy cargo shorts and XXL-sized Hawaiian shirts to hide their guts. Gross again. These titans of gambling wasted so much money you'd think the Golden Nugget could have afforded to pay us cocktail waitresses more. But no.

I tried to get used to the incessant ringing and jingling of those stupid slot machines but it was no use. All that gay ringing and jingling was designed to make it sound like everyone was winning. And that's a laugh right there.

Some of those highly sophisticated gamblers would sit on their stools in front of a slot machine for hours at a time. ("Good gravy Larry, we come all the way down from Missoula and you're gonna sit there all day?" "But Glenna, I can't give up my spot because this machine's the lucky one." "Well, suit yourself. I'm going to the souvenir shop.") Men with bad comb-overs and guts that drooped over their belts would swivel on their stools as I'd pass by, craning their necks in front of their wives who wore sequin blouses and too much hairspray. "Uh, hello Melvin darling, I'm sitting right here." Many of these women would glare at me as if it were somehow my fault they'd married a lecherous creep. Or they'd give me the withering stay-away-from-my-husband stare to hopefully keep my temptation over Melvin's charm at bay.

It was early in my shift at the Golden Nugget when I noticed two women in their late twenties hovered around a slot machine. They were about my age and had a naïve innocence about them, like they'd never been in a casino before. You could just tell because they were modestly dressed and way too excited. Regulars look bored, even when they're winning. One of young women looked up as I walked past.

"Katherine? Katherine Coombs? Omigosh! Is that you?"

I swiveled around with my tray at shoulder height to see Janet, my best friend from high school.

"*Janet?* What are you doing here?"

"We're on our way to Los Angeles for a girl's trip. We're trying to get on The Price is Right. Isn't that a hoot? We're going to wear Three Musketeer costumes and everything."

"Yeah, that sounds fun." I remembered that Janet had always been obsessed with TV game shows and we'd talked about trying to get on The Price is Right when we got a little older.

"Oh, sorry," Janet said as she motioned toward the heavyset young woman she was with. "This is my friend, Carol."

I balanced the tray stacked with empty cocktail glasses, dirty ashtrays, and crumpled napkins and reached out to shake Carol's hand. She reluctantly shook it but I think she was afraid she might catch a case of the wickedness-never-was-happiness bug which I presumably had in spades. "Hi, I'm Kate. I went to high school with Janet."

"You go by Kate now?" asked Janet. "Omigosh you look so different. You bleached your hair. It looks good."

"Thanks," I said. "You look good, too."

Remember what I said about being a pathological liar?

Janet had gained fifteen pounds with each child. And she had three of them, so far.

"So, like, are you married?" asked Janet. "Kids?" Meanwhile, her chubby friend Carol just stared at me trying to reconcile how one of Janet's high school friends from St. George could have become such an obvious slut.

"No, not yet," I said. "Just working, you know. How about you?"

"Yep. Me and Randy—you remember Randy Warner? Anyhow, we got married and have three kids so far. Here, I'll show you a photo." She rummaged through her purse which was large enough to hold a package of disposable diapers and a few auxiliary sandwiches.

"Here they are, the little stink pots."

"They're really cute," I said.

"Thanks. They're a handful but we love 'em. Hey, we missed you at the five-year reunion."

"Yeah, I was going to go but then something came up. Was it fun?"

"Omigosh, we had a blast! I wish you could've made it. Oh well, there's always the ten year!" Then that awkward lull. "Well, anyway, we need to get the ol' gang together one of these days." This was a long shot, but it's just what you say. "Sandra and Lisa live fairly close by. In fact, Sandra and her husband are in our same ward now if you can believe it."

"Oh wow," I said. "But, yeah, I guess I better get back to work."

"Yeah, for sure," Janet said. "But it was great seeing you again."

"You too."

As I walked away, I could feel their heads swiveling like that Linda Blair in *The Exorcist,* their eyes boring a hole in the back of my skimpy tutu. I didn't actually hear it, of course, but I'll bet their post-conversation conversation went something like this:

"That was your *friend?*"

"Yeah, I can't believe it. She was always straight-laced in high school. Her dad was the bishop and everything."

"What was up with that skirt?"

"I know, huh."

"I wouldn't wear one of those if you paid me."

"Yeah, I wonder what *happened* to her."

Janet and Carol Something would go their merry way to their TV game show, proud as punch they were on the straight and narrow. I'd be living proof to them about the dangers of leaving the fold, a perfect object lesson on the perils of sin. And me? I'd keep trolling through the ringing and jingling with my little tray and skanky tutu, trying to make a buck.

My parents were convinced I was going to hell. I could just tell. And they didn't even know the half of it. Can you imagine if they'd stumbled into the strip club? Obviously, that would never happen—my parents hadn't even made it through an R-rated movie. They boycotted *Sophie's Choice* and had to be coaxed into seeing *Tootsie*, sitting next to the aisle and ready to bolt at a swear word or the first sign of a bra.

Then again, I saw plenty of customers at Sugar & Spice whose families and friends would have been shocked if they'd known they'd slinked in. Bill? *Really?* But he's a good Christian with five kids! They'd be the antsy ones where their heads would practically disappear into their torsos like turtles. They weren't the regulars—they were the one-hitters who might have been passing through town on their way to Disneyland, the wife and kids back at Circus Circus, or the ones in Las Vegas for that risqué Certified Public Accountant's convention. They'd turn their collars up and pull their baseball caps down low. I always thought they were the creepiest ones. Now, I'm not saying I fully respected the men who came in with their heads held high but at least there was less hypocrisy and deceit. Still on the creepy side, but more on the honest side of it.

And then there was me. Who in their right mind would have dreamed *I'd* be there? Not me. Not in a million years. I grew up believing God had a plan for me, a plan that presumably did not include Sugar & Spice. I was supposed to listen to His spirit to figure out what that plan was. I often wondered why God didn't just come right out and tell me what it was. Why did He have to be so cagey about it?

Of course, my parents would've said that God hadn't been cagey at all. They would've said His instructions had been rather explicit, the blueprint spelled out in the scriptures and through the prophet. Come on, Katherine, you just haven't been listening! But I *had* been listening—I'd had my hand cupped to my ear since I was a child and all I'd heard was the word of God filtered through my parents. Be morally clean, marry a returned missionary in the temple, and have children that will be raised within the comfy confines of the church.

So, apparently, my parents *had* been told, point blank, how their life's plan was supposed to play out. I'm not calling them outright liars, but I had to wonder if God had ever really spoken to them. They would insist He had, of course—that His voice had come through loud and clear. But I don't think my parents had taken so much as a peek at anything else the world had to offer. They danced with the church like they were doing the tango, but it felt more like a compulsory 7th grade dance in the school gymnasium to me, the kind where you only touched your clammy hands together because you had to, and there was always a four-inch gap between your chests.

So, yeah, maybe I wasn't righteous enough to hear Him because of all the sin wax in my ears but I highly doubt God wanted me to be a stripper, even a very good one. What kind of grand design would that have been? Which brings me back to the grand design thing in the first place. Can you imagine God up there doling out the work assignments? Let's see here, I think I'll have Nancy Jones be a florist, Fred Smith will be a butcher, Bill Morris will be an accountant, and let's go ahead and make Katherine Coombs our stripper.

What if it wasn't up to God at all? Or what if He wanted me to break out of my little box and experience everything I could in life, doing it my own way? Knowing that would've made my life so much easier because then I could have stopped walking around with my head cocked, trying to hear to His still small voice. I could have stopped trying to interpret certain coincidences as "signs from God" and I could have saved all that time and worry trying to figure out how to figure out what God had already figured out for me.

I'd feel guilty whenever these thoughts would creep in, as if I was being disloyal to God and my church for merely having them in the first place, so I kept trying to tamp them down.

I drove home to visit family and friends in St. George about once a month and each time I braced myself for the *You Need To Set A Better Example* speech 101. This stirring speech was usually delivered by my dad, but my mom got her licks in too, and so did my dwindling group of St. George friends. If Grandma Coombs had still been alive, I would've also heard plenty from her.

It'd now been five years since I'd left St. George, Utah and it felt like fifty. I'd finally graduated from UNLV after taking a two-semester breather and decided to pay my parents a visit. We were sitting in their kitchen which needed a serious makeover, unless avocado-colored appliances and brownish linoleum were your thing. The spoon and fork wallpaper must have been fashionable in a post-World War II sort of way, but now it was faded and you could see a patch of the wallpaper's original color in the shape of a cuckoo clock above the window to the backyard. The clock had been a fixture in the kitchen for years until my mom finally got tired of pulling the pine cone chains twice a day.

My dad got straight to the point.

"We're worried about the example you're setting for your younger sisters," he said on cue.

"I'm sorry you think I'm such a disappointment."

"Katherine," my mom said, "of course you're not a disappointment. It's just that your sisters worship you and if you're not active—"

"What your mother is trying to say is that if you're not active in the church it sets a bad example."

"What am I doing that's so wrong?" I asked.

Now, if they'd known the whole truth about what I'd been up to then, yeah, I could see their point. But they didn't, and it bugged me.

My dad didn't hesitate to tell me what I was to do. "Now that you've graduated, it's high time you move back to St. George, get married, and have a family like you're supposed to. If you keep carrying on with this Richard character you might not be worthy enough to be married in the temple, and we know that's what you want."

There it was again, somebody telling me they knew what I wanted. I was looking out into the backyard at my little brothers throwing dirt clods at each other. My youngest brother, Kelly, was standing next to the rickety swing set with his legs crossed. I could tell he had to go to the bathroom but had waited too long. Even though he was in a perilous position, he didn't want to come in and miss out on the fun for two minutes, so he was trying to tamp down a problem of his own. He must've finally figured it was no use and he inched toward the back door, heels pressed together, cheeks clenched, pinching tight. I couldn't help but smile and my dad said, "So this is funny now?"

"No, it's not that. I was just thinking about something."

"Katherine honey," my mom said, "don't you want to meet a nice young man and get married in the temple?"

Kelly had almost made it inside by now and I was silently rooting him on.

"I don't know what you want me to say."

"Well," my dad said, "I'll say this just once." I knew what he was about to say because he'd said it just once about two million times. "It still bothers us that this Richard is not a member of the church. We don't think he's right for you, and you know it too."

I still liked to go home, for short spurts. After all, this was my family and even though there were things about my parents that bugged me, I still craved their acceptance. What I mostly wanted was for them to accept me the way I was without rigid conditions like church attendance and getting married in the temple—to have them shout *Ollie Ollie Oxen Come in Free!* and mean every word of it. But would they ever shout that? *Could* they ever shout that? Technically they could, of course, but I'm afraid they would have considered such a shout to be a betrayal of their orthodoxy. But isn't that what Jesus shouted? Wouldn't he be on the front porch imploring me to come home—that I was worthy of his love and acceptance without condition? I hate to judge my parents so harshly, but they knew how Jesus handled these situations, or at least they should have known if they'd paid attention during all that church going. So, no, they wouldn't have betrayed their faith by accepting me the way I was. The betrayal would be in *not* accepting me, stripper hair and all.

But what would be the point in arguing with them? It's simply the way it was. So, despite the awkwardness and the lectures, I resolved to temporarily inhabit my cage to keep the peace. But I would keep the cage door open.

I missed my sisters, especially Kylie. I'd give her a small gift each time I went home. Usually it was something dumb, like a book of matches from the Lucky Traveler (fun gift idea for a little kid!), or a roll of lifesavers. Maybe it was the fact that neither Kylie nor I fit the mold. I think Kylie must have felt it too because my mom told me the first word she learned was "Kafrun."

I'd become the highest paid performer at Sugar & Spice. Crock knew it and rewarded me with the best shifts. This distinction, however, didn't come with a trophy. I couldn't even brag about it. "Hey Mom and Dad, I thought you ought to be the first to hear the good news!" "What, Darling, you're finally getting married?" "No, I'm the highest paid stripper at a dingy little club called Sugar and Spice!"

I knew Ricky would eventually find out about my little hobby (which no longer felt like a little hobby), so I decided to get it over with. For the record, I didn't tell him to be a noble truth-teller or to rid my soul of guilt. I did it because it was inevitable that he'd find out anyway and it was becoming too stressful to hide it from him. Men tend to be dense but it was a stretch to think he wouldn't clue in on my wig in the back seat.

My preamble was pathetic. I basically explained that I needed to make more money to help him out. See, that's the pathetic part about it right there—justifying my actions by indirectly blaming him with my declaration of martyrdom. I figured this would soften him up. But it turns out he didn't need to be softened up. All he said was, "Yeah, I've heard that's a great way to make a quick buck."

I was upset that he wasn't upset. Here his girlfriend tearfully confesses that she strips for other men and he acts like it's no big deal? Are you kidding me? I wanted him to ask me to quit. No, I wanted him to *demand* that I quit, post haste. I wanted him to tell me that he knew the *real* me and that I was too good for that. But instead he just asked if he could tag along with me to my next shift. It turns out he was just as dishonorable as I was.

So he started to go with me, pretending it was his first time in a strip club. If it was, which surely it wasn't, he caught on pretty quick. He'd sit at the bar and get drunk while the girls shimmied on the pole and shook their money makers. I swear the only girl he didn't ogle was me (well, me and this one other girl who *nobody* ogled, which was beyond sad). I watched him flirt with a few of the other girls and I was surprised that it didn't upset me very much. Sure, I didn't like it but I didn't erupt in tears. I realize now that it's because, deep down, I was becoming apathetic about him. At least I think that's what it was but I can't confirm it because I've never been to therapy.

I thought Ricky would be jealous of all the men ogling *me*. At least I thought he *ought* to be jealous but Ricky was too vain to actually be jealous. But didn't it bother him that men were lustfully staring at his naked girlfriend? Presumably not. If the shoe were on the other foot, say he'd been one of those Chippendale dancers, I'm pretty sure it would have bothered me big time. I never cheated on him. But let's say I had. Would he have been ambivalent about that too?

I've already told you that some of the customers were women which I thought was a bit strange. They'd sit in the audience sipping their cosmopolitans and critique us like the judges in *Best in Show*, issuing demerits for flab and cellulite as if they were perfect. Ha! If they were so perfect without a wrinkle or stretch mark then why were their husbands dragging them to a strip club in the first place? Why not just install a pole in the laundry room? Maybe they looked for the cellulite so they could point it out to their husbands. "See, Dearest, I'm not the only one." The women also scrutinized our dancing. Of course, the men didn't give a shit about our dancing skills, all they wanted to see were big hooters. If they'd wanted to see dancing, they would've gone to *The Nutcracker*.

It was because of this fascination with big hooters that I decided to get breast implants. But I didn't want to go too big. I didn't want those ginormous party balloons that don't jiggle. You've seen them—the ones that start at the collar bone and are wider than the torso they happen to be crammed into. I wanted them to look natural, maybe hang a little, you know. But then Ricky got involved and he and the plastic surgeon decided a few more cc's oughta do the trick. On balance, I'm glad I had it done but I thought they were a little too big and made me look fatter in clothes.

Speaking of balance, I was drunk most of the time so it was understandable that my balance might have been off just a tad. Plus, there were the high heels and the additional 490 cc's of silicon (per side) that I was now lugging around. At least that's what I blamed The Incident on. Well, that and the fact that the pampered customer stuck her face too close to the action.

The customer was a beautiful young woman, I'll give her that, but she was obnoxious. Monique was her name. She thought she was better than me because I had to strip publicly whereas she only needed to strip in front of her rich sugar daddy who was, like, eighty years old. As they say, if there's a Will there's a way! The old geezer wore a pinstripe suit with a silk ascot, probably to hide his turkey neck. This whole Thurston-Howell look he'd been going for bombed because men don't typically wear pinstripe suits and silk ascots at a strip club. They just don't. This wasn't *Madam Butterfly*. Anyway, Monique was sitting there, pampered and perfect, looking down her perky little nose on us girls who groveled for money from lots of men instead of just one.

The tables and chairs at Sugar & Spice were set close to the edge of the stage—close enough for customers to slip us bills. I even got a few pesos from time to time. Olé! I spotted the rich old man sitting next to the lovely Monique and drifted closer to the edge of the stage. Maybe I was too close, I'll admit that.

I'd been working on my high kick and did it just as Monique leaned into her Louis Vuitton bag for some designer lip gloss. My heel barely caught her just above the left eye. I didn't even know I'd connected until I heard her start screaming like she'd been shot. A small trickle of blood ran down her lovely face and into her taut, enormously fake cleavage. A few drops got on her expensive dress that her geriatric boyfriend had given her in partial compensation for the exclusive right to remove it at his whim.

She grabbed a napkin and covered her face, then removed it to check for blood. When she saw a few drops of blood on the napkin, she screamed. "I'll sue, you bitch!" She was probably disappointed that it hadn't been drenched in red to justify the scene she was making, hoping even to be able to wring it out in front of the crowd. The old man was trying to lead her out of the club by her elbow, promising her another trip to Zales for the indignity as she craned her head back to the stage to screech about her forthcoming lawsuit. The crowd didn't know *what* to do. Some jeered, some laughed, and some just threw back another shot. Me, I just finished my set because I didn't know what else to do. I'd thought about grabbing a Band-Aid from my purse but then decided it might not have been necessary.

Well, she sued all right. Try $500,000. Her Las Vegas billboard-lawyer alleged "willful and wanton" misconduct. I didn't even know what wanton meant so I looked it up in the dictionary and it means a "deliberately cruel or violent action." It hadn't been deliberate, I can tell you that. And I've certainly seen more cruel things in my life. It hadn't even been violent. The lawsuit claimed Monique was a supermodel and the invisible scar hidden in her eyebrow cost her the cover of Vogue. Oh, please. It turns out she'd never actually been hired as a model, not even for a local tire store. Her only professional shoot had been one of those vanity glamour photos you get at the mall. I'll bet her real name wasn't even Monique. It was probably Barbara.

Crock was unhappy. "Dammit, Kate! What if Dean Martin had been here?" He probably would've fired most other girls on the spot but when the lovely Monique claimed a cool half mil for her horribly disfiguring scar (that didn't require a single stitch and was impossible to see), he switched his wrath over to that "goddamned sue-happy bitch." He even told me he wished I'd "poked her goddamn eye out" while I was at it.

Crock's insurance company settled the case for nuisance value to end the calamity once and for all, which is probably the only money she'd ever earned in her life. That's when Crock scooted the tables and chairs back another foot.

"Listen, Kate," Crock said, "you've got to slow it down up there. You've got to tease 'em a bit. You're done with a set before they've even settled into their drinks. I'll be goddamned broke at this rate."

After five years, I was just going through the motions. And the motions hurt. I had calluses on my hands from the pole and my legs were bruised from banging them against the pole or kneeling down on the hard stage. My knees became so swollen that I had to have them drained. If you haven't had it done, I don't recommend it. They take a long needle, stick it in your knee, and suck out the fluid. Occupational hazard, but no worker's compensation insurance because they don't extend that to hard working strippers. They just don't.

Ricky occasionally commented on the swelling and bruising but mostly pretended not to see it. One night we were sitting at the kitchen table smoking cigarettes. I usually smoked on the small balcony overlooking the apartment's parking lot but had otherwise pretty much thrown in the towel on the No Smoking policy. I was thumbing through a magazine with a bag of frozen peas on each of my knees.

"So you're going to the doctor again?" Ricky asked.

"Yeah, my knees are killing me."

"Don't the ice bags help?"

"A little bit."

"It's just that you rack up a bill every time you go to one of those quacks," he said, as if the money, any money for that matter, was coming out of his pocket.

"Quacks?"

"Well, they don't seem to do you any good. Sounds like a waste of money to me."

"You got any better ideas? I've got to do something."

"Can't you just wear knee pads or something?"

"What do you think, Ricky? Ever seen a pole dancer with knee pads?"

"Sorry, I'm just trying to help."

Hey, Ricky, here's a little tip: If you really loved me as much as you claim you could get a job and demand that I quit, not tell me to wear fucking knee pads.

It was a few nights later, after my shift at Sugar & Spice, when I'd hit what I thought was the bottom. I was in the bathroom taking off my makeup, staring at my face in the mirror. I felt disconnected from that face like it was a thing, a thing I'd become accustomed to but never really looked at. I put a Lortab on my tongue then stuck out my tongue and looked at the pill resting there. What was I doing? What had I become? I picked up the cup of water I used when I brushed my teeth and threw the pill back like I was taking a shot. Then I put both palms on the counter and leaned into the mirror, studying my reflection up close for a long time.

What had my decisions cost me? A dent in my self-esteem? Friends—real friends I could trust? The praise of my parents? A spot in heaven? In the final analysis I concluded it cost me only lies.

Ricky was still awake, sitting in the living room of my apartment, when I finally came out of the bathroom. I figured he was waiting up so he could romance me for four or five minutes. Let's just say there wasn't the attention to detail there'd been at the beginning. I understand. This happens. I'd gotten to the point where I would've rather just gone to sleep myself.

"I need to talk this through, Ricky," I said that night.

"Talk what through," he said as he whipped off his shirt, obviously disappointed that we actually needed to talk about something.

"I can't keep doing this, Ricky," I said. "I'm living this lie and I don't know what to do."

I was sitting on the sofa and he sat across from me, now shirtless, nodding along as I went through my tearful saga. He got up to get another drink, mid-saga. It was dark outside, and the sofa where I sat faced the window, so I could see his reflection behind me in the kitchen. As I was pouring my heart out, I saw him check his watch and then casually flip through a *People* magazine on the kitchen counter. You can only be so handsome.

I'd taken to wearing flesh-colored panty hose to hide the bruises and pills to hide the pain. It was easy to manipulate my doctor's testosterone and he gave me as many Lortab as I wanted. I was getting pain pills from my dentist, too. Was he stupid, or did he not care that I had a toothache twice as often as I had my period? Or did he think against all reason that we might have a future together? I'd convinced myself I wasn't an addict—I wasn't one of *those*. I just had knee pain.

Speaking of my dentist, between my jobs at Sugar & Spice and the Golden Nugget, I was making almost as much as he was, tax free. But it vanished as quickly as I could scoop it off the stage. Nails, clothes, booze, pills, and Ricky.

19

KATHERINE

I STILL COULDN'T BELIEVE I'd been on national TV and I'd freaking won. Sure, I'd been dressed like a Musketeer with a sombrero and handlebar mustache, but still. And I was over the moon about the boat. The kids were going to love it, but no one was more excited than Keith.

"This is going to be amazing!" he said when I got home to find the kids all in one piece. The floor had even been vacuumed which caused me some concern. I didn't even want to know what terrible event had inspired Keith to vacuum. "I used to go boating with Howard and his family when we were kids and I swore one day I'd buy one. I still can't believe it."

"So you're not upset it wasn't a new car instead?"

"No way! You can't have fun in a car." That's not what he would've said when we were dating.

I was on a high for two weeks. There was the new boat *and* another surprise in the oven. I swear anything would grow in my womb—it was the original Easy Bake Oven. All it took was the smallest dollop of sperm deposited anywhere within shouting distance of my monthly egg. Keith was flabbergasted but he shouldn't have been because we didn't believe in birth control, unless you call the rhythm method birth control. I mean, we weren't all weird about it, but we believed God would fertilize the egg only when, and if, He thought it ought to be fertilized. And, to be perfectly honest, I hadn't been in the mood very often those days so Keith took it when he could, even when it was slightly out of rhythm. I'm not apologizing for that because I had a lot going on. I'm just saying.

The local news channel was there to properly document the delivery of the new boat. I don't know who called them, but I bet it hadn't been Carol. In fact, I hadn't heard from her since she called to get her costume back. Just dry clean it and leave it on the front porch, she'd said, before reminding me they usually gave away a nice car to the Showcase Showdown winner.

We all stood on our front lawn near the KCPX Eyewitness News van. Extended family and friends were there, too. Even Vaughn and Dottie came. It's easier to mend fences when everyone is gaga over a new boat. It was hot out and our parents stood uncomfortably on the front lawn next to each other while we waited for the big moment. Vaughn wore his cargo shorts and flip flops and Dottie wore a sleeveless top. It was obvious which couple wore garments underneath their clothes because my dad wore long pants in the summer heat and my mom could never go sleeveless. When I think back, I don't recall my dad ever in shorts.

My parents were thrilled with my announcement of another baby on the way whereas Vaughn and Dottie treated the subject like a cold sore. This was one aspect of our religion they thought was crazy—accusing us Mormons of taking it upon ourselves to populate the entire planet, one by one. I made sure they didn't know about my morning sickness that wasn't just a morning thing or my throbbing varicose veins that looked like purple ropes down there. That would only have given Vaughn additional ammunition in his pursuit to prove my mental derangement. So instead of talking about our breeding habits, the two couples politely dueled to a draw over who were more devoted grandparents.

"Don't you think Jenna looks cute in that darling outfit?" my mom said. "I saw it at Kmart and just had to buy it for her."

"Did little Jacob tell you about the summer camp we're sending him to?" asked Dottie.

"No, but I'm sure he'll enjoy it. Say, we missed you at Jenna's birthday party," my mom said. "We had to cancel some other plans because we knew how much it meant to her that we be there. We were sorry you couldn't make it."

"We wanted to come but we brought her home a talking doll from our trip instead. She absolutely loves it."

"Oh, yes, I saw it under her bed while I was babysitting. I'm sure it's great to travel so much, but I don't think I could leave the kids for that long. They grow up so fast."

I'd changed my outfit three times because I knew the local reporter was going to interview me. "Does this make me look fat?" I'd asked Keith. "Not that much," he'd said.

A shiny black pick-up truck finally pulled to the curb in front of our house towing the boat which was wrapped in a colorful plastic banner that read: *ANOTHER PRICE IS RIGHT WINNER!* Unfortunately, the cameraman from the local news station had stepped inside to use our bathroom when they'd pulled up with the boat, so they had to turn the rig around and pull up to the curb a second time once he finished his business. I'm sure our reaction to the new boat appeared to be a bit subdued to those watching the Eyewitness News that evening because we all had to pretend we were seeing it pull up for the first time.

A few hours later we were crowded around the TV in our living room watching the news, balancing paper plates and pepperoni pizza on our laps. None of us had ever been on TV before. They didn't get to my story until the very end because they were still talking about how Ronald Reagan had been shot a few days earlier. We'd all seen the video clip about a thousand times. Meanwhile, the kids had given up on Reagan and were outside trying to climb into the boat.

"Okay, everybody, it's on! Shush! Get the kids! Omigosh, there we are on TV!"

Yeah, it was a pretty big deal.

My little brother, Kenny, had been home from his Mormon mission to Guatemala for five months and was getting married. You read that right—five months. I'm quite sure he proposed because he had ants in his pants. His fiancé was only eighteen and fresh out of high school, but everyone said she was a "mature" eighteen. So that was good. Her parents, who looked like they were in their mid-thirties, seemed eager to marry her off. Maybe that's why they threw such an elaborate $1,200 wedding in the gymnasium of their local ward house on the other side of town. Still, it was more than I got.

My new sister-in-law and I were standing under the gymnasium's basketball hoop that had been festively decorated with peach and gray streamers. She was wearing a conservative wedding dress with long sleeves and a lot of lace. "The Sounds of Silence" was playing from a boombox in the corner and my little brothers in their polyester tuxedos were going from the punch bowl to the dessert table and back again, bits of smeared chocolate on their untucked shirts.

"We're excited to have you in the family," I said.

"I'm way excited," she said. "I've waited sooooo long for this. I prayed about it and I'm sure Kenny's the one."

I loved my little brother and I thought he was fairly cute. But "The One"? She was too young to have auditioned many others. After all, they'd only dated for three months before he proposed and once he had there'd been no sense dallying. Mormons don't believe in living together before marriage because that's against the commandments—you know, the Sin Next To Murder. But a three-month courtship highlighted by weekly pizza and a movie? Geez, I doubt they even talked about mortgages and budgets, or whether they'd spring for the two-ply. Come to think of it, I doubt either of them had any proof that the other one even *used* the bathroom. Then again, I wonder if some couples overthink it. It might be just as sensible to take the first offer that comes along and make it work. Either way there are going to be ups and downs, and maybe the downs are more tolerable if you don't know any better. I say all this from a complete lack of experience.

"I heard you'll be going to Dixie State this fall," I said.

"Actually, Kenny doesn't think that's such a good idea," said my mature-for-her-age sister-in-law, "so we've decided I probably won't go to college because we want to start having kids right away. I don't want to wait until I'm, like, twenty-five or something."

My mom saw us talking and limped over in the peach chiffon dress she'd sewn to match the color theme. We all had to wear them and, to be brutally honest, they were ghastly. I noticed my mom was dragging her polio leg more than she used to.

"Hi, Mom," I said. "We were just talking about how she and Kenny are thinking about having kids right away."

"Why, that's wonderful!" my mom said.

"Yeah," said Kenny's new bride, "we want to have as many kids as we can."

"Oh, that makes me so happy!"

"We just hope they're all healthy and normal."

She didn't see my mom flinch, but I did.

20

KATE

I WAS HAPPY FOR KENNY and his forthcoming marriage but I thought he and his teenage bride were bat-shit crazy. I mean, *eighteen?* Actually, they'd rounded up her age when they pitched it to me. They'd said she was "almost nineteen" which, last time I counted, meant she was eighteen. My parents were good with it because they said she was a "mature" eighteen since she had a B+ average in high school. Hopefully she did well in Home Ec, that's all I can say.

I dreaded the trip back home to St. George for the wedding because my entire extended family would be there—including all my aunts, uncles, and three thousand cousins. Those cousins who were about my age would already be well on their way to breeding the next crop of blond hair, blue-eyed posterity, producing babies so fast it was hard to keep track of them all. My closest girl cousin already had three and a half kids and was roundly applauded for it, even though her OB strongly recommended she stop because of the toll it had taken on her, what with the gestational diabetes and all. I knew they'd be whispering behind my back about how I'd become a lost sheep, wandering aimlessly away from the herd because I was too lazy to keep the commandments. Oh, and that I was probably a lesbian to boot because I was "almost" twenty-six and still frightfully unmarried.

What bugged me was they didn't even know me, so how could they have known if I'd lost my way, or not? They would only know that I wasn't like them so, naturally, I was roaming perilously close to Satan's herd that would snatch me into their evil midst and they needed to rescue me before it was too late. I understand because that's the same way I'd felt about my Uncle Irv. My Aunt Beverly may have loved him, and he'd been a good father, but she'd basically been forced to divorce him after he drifted away from the church, seduced by the wicked black sheep and their baa'ing blasphemy. Everyone wrung their hands over poor Irv's dire everlasting lot. Come on, Irv! Can't you see you've been duped? It's time you came to your senses! I feel pretty stupid about it now because I'd also piled on with the judgment when I didn't know the first thing about him.

Anyway, Kenny was still in full-bore preacher mode when he got home from his mission and was good to remind me that my salvation was on the line. "What in the heck happened to you? Can't you see the church is true? Isn't it totally obvious?" Here he was, only twenty-one-years old, and he was already planning for his afterlife. Even worse, he was planning for mine. His self-righteousness was embarrassing, acting like he'd written the Sermon on the Mount all by himself. I could have reminded him about the stolen Playboy I'd found hidden behind a board in his tree hut or the time he'd shoplifted a Baby Ruth from the

7-11 down the street, but I was bigger than that. Then, to prove his utter devotion, he said he wished his mission had lasted four years instead of just the two. Seriously? What eighteen-year-old boy wants to wear a shirt and tie and knock on doors all day and night for four years? An insane one, that's who. Someone like Kenny.

"So," he said, "mom and dad said you aren't active." Of course, I knew he wasn't talking about my fitness routine because I was actually in the best shape of my life. He would've lost it if he knew why my calves looked so toned, what with the high heels and all.

"It's not really my thing these days."

"Are you saying you don't believe?" he asked incredulously, as if I'd testified under oath that the earth was square.

"I'm not really sure." I was actually pretty sure but I didn't feel like getting into the whole thing with him. I mean, what would be the point? I didn't particularly care what he believed. Even if I did, I wasn't going to budge him. And the more he acted like he was Moses, the less likely he was going to budge me either.

"You're not *sure?*" he asked as he reached to swipe his bangs from his forehead. For a moment there I thought this masterpiece of conviction was making a move to adjust his halo. "How could you not be sure? I know it's true for a fact."

For a fact, huh? I shouldn't bash on Kenny and his brainpower simply because he believed. But he wasn't smarter than me. I'm sorry, but he just wasn't. This was the same guy who wiped his butt with poison ivy at a scout camp and had to soak in the tub for two days. He walked like he'd just gotten off a horse and the bathroom smelled like Epsom salt for a week.

And when he was a teenager and tried to bake a cake for his girlfriend, he'd followed the Betty Crocker recipe to a T, greasing "the bottom of the pan" like any other idiot would. It's lucky he didn't burn down the house. I could go on. The point is that Kenny was not known for his smarts and this sort of factual declaration did nothing to disprove his reputation.

"I couldn't deny it for all the money in the world," he said.

That was the same line I'd used in high school. We all did. We talked ourselves into it which wasn't awfully hard to do because if everyone believed then it must be true, right? This certainty over the truthfulness of our church embraced an acceptable level of arrogance to the vast majority in the community. So maybe I shouldn't have been surprised when I got back to Las Vegas and found two missionaries at my door. I'm pretty sure Kenny had sic'd them on me. Or it might have been my dad. I invited them in because I didn't want to be rude. In fact, I felt sorry for them, pedaling a product door to door that no one was buying. One of the missionaries was a pimply kid from Idaho and the other one was some nerd from Provo. They tried not to look directly at my boobs as they laid it on the line pretty thick by telling me I'd go to hell if I didn't shape up and start going back to church. Actually, they didn't say the word "hell," they said the "Telestial Kingdom" which is about the lowest rung in the Mormon afterlife, basically a sprawling suburb of hell.

Quick doctrinal background tip: There are four levels where humans will be sent in the afterlife. You've got the Celestial Kingdom which is where you're sent if you've lived a righteous Mormon life. One rung down there's the Terrestrial Kingdom which is where you'll be sent if you've misbehaved a little bit, or if you were a good person but not a member of our church. And then there's the Telestial Kingdom which is where I was probably headed. There I would socialize with other degenerates who liked to have fun. Well, those folks and also people like Jeffrey Dahmer and Adolph Hitler. But the bottom of the barrel, the absolute pit of hell, is called Outer Darkness which is reserved only for those who once believed in the church and then campaigned against it. I figure I was slotted for the Telestial Kingdom because I didn't actively wage a campaign against the church so Outer Darkness was probably (hopefully) off the table. I'd feel okay hanging out in the Telestial Kingdom with other people who coveted or bore false witness, but Hitler? Personally, I thought they needed a few more kingdoms.

I was pretty upset when the missionaries left because all this Telestial Kingdom business was . . . well, it was insulting. But Ricky, who'd been eavesdropping from the other room while I was politely fending off the missionaries' heavenly blows, was amused. "You should've offered them a cup of coffee or invited them to Sugar & Spice."

"This isn't funny, Ricky."

Ricky's little joke hit a tender spot because I believed what I did at Sugar & Spice *was* wrong. Definitely wrong. I still do. I couldn't justify debasing myself like that. So, yeah, maybe the missionaries would've been right about that, but they weren't right about me.

That'd all happened a few months before Kenny's wedding and my family and I had fallen into a truce since then. They mostly honored the truce and left me alone in my debauchery but every once in a while they'd pull the pin and lob a heavenly grenade my way. They just couldn't help themselves. They'd say, "You're probably just going through a little phase." Or maybe it'd be, "We know you still believe deep down, so you'll probably be okay." This was no small relief.

Kenny's mature-for-her-age bride wanted my mom and all us sisters to wear peach chiffon dresses to the wedding. They had high empire waists and were pretty bad. No, actually they were worse than that. My mom looked like she was pregnant again, the poor thing.

My mom had sewn the dresses herself (with Kelly's eager help) to save money and had to ask for my measurements over the phone about three times. There was the larger than she expected bust and the smaller than she expected waist. I'd sacrificed dearly for my weight and shape, by the way. I ate about 1,000 calories a day and every calorie after that added roughly one pound to each hip. It upset me that Ricky ate whatever he wanted and just got more attractive. French Fries. Cinnabon's. Ice cream. You name it. About the only fruit or vegetable I ever saw him eat was an olive in the bottom of a glass. This was all very unfair, obviously.

I sat on the sidelines during the wedding reception in the church gymnasium and tried to avoid conversations with my aunts and uncles who asked me, for the billionth time, when I was going to get married and settle down. They were only trying to be nice. Besides, what else were they supposed to ask me? My thoughts about the Iran-Contra affair? The name of my plastic surgeon? My weight? They were probably as relieved as I was when someone would rescue them ("Phil, come and see Aunt Bonnie's photo album!"). I needed a smoke so I went out to my car to sneak a cigarette. I saw several of my aunts sniff suspiciously when I came back in for a few more chocolate strawberries.

I saw Kelly from a distance talking to some of my aunts. I smiled to myself because of course he was talking to the older women, it's just the way he was. While my other little brothers had been running up and down the halls of the church playing tag, slightly sweaty with their shirts untucked, Kelly stood tall with his shirt smartly tucked in and not a hair out of place, talking to these women about recipes and who did their hair. Ricky said Kelly was "pre-gay." Me, I couldn't have cared less about Kelly's budding sexual preferences because he was the most beautiful, sensitive, cool kid I knew.

Then I found my youngest sister in the crowd. Four-year-old Kylie looked like an over-ripe peach in her dress and I absolutely adored her—the other Coombs daughter who didn't fit the mold. Kylie (and maybe Kelly) was the only one who didn't judge me. She didn't whisper that I looked like a hooker, or that my soul was in jeopardy. She saw me watching her and ran up to me for a clumsy hug. Her hands were smeared with chocolate and bits of strawberries but I didn't care. I knew I'd never wear that ugly dress again.

"I wuv you, Kafrun!"

"I love you, too, Kylie."

21

KATHERINE

WE WERE ALL AT THE COMMUNITY swimming pool, a fairly low-budget affair with rusting lockers and unheated water. The lifeguard was a teenage boy who'd barely learned mouth-to-mouth in the Boy Scouts and hardly even watched the pool, so focused was he on his tan and a few teenage girls who pretended not to know he was ogling them. I was lathering sunscreen on Jacob when my kids started complaining to Keith.

"Why do I have to wear these stupid things?"

"Because you could drown, that's why."

"But mom doesn't make us wear them."

"Yeah, Dad, we'll only be in the shallow. Gol."

"I'm not mom. When you're with me you have to wear them."

"But that's not fair."

"Yeah, that's not fair."

Keith was an amazing father. I couldn't believe how much he'd changed in the past eight years. He was the fun one who patiently endured all the chaos in our house, the one who'd sit with the kids for hours helping them with their math even though they appeared to understand the concepts more than he did. And bedtime, that joyous two-hour nightly battle? I couldn't wait to put them down. Keith though, you really had to hand it to him. He'd lay on their beds and tell them homemade stories that were actually pretty creative. I got sucked into a few of them myself. After all, how *was* the little girl trapped in the tree going to get down? And the little boy who'd befriended the shark and let him in the rowboat? His stories would always wind up with a satisfactory conclusion without the little boys and girls getting killed.

He was a softy though and was easily manipulated by the kids. He waffled, which showed parental weakness in my book and he had an appalling lack of resolve. For example:

Kid: Can I have a sleepover at Ben's?

Keith: What? No. When?

Kid: Tonight.

Keith: I don't think so. What time?

He didn't waffle where the kids' safety was concerned though, even going overboard if you ask me. I let the kids ride their bikes down the driveway without a helmet, or soak in a hot tub without a life jacket, but not Keith. When he'd give them a bath, he'd practically put them in a headlock while he scrubbed them and pulled them out the second they were clean. They'd complain about the two inches of water he'd put in the tub and I had to agree with them—the water didn't even reach their clavicles. But Keith had them wrapped in towels like little burritos as the water dripped onto the tile floor before they knew what had hit them.

After Jim and Cathy's baby drowned, I'd been anxious whenever Keith watched Jacob. I didn't think he'd hand him a fork and plop him in front of an electrical outlet, or arm him with scissors for a relay race, but I was still anxious. When Jenna came along, something had to give. I had to trust that Keith wasn't a complete idiot. And by the time our third was born, Keith was handling everything—the envy of all moms in the neighborhood.

I wasn't used to living with a man like Keith. I grew up with a dad who'd sit at the dinner table with his arms folded waiting to be served. "I thought dinner was at six," he'd say, checking his Timex. "It's nearly ten after. Is everything all right?" In our house, Keith did the serving and most of the cooking, too. If a load needed to be put in the wash, he did it without being asked, and without acting like he was Joan of Arc. If Jenna's diaper smelled, he didn't pretend he couldn't smell it. And he didn't say, "I think Jenna may have messed her diaper. Can you check?" He even cleaned the oven and made perfect diamonds in the carpet when he'd vacuum.

Keith's "Husband and Father of the Year" awards bugged my dad and my father-in-law, Vaughn, because they liked things the way they were in the good old days. They knew generally what the oven did but had never used it. To illustrate the old school, Vaughn came over one afternoon to watch a football game when Jenna wandered by with a dirty diaper. Keith changed it, which seemed like the sensible thing to do. But then Vaughn goes all Stone Age and says, "Where's Katherine? Can't she do it? Geez, they're about to kick a field goal." My dad was no different. Let's say Karolyn spilled orange juice on the linoleum floor while my dad was treating someone to his opinions about family-value politics, or Jesus's atonement, or whatever. He'd simply call for my mom to "come quick" and she'd limp in with a mop like Edith Bunker and practically apologize for the disruption.

I'll tell you something else about Keith that made me smile. He wasn't a big hand holder but I noticed a trend. If we were out in public and a good-looking woman approached, he'd reach for my hand. Maybe he thought I'd worry that he'd been tempted to run off with that other woman, or that she might've been tempted to run off with him. Anyway, I thought it was sweet.

I also thought it was sweet that he wanted to get a dog, for the kids' sake, he said. I reminded him that we could have taken Enos when we first got married but he didn't like girl dogs, or wiener dogs for that matter. But Keith's insistence on a male, non-wiener dog backfired when we rescued Hank from the animal shelter. I suppose Hank was a smart enough dog but there's really no reliable test. He responded to his name most of the time but he was slow on the bathroom concept. That's probably why he'd been in the pound to begin with—his previous owner had run out of carpet cleaner. After several accidents (and I'm suspicious they'd been accidents—he was just too lazy to go outside), we installed a doggie door. Just when we thought he'd finally mastered it, I saw him stick his head out the doggie door, and while his head was outside and the rest of his body was in the kitchen, he promptly peed on the linoleum. I wanted to return him but Keith was too big-hearted.

Keith wasn't perfect though. His receding hairline was picking up speed and he was overweight. He'd fart in bed and then rollover and try to put the moves on me. I'll say this about Keith: He really knew how to dazzle a woman. He snored so loud, half the time I thought he was faking. I mean, how did that racket not wake him up? On the other hand, he'd be sure to mention it if I so much as purred. "Geez Katherine," he'd say, "you were really snoring up a storm last night. I had to nudge you about ten times." His table manners were medieval—he held his fork in his curled fist and never quite grasped the concept of putting the napkin on his lap. He only had three dad jokes in his repertoire, none of which were funny. Why do bees have sticky hair? Because they use a honeycomb.

I'd married him because I had to. I didn't think I had a choice because I was pregnant. We hardly even knew each other. He was the high school football star who had nearly gone to seed by the time we graduated high school. His teeth were small, his hair was ugly, and he already had a pot gut. I doubt he could even spell R-h-o-d-e-s S-c-h-o-l-a-r, and his dad was a jerk. But now, after all we'd been through and the beautiful kids we had, I felt like the luckiest woman in the world.

But. If Keith was so perfect and my life was so grand, why couldn't I stop thinking about Renaldo. Renaldo you ask? Yeah, Renaldo who lived a few doors down from us. I didn't even know his last name. I first saw him when he was mowing his lawn without his shirt. He was tall and lean with a six or twelve pack. He wore jeans that hung on his hips about two inches lower than pants are designed to hang. I didn't stare for very long but I wanted to. Then I started finding excuses to drive by his house hoping he might be outside without his shirt, maybe chopping down a tree with an axe and a light sheen of sweat on his body. A week later Keith said he met our neighbor, a guy named Renaldo, and wondered if maybe we should invite him over to our house for dinner. I had a momentary rush of excitement. This gorgeous man *in my house?* I casually asked if this man was married, as if I couldn't possibly have cared less, at once hoping he was and at the same time hoping he wasn't.

A few days later, I brought it up with Keith. "So," I asked, "do you still want to have that one neighbor guy and his wife over for dinner?" Keith, who was clueless about other men, said sure. So we had them over. His wife wasn't nearly as attractive as he was which made me . . . what? Happy? Sad? Indifferent? I mean, why should I care what his wife looked like? It was his freaking *wife* and Keith was my husband. I caught him staring at me a few times in a way that made me wonder if he wished I'd go out and mow our lawn without a shirt on, too.

So we flirted a little (a lot) and I felt guilty about it. Of course I felt guilty about it. I wasn't a home wrecker. And I loved Keith. But Renaldo, ugh. I even had a few dreams about him—the kind you don't want to wake up from and when you do, you try to fall back asleep as soon as possible to pick up where you left off.

I've considered lost possibilities and regrets in life plenty of times. I know I shouldn't whine because Keith was a *good* man, but he was the only man I'd ever been with, the only man I'd even been to second base with. So, yeah, that might have been a regret, with all due respect to Keith. I also regret that I didn't go to college or ever live away from home on my own.

I've also wondered about all the what ifs in my life. What if I'd been born into a family without a high-demand religion? What if my dad had taken that job up in Salt Lake when I was in fifth grade? Or what if Kylie had been born without that one extra chromosome? And then the biggee: What if I hadn't become pregnant? That stands out above all others when

I look back over my life—the turning point for better or worse. Maybe I would've stayed single. Maybe I would've moved out of St. George. I wouldn't be married to Keith Murphy with six kids, I can tell you that. And little Emily Blake would still be alive. Yeah, that's a tortured thought right there—that if I hadn't become pregnant when I did then we wouldn't have lived in the duplex and Emily wouldn't have drowned. Of course, you can go around and around on all of that because Emily *would* be alive but Jacob and Jenna *wouldn't.* In fact, hardly *anything* would've been the same. I might have gone to college, or moved away, or become a fashion model instead of the borderline frumpy mom I'd become. Who knows? I got what I got. But without that teenage pregnancy everything would have been different.

I had become a mom first, a wife second, and Sister Murphy in my church third. I was chauffeur, cook, laundry maid, barf cleaner upper, butt wiper, and all the rest. I felt guilty on the rare occasions I ever did something for myself, like the one and only time I got a pedicure (and even then I took a kid with me). I resented having to be everything to everyone else but then I'd feel guilty over that resentment. *Geez, Katherine,* I'd think to myself, *quit being so selfish and get over yourself.* Don't get me wrong, I loved being a mother but it seemed like Mrs. Keith Murphy had no identity other than "mom."

Maybe you'll think my life is a dud—just a boring stay-at-home existence without any excitement. No college or sorority sisters, no career, no exotic romance, no travel unless you count camping at Yellowstone in a collapsing pup tent, not a drop of booze, not a puff from a cigarette, not even a misdemeanor on my record. But let me tell you something; my life is anything but dull. What would you call a kingsnake let loose in the house, or Jacob starting the garage on fire, or Jenna throwing our pet gerbil down the stairs? (It didn't die—it was paralyzed, which was even worse and required Keith to declare it dead in front of the kids and then formally execute it in the backyard, shortly before the elaborate funeral the kids insisted upon.) Do you know how much barf I've cleaned up? And how do you put a price tag on seeing Keith with poo all over his hands when our youngest took her diaper off in the crib and finger painted a brown mural on the wall?

22

KATE

I CELEBRATED MY THIRTIETH BIRTHDAY by getting drunk and getting married—in that order. Ricky needed a gift for such a momentous occasion as my thirtieth birthday so he bought a cheap ring at a kiosk in the mall and asked me to marry him. I thought he was joking at first because it wasn't the sort of proposal girls ordinarily dream about. We'd been driving down Las Vegas Boulevard on our way to a two-star restaurant where I would pick up the tab and were stopped at a red light in front of the Tropicana when he looked over at me. "Hey, do you want to get married?" Before I could respond, he'd reached under the driver's seat and produced the ring box. It wasn't wrapped or anything. "Here, see if you like it."

It wasn't even a diamond. I mean, it was pretty, but had Ricky been living in a cave the past thirty years? Was he Rumpelstiltskin? You're supposed to give a diamond, not a ruby. Everyone knows that. He must have read my thoughts. "I know it's not a diamond, but that's all I can afford right now."

I was a bit tipsy because we'd had a drink before we left the apartment (pre-loading we called it) and I was feeling good. It's that feeling you get when everything looks rosy. So I said yes. A week later we drove to one of those tacky wedding chapels off the strip filled with fake geraniums covered by a fine layer of dust. The name of the chapel, *Si, Como No*, was fitting. It might sound romantic in Spanish, but the "Sure, Why Not" English translation didn't wow me. It wasn't the kind of place that inspired a commitment in sickness and in health. We hadn't thought to bring a witness, so for an additional five-dollar fee the *Si, Como No* threw in two witnesses who barely checked our ID's, our sexual orientation, or our level of sobriety. This wasn't the fairy tale wedding I'd envisioned but, sure, why not.

Ricky felt bad that I wasn't eager to tell my family about our glitzy nuptials. To be honest, I was embarrassed that we'd basically been married in a drive-thru and, besides that, I didn't want to burst my parents' bubble that I wasn't going to marry a returned missionary in the temple like I was supposed to. I had let them believe I was still going through my "confused phase" and would eventually come to my senses and tie the knot with a budding Mormon bishop.

"Ricky, I like my ring and all but my parents are pretty conventional. I know they'll wonder why I don't have a real one."

"A real one what?"

"A diamond, Ricky. You know, like married women have."

"We can't afford one right now but, yeah, we'll get you one soon."

"Maybe we can get a fake one before we go to St. George for Christmas."

"You mean one of those cubic zirconium ones?"

"Yeah, I guess."

So we went shopping. Ricky wanted to buy a big one so my family would see what a rich and generous groom he was. I told him it was so big it looked totally fake, like one that came from a bubble gum machine. We chose a smaller fake one—maybe half a carrot—because I didn't want to upstage my mom who wore about an eighth. My mom was a simple woman who might have liked her ring, and it wouldn't catch on a sweater but, personally, if I'd been my mom, I would've just gone with a band.

My dad was usually in a bad mood in the run-up to Christmas. First of all, it must have been expensive to buy presents for that many kids. Not only that, but there were all the lights he had to hang every year, standing in the cold on the stepladder under an eave while trying to untangle the string of lights. It was the same thing every year. I could never figure out why he didn't just wrap them up better when he took them down every year on January 2nd. Why just wad them up and put them in a cardboard box? It seemed to me like he was just asking for trouble. And this was back in the day when the entire string didn't work if just one of the damned bulbs was out, so he had to screw and unscrew every light on the string with frozen fingers to find and replace the offending bulb.

My younger sibs were jacked up for Christmas, especially Kylie. She told me she'd asked for a dog but I didn't think Santa would come through because my parents didn't need one more thing to feed. The family dog, Enos, our little wiener dog with bad smells, passed away a few years after I went away to college. My dad had lobbied for me to take Enos along with me to college but I obviously couldn't do that. Even if I'd tried to sneak him into the dorm room someone probably would have stepped on him and broken his back because he was so low to the ground. And my dorm room smelled bad enough as it was without Enos farting and breathing all the time.

Growing up, my family went through an assortment of pets. The common denominator was they were all free, usually the result of someone trying to get rid of them—goldfish, turtles, gerbils, and bunnies—and none of them lasted long. Maybe it was their diet because we fed them all the same thing: small bits of ground beef. If they didn't die within a week or two, they escaped. We'd wait for their return but they never did, not even for meals. As the death toll mounted, we'd console ourselves with the absolute knowledge that they weren't human and therefore couldn't feel anything; not hunger, pain, or cold. Santa had to know about our dismal track record.

My mom told me Kylie was convinced Santa Claus was real, even though Korbin kept trying to tell her that Santa was all a big lie. My mom smiled at the thought—at the thought that Kylie could be so innocent and naïve in her belief. I didn't tell my mom that Kylie's belief in Santa Claus seemed to be about as innocent and naïve as some of her own beliefs. After all, my fifty-year-old mom believed with all her heart in a magical, omniscient Caucasian male figure with a flowing white beard, a figure no one has ever actually seen. He is jolly and kind but also has a bit of a mean streak if he's crossed. He keeps a daily tally of who's been naughty and nice and gives rewards or punishments depending on what He sees. And He sees everything, even the things you do behind closed doors. So, yeah, mom, what about that? About the only difference I could see was that she was afraid of God year-round whereas Kylie just tuned in to Santa's mood during the Christmas season. I don't think my parents zeroed in on the similarities—that they used Santa Claus to manipulate our behavior as children just like the church used God to manipulate theirs.

Ricky was Ricky on our Christmas visit to St. George that year. He was just as smooth and gentlemanly as when I'd first met him. But when someone is that perfect you've got to wonder, don't you? At least some of it has to be an act, doesn't it? I mean, you can't be like that in real life all the time. You just can't, and he certainly wasn't, but my family didn't see it other than my dad who found reasons to be skeptical about everything except the golden tablets and Jesus's resurrection.

My mom was still a woman though, a fact that was usually lost on the rest of the clan because she'd become an overweight breeder who wore floral muumuus, did laundry, canned fruit, and made tuna noodle casseroles all day. Most of her amazing qualities remained hidden because she wasn't flashy or pretty. She was "salt of the earth" which usually means a good, plain, warm-hearted person. Salt of the earth is rarely used to describe beautiful movie stars and supermodels. It's used instead to describe someone like my mom who bakes banana bread for the neighborhood and volunteers for the PTA.

When I was a teenager I didn't want my mom to be salt of the earth. I wanted her to be more like Sandra's mom who wore fake eyelashes and drove a convertible, or Laura Clissold's mom who was a vegetarian and sunbathed in a bikini in their backyard. I wanted a mom who went to the gym and wore stylish clothes that didn't look homemade. And I will never forget how mortified I was when she took me and a few of my girlfriends to the community swimming pool. While I was busy trying to be popular, drenched in suntan oil and smelling like a coconut, my mom walked around the pool in her ugly, out-of-date one-piece bathing suit with a few curly black hairs sneaking out of her suit. However, now when I think of my mom I think salt of the earth with admiration, as it should be.

But, like I said, my mom was still a woman and had no immunity from Ricky's looks and charm. My dad, on the other hand, smelled something fishy. This was no surprise, of course, because my dad smelled something fishy in just about everything. And in Ricky's case you didn't need a certified fish sniffer.

I eavesdropped on their conversation the first night Ricky and I were there. I knew exactly which floor vent to stick my ear to. I used to do it in the days leading up to Christmas to see what I was getting. The vent was in my old bedroom and if you listened carefully, with a finger in your other ear, you could hear what they were saying in their bedroom. Ricky asked me what I was doing on my hands and knees with my head bent to the floor.

"Seeing if my parents like you."

"What in the hell are you talking a—"

"Shush!" I hissed.

I bent my head down low again, right ear over the vent.

"I don't like him," my dad was saying. "He's not right for her."

"Well, I think he's very nice," my mom said.

"He's too smooth. Something's not right with him. I think he's a little light in the loafers."

"What are you talking about, 'light in the loafers'?"

"You know, maybe he's a homo."

"A homosexual? Dale, be serious. He's married to our daughter for heaven's sake. Why on earth would you even say that?"

"I don't know," my dad said. "You know how they have that pretty boy look."

"The pretty boy look?"

"Yeah, you know. Like those guys who wear makeup and stuff. And he wears a turtle neck. Homosexuals wear turtle necks."

"What on earth are you talking about?"

"He's too . . . he tries too hard to be . . . handsome."

"So you think he's a homosexual because he's handsome?"

"I didn't say he was handsome," my dad said. "I said he tries too hard to be handsome." I'm afraid my dad thought if he agreed Ricky was handsome, that might make him a homosexual, too. "And that ring looks fake to me."

"Dale, you aren't being fair. I think it's lovely. We just need to give him a chance. And I thought he was very generous about taking Kylie."

"He's just trying to get on our good side."

"Then why don't we let him?"

Earlier that day, my mom had asked me if we'd take Kylie to Las Vegas for a week. I'd looked at Ricky who'd nodded, probably to get on their good side. My dad agreed, provided we didn't take her to "a bunch of casinos or anything." Yeah, dad, that's what we'd planned to do.

We made it through the weekend at my parent's house without any major crises, other than my little sisters preening for Ricky, hoping he might fall for them, too. Oh, and there were the not-so-subtle comments about joining our church. For example, one night over a rump roast my dad said: "So, Richard, I'd like to visit with you about joining the church." Ricky looked at me for help. "I've already talked to him about it," I said. Then my mom, who actually had a filter, touched my dad on the arm and asked him if he wanted another slice of that yummy peach cobbler.

I didn't know what to think when Ricky volunteered to do the dishes that night. Ricky? Dishes? My mom fell for it too. What an amazing partner! Me, I just chalked it up to Ricky being Ricky. Unless he was home alone with me, that is.

Kylie was thrilled about joining us for the week in Vegas. Ricky had acted like he really wanted to her stay with us—really wanted to be a part of the family. But he never said boo to her once we left St. George. "Hey, she's *your* sister."

Our apartment had a swimming pool and Kylie must have jumped off the edge no less than one thousand times. "Kafrun watch," she'd say, shaking with cold, her toes off the edge, until she confirmed I was watching. We walked the strip at night and Kylie was in awe of all the lights. We made quite a pair walking down the sidewalk holding hands; the tall, thin, thirty-year-old who looked like a stripper and her short, pudgy, nine-year-old sister who plainly did not.

Ricky and I never specifically talked about having kids of our own. I always assumed I'd have kids and I probably would have if I'd married almost anyone else. But instead Ricky and I said things like, "Yeah, we might at some point," when we both knew we probably never would. It felt better to pretend we hadn't ruled it out. "Let's just see what happens," we'd say, but the IUD stayed put as my biological clock ticked down.

Do you know the real reason we didn't have children? Do

you want to know the painful truth? It was because Ricky didn't want to take the breadwinner off the line. You'll rarely see a pregnant stripper.

I was now officially Kate Waters. I had my Hyphen Phase for about a year (me and my phases) and went by Kate Coombs-Waters until I realized it was a hassle and I wasn't Gloria Steinem.

I was now officially a stripper, too, even though I still thought of myself as a wholesome girl from St. George, Utah. Perhaps you'll roll your eyes at that. You'll probably say I was kidding myself, but people rarely change their fundamental character and I was still me, deep down. Stripping is what I did, not who I was. I was obviously no goodie-two-shoes but I truly believed I was different from the other girls who worked at Sugar & Spice because my morals had been baked into me from the crib. Then again, who was I to judge my fellow strippers? Maybe they were also good girls with baked-in morals.

Ricky was still Ricky, too. I don't know why I thought marriage would change anything. On the rare chance he held my hand in public, he'd yank his away whenever a pretty girl strolled by. This did not inspire great affection, or trust. He slept until noon most days, his string of unemployment nicely intact. Whenever I'd suggest a certain type of employment, he'd say he was overqualified. Exactly what made him overqualified, I cannot say. If the roll of toilet paper ran out he'd just leave it for me to change. If the kitchen garbage can was full he'd just keep packing it down to fit in one more candy wrapper. I didn't expect him to break out the Lemon Pledge every weekend, but it would've been nice if he'd walked his cereal bowl over to the sink from time to time.

"Ricky, you need to get a regular job," I'd say.

"I'm too busy. Besides, I've never been a nine-to-five kind of guy."

"But we could really use the money."

"When are you going to learn," he'd say. "People with regular jobs never get ahead because the system is rigged against them. That's why I've always been an entrepreneur."

I finally left Crock and his merry stage of strippers at Sugar & Spice without ever having seen Dean Martin (but I did see a few men from St. George who looked awfully familiar). The decision to leave had been easy because Lil' Secrets was the best strip club in Vegas and they'd come calling. The only catch was I'd have to strip *and* do lap dances at Lil' Secrets. It wasn't that much different to be honest, but it felt like a further capitulation—about a three-quarter spin in the downward spiral.

At Lil' Secrets we'd take our turns on the stage between shots of cheap vodka and spend the rest of our time roaming the club, half naked. I cannot tell you how weird it is to walk around topless in a public showroom. And that's exactly what it was, a showroom. Skinny dipping on a secluded beach without a soul in sight might be liberating to some people, but this surely was not.

I mentioned seeing a few people who looked familiar. Well, one of them was Brother Torgerson from my old ward in St. George. We all admired him because he was a popular college professor at Dixie State and was currently on a teaching sabbatical at UNLV where, coincidentally, he was my political science professor. I approached him from behind at the club without initially recognizing him. When he turned around and saw me standing there in a strip club without my top on it was, well, it was awkward to say the least, for both of us. I turned on my heels and went the other way without saying a word. We both pretended our little Lil' Secrets "encounter" had never happened as the semester wound down. I was a "C" student, but when grades came out a month later, I got a solid "A" in political science despite the fact that I hadn't turned in a paper and got mostly "B's" and "C's" on the quizzes. I took it for what it was, even though busting him was the last thing in the world I intended to do. Besides, who would I tell? His wife? His daughter Sherri who was my age and was in pep club with me? My dad? Tattling under these embarrassing situations would have resulted in our mutual destruction. I'm sure he felt the same way.

I'd wander around the club along with the other topless girls, prying tips out of the randy customers.

"Hi, I'm Kandy," I'd say. "What's your name?"

"John Smith."

It was always John this, or Robert that. No one volunteered that his real name was DeWayne and his wife was back home with the kids.

I'd sit close to them on the upholstered loveseats and large cushioned chairs that filled the dimly lit parlor, pretending to be smitten. Then I'd whisper into their hairy ear, "Wanna dance?" John, aka DeWayne, almost always said yes because he believed I actually yearned to run off with him—that I was practically in heat. Just how these fifty-year-old men with oily hair and protruding guts could think such a thing remained an ongoing mystery to me. What is it with men? Why are they so arrogant? Why do they assume we are merely objects meant to adore them? Don't they own a mirror? Sure, DeWayne, err, John, let's hop in your wife's minivan and skedaddle to the suburbs—just you and me!

I'd stand in front of DeWayne aka John when the DJ started a new song, looking at him seductively as I slowly removed my tank top. He didn't know that I was looking right through him, thinking about my grocery list or the fight I'd had with Ricky earlier that day about the laundry. I'd lean into him so my bare breasts were inches from his face, then I'd back away, just enough, and turn around. I'd unbutton my cut-offs and step out of them, exposing only the G-string I wore underneath. Three minutes later (or less if the blessed song was shorter) I'd bring DeWayne out of his love trance long enough to fish thirty dollars from his wallet, then go on trolling. Thirty bucks per song plus tips from the truly smitten all night long. You do the math.

The girls knew how to spot the Big Spender and we'd pay rapt attention to whatever bullshit he was droning on about over his rum and coke, pretending to care about his embellished life. And it was always embellished, for how could there be that many multi-millionaire, super achievers of truly astonishing feats in one little strip club?

"Hey, Robert," I'd whisper into Harold aka Big Spender's ear, "I'd love to give you a private dance."

"What would that entail?" Harold, the assistant manager at Costco would ask in the voice of Robert the neurosurgeon. It's odd, but they were always neurosurgeons or CEO's of something—I never did meet a plumber. I was more likely to meet an astronaut than a produce manager.

"Well," I'd breathe onto his scruffy neck, "there's a back room and I wouldn't be as . . . shy. It's only eighty dollars for two songs and I can be a little more, you know, relaxed."

I'd stand and take Harold's callused hand and pull him up from the love seat in the corner to encourage the exchange. Harold would usually follow because he'd bragged about having more money than Warren Buffet and he didn't want me to think he was cheap, especially when we were falling in love like we were. I'd get a little closer in the back room, but I still wouldn't let him actually touch me. If he tried, I'd pull back a tad and whisper to him that I'd *love* to let him touch me, love it more than anything in the world because I was so turned on, but my boss would be upset. Then I'd nod in the direction of the scary looking bouncer standing in the shadows who made sure the rules were followed, and the bill was paid.

Most of the men smelled. It was either cheap cologne, hair tonic, rubber tires, or BO. Many wore gold chains and there was often the indent on their fat fingers where the wedding ring had been an hour earlier. If they had hair, it was often dyed orange, which they thought made them look younger. Or it was dyed jet-black which looked plain ridiculous. "You're not really fifty," I'd say. "Come on, you look like you're thirty. Are you pulling my leg?" They'd suck in their gut and pull out another twenty.

Sometimes they'd ask me what I was doing after work. This was additional evidence that the DeWayne's and Harold's were convinced I was in it for the long haul.

"I'd really love to meet you, but I can't. It's against the rules here. If they found out, I'd get fired."

"Yeah, but they wouldn't find out. Here's my room number. I'm over at Caesars."

"Sorry, I'd love to, but I just can't."

"Even if I paid you?" DeWayne would ask, having somehow convinced himself against all reason that it hadn't been solely motivated by money up to this point.

"Sorry."

Another girl had been sacked on my first day for breaking this rule, the one about sleeping with a customer off the books. She'd been caught because the customer who'd begged for it had actually been an undercover vice cop. He'd been a fairly regular customer to make his cover more authentic, or so he'd said, and some of the girls had gone that extra mile and rubbed their bottoms near the zipper of his jeans. He sure hadn't been offended by their lawlessness *then* (unless that'd been a stun gun in his pants instead of his you-know-what). One girl agreed to have sex with him for a huge tip and he busted her on the spot because prostitution is illegal in Clark County. He also demanded further "consideration" from Lil' Secrets or he'd shut the joint down. Such a pig.

The girls tolerated each other because we were making $1,000 a night, tax free. But there were times tempers flared in the changing room. I should clarify that the "changing room" was actually just an extra-large broom closet in the back where the girls would stash their sensible shoes and sweaters.

You must remember the girls were rarely sober, for a variety of reasons, which didn't leave margin for error in the cramped changing room. Most were desperate capitalists, too. It'd usually go something like this:

"Stay away from that Russian guy by the bar. He's been asking for me."

"What are you talking about? He asked for me."

"Bullshit! I get up to get us another drink, and you start shoving your ugly tits in his face!"

And then away they'd go—on the verge of clawing each other, trading insults about the other one's tits, or hair, or you-name-its. This wasn't Wall Street. One girl got hit with a thrown shoe, and at least once a week someone would get slapped in the face. I even saw a girl pee into another girl's purse. Yeah, she sneaked the purse to the floor, squatted over it, and peed. Why, you ask? Because the purse owner had called the pee'er a bitch. And why had she called her a bitch? Because she was one. My particular issue with this particular Pee'er, aside from her bitchy-ness, was her moaning. She'd be standing in front of a man (and usually an unattractive one), rubbing her breasts and moaning like she was in the throes of an orgasm when she clearly was not. It was just so over the top that we hated her for it.

Sometimes we actually had fun with each other though. For example, we'd mess around with exotic accents and résumés from faraway places. Jessica, who'd been raised on an Idaho potato farm, claimed to be a southern belle from Baton Rouge. She'd perfected a rich southern drawl that was probably worth another twenty bucks an hour. And Tiffani spoke in a passable British accent even though she'd never been east of Denver. Another girl from Reno pretended she didn't speak a word of English so her DeWayne's spoke loudly and freely, assuming she must have been deaf, too. Then there was the Pee'er who could moan in any language. I was a medical student, an underwear model, a flight attendant, a rodeo champ, and a concert pianist; sometimes all in one night. I was anyone but myself.

Most of the girls at Lil' Secrets were attractive. In fact, there were several who were drop-dead gorgeous, and knew it. They strutted around like they were Madonna. Their hair was perfect, their nails were manicured, and they never ate more than 1,200 calories a day. When they weren't at the gym, they were in a tanning bed or getting waxed. You've got to respect their discipline because it was a lot of work and the burden to be beautiful is taxing. I don't know how many times I'd been sorely tempted to throw in the towel and eat a Big Mac or a Cinnabon.

The common assumption of all this sacrifice was that we were trying to impress the men but I found most of the pressure came from other women. They're more critical, they just are. That's why I cared more what Deborah thought than either Crock or Gulliver at my initial Sugar & Spice audition. Men don't resent us if we're too pretty or too thin—they're not jealous or competitive with us. The prettier the better. I think we have no one to blame but ourselves for buying into this concept that we must look a certain way, stepping on the scale every day to check our self-worth. We ought to call a truce but we won't. Society and the gazillion-dollar beauty industry won't let us. They say no one will love us if we don't buy this shampoo and that lotion, or these spanks and those jeans (that don't actually fit). And for some reason we believe them.

So, on the surface it may have looked like we were bad-ass women, confident and beautiful, but our self-esteem had been beaten down to a miserable pulp, one striptease at a time. That's why when drunk customers called us whores, we'd act all tough but cry in private because we knew it was true. Actually, that's not entirely accurate because there were times we had the last laugh when we'd take their money. Many of the girls were rather intentional in their career choice.

Our apartment wasn't in the best of neighborhoods. Tenants' cars had been stolen or stripped of their parts in our parking lot and there was graffiti on nearly every flat surface. A homeless man had taken up his vigil on our corner and I had to walk by him every day to the parking lot. His name was Reginald. I know this because I'd struck up a short conversation with him after giving him a few dollars. I asked if he went by Reggie and he told me his name was Reginald Johnson, and only Reginald Johnson.

There was nothing hostile about the way he'd emphasized his name and it struck me as a matter of pride for this man who held up a dirty piece of cardboard where a plea for help had been written without literary flourish. It simply read: *Money excepted.* I presume he'd meant to write money "accepted," and I can only hope he hadn't meant to write money "expected." He looked old but looks can be deceiving when you're living on the street and don't shave or have access to good dental care. We became friends, or at least I looked him in the eye and said hello whenever I'd see him. I know this alone did not make us "friends" and I had yet to invite him in for dinner but I had come to admire his dignity—yes, his dignity as he squatted on the sidewalk corner. He was appreciative and polite, and even though he was begging in a manner of speaking, he never groveled. I got the impression he believed that groveling was beneath him.

I remember riding in the car with my dad when I was about thirteen and we were stopped at an intersection when a homeless man approached our car with a cardboard sign written in poor penmanship. The sign said that he was hungry. My dad told him to go away and then rolled up his window in a show of irritation and disgust. He then shook his head and mumbled to no one in particular that the lazy moron just needed to get a job. Besides, he said, he doesn't want food money, he wants drug money. They're all the same, he said. I assumed at the time that my dad knew what he was talking about, an assumption that now strikes me as naïve.

I was with Ricky once as we were walking to my car to go to work at Lil' Secrets. Yeah, it will come as no shock to you that Ricky tagged along there, too. I'm pretty sure if I worked at Walmart he wouldn't have tagged along.

"Hello, Miss Kate," he said.

"Hi Reginald," I said as I handed him five dollars.

"Bless you, Miss Kate."

Ricky was upset. "What did you do that for?" he asked me a few steps later. "Do you *know* this guy?"

When I told him I did, he reminded me that honest people worked for a living and that I was only making the homeless problem worse. Now, I am no social scientist but I was pretty sure I wasn't going to cause a spike in homelessness by giving Reginald five dollars. The irony was rich, of course, because I was doing the same thing for Ricky who was also unemployed and living off me, only with substantially less appreciation. I'd given Reginald the money because I thought it was a charitable thing to do. At least I think that's why I did it. But then I'd begun to wonder if my acts of charity were actually a semi-subconscious way of compensating for my sins. Was it possible I was less charitable than I gave myself credit for—that I was merely trying to offset the charge of being called a whore? Then again, five dollars here and there shouldn't be much to brag about, or amount to much off-setting.

23

KATHERINE

I WAS PREGNANT WITH MY SIXTH BABY on my thirtieth birthday. Remember I said we were dripping with kids? Well, there's your proof. Keith celebrated the occasion by floating the idea of a vasectomy. *Happy birthday, Sweetie! I'm getting snipped!* Let's face it, we had to do *something* or we'd turn into India. My eggs got fertilized at the drop of a hat and I suspect Keith must've hung a feedbag of Miracle Grow near his nether-regions.

Keith knew I didn't believe in birth control. Okay, go ahead, call me a religious weirdo, I've heard it before. But, for the record, I wasn't the only one in my community who didn't use birth control, not by a long shot. We just weren't up to speed on it. To illustrate my point, my uber naïve twenty-year-old friend was considering the pill in the run-up to her wedding. "But how do you get them to stay in?" she whispered to me. See what I mean?

Anyway, Keith dearly wanted the unrestrained freedom to plant his seed without having it take root, so he called in the church cavalry. One randy evening he told me he'd done some research and found the church didn't specifically oppose vasectomies.

"But, Keith, God won't give us more than we can handle."

"I don't see what the big deal is. It's me that has to go under the knife."

"Why don't we just be more careful?" I said. "Maybe if we cut back some it wouldn't be a problem."

"But I don't want to cut back," he said. "I'd rather not have to worry about it every time."

See, that's the thing right there. Here I thought we already did it plenty and now Don Juan wanted to do it even more. If he had a vasectomy, I'd never get anything done.

"You know I don't feel good about birth control," I said.

"But the rhythm method's birth control."

"I guess, sort of," I had to agree, "but with the rhythm method God could still fertilize the egg if He wanted to."

"Listen, Katherine, it's pretty simple. If God wants you to get pregnant, you're gonna get pregnant. That's just all there is to it."

"Don't be ridiculous. God isn't going to get me pregnant if you've had a vasectomy. That's a medical procedure, and He doesn't interfere with those."

"What are you talking about? He could if He wanted to."

"Yeah, maybe," I said, "but He just doesn't."

I was obviously going out on a limb there because I didn't actually know what God would do in that situation, but I did know about the Virgin Mary and how God could work around these things if He wanted to. So even total abstinence is apparently effective only 99.999% of the time.

A few weeks later, we met with our Mormon bishop who gave us the green light. For the record, I didn't think it was quite as green as Keith did, but that's probably academic at this point. Maybe you'll think it's a bit odd that we felt like we had to ask our bishop if it was permissible for us, a married couple, to use birth control. But he *was* our bishop and the fact that he was a salesman for Myer's Meat by day did not detract from his role as an inspired spiritual leader. Anyway, this quasi-green light was exactly the ammunition Keith needed. He scheduled an appointment with a urologist the next day.

When the big day came, he paced the crowded medical clinic's reception room in those loose-fitting gray Russell sweatpants I liked so much. You know, the old-school types with the drawstring that Rocky wore.

He told me a nurse's aide came out and handed him a clipboard and patient history form. She also handed him a small cup and directed him to a bathroom down the hall. I can just picture Keith looking from the cup to the nurse's aide, and then back again at the cup. "No, Mr. Murphy. Just a urine sample, please."

Keith told me the whole story, embellishing the dramatic life and death "surgery" that he'd somehow survived by grit and bravery alone. He'd been asked to remove his pants and crawl up to the equivalent of a dentist's chair. Then the nurse told him to put his legs in the stirrups. "My knees were danged near waist high but I guess that wasn't good enough," he grimaced with the brutal retelling, "because the doctor then came in and kept asking me to slide down more until my butt was danged near hanging off the chair thingee."

He'd been told to arrive pre-shaved, and he had, but not according to their high standards. So, the nurse grabbed a razor and "really went to town" according to Keith, who gripped the arms of the chair for dear life. Such pain! Such suffering!

"You might feel a little sting," the doctor told him as he pointed a syringe at Keith's scrotum. To hear Keith tell the story, you'd have thought they'd slowly castrated him with a dull cereal spoon. He then saw a small puff of smoke from where the doctor had cauterized the ends of the sperm tube. "For a split second," he said, "I thought my pubes had caught on fire."

Keith felt like a martyr—taking the pain for our marriage. He thought the combination of the stirrups, the puff of smoke, and two sutures (one on each side) were on par with labor and delivery, times six. Typical.

We were very committed in our church attendance and enjoyed it very much. The adult's Sunday school class was referred to as "Gospel Doctrine" and our teacher was Brother Torgerson. Brother Torgerson was a spiritual giant in our congregation because he was a college professor with a sturdy testimony, beautiful wife, and smart as a whip. He'd recently returned from Las Vegas where he'd been a guest lecturer at UNLV for a semester or two. Anyway, our lesson that particular Sunday was on the importance of chastity and standing firm because these were the Last Days and Satan was pulling all the stops to tempt us into sin, making it look good when it clearly wasn't. Brother Torgerson reminded us that we needed to draw our line and not put ourselves in situations that could lead to sexual sin. He was a great role model for chastity and I suspected he'd rise in the ranks of Mormon leadership because of it.

Vaughn asked Keith to open a new store in Cedar City, a town forty-five minutes north of St. George. We didn't want to leave our hometown but we knew there was opportunity in Cedar.

Part of me, a big part if I'm being honest, was conflicted about leaving the street Renaldo lived on. I'll admit it. We hadn't technically done anything but I wanted to and knew all it would've taken was a nod of the head and a breath mint. In the meantime, I'd look at his house whenever I drove down the street and wonder what was going on inside, hoping he might walk out the door to get into his Jeep or take out his garbage cans. I even pulled over on the side of the street across from his house a few times and waited for some action. He'd called our house a few times when he must have known Keith was at work. He'd call for the lamest things, too, like asking if he could swing by to borrow a shovel (like he didn't own a shovel). And I about died when my little Jacob wondered out loud why that "one guy" called all the time. Naturally, I pretended to have no clue what guy he was talking about and, again, Keith was clueless, bless his heart.

There were times I wanted to freeze everyone else and take a break from my life with Renaldo. I had this fantasy that we would go to an exotic retreat for a few days, just the two of us. There would be discreet room service and swaying palm trees outside our suite's balcony. After a few hours of exploring each other's bodies, I'd slip into one of the complimentary plush bathrobes and watch him dress for a fancy dinner where we'd drink champagne(!) and play footsies under the table before hurrying back to our room. I didn't want to marry him or anything and I certainly didn't want to hurt anyone. I just had a crush that so far had been harmless. I knew it would be a mistake, and a big one with potential everlasting tenacles—not like washing whites in cold water, or mistaking a teaspoon of salt with a tablespoon. But, oh, I really yearned to make that mistake.

My parents were sorry to see us leave St. George, especially my mom who was worn to a frazzle. I took Kylie whenever I could because my dad didn't like to babysit and do the things that needed to be done with little kids. But, yeah, us moms just crave that stuff.

My dad would never admit it, but I think he was embarrassed that his own flesh and blood was "retarded." That's why he'd helpfully point out to anyone who would listen that there was no history of Down's on *his* side of the family.

We moved to Cedar City in October of that year, leaving behind friends, family, and the wall in the laundry room where we measured the kids. The kids showed unusually good posture on the days they'd stand with their back to the wall and we'd draw the new line. *Jacob at 9! Jenna at 7 1/2!* It was shocking to see the objective evidence of their sprouting because we couldn't see it on a daily or even monthly basis but it was happening right in front of our very eyes. All of them were growing taller, that is, except for Nathan who was stuck at 43" for three semi-annual measurements in a row. So I fudged, for his sake. I asked Keith if we could cut out that piece of sheetrock and take it with us but he said we ought to just take a picture of it instead, which we did, before Keith painted over it so we'd get our deposit back.

Jacob was now in seventh grade, Jenna in fifth, Emily in third, Nathan in kindergarten, and Josh was two. The new baby would be born a few months after we moved.

I already had my hands full but my mom asked if we'd consider taking Kylie for a few weeks. My dad was all over it. "Jackie," he'd say, "it'd be good for Kylie to spend more time with Katherine and her daughter. She needs a friend."

I'm sure my mom needed help, of course she did. Didn't we all? I was pretty busy myself with six kids. There was no time to put the seven decorative pillows on the bed every morning like I'd sworn to do when I became a homemaker. In fact, there were days I didn't make the bed at all. And I could count on one finger the number of times I defrosted the freezer. There were days I couldn't find five minutes to take a shower. Even going to the bathroom without one of them hanging on my leg or begging for something was a luxury.

My husband would come home from work "exhausted." Now, I don't doubt it must have been tiring to sit on a stool behind the counter of a plumbing supply store and consult with customers over the value of a good pea trap, but, come on. To his credit, Keith never once complained about the gourmet-less food we ate or the house that looked like a hand grenade had been detonated inside. If he stepped on a Lego buried in the carpet and cut his foot, or if there was no place to sit because all the cushions in the house had been used to build a fort in the family room, he didn't flip out. Instead, he'd crawl into the hut with the rest of them, pull down the beach towel they'd jerry-rigged for the door, and then hatch a plan to sneak in a package of Oreos. And when our family grew to include Kylie all he said was, "Hey, one more isn't going to make a big difference. It'll be fun."

I didn't know how "fun" it was going to be but we were determined to make it work. Like they say, they don't last forever but it seemed like they did when we were in the thick of it. Sometimes every *day* felt like forever.

We were all eager to use the new boat by the time summer arrived. Technically it was no longer new but we still called it the new boat. Keith had insisted that all good boats must be named. I suppose that's true because I'd rarely seen a boat without a dorky name attached to it. Why they do it with boats and not cars or appliances is a mystery to me. Anyway, our boat was christened *The Special K.*

"You're the one who won it, so you should pick the name," Keith had said as he sat before a bowl of cereal amid the chaos of another morning.

"I sorta like *Come on Down!* You know, because of the Price is Right."

"Nah, that's stupid," he said.

"All right," I said, "how about *Water Fun?*"

"*Water Fun?* Are you serious? That's even worse."

"Okay, how about *K & K Adventures?*" I said as I held a paper towel in one hand and the new baby on my hip. One ear was tuned to the other room where Jacob was yelling at Nathan to get out of his room and Jenna was asking no one in particular where her retainer went. Keith was fairly good at tuning those things out.

"Those are dumb," he said. "It's gotta be decent."

"If you're so smart, then why don't you just name it."

"No, it's your boat, so name it whatever you want. Just don't make it a stupid one. That's all I'm saying."

"What do you think would be good?"

"I dunno," Keith said. "It ought to have something about water. Maybe something like *Water Fantasy.*"

"And you thought *Water Fun* was bad?"

"Okay," he said, "how about *Wet 'n Wild,* or *Liquid Fantasy,* or *Wet Dream?*"

"I like that one," I said.

"Which one? *Wet Dream?*"

"Yeah, I like it. Do you?"

"Katherine, I was *kidding. Wet Dream?*"

"Oh, yeah, huh. Omigosh, that's disgusting."

Keith grabbed the box of cereal next to his bowl and said, "That's it! Here, let's name it this," and he handed me the cereal box.

"I love it!"

And so it came to be known as *The Special K.*

We planned a day at the lake for the Fourth of July. Our go-to place was Sand Hollow reservoir because it was close by and the beaches were shady in spots.

"Kylie's going again?" Keith asked.

"What, my little sister isn't welcome anymore?"

"No, of course she is. I just thought maybe we could take the kids this time."

"But, Keith, it's her favorite thing in the whole world."

Jenna overheard our conversation and asked if her friend Brittany could come. "It's my turn to take a friend this time. I never get to. Pleeeease, I'll do anything."

"But we thought it'd be fun to take Kylie," I said. "She's your friend."

"I want Brittany to go instead."

"You know how much fun Kylie has."

"But Kylie makes me embarrassed sometimes."

I knew it was inevitable—that day when Jenna outgrew her disabled aunt. That day when Jenna realized Kylie didn't wear the right clothes and had never even heard of the New Kids on the Block. She and Kylie had been best friends since they'd been born eleven years earlier. But now Jenna and her friends at school had seen that Kylie was different which, by definition, was embarrassing.

"Jenna, how can you even say such a thing?"

"Sorry, mom, but it's embarrassing when she talks to me at school and stuff."

Nathan said, "Kylie's not weird, is she mom?"

"No, Nathan, she's not. She's just a little bit different, but we love her just the same."

"Yeah but—"

"I'll tell you what," I said, "if you really want to invite Brittany, that's okay if it's all right with your dad."

"Thanks mom!" She turned around and headed for the phone, then paused and turned back around. "Does Kylie still have to go?"

"Yes, I think we should take her, too."

"Then I don't want Brittany to come."

We dropped off the three youngest at my mom's house when we picked up Kylie. She was short for her age, and chubby. Her chin was abnormally small and her round head sat on top of a short neck. She wore glasses that were so large you could clean them with a squeegee and they were so thick they made her eyes look too big for her face. Of course, Kylie didn't know any of this. She was always happy, smiling back with small teeth at the kids who teased her, oblivious to their judgment. She came out to the car that morning wearing the same bathing suit she'd worn for years—a yellow one-piece that was noticeably too small. Her middle stuck out like a pot belly. My parents had learned to pick their battles and let her wear whatever she wanted. Unfortunately, Kylie had no taste in fashion.

Jenna tried to like her, bless her heart, but it was hard because Kylie didn't pick up on social cues. She thought Jenna loved it when she'd run up and hug her at school while she was talking to her friends and trying to be popular, or demand to sit by her at lunch. I'm sure Jenna tried to ditch her plenty and it broke my heart. But I understood.

"We're going to the lake, huh Jenna!" Kylie's speech was thick because her tongue was too big for her mouth.

"Yeah, sure."

She picked up Jenna's hand and held it with her short, fat fingers. "We're going to the lake in our boat! My mom said I get to ride in the front, huh Kafrun."

"She sure did," I said.

"We're going in our boat Jenna and I get to ride in the front!"

"Yeah, I know."

Despite all the practice, Keith still struggled with properly backing up the trailer. I shouldn't be critical because I tried it once and it was a disaster, the trailer jack-knifing within five seconds and the more I tried to straighten it the worse it got. Keith was only slightly better than I was and we stem-christied our way down the boat ramp in reverse, herky jerky, the kids ducking down in their seats in case anyone recognized them. We finally launched *The Special K* and piled in. Keith pulled Jacob on two skis and then the girls in a rubber inner tube. Meanwhile, Kylie sat in the front staring straight ahead like the figurehead on the bow of a Viking ship, letting the full force of the wind hit her face. She was so happy. I watched her with a mixture of compassion and envy. Maybe more envy.

"It's your turn," I told Keith. "You haven't been in a while."

"Yeah, come on, Dad," Jacob said. "It's easy."

"Okay, if you're going to twist my arm." He tied the end of the orange ski rope to the back of the boat and tossed the tangled slack into the water, then picked up the ski and threw it where it slapped onto the water's surface next to the floating rope. His suit was too tight and looked like he'd owned it since high school, which I think he had. I made a mental note to buy him a new one that fit. He was pasty white with generous love handles and didn't seem to care a bit. What was it with men? Didn't he know he was no longer the show-stopper he'd been in high school? Or did he just not care? I look in a mirror and see every flaw. In fact, that's all I see. That's why hardly anyone saw the swimming suit I wore under my sundress. I don't even know why I bother with the suit. It's not like I'm actually going to go *swimming*. And then there's Keith (and just about every other guy I know) who looks in the mirror and sees a fighter pilot. Why didn't he feel the need to hide his imperfections the way I did? So, yeah, I envied him, too.

"Okay, here goes nuthin," he said, and dove into the cold water.

"Take out the slack nice and slow!" he yelled from the water.

When the rope was fairly taut Keith yelled, "Hit it!" and I thrust the throttle down with my right hand. The boat fought the drag of Keith's 215 pounds of hold-over muscle and flab, finally pulling him out of the water. He had declared, rather unambiguously, that he weighed in at 183 pounds. So, basically, we both fudged on our weight. I think that by putting such a fine point on it, Keith must've figured his weight pronouncement was more believable than if he'd declared his weight to be an even 190, or 200, or even 185. He teetered but regained his balance long enough to release one hand from the rope's handle to wave at the kids in the boat before wiping out.

I made a wide arc and swung back around to where he was bobbing in the water trying to put the ski back on.

"Wanna go again?" I hollered over the noise of the engine and the lapping water.

"Dad, you gotta lean back more," said Jacob. "And keep your arms straighter."

"Yeah, Keef," said Kylie too loudly, "keep your arms straighter." Her voice regulation was iffy—she usually spoke at twice the volume she needed to.

"All right, one more," Keith yelled from the water. "The old man's still got it, huh?"

"Yeah, you look good Dad!" shouted Jenna.

I pulled the boat around to where I thought the rope was fairly straight in the water. Keith was trying to untangle a loop of rope floating a few feet in front of him just as Kylie came back from the front of the boat and sat next to me on the driver's seat. "I'm sunburned too much," she was saying. The boat was in gear but barely idling forward, just enough to keep the slack out of the rope.

As Kylie was trying to show me her sunburn, I thought I heard Keith yell "Hit it!" So I did. In the noise and confusion with Kylie, I hadn't heard him yell "Hold it!" instead.

"Mom! Stop! *Mom!*"

I looked back and saw Keith being pulled through the water headfirst like Superman with his arm in front of him. I yanked the throttle up to stop.

"Sorry!" I yelled back. "Are you okay? I thought you said to hit it!"

Keith lifted his head out of the water and I could tell he was hurt. I turned the boat around and idled up next to him, the boat bobbing with the wake. The ski had come off and was floating twenty feet behind him. I killed the engine and leaned over the side of the boat to help pull him in.

I screamed when he lifted his arm above the surface of the water because the orange ski rope was cinched so tightly around his bicep that his arm looked like an hourglass. By the time I could untangle and untie the knot, the lower half of his arm was white. We both looked in horror. The circumference of his bicep was the thickness of a garden hose.

24

RICKY

I'D BEEN MARRIED TO KATE for a few years now. I never thought I'd get married. Who wants to be tied down like that? I just don't think monogamy is my thing if you know what I mean. I've got nothing against Kate. She's easy going and makes good money. She's beautiful, too, and has a great body. But there are plenty of fish like that in the sea and it made no sense to use just one pole. Did I cheat on her? A few times, yeah, but they didn't mean anything.

I basically married her to keep the peace. I don't mean that as a slight but it's just the truth. She and her family were weird that way and I figured there was no harm in it so long she didn't insist on a bunch of kids. Besides, like I said, she made good money as a stripper.

I know how to make money, too, and it's not working for wages, I can tell you that. Working for wages is a total scam—it's rigged against you. Just look around. Who's making all the money? It's the entrepreneurs, that's who. I don't think Kate ever got that. I mean, look at her. She works her ass off and I appreciate it because she's keeping us afloat, but it's the *owner* of Sugar & Spice, and the *owner* of Lil' Secrets who's making it big. So if you can't be the owner for whatever reason then you've got to find an angle.

When I was a kid, my dad was an auto mechanic and used to take me to work with him. I thought I was indispensable because I'd sweep the shop and sometimes hand him a tool. I remember how hard he slaved away, crawling under cars and working with wrenches. He wore gray coveralls with his nametag sewn in cursive near the chest pocket and always had a dirty yellow rag hanging from his back pocket that he'd constantly use to wipe his hands of the grease. At the time, I thought he knew what he was doing working hard like that and I wanted to be just like him when I grew up and have my own shop, too. My shop would be like his with old license plates from different states nailed to the wall, a pin-up-girl calendar above the work bench, a Goodyear Tire clock, and a soda pop machine.

I'm glad I wasn't there when the car slipped off the jack because I was just a kid and wouldn't have known what to do. He'd been flat on his back, pinned down near his stomach by the rim of a wheel for an hour before anyone noticed. By then it was too late. I still see images of him on the shop floor in my mind. I knew something horrible had happened when my grandma checked me out of school that day.

My mom and I got virtually nothing when he died. A competitor bought his shop and we used the money to pay off debts. All that hard work, all that sacrifice, for nothing. My dad got caught up in this American Dream bullshit that if you work hard and play by the rules you'll get ahead. We lived in a trailer park just outside Reno and there was a casino nearby. I was underage but my buddies and I snuck in and I put a quarter in the slot machine and won ten dollars. I was hooked. My mom wanted me to get an "honest" job, whatever the hell that means, but I've always been a hustler.

And now, all these years later, Lady Luck was in a bad mood. I'd never seen anything like it before. How many times can you come up snake eyes? The odds were in my favor and I knew I'd come out of it but in the meantime I was getting in deeper with my bookie, a creep named Victor Spanos. He was a real piece of shit but I went along with him because I needed his money.

"I hear the bitch finally got you to marry her."

"Yeah, Kate and I got married."

"What, she cut you off?"

"We just decided to get married, that's all."

"Yeah, you can only bang 'em for so long before they start whining about it. 'If you loved me Vic, you'd marry me.' Same old whiny bullshit with these broads so you just marry 'em to shut 'em up. Am I right? What else you gonna do?"

He was a total pig but I needed his money, so I pretended to agree with him. Besides, I tended to agree with much of what he said.

"But I've seen her around and you got lucky, Waters. Whaddya say her name was? Kate was it? I'll bet she's great in the sack, huh?" he said as he nudged me with his elbow. "Got them nice long legs. Am I right?"

I wanted to hit him, I really did. Kate was mine and I didn't appreciate this piece of shit talking about my wife like that. But this was a man you didn't hit because if you did you'd get killed. I mean it—you'd literally get killed. Victor Spanos had no conscience, and he had guys, if you know what I mean.

"Come on, Vic, she's my wife. Okay?"

"Settle down, Waters. You oughta be glad. The bitch I'm married to is a whole different story." I think it was his fourth or fifth wife he was talking about. "Course, I'm sick of her fat ass anyway."

Victor Spanos crawled around the sewers of Vegas taking advantage of people in trouble. He could smell desperation and he pounced whenever he got a whiff of it. There's profit in desperation and this Spanos guy knew it. He was Italian, or at least he wanted people to think he was—you know, that whole tough-guy mafia vibe. I know it was stupid to have borrowed money from a prick like him but it's not like the bank was going to loan me anything. My mom still lived in Reno and she didn't have much, just her social security and a few bucks left over from my dad's small life insurance policy. She'd given what she had and that well was now dry. Kate said she was tapped out, too, and I had no choice but to believe her. The way I saw it, I had no choice.

We were sitting at a table in a café off the strip. It was early afternoon but Victor had already slurped down his second Chivas on the rocks. He'd asked me to meet him there and I knew the reason why—I owed him money and it was time to pay up.

"I like you Waters, I really do. We've done business before and I know you understand how this works. I give you money and you pay me back. You don't pay me back and someone gets hurt. Very simple." He was doing his best Marlon Brando and I would have laughed if he hadn't been so serious.

"Yeah, of course," I said. "It's just that I've been getting screwed and I was going to—"

"Shut the fuck up, Waters. I don't wanna hear it. We're friends and friends can be patient where need be. Now, I'm a reasonable man," he said before throwing back the rest of his drink. "How much time you need?"

"Another month and I swear I'll pay it back, with interest."

"I said we were friends, Waters. I didn't say I was a stupid. You got two weeks. And that's twenty grand."

"Twenty grand? Come on, Vic, I only borrowed ten. Can't you cut me some slack? That's double."

"I don't negotiate, Waters. You know that. But I'm not worried; you'll come up with it."

Victor was middle-aged and stocky—like a guy who might've once been fit but had let it go. He looked like a mid-life crisis. His brown silk shirt was unbuttoned to his chest where a gold medallion rested in gobs of chest hair. His armpits were wet and the bottom four buttons of his shirt looked like they were about to pop because of his gut. Seriously, the guy looked like an upholstered brown sofa.

Then there was his hair. A line of hair plugs were planted around the perimeter of his shiny scalp where his hairline used to be. They'd been plugged in about a quarter inch apart from each other and it looked ridiculous.

I'd borrowed ten grand to cover my gambling losses, robbing Peter to pay Paul, even though I knew it was pretty stupid to rob either one of them. Once I got out of the hole, I'd sworn to never borrow from this thug again.

Victor stood and took a French fry from my plate. "Whaddya say we get the gals together for some drinks. The four of us, ya know?"

"I don't know what Kate's schedule is but I'll ask her."

"Tomorrow night. Let's make it eight o'clock at Carlucci's."

"Yeah, that might work but I gotta check with—"

"Make it happen, Waters. I'd like to get to know your wife better."

That night I told Kate we had this dinner thing with a business associate of mine. She bitched about it when I told her who it was. She'd only briefly met him once before and was unimpressed. Said the muscular thug looked like a fucking steak.

"And what if I don't want to go to dinner with that ugly creep and his, what, sixth wife?"

"Hey, I don't want to go either but what was I supposed to say? He totally put me on the spot."

"What, you couldn't say no? You couldn't get us out of it? Come on, Ricky, that's the last thing I want to do."

"I tried but he wouldn't take no for an answer and I have to stay on his good side because I owe him some money."

"What do you mean you owe him some money? I just gave you $2,000 last week. I thought that was supposed to cover everything."

"Well, I had to get a little more but I'll be able to pay it back. He gave me some breathing room."

"How much did you borrow?"

"Just ten thousand."

"Ten thousand!"

"Yeah, but I'll work it out. Don't worry about it."

"How? How are you going to work it out? Ten thousand dollars? Are you being serious right now? I gave you everything I had!"

She would have totally freaked out if she knew I really owed twenty. She obviously didn't understand business and compounding interest and all that and I didn't feel like explaining it to her.

The next night Kate and I were heading out the door to meet Spanos and his wife when I noticed what she was wearing.

"I'd wear something different," I said.

"What do you mean? I thought you liked this top."

"Yeah, but I think you should wear something different tonight. It's too . . . you know . . . it shows too much."

"And since when has *that* bothered you?"

"I don't know. I'm just saying it might not be right for a business type dinner."

Kate agreed to change into something more conservative. Of course, she didn't own a turtleneck—most of her clothes were designed to show off her figure, which was amazing by the way.

I felt Kate recoil from the way Victor was staring at her when we walked into Carlucci's. I'm sure she wanted to turn around and go home to shower. He even licked his lips, the creepy bastard. He and his wife were already seated at a table near the back of the restaurant but he stood when we walked up to the table so he could hug Kate. I could tell she was pissed. She'd never even said hello to him but he'd still felt entitled to maul her with his sweaty body pressed into hers, holding it there for an extra count or two. What a prick.

Victor didn't even bother to introduce his wife and her huge hair. I mean, it looked like she was wearing a fucking helmet.

She must've used an entire can of hairspray because it could have withstood a tornado. And her make-up was so thick it looked like part of a Halloween costume—like a raccoon who'd decided to experiment with blue. A lightweight pink sweater stretched over her gigantic fake tits. I'm like most guys—I like big tits, okay? But these were a total joke. I doubt she could have even seen the salmon on her plate. Later that night, Kate yelled at me for staring at them. The truth is I did, but not in the way Kate thought. I stared at them in utter amazement that they could be so big, and so fake. By the way, I saw Kate staring at them, too. But Victor didn't even appear to notice because his eyes were aimed exclusively at my wife.

"Where did you find *her?*" Victor asked without taking his eyes off Kate.

"Oh, Kate and I have been together for several years."

"She's hotter than I remember," he said, as if Kate wasn't sitting right there next to his fifth wife.

"Uh, thanks," I said just as Kate kicked me under the table. It wasn't a flirtatious tap either. We're talking a sharp kick right on my goddamned shin.

"Is she still givin' it up?"

"*Excuse me?*" Kate said.

"Oh, sorry. I was just wondering if Ricky was as lucky as it looks."

Kate glared at him and I thought for a minute she was going to reach across the table and slap him, or maybe grab a fistful of his ape-like chest hair. I desperately tried to think of something to say to change the conversation.

"So, let's see, what's good here?" I asked as I pretended to be absorbed in the menu.

Kate then turned her glare on me.

Victor obviously saw the look because she wasn't trying to hide it. "Looks like she gets sassy," he says. "I like it."

Before I could say anything, Kate jumped up from her chair, knocking it over in the process. She didn't even bother to pick it up. She threw her napkin onto the table and turned for the bathroom.

"We'll be just a second," I said and followed her out.

I caught up to her in the small hallway outside the restrooms when she suddenly turned on me.

"What the hell is wrong with that man? He's a pig!"

"I know, I know. But what do you want me to do about it? It's not my fault."

"Aren't you going to say something?"

"I'll ask him to stop if he keeps talking like that."

"That's great, Ricky. Thanks a lot. And let me know when he goes too far."

Oh, she was pissed. Kate comes across as this nice, friendly, easygoing type but she can also be tough as hell. Trust me, I've seen it. I wouldn't say she has a bad temper, but she's no pushover when she sets her mind to something. I could understand why she might be upset with Spanos but I still thought she was overreacting. I mean, he hadn't touched her or anything and it's not like she wasn't used to guys staring at her. Guys pay good money to look at her. Anyway, I finally convinced her to return to the table.

"Hope I didn't start a little lover's spat," Victor said and chuckled to himself. Meanwhile, his helmeted wife sat twirling a glass of chardonnay, seemingly unperturbed by the whole scene. She finally looked at Kate and shrugged her shoulders as if to say, "Yeah, he's a pig but what you gonna do?"

Victor spent the next half hour telling us how rich he was. "This Rolex here cost me ten grand," and "I got me one of them Jaguars. Cost me seventy G's." On and on he went as I sat there furious with myself for having gotten involved with this asshole. He also treated us to his views on race: "Goddamned blacks everywhere in this town." And sexual orientation: "That waiter's probably a goddamned fag." And gender: "That broad over there's a real looker." My shin was being kicked every few seconds but what was I supposed to do? Just get up and leave? I tried to shift in my seat to get away from the kicks and hoped Victor would wrap it up.

The waiter finally brought the bill. Now, you'd think Victor would've paid after all the talk about how rich he was but instead he slid the bill over to me. Un-fucking-believable. His wife just sat there acting like she didn't know what a bill was, as if it'd never occurred to her who might pick up the cost of her not one, not two, but three twenty-dollar glasses of chardonnay. Kate was too pissed to react. I paid with a credit card that was already at its limit.

We tried to beat them out of the restaurant because I knew Kate had had enough, more than enough, and so had I. But, unfortunately, we had to walk behind them out to the parking lot. Victor then hocks a loogie right there on the sidewalk ten feet in front of us. We had to step over it—a shiny wad of phlegm like a freshly shucked oyster. I thought Kate was going to barf.

I got the silent treatment until we were halfway home when Kate finally looked at me. "I will *never* see him again."

"Yeah, he's really something."

"No, Ricky," she said. "I never want to see him again. Do you understand?"

"Okay, I know."

"I'm serious."

"Okay, fine."

We drove down Flamingo for a few more minutes in silence, past the well-lit sprawl of tacky souvenir shops and racks of cheap T-shirts on the sidewalk that all those dumbass tourists buy. Look at me! I've been all the way to Las Vegas and I have this T-shirt to prove what a goddamned loser I am! And then you wonder how Vegas makes its money.

"That was unreal," I said. "Could you believe that guy? What a jerk."

Kate said nothing for a few more seconds and I thought she'd never speak to me again. Finally, she said, "Oh, and did I mention my Rolex?"

Thank God she was in one of those moods where she'd get so mad she'd actually make a joke out of it. I think it was her way of winding down or something.

"And did I tell you my jacket was hand-stitched?" I said.

"Yeah, I'll bet it was," Kate said. "And see these hair plugs? This ain't synthetic hair, mister. No siree. She's as real as she can be!"

"Hair plugs? What hair plugs?" I said.

"And see my wife's tits?" Kate said. "Them things cost me a goddamned fortune! You wouldn't believe how much silicone's in them puppies! Am I right? Huh? Just look at 'em, will ya!"

25

KATHERINE

KEITH'S ARM WAS DEAD by the time we got to the hospital and there was nothing they could do to save it. But first there'd been the frantic boat ride to the marina. Kylie took her position up front, the Viking figurehead, and we rode as fast as we could, the poor kids hanging on for dear life. We were all soaked from the spray made by the boat banging against the waves. We'd draped a Mickey Mouse beach towel over Keith's arm because no one could bear to look at it. Like I said, it looked like an hourglass. There wasn't any blood or anything, just his white arm. The kids were all bawling and kept asking me if dad would be okay. I lied and said he would. Meanwhile, Keith sat next to me in the boat with this blank look on his face—the same face he wore when eighteen-month-old Emily drowned on his watch. He had to be in shock.

An ambulance met us at the marina. A nice man in coveralls who worked at the marina's gas station agreed to drive the kids home, and I let him. At least I thought he looked nice, but he could have been a serial killer for all I knew. Now I can't even remember what he looked like. I rode in the ambulance with Keith who was quiet and shellshocked.

The amputation was traumatic. They removed Keith's wristwatch and wedding ring and then cut the bone off with a power saw a few inches above his left elbow. I wasn't there when they did it, of course, but I had dreams about the noise it made when they were sawing, and all the bone dust. They sewed a stump with the extra skin like they were darning a sock. I have no idea what they did with his dead arm. Threw it in the garbage I suppose. I have dreams about that, too—a hairy forearm attached to a lonely hand just lying at the bottom of a trash can.

I think the kids were also in shock. They'd never seen someone with an amputated limb and it freaked them out. Keith said they could touch his stump but they wanted nothing to do with it. After all, who wants to touch a stump, and especially a fresh one? They didn't even want to look at it.

Word traveled quickly through our neighborhood and the community came out in force. I've been there. I know what it's like when you hear about someone else in the ward who'd died, or had cancer or something. You don't want to act too excited because that would just be mean and inappropriate. But it is sort of exciting, in a way, and you want to tell everyone you know as soon as possible before someone else beats you to the punch. I could hear them now.

"Did you hear what happened to Keith Murphy? He got his arm cut off!"

"I know. Isn't it awful? Katherine called me right after it happened."

"She called us, too," they'd say, not to be outdone. "She was still at the hospital when she called us."

"Yeah, same here. I heard he was dragged a quarter mile before she cut the engine."

"She must feel horrible."

"No kidding. I heard Keith's dad is pretty upset, too. He thinks Katherine had no business driving that boat in the first place. Not with all those kids on board."

"We're taking a casserole over tonight."

"We took a chicken pot pie over yesterday."

See, I know how it goes. The excitement. The competition. I couldn't wait to tell everyone after I learned that our bishop had an affair with his secretary at the insurance agency. And I was calling people off the hook when my neighbor got breast cancer. That it appeared to be terminal just made it more sensational.

The kids and I decorated Keith's hospital room with cheery banners and made posters with messages written out in candy bars. *You're a **Big Hunk**. We hope you get **Mounds** of care and get **Good & Plenty** of rest. We'll have **Whoopers** of fun when you get your **Heath** back. Soon you'll get over this **Rocky Road** and feel like **1,000 Grand!*** Neighbors brought flowers, cards, and balloons, their strings hanging limply from the ceiling of his hospital room like the tendrils of jellyfish. Emily and Nathan drew pictures of our family with crayons which I taped on the wall next to his hospital bed—Keith standing the tallest among the row of stick figures with both arms still attached.

Keith's parents were devastated. Vaughn wasn't a water skier, so he didn't understand how the ski rope could have cinched around Keith's arm if I'd been paying an ounce of attention. He tried to hold his tongue and only outright blamed me to anyone who would listen. He persuaded Dottie to blame me too, which I thought lacked credibility because Dottie barely knew how to drive a car, much less a boat.

Vaughn and Dottie were good grandparents, I'll give them that. They'd been thrilled when Jacob was born, fighting for babysitting time, but I think their interest had been watered down by the time our sixth kid came along. Let's just say they no longer insisted on babysitting and their repertoire of pre-made excuses was impressive. And, really, who could blame them? Six kids? But these were difficult times for us and Dottie pitched in without complaint (and Vaughn was good to let her).

Keith had become an overnight sensation because his arm had been caught in a rope. He went to church with the rest of us a week later and you would've thought he was a Beatle the way they gawked. People tried not to look down at his arm, or what was left of it, disciplining themselves to look him in the eye and only staring at his empty sleeve from a distance. The bishop spoke glowingly about Keith's bravery. This was the new bishop who'd taken over on an emergency basis after the former one was caught red-handed at the Days Inn with his secretary—the bishop who claimed this particular secretary had beguiled him. Had I been his PR manager I would have told him to drop the victim bit because it just added insult to injury.

Keith said he felt stupid being treated like a hero. "I didn't do anything brave," he said. "It's not like I just bit down on a stick when they cut the danged thing off." He also appropriately acknowledged that he hadn't donated his arm to charity or anything, like a selfless kidney donor.

After the church service, he'd been mobbed in the foyer by well-wishers who tried to keep their kids from gawking. There were a few awkward comments which were meant to be inspiring. For example: "At least you're right-handed, so that was lucky," and "Jerry's uncle lost his arm in the war and he ended up having a pretty normal life."

Keith just wanted to go home and take another pill because the pain was so bad. I worried he'd get addicted to them because that can happen after you've taken a few in a row. You also tend to get constipated, something that'd never once happened to Keith as far as I knew. He'd wake up and do his business just as predictably as can be, rain or shine. Not me, especially when I wasn't in my element. Like if I was traveling? Forget about it. It must be a mental thing. Anyway, I wasn't a pill popper myself. You grinned and bore it when I was growing up in our house. If a wet towel on your forehead, Vicks vapor rub, and drinking five gallons of water didn't do the trick, my mom might dole out a Bufferin. One Bufferin, max, and even then it was an unusually momentous occasion.

The doctors warned us that Keith might have recurring pain in his left hand, the one that had been chopped off and was in a garbage can somewhere. Talk about weird. They said the brain gets its wires crossed and sends electrical signals to the missing arm. Hey, left arm, you there? Don't you hurt? And the obvious problem with that is you wouldn't be able to rub it out. It was sort of like the time I fell out of a wheelbarrow as a kid and broke my arm. It was casted for six weeks and when I had an itch I had to straighten a clothes hanger and poke it down the inside of my cast to scratch it. In Keith's case, a hanger wouldn't cut it.

His therapist told us to use a mirror to trick the brain into seeing the missing limb which is supposed to help with the phantom pain. Keith would hold a large mirror vertically down the center of his upper body—right down his sternum. Then he'd look into the mirror while moving his right arm which gave his brain the illusion that he really had two arms after all. I know it sounds strange but it worked.

It wasn't the missing arm so much as the missing hand. The therapists taught him how to tie his shoes with one hand and cut a steak using a utensil that looked like a miniature scythe and a fork. I got the Soviet Union flag vibe whenever I saw it. Bathing the slippery kids was also tricky, but still he tried. And how about changing a diaper? Most men I knew would've taken early retirement from that job, but not Keith. He'd have to stick his chin on the diaper to hold it down while he yanked the tape on each side with his only hand. I know I shouldn't laugh, but the first time I saw him do it with a dirty diaper—the look on his face—I thought I was going to pee my pants.

I was surprised how little he complained because normally he was a real boob about any ailment. For example, if he had a hangnail he'd make sure I knew about it. "Geez, this bugger's really been killing me." And I heard more than once about how the two scrotum stitches from his vasectomy "pulled" for three months. He'd ask me where we kept the ibuprofen three times a week just so I'd know something hurt. And yet he was a trooper when his arm had been cut off. Go figure.

I was holding it together—but just barely. It's not easy having a house full of kids and a one-armed husband. And knowing it'd been my fault didn't help. I felt like a knitted sweater with a loose strand. If someone had pulled the strand, even gently, the entire thing would've unraveled into a pile of tangled yarn.

I was out of sorts, frazzled to within an inch of a complete meltdown. I even found myself employing the occasional swear word. On those rare occasions when one slipped out, however, it would be a relatively harmless one, like a hell or a damn. And I never swore in front of the kids because I didn't want to traumatize them. Instead, I just told them fairy tales which weren't the least bit traumatizing. Like the one about the wolf who dressed up like grandma and tried to eat the little girl, or the trio of little pigs who lost their home to the wolf. Or the cannibalistic witch who tried to throw Gretel into the oven but was outwitted and found herself cooked instead. Or how about the poor little mice who happened to be blind and had their heads chopped off by a carving knife. But I never swore in front of the kids because I didn't want to upset them.

Kylie was over at our house a few weeks later, sitting at the kitchen table with a coloring book and crayons. She was unusually quiet, mumbling or singing to herself. Finally, she said, "You're mad at me, huh Kafrun."

"No, of course not. Why would I be mad at you?"

"Because I got sunburned."

"When did you get sunburned?"

"When Uncle Keef almost got dead."

"I'm not sure what you mean. I didn't know you were sunburned. Did it hurt?"

"Cause it's my fault, huh."

"What's your fault?"

"I got sunburned and Jenna said that's why you drove the boat fast and Uncle Keef almost got dead."

I had to think back to the day of Keith's accident. I vaguely remembered that Kylie had distracted me, complaining about a sunburn. That's when I'd misheard Keith.

"Oh, no, Kylie. That's not why the accident happened. You didn't do anything wrong."

"But Jenna said it was my fault."

"Well, that's just silly, Kylie. Of course it wasn't your fault."

Kylie went back to her coloring book where staying within the lines was a low priority, for she was crossing them constantly. I found Jenna propped up in her bed reading *The Hidden Staircase*, a Nancy Drew staple. A large metal "J" hung on the wall above her headboard and my grandmother's small antique jewelry box sat on the nightstand next to her retainer. A little ballerina twirled to *Für Elise* whenever the jewelry box was opened. One of the ballerina's tiny arms was broken off, too.

"Jenna, did you tell Kylie the accident was her fault?" We always called it "The Accident." No one ever said anything about a chopped off arm.

"She's always trying to get me in trouble. Why does she have to stay at our house all the time?"

"But why would you tell her it was her fault?"

"Because it was! It's all her fault! If she didn't bug you about her stupid sunburn the accident wouldn't have happened and dad would be okay."

"Jenna, that's not fair. It was just an accident. Kylie didn't do anything wrong."

"Yes she did! She always messes things up. I hate her!"

"Stop it, Jenna! You stop that kind of talk right this minute!"

"But I do! I hate her!"

"You don't hate Kylie. She's my little sister and she's one of your best friends."

"No she isn't! I hate her! She's embarrassing!"

"She has Down syndrome, Jenna. She can't help it."

"Yes she can! Why does she always try to talk to me when I'm with my friends? It's embarrassing! She always tries to kiss me. It's gross and I hate it!"

Jenna was in the sixth grade. I get it. How was she supposed to be popular when there was a girl with Down syndrome running around trying to kiss her all the time?

"We let her stay with us a lot because Grandma Coombs needs help and we're her second family. It makes me sad that you'd say such mean things about her. I'm really disappointed in you, Jenna."

It was bad parenting, I know. Jenna's complaints weren't unreasonable. I wouldn't have wanted to deal with Kylie in the sixth grade either. Who would? But I hurt so much inside. I hurt for Kylie, and Jenna, and Keith. I hated God, or biology, or whatever it was that caused my little sister to have that extra chromosome. One stupid little chromosome had caused so much pain.

We tried to disguise the pain by calling it a blessing from God because that's what we do to make ourselves feel better about our plight. But I didn't feel like dressing it up as some kind of blessing because it wasn't. I'm sorry, but it just wasn't. So just stop it already with how challenges are such wonderful blessings in our lives. And it didn't make me feel any better to believe God may have had a hand in all this. If anything, it only made it worse to believe He'd foisted this on her, on us. I mean, why would He do such a thing? That's not something a loving Father would do, is it? That's why I chose not to buy it, or at least not to think about it, because I didn't want to compound my inner turmoil by putting my faith on the scale. Kylie just had an extra chromosome and that's all there was to it.

Later that afternoon I drove Kylie home to my mom's house. Emily and Nathan were also in the car.

"Kylie, I talked to Jenna and she's sorry about saying Keith's accident was your fault. Because it wasn't your fault. Not at all."

"Oh." Kylie no longer seemed to be concerned about it. She was trying to clean her glasses by breathing on them the way she'd seen adults do which only smudged them worse.

"And Uncle Keith will be okay," I said.

"I know," said Kylie.

"Me too," said Emily, "because I said my prayers."

"Me too," said Kylie.

"I did too," said Nathan, not to be outdone.

"It's going to grow back, huh, Mom," said Emily.

"Yeah, Kafrun, it's going to grow back, huh," said Kylie. "Because Jesus loves me."

26

RICKY

I'D HAD LOSING STREAKS BEFORE but never one like this. This was a joke. My plan had been to parlay the final $2,000 Kate had given me into enough to repay Victor Spanos but I swear to God the cards were stacked against me and I'd lost it. And now Spanos was turning up the heat.

I knew Kate kept a stash of hundred-dollar bills in an old pair of socks in the back of her drawer. I'd found the secret stash when I was looking for the match to one of my own socks. There were five hundred-dollar bills rolled up tighter than a fuckin' drum in that sock. That had been three months earlier and it'd bugged me that she'd hidden it from me. Where's the marital trust in that? I wondered what else was she hiding from me. I never said a word about the money even though I'd obviously wanted to use it. I figured I'd wait until I was desperate. Well, now I was desperate.

Kate was working that night at the Golden Nugget and I knew she wouldn't be home until after midnight. I opened the drawer and removed the sock. Now there were eight hundred-dollar bills. What the—! How could Kate hold out on me like this? We were *married* for God's sake. The fact that she was sneaking it from me made it easier to take. I'm not sure why, but it did. After all, how can you steal from your own wife? Half of it was mine anyway, right? Besides, I'd smuggle it back into the sock within a day or two anyway.

I dressed in my blue pinstripe suit and a white French-cuff shirt with no tie. It's not like I'm overly superstitious, but I swear I win whenever I wear that pinstripe suit. Is it scientific? No, it isn't. I know that, but why mess with it if it's working? I took Kate's $800 sock money to my favorite blackjack table at Caesars. It was eight o'clock at night and the casino was already jam-packed. God how I love the energy in a packed casino—the sounds of ringing slot machines, shuffling cards, and the occasional cheer from a craps table. Call me crazy, but I like the smells, too. I think it's the combination of a freshly struck match, cigarette smoke, perfume, and carpet. The halter tops and skanky dresses don't bother me either, but you've got to overlook the flabby women there who've let themselves go.

I waited for some loser to leave the middle seat and jumped in. The woman to my right was squeezed into a blue pantsuit three times too small and spent five minutes trying to decide whether to hit a nineteen. I mean, who were these idiots? The guy on my left was just as bad—a drunk moron in a sleeveless tank top with hairy shoulders who asked the dealer if he should split his eights. No wonder the house is so goddamned loaded.

The dealer was a hot Chinese woman I knew. Or maybe she was Korean or Japanese or one of those other ones, it doesn't matter because they all basically look the same, you know what

I mean? I once told Kate that and she went off on me—called me an ignorant racist. But since when is it racist to state a fact? I knew this dealer was into me and I could have had sex with her anytime I wanted. And I wanted to, in a way, but Asian women don't really do it for me. Too skinny. Anyway, I put down $100 and drew an eighteen. She busted. I left the $200 on the table and she busted again. I left the $400 on the table and was dealt a twenty-one. I knew this was no time to be timid with the dealer this cold, so I put $500 down and was dealt a fourteen. The dealer showed a ten. I hit it, and she dealt me seven. Hell yes! Speaking of hot.

I can't describe the adrenaline rush when I'm winning. There's no better feeling in the world. I feel invincible, like I just *know* I'm going to win. There's probably no scientific explanation for that either, but it's real, I'm telling you. I won six thousand bucks over the next two hours and wanted to celebrate with that dealer but I needed to get home and put the eight hundred dollars back in Kate's sock before she got home because if she knew I'd found the sock she would have been pissed, even though *she's* the one who was cheating her spouse. Then she would have re-hid it in a place I would never find.

I called Victor first thing the next morning. "I've got a good chunk of it for you."

"How much is a good chunk?"

"Five thousand."

"That's a small chunk, Waters, not a good chunk. Meet me at the Lucky Traveler this afternoon. Pay me the five G's and we'll work out some new terms."

Victor seemed pissed on the phone which bugged me. I could see it if he thought I was trying to duck him, but don't forget that I'm the one who'd called *him*. I chalked it up to his tough-guy act. That afternoon I drove to the Lucky Traveler for our meeting and found him sitting in a booth wearing one of his godawful brown silk shirts unbuttoned to the sternum. Was he trying to show off his chest hair? Was that it? Did he think it was sexy to have pubes that extended clear up to his throat? My God, he looked like an ape. And the guy needed to buy some antiperspirant.

I slid into the bench seat opposite him where he sat twisting this huge gold ring around his pinky, a ring that was chunkier than a class ring and twice as gaudy. I mean, it must have weighed a full pound. I gave him the thick envelope with fifty one-hundred dollar bills which he stuck in the back pocket of his pants without counting it, or even looking at it for that matter.

"I said two weeks, Waters. It's been two weeks. When am I getting the next fifteen grand? And no more chunks. I want the whole thing."

"Soon. Can you give me another two weeks?"

"I'll give you one week."

"I'll try but it's been tough lately."

"Ever heard of Al Gonzalez? Goes by Gonzo?"

"Yeah, I know who he is," I said. "Wasn't he in some accident a while back, broke his jaw or something?"

"Oh, he broke more than that," Victor said. "I'd hate to see you have the same kind of accident, Waters. I really would."

That was obviously meant to scare me. And it did, I'll be honest. Gonzalez was a huge dude. So, yeah, he'd made his sick point and the sick point was that he was an asshole.

He ordered a chicken fried steak from the attractive twenty-year-old waitress. I wasn't very hungry but ordered a turkey sandwich. The restaurant was busy with the lunchtime crowd and you could tell the waitress was in a hurry. Victor tried to flirt with her anyway, even though it was obvious that she was fairly repulsed by him. After all, he was a repulsive person. When she left the table, he told me she was really into him. He said he'd probably get her number on the way out. I didn't know where to start. When our food arrived, Victor reached over and grabbed half of my sandwich and took a bite, then put it back on my plate. Who does that?

He cleaned his plate then threw back the rest of his Chivas. As he walked out of the restaurant, I saw him talk to the maître d' and then point at me, to make it clear I was picking up his tab.

That night, after Kate left for work at Lil' Secrets, I drained the sock again and went back to Caesars. I wore the same suit, shirt, socks, and shoes from the night before. I would've worn the same goddamned underwear but Kate was behind on the laundry. I'm not as superstitious as it sounds—not like some gamblers who'll eat the exact same food, wear the same clothes, and park in the same spot—but why jinx it, if you know what I mean.

I had to wait for the middle seat at my favorite blackjack table because some jackass who had no idea what he was doing had taken it. This idiot was wearing a Def Leppard World Tour T-shirt, like he'd be the kind of guy to go to a Def Leppard concert. I got more of an Air Supply vibe from him. He was guzzling the free screwdrivers and fingering his puny stack of five-dollar chips. Total rookie. I jumped in when he finally got up to take a leak.

I started small with $50 and lost. No problem, I thought. I lost the next three hands, too. And then that hot Asian chick came to sub out the dealer. She smiled at me and said, "Let's do it again, huh?" Yeah, I could've had my way with her but, as I said, Asian women really aren't my thing. Anyway, the first card she dealt me was an ace, followed by a king. Then I doubled down on a ten and was dealt another ten to win. Then a loss. Then two more wins. I could smell another big night. I split eights and she busted again. I was up $7,000 and had the discipline to call it quits.

I returned to the apartment and stuck the $800 back in the sock before Kate got home. It pissed me off to have to do it but it made no sense to expose my knowledge of the golden goose. And why in God's name did she have so many socks, anyway. The drawer was filled to the top with balls of socks—you had to press them down to close the drawer. And don't even get me started on her collection of swimsuits. Sure, have two or three, but I counted ten. But unlike the socks, at least she used use them all. She'd go down to the condo's pool to lay out and everyone gawked behind their sunglasses when she'd remove her swimsuit coverup.

I was lying in bed watching TV when Kate got home after midnight. "Hey," she asked from the bathroom where she stood in front of the mirror taking off her makeup, "whatever happened with that creepy Spanos guy? How are you going to pay him? Wasn't it ten thousand dollars?"

"Yeah, but I had a good night and won three grand, so I should be okay. He's giving me more time." Hey, if she's going to lie to me then fuck it, I'll lie to her.

"Promise me you'll never do business with that guy again."

"There's no way. I hate the sonofabitch."

And I'd meant it. That's what a winning streak will do for you. The odds should technically be the same every time, but when the dice are hot, they stay hot. Again, maybe not scientifically based but true.

I earned another $1,000 over the next five days making it a total of $8,000 in less than a week. That left me just $7,000 short. I made arrangements to give Victor the $8,000 and assured him that I'd come up with the rest. "You've got two more days, Ricky," he says. "Don't fuck with me on this."

The next night I went back to the sock, hopefully for the final time. It had been moved. Now it was on the other side of the drawer. I reached inside and pulled out eleven hundred-dollar bills. She'd put another $300 in the sock! I couldn't decide if I was happy or even more pissed. I took out $1,000 and headed back to Caesars. All I needed was one more big night.

I was up $8,000 within an hour. I had enough to repay Spanos plus a little cushion. My head told me to stop but why stop when I was hot? It didn't feel right. So I kept going and lost my cushion, and then some. By the time I finally walked away from the table I'd lost $6,000 of the $8,000 I'd worked so hard to earn. I was so pissed. But I was still up $2,000.

I put "Kate's" $1,000 back in the sock before she got home. I had to meet with Victor the next day and I was still $5,000 short.

When Kate got home that night she asked me if I'd made any more progress with Spanos.

"I'm still a little short but I'm sure he'll work with me."

"I have a few hundred if you really need it," Kate said.

"Really? That'd be great," I said. "But I thought you'd already given me everything you had."

"I made a little more tonight. Here, I'll go get it," she said as she left me sitting on the sofa to go fetch the money from our bedroom. I felt guilty that I'd judged her for holding out on me; that is until she returned from the bedroom and handed me three hundred-dollar bills. "Ok, that's all I've got, so I hope it's enough."

"Uh, yeah, thanks," I said, my short-term guilt having vanished.

"I'm getting in the shower," she said. Kate always showered when she came home from work at Lil' Secrets. Always. It didn't matter what time it was. They were long showers, too.

I followed her into the bedroom and when she stepped into the shower, I checked the sock. It hadn't been touched—there were still eleven hundred-dollar bills rolled up in it. What the absolute fuck? Maybe, I thought, there were more socks. I squeezed every pair in the drawer. Nothing. I searched her purse, but there was less than $100 there. I took a twenty.

Victor was sitting at a both rubbing his temples with his eyes closed in front of a cup of black coffee when I walked into the Lucky Traveler the next day. Same ugly chest hair. Same pit stains. I wanted to reach out and yank on that hair, or at least tell him how pathetic he looked, but instead I just handed him the money. This time he counted it slowly and deliberately. Then he counted it again with a dramatic frown on his ugly face, like he'd miscounted. He looked up at me. "You're five thousand short."

"Yeah, I know, but that's fifteen grand and I only borrowed ten. Can't you cut me some slack?"

He leaned back and stared at me, tapping the envelope on the table with his index finger without looking away. That ridiculous fake-gold medallion still nested in his upper pubes. He said nothing and showed no emotion.

"You know I'm good for the money, Vic. Come on."

He reached into his jacket that was next to him on the seat and pulled out a large manila envelope that had been folded in half. He slid it across the table to me like he must've seen a mob boss do in a gangster movie. I picked it up and unfolded it. Inside was an 8" by 10" photo of some poor bastard who'd been beaten. I didn't know who it was because his swollen face was unrecognizable.

"Don't worry, pal. He's still alive because I need the rest of what he owes me."

"Come on, Vic."

He just stared at me.

"What do you want, Vic. You know I'll pay you back. I just need more time."

The dirty little hair ball just kept staring. He had a toothpick in his mouth and moved it from one side to the other with his tongue. Then a faint smile came over his face, a goddamned smirk that I'll never forget for as long as I live.

"I'll tell you what, Waters," he said. "You still owe me five grand, and that's a lot of money. But I'm a reasonable man. So, here's what I'll do." He paused for dramatic effect just like in the movies. Another shift of the toothpick. "You let me fuck your wife and we'll call it good."

I don't know if you've ever had that feeling—the one where you'd actually, dead seriously, kill someone if you could get away with it (and maybe even if you couldn't). You'd tie them

27

KATHERINE

VAUGHN BLAMED ME AND THE CHURCH for Keith's amputation. You read that right, he blamed me and the *church*. Me I could see, but the church? That was ridiculous on its face, of course, but Vaughn felt entitled to spread the blame to anyone or anything he disliked. So, yeah, it'd been the church's fault all right. Clear as a bell. I heard he even blamed the manufacturer of the ski rope. Why, you ask? Because the rope had been *too* strong.

I try to be nice. I have my moments like everyone else but I'm naturally a kind person. About the only thing I ever said on the subject was, "Geez, Keith, I'm so flippin' mad at your dad! What's he got against me anyway?" That's all I *said*, but I thought worse. I'll admit it. I'm not Jesus.

Keith was more mature about it—he only blamed himself.

We were over at Keith's parent's house and I was in the kitchen helping Dottie do Vaughn's dishes when I overheard Vaughn spouting off to Keith in the living room.

". . . and she was distracted by that retarded sister of hers—the one you're raising. That's the problem right there."

"We aren't raising her, Dad. We're just helping her parents. We've got little kids so we're more used to it."

"Well, as long as that Dale and Jackie keep having kids, something like this was bound to happen. What've they got now, ten?"

"Eight."

"Oh, sorry, just the eight, huh?"

"Dad, we have six."

"That's because Katherine wants to keep up with her mom for some strange reason. How does she expect you to pay for that many kids? It's not fair to you, son."

"Come on, Dad. They're my kids, too, and we've wanted every single one of them."

What a jerk. I wanted to march out of the kitchen and strangle Vaughn with the damp dish towel. Dottie could see me trying to eavesdrop and she didn't want a scene so she started talking louder about the lasagna recipe. She knew exactly who she was married to.

My dad claimed Vaughn was just a bitter ex-Mormon who went looking for whatever he could find to blame on the church. "That Vaughn, he doesn't like us because we have the truth and he knows it. Knows it clear as day." It was always "that Vaughn" or "that Dale" when our fathers referred to each other. Our moms, on the other hand, got along pretty well. This was mostly due to the fact that my mom never made waves. She was reliably deferential, just sort of blending into the woodwork. She was a homemaker, and a good one, but that's about all she did. Dottie had girlfriends. My mom did not. Dottie played bridge and was in a book club. Not my mom. When Dottie said she voted for Clinton, my mom sweetly changed the subject to the grandkids. She obviously hadn't voted for a Democrat, for how could she?

The rift between our dads was temporarily healed when Vaughn had his heart attack. He'd been mowing his front lawn when it happened. Dottie had just returned from having her hair done and was looking out the living room window just in time to see him slump over the steering wheel of the riding lawn mower he just had to have, even though his lawn was so small it took forever to mow it with that thing—what with the ten million three-point turns he had to make—backing to and fro, in and out of the petunias. And he insisted on wearing safety goggles and gloves whenever he rode it which, I'm sorry to say, was just plain ridiculous. I mean, its top speed might have been that of a tortoise. But he made sure everyone knew it was a top-of-the-line John Deere! An XL-150! And you just can't do any better than that.

So, Dottie saw him slump over the steering wheel and a moment later saw the coveted XL-150 crash into the trunk of a maple tree at the brisk pace of two miles per hour. Vaughn toppled over from the mower's seat to the grass clutching his chest with his safety goggles twisted from his eyes to his nose and cheek.

Dottie screamed and called 911. A neighbor across the street was sitting on his front porch with a glass of lemonade in his hand and just happened to see the collision with the tree. "Hey, Marlene!" he shouted from his porch swing, "You gotta come check this out! Vaughn Murphy just ran into a tree with his riding lawn mower! Funniest thing I've ever seen!" Then he felt bad for laughing when he saw Vaughn lying on the grass, clutching his chest like that. It was something of a surprise that this particular neighbor felt any sympathy at all for Vaughn because there had been bad blood between them ever since Vaughn had wrongfully accused him of backing into their garbage cans and knocking the trash all over. Knowing Vaughn, he'd most likely made the accusation simply because this particular neighbor happened to be an active member of the church.

Vaughn had been propped up with his back to the maple tree by the time the ambulance arrived. The neighbor told me Dottie was practically waterboarding him with lemonade because she thought the sugared liquid would help. And another neighbor who lived a few doors down took over by putting a wet cloth on Vaughn's neck. The other neighbors had collectively deferred to this guy's medical knowledge because he happened to work in hospital administration.

Dottie frantically paced back and forth over the freshly mown lawn, her hands clamped to the sides of her head without even thinking about the new perm she'd had an hour earlier, and I know how fastidious she is about her hair. She asked everyone on the lawn for their expert medical opinion about whether or not Vaughn would survive, including one neighbor who dabbled in cabinet making and another who couldn't diagnose a cough.

Vaughn survived, flourished actually. And it might very well have been because of all the neighborhood prayers. Dottie had always believed in God but she'd been afraid to say so in front of Vaughn who would've made her feel stupid. He ridiculed anyone who had faith; that's just what he did. She'd called their local bishop as soon as they got to the hospital who'd up and take your time. Maybe you'd use pliers on their fingers first, or start out by shooting them in the leg, so they wouldn't die right away. You'd talk calmly to them about how pathetic they were, smiling sadly as you detailed all the reasons why you had no choice, no choice, but to kill them slowly and painfully because they deserved it. Then maybe you'd reluctantly, out of civic duty, cut off another finger to drag it out. Then maybe a thumb. You'd force them to look at you the whole time too, emphasizing that they'd left you no other option. Then there'd be the satisfaction when you finally took them out of their misery. But you'd still be left with a bitter aftertaste because the dead bastard hadn't suffered enough—that his suffering could never be as awful as what he'd deserved. Well, that's what was going through my head.

"Think about it for a day," he said and got up to leave. "Oh, and keep the photo. I've got others."

dropped what he was doing (he was an electrician by day) and gone straight to Dixie Medical Center to give Vaughn a blessing. Vaughn allowed it because he thought he was on the verge of death. And isn't that the way it is when the chips are down? I wasn't there, but I heard the bishop blessed him with good health and promised he'd heal up, good as new. When he recovered, Vaughn allowed for the possibility that it'd been the blessing that'd done the trick.

Word quickly spread of Vaughn's miraculous recovery and the role his faith had played. My parents were thrilled because now the bad grandpa had finally embraced the faith. Hallelujah! "That Vaughn," my dad said, "has always been a stubborn son of a gun and if it took a heart attack for him to come to his senses, well, then I guess it was worth it." My mom simply reminded everyone that God worked in mysterious ways. It's such a good line because of its universal flexibility. You can apply it to just about any situation. Seriously, you should try. As for me, I believed in prayer but I was suspicious that Vaughn did. Oh, he said he did, but I think he'd been so desperate that he would have taken Catholic communion and the help of a Ouija board if he thought it'd save him. He really had nothing to lose.

Dottie was delighted when Vaughn started going back to church. There he was in his only suit and tie on the third pew for three weeks in a row. The suit had been tailored twenty years and about forty pounds earlier so he couldn't make the button on the jacket reach but, dang it, he was there. Dottie had always wanted to renew their church activity but Vaughn had been a stick in the mud. So, you can only imagine how terribly disappointed she was when, a month later, he got back on the riding mower with the tiny dent on the front bumper instead of going to church. Whaddya know, he'd forgotten all about the prayers that had healed him. In fact, he acted embarrassed by his near-death-bed conversion. "I'm not that gullible, okay?" he said. "What, you've never heard of nitroglycerin? I would have recovered anyway."

My dad wasn't surprised. All he said was, "That Vaughn wouldn't know the truth if it smacked him upside the head."

28

KATE

RICKY COULDN'T BEAR to come right out and ask me for this favor. I'll call it a "favor" here because I don't know what else to call it. But let's be honest; a favor is asking your neighbor if you can borrow a cup of sugar, not asking your wife to have sex with a disgusting loan shark with hairy shoulders.

Seems my devoted husband didn't have the guts to ask me straight up, he left the manila envelope with the photo of the man beaten to a pulp on top of my dresser hoping it would inspire me to action!

We were getting ready for bed and it was late. I'd just stepped out of the shower after returning from work at Lil' Secrets, both my body and hair wrapped in separate towels. My black bra was smeared across the carpet like a skid mark and my black wig was resting atop the head of a faceless Styrofoam mannequin on the dresser.

"What's this?" I asked as I pulled the photo from the envelope. "What the— What *is* this? It's disgusting."

"Oh, that? It's nothing."

"Nothing? What do you mean it's nothing? You have a photo of some guy who looks like he's been beaten to death."

"I don't know. Some guy just gave it to me. It's no big deal."

"What guy, Ricky? What's going on?"

"Don't worry about it, Kate. It's something I've got to work out and I don't want to involve you."

"Talk to me, Ricky. What the hell is going on?"

"It's that Spanos guy."

"What's this got to do with him?"

"It's somebody he beat up," Ricky said.

"Are you serious?" I said and looked again at the photo. "And he took a photo of it? Why would he beat a guy like that and then take a photo of it? And why, Ricky, would he give that photo to *you?*"

"He's just being a prick. Don't worry about it."

"Has he threatened you? Is that what this is?"

"Not really."

"Not really?"

"He's just pissed because I haven't paid him all that money I borrowed."

"But I thought you already paid him back."

"Well, that's what I thought too. I repaid him the whole $10,000 and I even gave him another $5,000 for interest, but now he claims I still owe him another $5,000."

"He can't blackmail you like this! It's extortion or whatever you call it. You need to show this to the police."

"I can't do that," he said.

"Well, if you won't, then I will. This is serious, Ricky."

"If either one of us shows that to the police, I'm a dead man.

You don't know what this guy's capable of. I have no choice—I come up with the $5,000 by tomorrow or that's what'll happen to me."

Ricky sat at the foot of our un-made bed with his head down. He was so weak and incapable, relying on me to bail him out of yet another problem of his own making. I'm no expert on these things, but bobbing through life on your charm and good looks doesn't build strength, or character. I often wondered in those days if I'd been his buoy or his anchor. Maybe I'd been both. Was I aggravating the situation by not demanding he get a job? Was I enabling him by single-handedly funding our lives? Is someone guilty of aiding and abetting their gambling addicted husband by giving him money? Is the spouse of an alcoholic complicit by handing them a drink, or even turning a blind eye? I don't know because these seem like fine lines to me. But I still loved him. You can't always change that.

"So what are we going to do?" I finally asked. There was that "we" again—me adopting his problem.

"I come up with the money or give him what he wants."

"What do you mean 'or give him what he wants?'" I waited. "What does he want, Ricky?"

"You don't want to know."

"What the hell is that supposed to mean? What does he want, Ricky?"

"It's nothing. I shouldn't have said anything."

"Ricky, you tell me right now or I'm calling the police. I swear it."

He drew a breath. "You. He wants you."

"What are you *talking* about?"

"I wasn't going to tell you. It's crazy and I'd never agree to it anyway. So let's just drop it, okay?"

"Drop what? What the hell does he want with me?"

Ricky was such a coward. He was still sitting there on the edge of the bed looking down at the floor, then out the window, then at the door, then back at his shoes. When he'd run out of places to look, he finally looked back at me. "So, whew," he said. "I'm not sure how to put this."

"Put what? Just tell me, Ricky. What in the hell does he want with me?"

"He says he'll forgive the debt if he can have you. If not, I'm dead."

"Have me?"

"Yeah. Don't worry. I didn't even consider it, and I know you wouldn't either."

"Have me?"

"Yeah, he wants to sleep with you and then he'll call it good."

It took a moment to register. I looked down at Ricky and then at the photo from the manila envelope. The anger and revulsion welled up and the urge to vomit was there—that feeling you get when you start to flush and sweat from every pore and you know it's coming. I threw the photo at him and ran into the bathroom, slamming the door.

I opened the medicine cabinet and tried to pry the lid off a bottle of Lortab but I was shaking so hard I couldn't do it. I slammed the medicine cabinet shut and sat on the toilet seat and cried.

After a few minutes there was a tap on the door. "Kate, listen, I'm sorry, okay?" It sounded like his head was leaning into the door. "Don't worry about it, okay? I wouldn't let you do it even if you wanted to."

"Even if I *wanted to?*" I practically jumped up from the toilet seat, totally hysterical by now. "Geez, Ricky, thanks! Thanks a lot for that!"

I heard him turn the knob but I'd locked it. "Come on, Babe, open the door. I'll work something out."

"Fuck you!"

"Come on, Kate. I never agreed to it. I only told him I'd talk to you."

"You told him you'd *talk to me* about it? You're an asshole, Ricky!" I screamed. "I'm your *wife* for God's sake!"

"I know, I know, and I'm sorry. Just open the door so we can talk about this like adults."

"Oh, so now you want to be an *adult?* Well, fuck you!"

"Settle down, Kate. You're overreacting. It's not that big of a deal. Come on. Be reasonable here."

Right. I was overreacting. And it wasn't that big of a deal. Ricky always had a way of turning it against me—painting me as the one who was bitchy and unreasonable. It was his good old mind fuckery at work again. The way he'd twist things to manipulate me. Why was I overreacting when he was always so right about everything? Why, according to Ricky, did I always have PMS whenever I was in a bad mood, meaning I wasn't in the mood to adore him?

"I'll fix it, okay?" he said.

"But you asked me, Ricky. You asked me and you know it! So what am I supposed to say? Huh? You know I can't say no. So fuck you!"

"Can't we talk about this? Come on, open the door."

"You want to talk, Ricky? Well then, let's talk! Let's talk about how you lied to me about how much you owed him. Let's talk about how you left that photo so I'd see it. Let's talk about how you'd hand me over to that bag of shit to save your own skin! Yeah, Ricky, let's talk about it!"

"You act like I wanted this to happen. I did everything I could to leave you out of this."

"Bullshit!"

I could still hear his forehead leaning into the door. "Listen, Kate, you haven't had to do anything yet. I'm only telling you what he said."

"I haven't had to do anything yet? Is that what you just said? To hell with you, Ricky! I've given you every dime I had. I've worked my ass off stripping for dirty old men while you sit around and gamble all day. But no more, Ricky. No more!"

"You've given me everything you have? Really, Kate?"

"You're damned right I have!"

"What about all the money in the sock? Huh? You think I'm stupid? You give me a little money here and there and then act like I owe you my goddamned life! Well, fuck you, too!"

I threw open the bathroom door. My make-up was smeared with tears and snot and the towel around my wet hair had come undone and fallen to the floor. "You want the money I've been trying to save? You want to take every last dime we have and blow it on your insane gambling addiction? Huh? Is that what you want?" I was screaming in his face, spittle flying. "Then take it!" I pushed past him and opened the dresser drawer and threw the sock at him. Then I pulled out the whole drawer and flung that at him, too. He jumped out of the way and it crashed to the floor sending balls of socks everywhere. "Take it! Take everything we have and give it to that goddamned pervert!"

Then I lowered my voice and said each word slowly for emphasis, but it wasn't an act, I can tell you that. "Don't you *ever* ask me for another dime." I was now heaving with breath, more upset than I'd ever been in my life. "Not a fucking dime."

I threw on the nearest clothes I could find, my hair still wet and uncombed, and grabbed my car keys that I'd left on the kitchen counter.

"Where are you going?"

I left and slammed the door. I had no plan, no other place to go, but I couldn't stay with Ricky. Not that night. I called my old roommate, Deborah, who was willing to let me crash on her sofa. I didn't tell her that Ricky had negotiated to sell me to a pig for $5,000, only that we'd had a fight. It would have been too humiliating to tell her the godawful truth.

I lay on the sofa trying to think rationally. In the dark I could not see how messy the apartment was but the coffee table was littered with ashtrays, papers, fashion magazines, and a few dirty dishes, one with the crust of a pizza slice. It was quiet except for the ticking of a clock. What would Deborah have said if I *had* explained it all to her, if I'd laid it all on the line? Would she have been as mortified as I was? Who would she have killed first, Ricky or Victor? Or would she have told me to calm down—that it was only sex. Sex with a disgusting hairy pig to be sure, but still only sex. Would she have reminded me that I wasn't living in a nunnery, after all—that the convent hadn't sold me to a pack of lecherous, heterosexually starved priests?

I was no prude where sex was concerned, obviously, but being coerced into having sex with a fat sexiest scum bag without a conscience? To cover my dear lying husband's gambling debt? It was so repulsive that I wanted to shower and throw up on him, on both of them actually.

It was more about Ricky's betrayal than it was about Victor Spanos, disgusting as Spanos was. I could plug my nose and tolerate his disgusting hands on me long enough to save Ricky from a potentially fatal beating. It would not kill me. But what I couldn't tolerate was Ricky's willingness to let me do it—no, *asking* me to do it.

I dialed my parent's telephone number early the next morning from Deborah's apartment. I took one more drag from my cigarette while the phone was ringing, then crushed it in the ashtray on the coffee table next to the sofa where I'd slept. Maybe my mom had stashed some secret cash of her own to help a daughter in need.

"Hi, Mom, it's me."

"My goodness, Katherine! It's so good to hear from you. You never call this early in the morning. Are you all right?"

"Yeah, Mom, I'm fine. I was just calling to . . ." my voice cracked with emotion.

"Katherine? Honey, are you okay?"

I regained control. "Yeah, Mom. I was just wondering what you guys were up to. How's Kylie?"

"Why, she's doing very well. We all are. But I'm worried about you, Sweetheart. Is everything okay?"

"Yeah. I've just run into a financial bind and wondered if you guys could help me out with a little loan."

"What on earth is the matter? Is it serious? How much do you need?"

"It's not too serious, but I need about $5,000."

"Five thousand dollars? Oh my goodness, I'd have to ask your father, but I know we don't have that much anywhere. Maybe your father would be willing to cosign on a loan for you if it's that important. He makes all the financial decisions, of course."

"I need it sooner than that. I just wondered if you had, you know, some money tucked away for emergencies. Something like that. I'd for sure pay you right back."

"I know we did, but we spent everything we had on a down payment for the kids' braces. The orthodontist put us on a monthly pay plan for the rest. Maybe you could do something like that. Why do you need it?"

Like I, the pathological liar, was suddenly going to spring forth with the truth. *"Well, Mom, see, here's the thing. I'm married to a gambling addict who borrowed money from a scum bag and now this scum bag is going to beat him to death unless he comes up with $5,000 by tonight. But here's the good news, Mom: This scum bag will forgive the gambling debt if I have sex with him. Isn't that just grand?"* Instead I said, "It's just to pay off a stupid debt."

"Debt is one of Satan's tools," she said. "That's why church leaders always caution us to stay out of debt."

"I know. But this is something that just came up."

"I wish we could help you, Katherine. But I'm sure you'll be able to work something out. I'd try to get on a monthly payment plan if I were you. Maybe dad can walk you through how you go about doing that sort of thing."

"No, that's okay, but a monthly plan might be a good idea," I said. It would've done no good to say, *"Yeah, maybe you're right. Let me run it by him. He might be willing to settle for monthly blow jobs until he feels like he's got his money's worth."* It would've only confused and upset her.

"Say, Katherine, before I let you go, I just heard that Keith Murphy's father, you know the boy you used to date? Anyway, I just heard he had an awful heart attack."

"Oh, I'm sorry to hear that."

"That Keith was such a nice young man. I know your father didn't always care for him, but I thought he was a good boy. I heard he married a girl from over in Santa Clara."

"That's nice, Mom, but sorry I kinda have to go. Say hi to dad and the rest of the fam."

I called Ricky at noon. There was sleep in his voice and that struck a nerve. He could sleep until noon? On a day like this? If I were him I'd be on a Greyhound going somewhere remote, not sleeping the day away. But not Ricky who'd once again shoveled his shit over to make it mine.

"So what are you going to do, Ricky?"

"Um, I'm not sure. What are you thinking?"

"Can't you get it from somebody else?" I asked. "Don't you have any friends who can loan you the money?"

"I've already tried."

Ricky didn't have many friends. The few he had probably refused because Ricky had reminded them for years that he wasn't a nine-to-five kind of guy. They must've known the only way they'd ever get their money back was if he robbed Peter, or pulled the ol' Rent-A-Wife routine.

"Are you waiting for me to say I'll sleep with him?"

"Only if you want to. Wait, I didn't mean it like that. But . . . yeah, if you'd be willing to that'd be great."

"What if I didn't?"

"You saw the photo."

"Yeah, Ricky, I saw the photo. You made sure of that."

"So, then should I . . . go ahead and call him?"

Ricky had no other plan. I was his wife and he was on the verge of being beaten to within an inch of his life. What would *you* have done? No, really, what would you have done if you'd been me? Am I the only one who thought I had no good choices? Was I so far gone to believe it was the least worst option? I'm not sure the "in sickness and in health" provision quite fit this circumstance, but I had vowed in that sacred drive-thru ceremony at the *Si, Como No* to help him out whenever I could. And technically I could. But here he was, once again, looking for me to save him and I didn't see much reciprocity. Like I said, it was the ask that broke my heart—that he would ask me to do such a thing, and then hope I'd do it. And what really hurt was to accept what we both knew, that when push came to shove, I would do it.

"I'll do it, Ricky. But I swear to God I'll do it only if you promise to get a real job. I'm not going to do this just to get you out of some temporary bind."

"I'll look into that for sure."

"No, Ricky. You won't look into it. You'll do it, because if you don't, we're through. I swear to God, Ricky, we're through."

"Okay. I know this is a big deal, but it's not like you, you know, you haven't been with other guys."

Was he serious? And was he really that stupid? To say a thing like that at a time when I held his life in my hands? Maybe he thought my job made this easier. Maybe he thought there was no difference between being a stripper and a whore. Or maybe he just didn't care. "Fuck you, Ricky!" I slammed down the phone.

I presume most men who'd seen me in the previous handful of years assumed I was more sexually active than I actually was, and that assumption probably would have been a reasonable one to make. It might even have been a reasonable assumption if I worked in a bakery shop instead of a strip club. But despite my jobs at Sugar & Spice and Lil' Secrets, I'd only had full-blown sex with two men in my entire life; Keith Murphy a few times in high school and Ricky. That's it. I'm not claiming to be all virtuous with that admission, only that it might surprise a lot of people who thought they knew me.

I overheard the phone call later that afternoon and it's a miracle I didn't vomit on both of them. Ricky picks up the phone and dials up Scum Ball. Scum Ball talks loud, so I could hear his end of the call.

"Okay, Vic, she'll do it."

"So you're saying I can have sex with your wife?"

"I don't have any more money so, yeah, I guess the answer is yes."

"I'm giving you a deal, Ricky. I don't normally pay five grand to get laid. You remember that."

"So, like, when . . ."

"How about tonight. I'll get me a room at the Tropicana. I'll call you with the room number. Have her there at nine."

"Okay."

"Oh, and Ricky."

"Yeah?"

"You owe me one."

I walked through the Tropicana casino to the bank of elevators in the back and took one to the eighth floor. The elevator ride was too fast. I'd dressed in the baggiest, un-sexiest clothes I could find and hid behind an extra layer of make-up. I knocked on his door. When it opened, he stood there with his silk shirt unbuttoned to the bottom of his chest. I could practically taste the pre-vomit bile in my mouth.

"I knew you'd come," he said. "But what's with the wig?"

I said nothing. The wig was just another shield, albeit a flimsy one. I walked past him to the middle of the room where I immediately began taking my clothes off. I wanted to get this over with as quickly as possible.

"Whoa, whoa, whoa, slow down." He came up to me from behind and put his hands on my shoulders. I recoiled. His cheap cologne smelled like a urinal cake but at least it compensated for his rank BO, or at least it tried to. Wouldn't you think he would have showered? When I was finally undressed, he threw me onto the bed. There was no romance, thank God, and zero excitement. He tried to kiss me but I turned my head. He then got on top of me, this hairy beast of a human being, and I closed my eyes tight. It hurt, but not because he was big. In fact, it gave me a slight measure of satisfaction that his penis was so small.

I was out into the hallway within fifteen minutes, Scum Ball having paid the equivalent of $20,000 per hour for the right to lie on top of a woman who was repulsed by him, held her breath, and barely moved.

I didn't feel like going right back home, so I drove around for another half hour. Ricky was in the apartment when I returned an hour later and do you want to know what he was holding? A vase of roses. I swear to God. A fucking vase of red roses with the little card on the end of a long stick that looks like a devil's spear. The card read: "Thanks for helping me out of this bind." He had never given me flowers before.

"Here," he said. "I hope you like them."

I took the vase of flowers and threw it at him. He ducked and the vase shattered against the kitchen cabinets sending water and shards of glass everywhere. I ran into the bathroom and locked the door, then I knelt in front of the toilet and vomited until there was nothing left but acid-flavored strings of spit. I turned on the shower and stood under it with the water scalding me, my hands pressed against the tile and my head hanging under the faucet. I spent thirty minutes trying to scrub him off me.

When I returned to the bedroom, Ricky was lying on the bed with the TV remote in his hand. I crawled into bed and turned toward the wall, hugging my side of the bed.

"So, like, do you want to talk about it?" he asked.

I ignored him. Besides, what was there to say? You're welcome? These two men had forced my hand in the most despicable of ways. A few minutes later, I felt him scooting over to my side and he put his hand on my shoulder and then started to rub my back.

I partially rolled over to face him. "You've got to be kidding me."

"I just thought, you know, maybe we could, you know . . ."

I turned toward the wall again. "Do not touch me."

I had crossed another line. A big one. I had sex with another man for money. There are many shades of gray, but this was black and white.

29

KATHERINE

THE FEUD GOT STARTED when Kenny was a teenager. Nobody knew at the time that it would lead to a political campaign. I wasn't present for all of it, but I'd talked to enough of the participants to give you the gist of what happened.

Kenny got his new driver's license and was antsy to drive. Our next-door neighbors, the Rasmussen's, were out of town and Kenny and his buddies got this harebrained idea to drive my dad's car over their front lawn late one night. Doing donuts on your neighbor's front lawn might sound like a stupid thing to do, I know, but you don't know Kenny. I think his brain had been tampered with.

The Rasmussen's had been neighbors for as long as I can remember and were in the same ward as my parents but I never got the sense that my dad liked Brother Rasmussen, probably because he drove a Cadillac Seville and my dad thought anyone who drove a Cadillac was too full of himself, especially when all we could afford was a hand-me-down minivan and an old Ford station wagon. On the other hand, the Rasmussen's had one of those above-ground swimming pools in their backyard, so their level of pretentiousness was highly debatable. In addition to the showiness of driving a Seville, the Rasmussen's only had two kids so my dad was suspicious of their commitment to the gospel of multiplying and replenishing the earth. They were selfish, he said.

Anyway, the Rasmussen's noticed the tire tracks when they returned from their trip and began a neighborhood investigation. Sister Felt, who was an incorrigible busybody, lived across the street and monitored all the neighborhood coming's and going's. Unfortunately for Kenny, she'd been up taking her obnoxious little schnauzer out to pee in the middle of the night when she saw the boys go on their joy ride in my dad's car. She couldn't wait to tell Brother Rasmussen who'd done it, and a neighborhood feud was born.

"I'll talk to Kenny," my dad said to Brother Rasmussen, "but that doesn't sound like something my son would've done."

"Well," said Brother Rasmussen, "it was your station wagon and Maxine Felt said she saw the whole thing."

Kenny eventually confessed after initially claiming he couldn't quite remember whether he had driven across their lawn in the middle of the night, or not. My dad made him call Brother Rasmussen to apologize, which Kenny did but with less sincerity than Brother Rasmussen would've liked (again, you'd have to know Kenny). That should've ended it right there, but then Rasmussen's nineteen-year-old son thought it'd be funny to return the favor to my dad's lawn a few weeks later. I hadn't seen my dad that mad since Kenny took his pea-shooter to church and hit Sister Collingsworth in the back of the head from two pews back. My mom was mortified because Sister Collingsworth was the unofficial matron of the ward and everyone was nice to her because she was in charge of the ward bazaar and doled out the assignments. My mom reminded Kenny that he could have put an eye out. I don't know what her fascination was with putting eyes out, but my mom used that line whenever there was a dirt clod, snowball, peashooter, or frisbee in the vicinity, even though in all my years I'd never seen an eye put out. There's always a first time I suppose, but I would have been surprised if you could put an eye out during the commission of a joy ride across the neighbor's lawn.

Kenny's joy ride had been a few years earlier but the wounds had festered. The Rasmussen's and Coombs's still waved to each other out of neighborly duty but the waves had been lukewarm—the obligatory wave followed by muttered condemnation under the breath to no one in particular.

Then the Rasmussen's got a dog named Puffer.

Puffer may have been a good dog and he didn't bark but he had no sense of boundaries and liked to wander. The grass on my dad's side of the driveway got him going for some reason. Maybe it's because my dad has always been a fertilizer freak, I don't know. Anyway, Puffer liked to be comfortable when he did his business and he happened to be more comfortable on the Coombs side.

My dad let it go, at first. He'd been the bishop several years earlier, during my teens, and was determined not to hold a public grudge (his grudges were mostly private ones). But Brother Rasmussen knew darn good and well where Puffer did his Number Two's. And did he care? Nope. My dad retaliated by scooping it up and piling it just inside the Rasmussen's boundary. This seemed awfully petty to Brother Rasmussen, so rather than clean it up and discipline Puffer like he probably should have, he'd simply scoot the pile back over to my dad's side. Back and forth the pile of poo went. The driveway had become the DMZ for dog feces.

Nothing was said about this trying situation between my dad and Brother Rasmussen. Not a word. Not even when my dad stepped in it while mowing the lawn. He did, however, make an exaggerated scene scraping the poo off the bottom of his shoe with a popsicle stick. They still waved to each other but there was bad blood in the system. My dad wanted to catch Puffer in the act and have the dog catcher haul him away. In fact, he'd become so obsessed with Puffer's bowel movements that he'd come to know his schedule. (Puffer, it turns out, was quite regular.)

One day after mowing around the pile, my dad scattered some Bacon Bits about ten feet onto his side of the property line and then crouched behind a laurel bush with his new Sony camcorder, recording Puffer in the act. He narrated the entire video, describing the date, day, and time. *My name is Dale Michael Coombs. I live at 3454 Sun River Drive, St. George, Utah. Today's date is Wednesday, June 14th. I'm standing approximately fifteen feet inside my property line and . . .* Then, with the recorder still on, he zoomed in on the pile and then back out again to properly document that the deposit was unmistakably made on a patch of grass where my dad paid property taxes. Armed with this unimpeachable evidence, he called animal control.

My mom was embarrassed by the whole thing, and so was Sister Rasmussen. "Please, Dale, let it go," my mom pled. "This is ridiculous."

My dad, however, was unmoved. "Well, Jackie, you might feel differently if you were the one who had to scoop it up."

The wives tried to reason with their stubborn husbands but neither one would budge—not until the other made a full public apology. My mom even smuggled some homemade zucchini bread over to the Rasmussen's with a sweet little note and Sister Rasmussen reciprocated by refusing to accept payment for Korbin's weekly piano lessons at her house.

Animal control chose not take Puffer into custody, but they did speak to Brother Rasmussen who called it a classic case of entrapment. "Wait just a second," my dad said. "*He's* mad at *me?* It's not my dog and I'm not the one who started this." My dad was also upset that his tax dollars didn't protect the citizenry from dogs with roaming bowels. He earnestly believed this lawlessness amounted to a denial of his right to life, liberty, and the pursuit of happiness.

"I'm running for County Commissioner," my dad declared. "I've about had enough."

"Why, I think that's wonderful, Dale," my mom said. "I think you'd do a fantastic job. But I hope you're doing it for the right reason."

"You're darned right I am. Government should enforce its ordinances and I intend to make a difference."

My dad liked the sound of that phrase so much that he made it his campaign slogan: *"Coombs, Making a Difference."* There was an open seat on the three-member county commission and several candidates wanted the job. All of them were Republicans, like my dad. No big surprise there—just about everyone in my town was a Republican. In fact, when I was a kid, our neighbors three doors down were Democrats, and I'd heard that Democrats were sort of like communists. That's why we needed the bomb shelters at school—to protect us from the communists. I was even leery about walking past that neighbor's house on my way home from school because no one wants to be kidnapped by a communist.

A few friends and extended family members made contributions to my dad's campaign after my dad guilted them into it. One neighbor finally relented to get my dad off his back and because he thought it was tax deductible. When he learned it wasn't, he politely asked for his money back, which was awkward because my dad had already used the money to buy a stack of flyers. I doubt the guy ended up voting for him. The flyer was a big hit though—a glossy headshot of my dad with an American flag unfurled in the background. It looked very patriotic to me.

My dad's campaign staff consisted of us kids. We passed out the flyers and talked to the citizenry about the importance of electing our dad. What a hoot. Who'd vote for a guy just because some fourteen-year-old kid pulled a bent flyer from his pocket and told them to vote for his dad? Nothing was said about the dog, but I assumed my dad's first official act as county commissioner would be to order Puffer's immediate incarceration at the pound.

My dad rented three large billboards along the freeway that ran through the county. The billboards were essentially a humongous family photo of my dad with his brood. We all wore matching denim shirts for the photo. Kylie was in front (by design, I think, for the whole compassion angle). She stood next to my daughter Jenna, who didn't look happy at all. *Dale Coombs, Protecting Family Values!* the billboard read.

Now, you tell me. Who wouldn't vote for that?

30

KATE

I WAS STILL REELING from being leased out by my husband. And, honestly, who could blame me? Adding insult to injury, the next morning I stepped on a shard of glass from the flower vase I'd thrown. Ricky had been good to pick up most of the larger pieces but hadn't bothered to sweep. I hobbled over to the sofa on the side of my foot with my cup of coffee in one hand and a pair of tweezers in the other.

I'm sure Ricky felt bad about renting me out to Victor Spanos but I swear there was a new spring in his step, just knowing he was off the hook. He'd promised to never borrow money again, and I believed him. Sort of. At least I believed he'd never borrow from Spanos again.

Ricky also bought me a diamond necklace, which was awfully big of him because he'd used my sock money to do it. I told him I didn't want the necklace and threw it in the kitchen trash can, but I retrieved it when he wasn't looking because it made no sense to throw away a perfectly good diamond necklace, especially one I paid for.

"So, are you ever going to talk to me?" he asked.

"You have no idea how awful that was for me, Ricky. No idea."

"Hey, I already said I'm sorry."

This was true. He'd said he was sorry about ten times, but he'd essentially been shamed into it and it didn't feel heartfelt. Besides, there are only so many times a person can apologize before it just becomes annoying. And he had reached beyond that point.

The next day Ricky conspicuously left a copy of the classified ads from the newspaper on the kitchen table after he'd read the sports section. Notice I said the next day and not the next morning. He didn't get out of bed until 10:30—conduct from a less than sincere job hunter. He'd circled a few jobs for my benefit, but I doubt he actually called on any of them. After all, I highly doubt he was qualified to be the "supervisor of a mid-size engineering firm specializing in munitions." Racking my brain here, I can't think of a job he *would* be qualified for. How would he even fill out a resume? Education: none. Career goals: none. Experience: gambling. Hobbies and extracurricular: gambling. References: casino cocktail waitresses and strippers. So I don't know for the life of me who would actually hire him. Fair enough, I suppose he might make a decent pimp.

A few days later, my mom called me with the exhilarating news that my dad was running for public office.

"Hi, Mom. How's the family?"

"We're all doing very well. Kenny and Alison are expecting and we're over the moon about that."

"Yeah, you told me. I was a little surprised because they've only been married for a few months?"

"I know. Isn't it exciting?"

Personally, I thought it was more depressing than exciting, but my new "almost nineteen-year-old" sister-in-law was apparently pleasing everyone with her fertility.

"Is everything else okay?"

"Well," my mom said, "you're not going to believe this, but your father is running for County Commissioner!"

"Wow, that's great. Right?"

"Oh, he's so excited. I haven't seen your dad this worked up since he was called to be the bishop."

"So, like, when is it?"

"The election is in November, so we only have a few months to get ready. Honestly, I don't know *what* I'll do if he wins. I'm a nervous wreck because we've never been famous or anything. Your dad wants to have a family photo for the campaign and he's going to put it on a huge billboard—right on the freeway!"

"Wow."

"We've got the photo shoot lined up for this Saturday. Your dad wants all of us in the photo and we're so excited around here. Uncle Reed has all the camera equipment and everything."

"Well, I had plans but if—"

"I know it'd mean a lot to him if you came."

"Okay, yeah, I'll see what I can do."

"And after the photos we thought it'd be fun if we all fanned out across St. George to pass out flyers. We'll have a ball!"

I would've rather passed a kidney stone than traipse around St. George rounding up votes for a candidate who didn't think I should go to college because I was a girl. I love my dad and was happy for him if that's what he really wanted to do. However, if given a truth serum, I probably wouldn't have voted for him. Then again, his opponent would probably be just as bad. These were the same politicians who'd put the kibosh on the play *Mama Mia* that had planned to run at the local playhouse because they said it didn't meet community standards. It didn't meet community standards? *Mama Mia?* Yeah, because the lead's daughter could have been the biological daughter of three different men.

"I think I can make it for the photo, but I have to get back Saturday night for work. So, yeah, I probably won't be able to pass out the flyers."

"We scheduled the photo shoot for early morning so you could be there. That'll give us plenty of time to pass out the flyers. You'll be back to Las Vegas by three, at the latest. It'll be a fun family activity!"

I'd been outmaneuvered.

"Oh, and Katherine, I think dad would like it if you wore something nice for the photo. You know—something modest."

I showed up that Saturday morning without my wig and makeup in the most conservative blouse I had because I didn't own a prairie dress. In the meantime, my dad got this brilliant idea that we'd all wear matching denim shirts. Talk about dorky. There we were, a huge family portrait right off the freeway, a regular old Brady Bunch in matching denim. I was slightly mortified. And it bugged me that I had to suffer this public humiliation all because the Rasmussen's dog kept shitting on our lawn.

I was given a stack of flyers after the photos were taken and assigned to the Valley View 10th ward boundaries. That's the area on the other side of the high school. In our town, the locals describe areas of town by ward boundaries. The library? Oh, that's over in the Santa Clara 5th ward. The courthouse? That'd be over in the Desert Hills 7th ward. So, anyway, I walked several blocks in that denim shirt ringing doorbells. Ding dong. "I hope you'll vote for my dad. Here's a flyer." Next house.

I think my dad had mixed feelings about me being on the team to pass out the flyers. He needed the manpower but he also knew I didn't present the right image. Sure, I had the denim shirt but it was a little snug fitting with my implants and there was the platinum hair and, well, you know the look. I didn't look like a girl from *Little House on the Prairie*. But, alas, the ward boundary I'd been assigned to was where most of the non-members in town lived, the brave souls who'd moved to St. George even though they weren't members of the church. I'd say it was "only" seventy percent Mormon. So, who knows, maybe I'd inspire one of the gentiles to vote for my dad.

My dad's opponent, Red Harman, tried to outgun my dad on the whole "family values" theme. According to Red, my dad's family-value roots were pretty shallow because he didn't own a single gun. And how could you be a genuine family values candidate if you were some namby-pamby citizen who wasn't properly armed? How would you protect the homestead from a Russian invasion? How could you claim God inspired the U.S. Constitution and then turn around spit on the 2nd Amendment? How could you look a voter in the eye and tell him you honor freedom and give a hoot about our beloved county?

What did my dad do to rebut this scandalous charge? He went and bought a rifle, that's what. But politics being what they are, Red then switched his line of attack. He said he'd been contacted by my dad's neighbor, a Mr. Phillip Rasmussen, who claimed my dad was a petty tyrant who threw dog shit onto his yard. "And in the most diabolical and twisted turn, my opponent, Dale Coombs, even recorded it on video." My dad was so mad I thought Red Harman and Brother Rasmussen were going to be the first two victims of his brand-new gun.

31

RICKY

I WAS HAVING A SMOKE with Kate on the balcony of our apartment two weeks later when Spanos called me again. I walked inside to take the call when I saw the caller ID because I was never supposed to speak to him again. And, trust me, I didn't want to.

"Hey, Ricky. It's me. Vic."

"What do you want? We're square."

"Actually, that's what I wanted to talk to you about. See, your wife really got off on me, but she didn't really rock my world. You know what I mean?"

I was so pissed I couldn't speak.

"So, I've been thinking that I'm gonna need that five thousand you still owe me."

"No way, Vic." I was shaking with rage. "No fucking way! We had a deal!"

"No, Ricky, that's not entirely true. I told you if your wife had sex with me, I'd *consider* calling off the debt. Well, I've done some considering and she was so bad I can't forgive the whole thing in good conscience."

I would have killed him if he'd been in front of me. I'm serious. I would have repeatedly stabbed the motherfucker in the heart with a butcher knife until someone pulled me off.

"But I'll tell you what," Spanos said. "How about I knock off $500. That's more than she was worth, but I'll do it because we're friends."

"Go to hell, Vic!"

"Listen, if she wants to do it again, I'd probably knock off another $500."

"Fuck you, Vic! We're done!"

"No, Ricky, we're not." He was calm, which infuriated me even more. "You still owe me $4,500 and I'm gonna need that right away. But I'll give you a few more days because we've been able to work so well together."

"No way. We had a deal."

There was only breathing on the other end of the line. "I'll get it from you Ricky, one way or the other."

I slammed my fist into the kitchen wall, busting a hole in the sheetrock next to the pantry. There went Kate's security deposit. It turns out I sprained my hand, but I didn't even feel the pain until later. I only wished it'd been his ugly face.

"Shit!" I yelled after he hung up on me.

Kate had come in from the balcony when she heard me yelling. "What's the matter? Is everything okay?"

I was facing the refrigerator and didn't turn around.

"Ricky? Are you okay? What's going on?"

"That was Spanos."

I turned around to face her.

"You promised me, Ricky. You promised me you'd never do business with him again."

"I know."

"You promised me and now a few days later you're already talking to him again? How could you do that to me? He's a scumbag, Ricky, and you know it!"

"I didn't call him—he called me. I swear."

"Then what does he want?"

"He's reneging on the deal."

I can't adequately describe the look on her face. I guess I'd have to say it was equal parts disbelief, revulsion, and more anger than I thought was humanly possible. I think she would have stabbed the motherfucker in the heart, too.

"No he didn't, Ricky." She was shaking her head back and forth. "No, no he didn't. No he didn't."

I didn't say anything because what *do* you say in moments like that?

"He promised you." There wasn't the visible rage. Not quite yet. But I knew Kate, and it was building. She was ready to blow.

"I know."

"I'll kill him," she said slowly and deliberately. "I swear to God I'll kill him if he tries to touch me again." She turned around to face the balcony. "I'll kill him," she whispered to herself.

"He says I still owe him $4,500." She didn't move. She didn't flinch. Her back was to me and I wasn't sure if she'd heard me. "I owed him $5,000 but he agreed to knock $500 off because of, you know, what you did." What a stupid thing to say. I should've kept my mouth shut.

She turned toward the kitchen counter and picked up the large ceramic bowl that held our spatulas. It was glossy yellow with a black rooster on it. I'm not a sentimental guy but the bowl had been the only thing I inherited from my grandmother. Every time I looked at it I thought about the way she'd fuss over my favorite lunch of grilled cheese sandwiches and potato chips in her small kitchen with the cornucopia wallpaper and that ceramic bowl on the counter next to her Sunbeam Mixmaster. Kate picked it up and threw it at the kitchen cabinets where it shattered, spatulas flying everywhere and the rooster now officially extinct. She looked for something else to throw because now she was completely out of control. The only thing in range was a framed photo of the two of us standing outside the wedding chapel at *Si, Como No* that someone on the staff had taken. She threw it at me but her aim was off and it cracked the microwave door.

"Calm down," I yelled. "Get a hold of yourself."

"I will not calm down. This has got to end."

32

KEITH

I WAS AN ONLY CHILD and it was quiet, orderly, and boring at my house when I was growing up. Both my parents worked and I was a solitary latch-key kid. So it was quite an adjustment when I married into the Coombs family. There was always so much *action* and I loved it. I loved it so much I decided I wanted a big family, too. I didn't think they'd come all at once though. Sometimes I still pinch myself that I got married to Katherine Coombs who was the hottest girl in high school. It hadn't been in the plan. At all. But it turned out pretty well. Except for maybe my arm. I even got along with Katherine's dad who wasn't much fun. He was just so buttoned up. Katherine told me stories of growing up with him and it sounded tough.

Even though Katherine grew up with all those brothers, it was pretty obvious she didn't understand boys. Take the case of Jacob, our oldest. He was a great kid but Katherine freaked out when his school's principal called. She'd sent him to his room and threatened Armageddon when I got home from work. Jacob probably figured I'd take a belt to him, even though I'd never taken a belt to anybody in my life. I was more of a guilt guy.

"The principal called," Katherine said the second I walked in from work.

"Which one?" I wasn't trying to be a smart aleck. We had kids in junior high, elementary, and pre-school.

"Mr. Carter, from Cedar Middle School, and he wasn't happy, I can tell you that. We've got a big problem on our hands."

"What happened?"

I got the whole dramatic story. It turns out the principal had planned an end-of-school-year barbeque for the faculty hosted by the PTA president who lived a few streets away from us. Jacob and his buddies found out about it and spent an hour filling water balloons, then hid in the bushes in a field behind the PTA president's backyard. When the party was in full swing, the boys started lobbing the water balloons over the fence, one after the other, like a naval artillery barrage. Bombs away! Water balloons landed in the potato salad and bowls of chips. The buns got soaked and so did the brownies.

The teachers ran for cover from the pelting but they got soaked, too. Mrs. Ronstadt (who I hated from the parent-teacher's conference), was livid when her platinum bouffant got drenched. There was a direct hit on Mrs. Duckworth, too. She said she feared for her very life. "I thought I'd been shot," she'd said. The boys also landed a direct hit on Mrs. Tucker's upper back, right between the shoulder blades. Mrs. Tucker was the drama teacher and was a towering woman who was "big boned" as they say and wasn't one to trifle with. She could've been an offensive lineman on the high school football team had her eligibility not expired thirty years earlier. Rather than run for cover like the other faculty members, Mrs. Tucker heroically turned toward the incoming fire and ran toward the fence in an impressive show of bravery. It was brave but dumb because she got hit again in the face which knocked off her eyeglasses. I was relieved to know Jacob wasn't enrolled in drama that year.

After draining their arsenal, the boys ran through the field and then cut through the Livingston's backyard. That's when thirteen-year-old Brittany Livingston spotted them and ratted them out, just like a girl would. There was even talk of a citizen's arrest by Mrs. Tucker who was determined that these boys, these felons-in-waiting, face the full weight of the criminal justice system. Me, I didn't even know how to go about making a citizen's arrest. I mean, I'd heard of them but never seen one properly executed. Anyway, the boys had all eventually come clean in the principal's office the next day and were expelled for the last two days of school. Seriously, the last two days when all they do is sign yearbooks anyway. The expulsion backfired because it made them the most popular kids in the ninth grade and summer vacation heroes—something the principal should've seen coming.

Katherine breathlessly told me all this after dragging me down the hall by my elbow and into our bedroom before I even had time to change out of my work clothes. She thought we should check out one of those wilderness camps for wayward teens because Jacob was destined for a life of crime. She imagined him featured on one of those Dateline shows where they reconstruct the crime and nobody, I mean nobody, seems to get away with anything. They always make a mistake—they always leave a trail of evidence. The bottom line is this: Never kill anyone and in particular not your spouse, especially if you've just taken out a big life insurance policy on her and have a girlfriend on the side.

Personally, I didn't think Jacob's theatrics were anywhere close to Dateline material. Not even wilderness boot camp material. In fact, I thought it was actually quite funny and was something I probably would have done when I was his age. Of course, I had to pretend this was something that required strict parental attention because Katherine was flipping out. "You need to discipline him," she said. "You need to call him in *this second*." Okay, fine, I said and we called him into our bedroom.

Jacob walked in, head down and utterly repentant, for he had already learned the valuable lesson that everyone loves a repentant sinner. And because he appeared to have learned this vital lesson, it was hard to know if he was truly repentant or just faking it. My guess is it was more act than not, that he and his friends were still laughing their guts out about it, but I figured I'd give him the benefit of the doubt. Before closing our bedroom door behind him on the way in, I overheard the other kids gleefully shout that Jacob was in big trouble from mom and dad. I imagined at least one of them was hovering just outside in the hallway, ear cupped to the door and finger to lips, shushing the others so they could be given a full report.

Jacob sat on the upholstered bench at the end of our bed. The bench was only about eighteen inches tall and his knees angled sharply up from the bench because he had grown so tall and all, it seemed, within the past year.

"I'm so disappointed in you," Katherine began.

"Sorry, Mom. We just thought it'd be funny."

"You thought it'd be *funny?* Do you realize you could've put an eye out?"

"But they were just water balloons."

"They could be dangerous weapons," she said.

I know I shouldn't have undermined her because he needed to be disciplined but I couldn't resist. "Yes, son," I said, "this is very serious. Those teachers could have drowned."

Katherine turned on me. "So now you think this is *funny?* Is that it? You think getting a call from the principal is all fun and games?"

"Come on, Katherine," I said. "I'm sorry, but it wasn't *that* big of a deal."

Jacob was relieved that I'd partially saved him and it must have emboldened him when it shouldn't have.

"Yeah, Mom, it wasn't that bad. Haven't you ever made a mistake? Gol."

"Not a mistake this serious. And don't you dare try to twist this. This isn't about me. You've been expelled from school, young man."

"What about when you were driving the boat? It's your fault dad got his arm cut off."

Silence. We both looked at Jacob in shock. Here he'd gone and ruined a perfectly good character witness because now I was mad. I stood from the bed where I'd been sitting. "Don't you *ever* talk to your mother like that again! Do you hear me?"

"But dad—"

"Don't you but me. Go to your room. You're grounded for a week and then we'll see how funny this is."

He opened the door to leave with his head bent low, just like he'd come in, and the other kids scattered.

After Jacob had slinked away to his bedroom, Katherine said: "He's right, you know."

"You know that's not true. It was an accident."

"Yeah, yeah, I know," she said. "You always say that just to make me feel better."

"No I don't. It was a fluke."

She looked down and started to cry. "How many times do I need to say I'm sorry?"

"You don't. I know how you feel," I said.

"No you don't. How could you?"

I stared out the window, not really looking at anything. Even though it had been several years, I thought about it all the time. A mistake. A misjudgment with catastrophic consequences. I turned around and sat on the edge of the bed next to her.

"You know, she would've been almost thirteen now. I've gone over it a million times. If only I hadn't gone inside to take that phone call. If only the water hadn't been quite so deep. If only this, or if only that. If only I could go back in time. But I can't and there's nothing I can do about it now."

"Keith, you can't beat yourself up for that." She reached over and took my hand. "It was an accident."

"I know, just like the thing with the boat. It was just an accident and it wasn't your fault."

"Do you mean it?"

"Of course I do. Besides, it's not that bad. I mean, look at me. I've hardly missed a beat." I stood on the bench at the end of our bed where Jacob had been sitting and pretended to be leading an orchestra. Then I started doing jumping jacks. It looked ridiculous and Katherine smiled, and then laughed.

"You're crazy, you know that?" she said.

"I haven't blamed you for one second. And I never will."

This was the gospel truth, and she knew it. She started crying again, but these were happy tears.

I put my stump on her shoulder and said, "I know you're upset but you've got to admit it. Jake's prank *was* pretty funny. I mean, seriously."

She pulled away with a shocked expression. "Never!"

"I would've paid fifty bucks cash to see that old Ronstadt hag get pelted with one of those water balloons. Have you seen that hairdo? It looks like a freakin' beehive."

"How dare you! That hairdo is stunning."

"If you like Marge Simpson, I guess. And isn't Duckworth the one who gave him a C- because he couldn't name all the state capitals? Which one did he miss? Was it South Dakota or North? I mean, who cares. I would've paid good money to see her get drenched, too."

"Keith Vaughn Murphy! Listen to you!"

I wish Jacob could have heard his mom laughing because he was a great kid. I also wish they had videotaped the bombardment.

33

KATE

I COULDN'T JUST *move on* like it was no big deal. You move on when someone cuts in front of you in the grocery line, not when you're forced to let a naked hairy scumbag crawl on you. What happened to me was about as close to rape as you can get, and I had allowed it. Yeah, quasi-consensual rape. Men know rape is awful, but I don't think they fully appreciate just how traumatic it is, on so many levels. I recently heard an ignorant right-wing male politician say as long as you're getting raped, you might as well lay back and enjoy it. He actually said that. And people will still vote for him. *Women* will still vote for him. I don't get it.

I felt dirty, obviously. I felt used, obviously. But you can only shower so many times, scrubbing the outer layer until it's raw and still not get to the part that needs to be wiped clean. I'd need to have my brain removed and thoroughly dry cleaned to get rid of all memory, and then put back into my skull.

And now this thug was back.

"Listen, Kate," said Ricky, "I know you don't want to talk about it but this Spanos guy is serious. If I don't come up with the money today he'll come looking for me, or he'll send his guys."

Here we go again. My husband, the suave and charismatic weakling, relying on me to fix it. "What do you want me to do, Ricky? Huh? I don't have any money."

"All I'm saying is we've gotta get out of here, like right now, before they get here."

"And where exactly would we go? You don't have any money, or have you forgotten that already?"

"I know a guy who has a room he'll let us use down at the Motel 6 off Charleston Boulevard. We can stay there for a few days until this dies down."

We threw a few things into an overnight bag and were off, now officially on the run. On the run from a lecherous and hairy murderer. Un-fucking-believable.

The motel room was cheap all right and Ricky didn't leave it for two straight days, hiding out with the curtains drawn like he was Anne Frank. But unlike Anne Frank, Ricky had the luxury of ordering in pizza and watching television. Of course, I had to leave each night because I actually had a job.

I came back to the motel room after midnight on the third night. Ricky was still up, lying in bed watching television with all four pillows propped behind him, just as comfy as can be. The slippery bedspread in a dark, stain-concealing color was crumpled on the floor at the foot of the bed and there was an empty pizza box on the bedsheet next to him. On the nightstand there was an ashtray full of cigarette butts which he'd been too lazy to empty.

"This is how you look for a job?"

"Come on, Kate. You know I can't leave. I'm a dead man if Spanos sees me."

"So, what, you plan to hide out here for the rest of your life? How's that going to work? Why don't you just call him and work something out. Maybe he'll take payments or something."

"You don't know Spanos."

I just glared at him.

"Let's just say you don't know him as well as I do. The guy has no conscience."

Just then there was banging on the door and we both jumped. Ricky shot up in bed. I didn't move. It was dark inside our motel room except for the light from the television and a ray of light from the bathroom where the door was ajar. The curtains were drawn but slightly bunched in the middle, directly above the air conditioning unit, allowing for a sliver of visibility into the room.

The door handle shook. Someone was trying to turn it from the outside.

More banging. "Open the fucking door, Waters!"

Ricky slowly stood from the bed and tiptoed over to the door. He was wearing only his boxer shorts. He looked into the peep hole just as Spanos banged on the door again and Ricky jerked back. It reminded me of when you're driving on the freeway and a bird just misses your windshield and you flinch as if the bird was going to hit you in the face.

"I said open the fucking door! I know you're in there!"

Ricky was petrified, and so was I. We were trapped and there was nowhere to run. You see those movies where they crawl out the bathroom window to make their escape but there was no bathroom window. He mouthed the word "hide" and motioned to the bathroom. I ran to the bathroom but realized that was stupid. What, like Spanos wasn't going to look in there? I dropped to the filthy carpet next to the bed but there was a board that prevented me from crawling under it. I saw the small closet next to the bathroom. I opened the louvered accordion door and stepped inside.

Another bang on the door. "Goddammit, Waters! I'm warning you!"

"Just a second," Ricky said into the door. He grabbed his pants and pulled them on. He looked through the peephole again, then took the chain and tried to slide it into the groove for more protection but his hands were shaking. Spanos must have heard it and he banged on the door with his shoulder which made Ricky jerk backward again.

"We had a deal!" Ricky yelled through the door.

"Open the goddamned door or I'll bust it down. Don't push me, Waters. Open the fuck up!"

"What are you going to do?"

"I'm gonna collect my five grand."

"I don't have it yet. But I'll get it to you soon."

"You take off and try to hide from me and you think I'm just going to *forget* it? I'm not stupid, Waters. Now open the fucking door. I'm warning you."

"I'll call the cops!" Ricky yelled through the door.

"No you won't because I'll kill you if you do, and you know it."

"I'll open it if you promise not to hurt me."

"Open the door, Waters. We'll talk."

Ricky slowly slid the chain back and then reached for the door handle just as Spanos thrust his shoulder against the door again. I thought for sure the door jamb would splinter.

"Okay, I'm opening the door. Just put the bat down. Okay?"

Ricky reached down and turned the handle. Spanos pushed past him and came into the room. He then closed the door behind him and slid the chain into the groove so we were sort of locked in.

Ricky backed up a few steps toward the bed, cowering. "Come on, Vic. We had a deal," he pleaded.

"Where's my money, Waters?" He was holding an aluminum baseball bat and thumping it into the palm of his left hand. It clicked every time it struck his wedding ring. "Just give me my money and I'll leave you and your cold bitch alone."

I was standing in the dark closet in my cocktail waitress uniform, shaking so hard I thought he could hear it, or maybe even feel the tremor of it. I could see through the slits in the louvered door that Spanos was facing me with his back to the motel-room door. Ricky had backed up, almost to the bed now, holding his arms out in front of him.

Spanos flicked the light switch and the lamp next to the curtained window came on. "Where is she anyway?" he asked. "Where's that lousy fuck?"

"She's not here."

"Bullshit! I heard you talking to someone."

"That must've been the TV. She's not here, I swear."

"That's a shame because I'd like to see her. She wanted me bad, Waters, she really did. A real moaner. But she just ain't my type, you know what I mean? Got the nice long legs but too scrawny. I like 'em with a little more meat."

More thumping of the bat into his open palm as he swept the room with his eyes. Click, click, click of bat to wedding ring in the silence. I've never loathed someone more.

"See, the thing is, I gave you a break. Said I'd knock $500 off, just to be nice. But you thought you could hide from me." His appraisal of our situation was spot on. "You're pathetic, Waters, bringing your whore to a dump like this." Again, spot on.

"Listen, I'll pay you, okay? I just need more time."

"Times up. You need to be shown I'm serious."

He swung the bat at Ricky's legs, but Ricky jumped back against the bed and it only grazed the flesh of his thigh.

"Please, Vic, I'll pay. I swear! I'm begging you."

Spanos looked around the room again. "She ain't here, huh? Then what the fuck is that?" he asked as he aimed the bat at my purse that I'd set on top of the dresser, next to the television. He stepped forward a few feet and tried to look into the bathroom, keeping one eye on Ricky.

"She's here. I can smell the bitch."

He stepped closer to the closet and I backed into it as far as I could. I could see he was now standing with his back to me, just a few feet in front of the louver doors. It was dark in the closet but I felt something metal up near my left shoulder. It was the metal bracket for a clothes iron. I slid the iron up and out of the bracket with my right hand as quietly as I could, but it scraped on the bracket and Spanos heard it. He swung around, faced the closet, and raised the bat.

"When are you going to learn that you don't fuck with me? Huh?" He grabbed the knob on the louvered door and yanked it open. He probably expected to find me curled up in the fetal position on the floor of the closet. But he was mistaken. My right hand came down with all my rage.

The heel of the iron caught him flush in the face.

He fell back and dropped the bat as blood spurted from his shattered nose. I looked over at Ricky who was now holding his shirt and shoes. He'd slid the safety chain from the door, opened it, and had been about to run when he saw Spanos turn toward the closet. Now he stood frozen with a look of shock at me as I held the bloody iron in my hand. He stepped back into the room and closed the door. I think he was ashamed, or at least I hope he was, because we both knew damned well that he'd been planning to make a run for it as soon as Spanos opened the louvered door and found me in the closet. He had to know Spanos would have either raped or beaten me, and probably both.

"Is he dead?" Ricky asked in a whisper as he took a few tentative steps closer to Spanos who was splayed out on the floor, face up.

"Fuck you!" Spanos mumbled from the dirty shag carpet now splattered with blood. "I swear to God I'm going to kill you." It was hard to understand him because his hands were covering his face and the words were gurgled by blood.

"We gotta get out of here!" Ricky said. He carefully reached out a foot and rolled the bat a few inches closer to where he stood and then bent down and picked it up. I think he was afraid Spanos would jump up and use it to bludgeon him. But Spanos was in bad shape, he really was. I figured he'd probably survive, but not by much, and I couldn't decide how I felt about that.

I looked down at the pitiful creature with the gold, blood-speckled medallion nestled in the gob of chest hair, blood burbling up through his thick fingers that still covered his face. There was already a metallic smell in the room. I was still wearing my high-heeled boot over my fishnet stockings and brought it down on his groin as hard as I could. He tried to rollover to deflect another blow, but he was too busy trying to hold his nose somewhere on his face. I lifted my boot and brought it down again. Then again.

I was having another out of body experience, only this one was strangely exhilarating. I felt so powerful over this monster. For one of the first times in my life, *I* was the one who held the power over a man and I squatted down next to him so he could look me in the face. I spit on him.

"If you ever touch me again, I'll kill you. Do you hear me, you fucking asshole? Next time I will kill you."

I stood and stared down at him, taking in all I had done to this man who intimidated and tortured everyone else. "You don't seem very tough to me with your tiny little dick, you ugly son of a bitch." Then I kicked him again as hard as I could in the ribs. I realized I was still holding the bloody iron, the cord dangling above his face. I dropped the iron on his hand-covered face and turned for the door.

"Say another word to me and you'll regret it."

"Fuck you," he mumbled through the blood.

I turned back toward him. "I thought I told you not to say another word to me," I said and kicked him as hard as I could in the ribs, then headed for the door.

"Are we just going to leave him here?" asked Ricky.

I didn't answer. I picked up my purse and walked out the door. Ricky followed me, still holding his shirt and shoes in one hand and the aluminum Louisville Slugger in the other.

"Now what do we do?" he asked as we drove to our apartment. "You shouldn't have done that because now he'll be coming after us for sure. Only next time he'll try to kill us."

"So I've should've just let him rape me and beat me? Is that it?"

"We don't know for sure that's what he'd would've done."

I had to drive because Ricky was shaking too hard. This might sound strange, but I wasn't scared at all. In fact, I wanted to go back to the motel and finish him off. That hairy, fat pig with the little penis was lying on the floor of a cheap motel room with half a face. And I had done it to him.

"Where are you going?" Ricky asked as I began heading in the direction of my apartment. I'll call it mine because I'm the one who paid the rent. And the utilities. And the cable bill. "We can't just go home and stay there like nothing's happened!" Ricky said. "Are you crazy? He'll be looking for us!"

"I'll call Crock. He might know a place we can crash until I figure something out." Obviously, it was taken for granted that I'd be the one who'd have to figure it out—that I'd take over this problem by default like I always did with Ricky.

There were no people or suspicious cars in our apartment parking lot. Still, Ricky didn't want to get out of the car.

"You coming?" I asked him.

"Maybe I should just wait here."

"Whatever," I said as I started up the exterior steps to our second floor apartment.

"Wait up," he said and then tentatively followed me up, several steps behind.

Our apartment door was ajar. I pushed it open with my fingertips without stepping inside. Ricky stood behind me with the bat lifted just in case the bad guys got through me. When the door swung open, I saw that our apartment, my apartment, had been ransacked. Sofa cushions thrown around, kitchen cabinets opened, and drawers pulled out. Now I *really* wanted to return to the motel to smash his face with the iron until he was dead. While I was surveying the damage in the apartment, Ricky had picked up my car keys that I'd dropped on the kitchen counter. He said he had to go pick up some things and would be back in a few minutes, but I was hardly listening.

I made my way down the hall and into our bedroom which now looked like a war zone. My clothes were scattered everywhere and the mattress was drooping halfway off the frame. Dresser drawers were opened and my jewelry box with all my pricey costume jewelry was on the floor. A pair of my panties was hanging on the ceiling fan as some sort of sick joke. I felt violated all over again.

I called over my shoulder for Ricky. No answer. I walked back into the living room to find him.

The front door was wide open, and Ricky was gone.

34

KATHERINE

A FEW DAYS AFTER JACOB'S water-balloon fiasco, Keith called me from work to say he got a call from our former neighbor asking for some plumbing advice. "Hey, remember that Renaldo guy?" Um, *yeah*. "He wants to drive up after work and borrow some of my tools. I'll try to be home before he gets there but just let him in if I don't make it home in time."

Renaldo was going to drive forty-five minutes up to Cedar City just to borrow a tool? What, they don't have tools in St. George? He was a real estate agent so I could understand if he didn't have a garage full of plumbing supplies, but this seemed a bit extreme when he'd be passing two Home Depots and an Ace Hardware before he even got on the northbound freeway to Cedar City. I got a pit in my stomach and tried on two different outfits so I'd be ready when this guy I hardly knew dropped by to pick up a monkey wrench.

Keith came home a bit earlier that day, predictably oblivious as to why Renaldo would drive all that way to borrow a tool.

"Gol, you look great," Keith said. "What's the occasion?"

"Whaddya mean?"

"Yeah, Mom, you look all dressed up," said Jacob.

"I do?"

"And you smell good," said Jenna.

Just then the doorbell rang. Keith opened the door and then walked out to the garage, Renaldo two steps behind. We had an unattached garage and I saw Renaldo look back over his shoulder to the house a couple times house where I was peeking out the kitchen window in my favorite pair of jeans. Two squirts of Chanel basically down the toilet.

I wanted to put Jacob in a wilderness survival program after he was expelled from school—the ones where they drop teenagers off in the middle of nowhere and dare them to survive and they come back saying *Yes Sir*, and *Yes Ma'am*. Keith, however, talked me off the ledge.

Keith had a way of reducing the drama, no matter what it was. There were times I wished he would've taken things more seriously, but I preferred his laissez-faire approach to someone more volatile. I never had to worry that he'd suddenly fly off the handle, requiring us to tip toe around him like we used to do with my dad. He just wasn't scary and stern. Besides, my other kids were acting out, too. Jenna was sneaking into my make-up and Nathan and his friends were practicing swear words in their tree hut. We couldn't afford to send them all to wilderness boot camp.

Just when everything settled down, I was changing Jacob's bed sheets and had to lift his mattress a few inches to yank the fitted sheet into place. And what do you think I found between the mattress and box springs? You guessed it. I hardly dared touch the thing but I couldn't just *leave* it there. I wasn't about to just "go along" with this like some moms who try too hard to be popular with their kids. I'd heard one mom down the street had even given her teenage son a year's supply of condoms if you can believe it. I can only hope the supply came with a lecture and a gift-wrapped set of scriptures.

I sat on the corner of Jacob's bed and thumbed through a few of the pages. Gorgeous, airbrushed women were on the beach, on silk sheets, on bear skin rugs, you name it—all of them presumably in heat, just lying there looking back at my innocent teenage son with the look of erotic passion.

And he *was* innocent, right? Then again, that's what my parents had thought about me and we all know how that turned out. But Jacob had only been exposed to the mild vices in life because we lived in such a safe, conservative community. Maybe a swear word at school here and there but nothing worse. I was certain of it. Well, I was pretty sure of it. Okay, fine, I was hopeful of it. On the other hand, he was now looking at pornography and there was no denying his maturation happening right before my eyes. He'd grown to be as tall as I was, his skin was pimply, and he had a knobby throat. His voice was a steady low baritone too without the interrupting squeak.

I pulled Keith away from the fridge as soon as he came in from work and gave him the ugly low down about Jacob's porn addiction. Obviously I had to do it in the privacy of our bedroom because our kids all had rabbit ears, especially when they suspected someone was in trouble.

"So, what are we going to do?" I asked him.

"Nothing."

"*Nothing?* You're just going to stand there and pretend we don't know he's looking at pornography? Is that what you're saying? Because if it is, I think they removed more than your arm in the operation."

"It's not that big of a deal. All boys do that at some point."

"Did you?"

"Not really."

"Not really?"

"Hey, I'm not saying I liked it."

"Come on, Keith. Be serious. You know darn good and well where this leads."

"And where is that?"

"To reckless, permissive sex, that's where."

"Where is it?"

I eyed him, trying to decipher if he was serious. When he didn't smile, I handed the *Playboy* over to him. He opened it on his lap and slowly, too slowly I might add, turned the pages, pausing whenever he'd come to a beach, silk sheet, or bear skin rug.

"Is this really necessary?"

"Hey, I need to know what we're dealing with here."

I snatched it away from him before he got to the centerfold (a "journalism major" who wanted to save stray kittens. Oh, please.)

Keith said I was a worry wart, which I refuse to apologize for. After all, *someone* had to worry about our kids, didn't they? Then again, maybe there was a good balance—Keith worried about their physical safety and I worried about everything else. And now that they were becoming teenagers the everything else was taxing.

I very reluctantly returned the magazine to where I'd found it, but scooted it a little farther under the mattress so at least Jacob would have to stretch for it. I also put a note on his pillow to guilt him into repentance: "Clean sheets! I'm proud that you're such a great young man!"

Jacob acted normal the next day. Hmmmm . . . what was I supposed to make of that? Where was the guilt on his face? Where was the shame? As soon as he left for school, I checked under his mattress and the magazine was no longer there. Keith told me there's no way Jacob would have thrown it away. He said such a treasure trove would've been too hard to come by at his age. Treasure trove? Did I even *know* my husband? Geez, maybe Keith took it for all I know.

I shouldn't have been that surprised when I think back on it because I'd found a stack of *Playboy's* at Vaughn's house. He hadn't even bothered to hide them and I felt sorry for Dottie. I imagined her dusting around them, careful not to disturb Vaughn's treasure trove. So this may have been a hereditary thing—the one thing Jacob inherited from his paternal grandfather. Keith said Jacob had probably smuggled it out of the house under his shirt and re-hid it. Probably stashed it someplace like the Tuff Shed in our backyard where we kept the lawnmower. This made me feel a whole lot better; just knowing that the entire Murphy line of males were all perverts.

Oh, and then to further cause me to wonder about my son's erupting hormones, I saw that he was reading *A Scarlett Letter* which was one of my favorite books in high school. Maybe Hester Prynne's sexual history sparked his interest because I'd never seen him read a book in his life, not even *The Hardy*

Boys. He said it was a high school reading assignment, and it probably was, but I didn't see him peeling through the pages of *Pride and Prejudice*. Was I upset that he was reading the book? Of course not. I'm simply saying it was slightly out of character. If he was determined to read a book, I would have preferred it be *Old Yeller*. That's all I'm saying.

For the record, I wasn't one of those moms who snoop through their kids' diaries. I respected their privacy, to a point. I'd gently pry and I certainly won't apologize for that. And neither did I try to micromanage every aspect of their existence, catering to their every need. I didn't have the energy or interest to fawn over my kids like some moms, reminding them to eat and wear a coat. I figured my kids would eat when they were hungry and wear a coat when they were cold. I knew they wouldn't starve or freeze to death if they forgot. How were they supposed to become independent people if I did everything for them, trailing along to make sure they were never put out, or offended, or bored, or the least bit uncomfortable?

I often thought about the way moms parented back in the day. I know they didn't hover. For one thing, they probably didn't have time, what with their washboards, clotheslines, and making every meal from scratch. I'd bet my life that Grandma Coombs didn't peel and slice the apples for my eight-year-old dad and then ornately display them on his plate in a perfect fan. And I wonder what she would have said if my dad had demanded that she make him a peanut butter sandwich instead of the tuna fish. Would she have fainted? Would she have washed his mouth out with soap? Kids weren't entitled like that. Grandma would have made him sit in front of that tuna fish sandwich for a week until it was gone. If the tuna went bad, so much the better.

I don't think parenting had changed much one generation later. For example, I don't recall my parents rushing to call the teacher when I hadn't been rewarded with a first place ribbon for my seventh-grade essay on the Industrial Revolution. And my parents didn't obsess over where I was every split-second of the day. I walked to school and so did my friends. Was it perfect? Were there potential kidnappers? Maybe, but I don't remember all the kids getting kidnapped.

And now a generation after that? Was I expected to march in protest against the inequity when my precious, fragile child didn't get a participation trophy for everything he did? Was I a neglectful mother when I let them climb a tree or made them walk two blocks to church? Would the state's child protective services come knocking on my door if I didn't hound them incessantly about their homework and then do it myself when they waited me out? Did I not do enough to ensure that they were entertained and amused at all times. Whatever you do, Dear Moms, don't let them fail at anything! Good heavens, my neighbor called me the other day to express concern that Jenna hadn't included her daughter in a game of Four-Square at recess. What on earth was wrong with these people? Did they think they were doing their kids a favor and then salute themselves for their selfless martyrdom? Wow, look how great *that* mom is, sacrificing everything in her life for her children! Didn't they know it would probably backfire?

Maybe I was a better parent out of necessity and not because I was so enlightened. After all, it's pretty hard to hover over your little angels when you've got six of them. I hope they'll grow up to be more independent, capable adults than some of their friends who had "better" moms. And I'll probably take most of the credit if they do.

Our lives were actually going well, all things considered. I would often see Keith and think *Oh that's right, he only has one arm.* I'd begun to forget that he'd once had two hands. You tend to adapt and get used to the way things are. We were very active in our church-related activities. In fact, Keith was moving up the ranks of leaders in our neighborhood ward and there were whispers that he was destined to become the bishop one day, just like my dad had been. And who would have ever dreamed Keith Murphy might one day become a bishop?

I'd like to think we were a poster family for the church. We weren't perfect, obviously, but we didn't smoke, drink, gamble, or watch R-rated movies. Keith wanted to see *Indecent Proposal*, that new R-rated one with Robert Redford about the husband who rented out his wife for a night in exchange for money, but I said no way. I mean, what husband would ask his wife to have sex with another man for money? And what wife would actually agree to do it? I can't imagine.

The election for County Commissioner was heating up. My dad's opponent, Red Harman, passed out a flyer implying that my dad was anti-gun. This was an inflammatory charge in our community. "I've shot plenty of deer and rabbits in my lifetime," my dad boasted. "I also killed an elk once, a big one too, but then I gave my gun to my brother-in-law. Now, if Red Harman is so hell bent on me owning a gun to prove my family values, then I'll go buy a danged gun."

And so he did. That very day he drove the family minivan down to Duce Sporting Goods and bought a danged gun to prove he was rock solid on family values. Take that, Red Harman!

My dad figured his neighbor, Brother Rasmussen, must have been in cahoots with Red Harman. How else could Red have known that my dad had once displayed a political yard sign for a Democrat? It'd been his boss at work who was running for the local school board and my dad couldn't say no. So he'd hammered the smallest yard sign they made into the front lawn, partially obscured by a lilac. The small image of a donkey was tucked into the corner of the yard sign to hide the fact that the guy had actually been an unpatriotic Democrat, but it was there if you looked close enough. To offset this blockbuster charge, my dad's yard signs this time around had huge elephants on them.

Red was fond of flyers. His latest was a montage of his family designed to show the electorate that he could be counted on to uphold family values. There was a photo of his family standing in front of the Mormon temple, and another with Red standing next to his sons in their Boy Scout uniforms. The final photo on the montage was one of Red in an orange hunting vest crouched down next to a dead deer. One hand rested on the large set of antlers and the other held a Winchester rifle. He wore a satisfied grin—proud, heroic, and as patriotic as can be.

Not to be outdone, my dad fired back with a new flyer of his own. It was also a montage of photos. One depicted my dad working on a church welfare farm, bent over a shovelful of dirt with his sleeves rolled up. Other photos were of the kids including a large solo of Kylie, which was the whole point of the flyer I think because my dad wanted to make it perfectly clear that his daughter had been born with an extra chromosome, and yet he still loved her. And if that didn't spell family values then, pray tell, what did?

They had a debate in the junior high school gymnasium a month before the election. The gym was jampacked with about seventy-five citizens, only half of whom were old enough to vote. The other half were the candidates' kids and grandkids. Red's large brood in the crowd all wore these stupid *Seeing Red for Harman!* T-shirts. So dorky. Even worse than the denim billboard.

They got right down to the serious issues a rural county commissioner would have to tackle, namely abortion.

"So, Mr. Harman," the moderator asked, "as County Commissioner, what would you do to decrease property taxes?"

"Well, I'd limit the size of the federal government. But let's not take our focus off society's moral corruption, what with all this rampant abortion."

Those with T-shirts in the crowd cheered. You tell 'em, Red!

"I agree," my dad said. "Life begins at conception, and that's why I'm in favor of a constitutional amendment to support life." This put Red in a pickle because he couldn't do any better than that. He couldn't say it began even *before* conception. But he wanted to, I could just tell.

My dad won the election by 103 votes. We were all pretty excited. Calls poured in to campaign headquarters (my parent's kitchen). There was even a call from the Governor. My dad also got a note from Brother Rasmussen complaining that some yard signs had blown onto his property and could he please remove them immediately. We watched from the living-room window as my dad walked over to collect the signs, dodging dog poo near the DMZ. My mom was furious when we saw him write something on one of the signs and leave it propped up on Rasmussen's front porch.

"And what was that about?" my mom asked when he came back in the front door.

"Nothing much. I just thought Brother Rasmussen might like an autograph from the new County Commissioner."

I was happy for my dad, but I feared for Puffer's life.

35

KATE

I WAITED ALL NIGHT at our burglarized apartment for Ricky to come back home but he never did. He didn't call either. Where in the hell was he? I lay in bed, freaking out with every sound—holding my breath until approaching cars passed safely on by, or bolt up in bed, frozen with fear when the air conditioner kicked on because I knew Victor Spanos or his goon squad would come for us.

I wished I'd killed him. I wished I'd taken that iron and crushed his dirty-rotten skull with it. Then, after he was dead, I could've plugged it in and turned it to the cotton setting, pressing it down on his face or his bare crotch until he'd be forever branded with the upside-down V. That would've become my infamous trademark—The Iron Murderer. After branding him, we could've wrapped him up in plastic garbage bags and dragged him out to the trunk, freshly pressed.

But what to do with the body from there? That, and the murder weapon, always seem to be the tricky part. There were plenty of places we could have buried him, including the county landfill where he belonged. And I suppose we could have incinerated him or chopped him up and fed him to a pack of feral dogs. It would have been easy to dispose of the clothes iron too, once we scrubbed it clean from the blood. But could I have actually done it, I wondered? Could I honestly have killed the scum bag? Probably not. In fact, I know I couldn't have actually done it. Then again, there were things I'd done that I never would have believed I could do. Not in a million years. And where in the hell was Ricky?

I called Crock at daylight.

"Hi, Crock, this is Kate. Sorry to call so early."

"What time is it anyway?" He must've looked at his clock. "God Almighty, Kate, it's not even seven!"

"I'm sorry, but I didn't know who else to call."

"This better be good. What's up?" His voice was still husky from sleep and I heard murmuring on his end of the line—probably a girl who hoped to sleep her way to the bright lights of the Sugar & Spice stage.

"It's Ricky. He took off with my car."

"And you're calling me at seven o'clock in the morning?"

"No, it's not that. We're in trouble. You know who Victor Spanos is?"

"Yeah. Real prick. What about him?"

"Well, Ricky owed him money and he came looking for him with a bat and I hit him with an iron and almost killed him and now he's after us and Ricky took my car."

"Whoa, whoa, whoa, slow down. You hit who with an iron?"

"Spanos. But I didn't kill him and now he's coming after me. He tore up my apartment and everything."

"When?"

"Last night. We were hiding out at a motel because Ricky didn't have the money he owed him and Spanos tracked us down. I got scared and hit him with an iron."

"An iron? Where'd you get an iron? I didn't know you played golf."

"No, it was an iron, iron."

"Like a clothes iron?"

"Yeah, I thought he was dead, but I probably only broke his nose."

"So where's Ricky?"

"That's what I'm trying to tell you. He took off after I hit Spanos. I don't know where he went but he took my car and now I'm stuck at my apartment and Spanos is probably going to show up any second."

"So what do you want me to do?"

"Can you come and pick me up? Maybe I could stay a couple days at your place until I figure out what to do? I know it's asking a lot."

"Now? At seven o'clock on a Saturday morning? God Almighty, Kate." There was more ruffling on his end of the line. "All right. Give me twenty minutes. Be waiting outside."

"Thanks, Crock."

"Shit," I heard him mumble as he hung up the phone.

I left my second-floor apartment but only after peeking through the curtains to be sure there were no suspicious henchmen lurking, or anyone with their face wrapped in bandages. There was a vending machine at the bottom of the outdoor stairwell and I hid behind it next to a rat poison bait box while I waited for Crock. I listened for approaching cars, squealing tires, or the sounds of angry men. I almost fainted when the vending machine motor automatically turned on.

I'd changed out of my cocktail-waitress uniform into jeans and a T-shirt and I wore my hair in a ponytail underneath a baseball cap. I looked nothing like an iron-wielding murderer. I held an overnight bag filled with a few things I'd picked up off the floor of my burglarized apartment. When I saw Crock's old Lincoln pull into the parking lot, I ran out and jumped into the front seat.

"Thanks, Crock. Honest. I didn't know who else to call."

"Don't worry about it. You shoulda just killed the scumbag—do everybody a favor."

Crock lit a cigarette before starting the car and asked me if I wanted one, like we had all the time in the world.

"By the way," he said, "did I tell you Wayne Newton came in a few months ago? At least we think it was him."

"No but, um, we gotta go," I said as I scanned the parking lot. "He'll be coming any minute."

"Relax. All I wanted was a goddamned cigarette. I haven't even had my coffee."

He finally put the car in drive and we were on the street.

"Do you think I could crash at your place for a few nights? I told Ricky I was going to call you, so he'll probably try to reach me there."

"We'll find some room."

"Thanks so much. Like I said, I didn't know who else to call."

"Hey, don't worry about it." He smiled at me across the wide bench seat and reached over to pat me on the thigh. "You'll be okay." He'd grown a mustache, so it looked like a curtain was being raised and lowered over his two large teeth whenever he smiled.

I'd never been to Crock's house and was surprised it was so small. I'd always assumed he was a rich businessman who lived in a mansion with a uniformed maid or two. Instead, it was a tract house with faded stucco, graveled yard, bar-tile roof, and a fake cactus in front. The living room had been decorated in traditional bachelor with a leather sofa, two chairs, and a coffee table. That's about it. No art, no books, no lamps. A beleaguered Ficus tree slouched in the corner surrounded by half its leaves on the carpet. There were a few empty Budweiser cans on the coffee table along with about five TV remotes. Just looking at all those remotes gave me anxiety.

The photo of a thirty-something-year-old woman was perched on the fireplace mantle next to the photos of three young girls—elementary school photos showing crooked, pre-braces teeth. The youngest of the girls was missing her two front teeth altogether.

"Make yourself at home," Crock said as we walked in. "I'm going back to bed."

I was starving. There wasn't much in his fridge—mayo, mustard, and a take-out box of chow mein with a fork sticking out from the upper corner. I pried the lid off of a small Tupperware container and took a whiff of egg salad that had gone bad and staggered back a step or two.

Just then, a large Hispanic woman walked into the kitchen, yawning and half naked. She acted like I wasn't even there, as if it were perfectly normal for a strange woman to be standing in their kitchen sniffing Tupperware cartons at seven thirty on a Saturday morning. She re-opened the fridge and stared for a while, then finally picked up the take-out box of chow mein and took a whiff herself. She debated before putting it back in the fridge where it toppled over from the weight of the fork. She didn't bother to straighten it back upright. "Sheet, Crock he never gots nuthin' good to eat."

"Who's makin' all the racket?" A bald head popped up from the living room sofa next to the kitchen. The head belonged to a skinny elderly man whose lower face had sunken in which caused him to look like a light bulb. "Can't you see I'm tryin' to get me some goddamned sleep?" His head disappeared again.

I noticed a shadow pile up against the frosted-glass on the front door and froze. Shit, this is it, this is how it ends—one of Spanos's goon squad had already tracked me down. The doorbell rang, which slightly comforted me because I figured a hit man wouldn't have bothered with the common courtesy of politely ringing the bell. He'd probably just knock it down or simply start shooting through it. I hid in the kitchen pantry, holding my breath, when the large Hispanic woman padded over to the door.

Turns out it was only the newspaper boy coming to collect the fare. Would this be my fate forevermore, hiding whenever a doorbell rang? Afraid even of the newspaper boy?

Crock walked back into the kitchen being trailed by a calico cat. I'd never taken Crock for a cat guy. "I can't get back to sleep so might as well make coffee." He started opening up cabinets until he found a can of Folgers. He tipped it up and dumped a mound directly into the coffee maker with no filter. "This here's Lucinda, by the way, and that's Wayne," he nodded to the sofa. "Kate's an old friend who's going to be staying here for a few days." Lucinda only grunted and Wayne farted from the sofa.

"Has anyone called here this morning?" I asked.

"Who in their proper mind'd call at this hour?" asked skinny Wayne who now stood in the middle of the living room in a pair of stretched-out tighty-whities, his bony thighs not even close to filling out the leg holes. He picked up a dirty pair of trousers from a pile on the floor. "I needed to get some sleep, goddammit. Got me a big day." It looked like his idea of a big day was to push around a stolen grocery cart filled with junk. I later found out that Crock had taken him in a week earlier when he'd found him nearly unconscious in the Sugar & Spice parking lot.

Lucinda was skinny Wayne's polar opposite. She looked like a linebacker, the poor thing. She had a big round upper body with enormous breasts and a small, flat bum—like a giant had squeezed her around the thighs, forcing all the fat up. I thought of a Genie when he's about two-thirds of the way out of his lamp. Apparently, Lucinda was a street walker who'd eked out a living giving blow jobs in dark alleys off the strip. Crock had taken her in when she'd come to Sugar & Spice looking for a job as a stripper. He didn't have the heart to turn her away, so he hired her to do "odd jobs." That was Crock for you.

"Sheet," said Lucinda, "less go eat."

"Fine," said Crock. "I'll pay. Come on, Kate, you're probably hungry, too."

"What you do weeth the skeeny senorita?"

Crock looked in the direction of his bedroom. "She wants to sleep in. Come on, let's go."

Denny's was crowded. Wayne gummed on pancakes and Lucinda scarfed down the Grand Slam because Crock was paying. I pushed my fruit medley around the plate and jumped whenever the door opened and the chime sounded. I watched

Lucinda with envy as she mopped up the last of her syrup with a pancake. Just once I would have loved to eat a Grand Slam in peace without worrying about my figure, or about some guy barging into the place to whack me.

"So why you stay weeth Crock?" Lucinda asked me.

"I owe some guy who's after me."

"Sheet. He go fuck self."

"I need to earn some money to pay him back."

"You pay *heem?*" She looked at Crock, shook her head, and jerked her thumb in my direction. "Sheet, theese one here is crazy."

A day went by and still no word from Ricky. I hunkered down and didn't leave Crock's house. After all, where could I go? The Wayne Newton show? I didn't even have a car. But I did have a lot of nervous energy so I cleaned Crock's house but generally stayed away from the windows.

"You can stay her as long as you want," Crock told me, "but you need to make some money at some point."

"Thanks, Crock. I really thought Ricky would've called by now. Maybe Spanos got to him."

I couldn't bear the thought that Ricky would abandon me to save his own skin. On the other hand, I had to acknowledge that he'd been halfway out the motel room door before I clobbered Spanos with the iron. The longer it went without hearing from him I started hoping that maybe Spanos *had* gotten to him, because at least that would've meant my loving husband hadn't intentionally left me high and dry.

"Listen," Crock said, "I know a guy out in Pahrump. Ever been there?"

"No."

"Well, he owns the Kitty Kat. It's a brothel, but it's a pretty nice one."

"I'm not a prostitute, Crock."

"I know that. But you'd be safe out there. And if you need to make some fast money, that's an option. I know that's not what you want, okay? I get it. But the guy who owns it is a friend of mine and runs a clean operation. Treats the girls fair."

I couldn't believe we were even having this conversation. Then again, what *hadn't* I done? Still it made me sick to know Crock thought working in a brothel might actually be an option for me. Was I about to start wearing a sweater with a scarlet "A" embroidered on it like that Hester Prynne girl I read about in high school? Um, I don't think so.

"I'm just saying it'd be a safe place to lie low until things settle down," he said. "You could stay with me, but you can't go back to the Golden Nugget or Sugar & Spice, not with that Spanos prick out there. Shit, you can't even go back to that lousy Traveling diner place you worked at. I don't want trouble, you understand?" Yep, perfectly understood—even the Lucky Traveler wasn't an option.

I may have hit rock bottom, but a *prostitute?* That's a whole new level of bottom. "I'll think about it, Crock, but don't count on it. I'm not a hooker."

I slept in a spare bedroom for two more nights at Crock's house and shared a bathroom with Lucinda and skinny Wayne. I planned my trips into the bathroom to limit them as much as possible. There was the smell, for starters, and it was disconcerting to brush my teeth while straddling a pair of dirty underwear on the tile floor. The final straw was learning the lock on the bathroom door didn't work. I learned the hard way, too, when I stepped out of the shower to find skinny Wayne splashing pee into the toilet not three feet away. He didn't even look at me.

I was quite sure I could never actually work at the Kitty Kat, but I did think about it. And that's the thing right there—I actually thought about it. If you open the door to a thought, even slightly, the tortured justifications start creeping in. So, yeah, here's a nugget of truth for you: You'll know you're approaching the sea bed when you start justifying the benefits of prostitution.

I waited for Crock to wake up on the morning of the fourth day. The young starlet he'd been with a few days earlier turned out to be no starlet at all—just another soul trying to find her way and who had taken about ten wrong turns. You couldn't blame Crock for those wrong turns any more than you could blame men in general. Then again, why blame men in general? Was it their fault that they'd been programmed to lead out with their penises? Maybe the blame rests somewhere else. God? Nature? About the only group you couldn't blame is women. At least I think women are mostly blameless for the world's debauchery. There are exceptions, of course, like Lizzie Borden, but it's mostly men. Anyway, when Crock woke up that morning, I asked him if he could drive me over to my apartment to pick up some things.

"Can I at least get me some goddamned coffee? You early risers are starting to annoy me."

On the drive over to the apartment I asked him how much the girls at the Kitty Kat made. "I'm just curious," I emphasized.

"I'm not sure but I'd guess the good ones probably make about a thousand a night or something. What, you thinking about it?"

"No." I dropped my head. "I don't know. I need to get out of Vegas for a while and I can't go home to Utah. I just can't. What if he tracked me down there?"

Crock walked me up the exterior flight of stairs to my apartment. It hadn't been touched since I'd left, still ransacked like you see in the movies when the bad guys come looking. The light was blinking on the answering machine. I pushed the button. *Kate, it's me. Sorry I had to bail so fast. I knew Spanos would come looking for me and I didn't want you to get into the middle of it. And sorry I took your car. I can't tell you where I am, but I just wanted you to know I'm safe. I'll be in touch later.* There was a beep, and then: *To save this message, press nine. To erase this message, press seven.* I looked at the machine for a moment and then pressed seven.

"I'm sorry, Kate," Crock said on the drive back to his place. He'd never liked Ricky, I could just tell. Men didn't like Ricky in general. There were probably several reasons for this. Among other things, he was too obsessed with his looks. He was pretty like a woman and had a manicure about as often as I did. There was also the undeniable fact that he never asked anyone else a question, so absorbed was he. Crock had never come out and said he didn't like him but he'd seen Ricky come into Sugar & Spice with me—seen the way he'd sit at the bar and flirt while his own wife was on the stage. "Maybe it's just as well that he's gone." And maybe it was.

The next day I asked Crock if he'd drive me out to Pahrump and he agreed. What would I wear? Do I go skanky or wholesome? I decided to go neutral and wore workout clothes with my hair in a ponytail. I hadn't yet decided if I'd do tricks for money, but I hadn't officially decided that I wouldn't either. And that's the Danger Zone right there—being wishy-washy about it, just like we used to say to each other in high school. Draw your line and don't cross it, girls! I've since come to believe there is wisdom in that line drawing business because that treacherous, wishy-washy Danger Zone practically becomes the Go Zone—the default when things don't go perfectly according to plan.

Crock was quiet on the hour long drive out to Pahrump. He'd never told me his story—how he'd come to own Sugar & Spice, whether he'd ever married, and who the children were in the photos. He knew my story, or at least the ugly part of, so I felt it wasn't off limits to pry into his a bit. After all, he'd seen me naked which usually creates a bond, or at least a familiarity.

"You have photos of a woman and three little girls at your office and in your living room."

He didn't respond.

"Is that your wife? Are they your kids?"

He remained quiet.

"I'm sorry, I didn't mean to pry."

We drove in uncomfortable silence for another mile or so when Crock slowly nodded. "Yes, that was my wife, and those were my girls."

I waited this time, figuring he would fill me in if he wanted to.

"It was ten years ago and we had to take my car into the shop. Linda, that was my wife, drove with the kids in another car behind me. They were following me to drop off my car at the repair shop."

I shifted in my seat to look at him.

"I ran a yellow light and Linda, who didn't know the way, sped up to make the light so she wouldn't lose me. I saw it all in my rearview mirror."

This was awful. I didn't know what to say. I reached out and touched his arm. "I am so sorry."

He lifted his hand to wipe a tear with his thumb before clearing his throat. "The cat you saw at my house was Nicole's. She was my youngest."

Pahrump is a small town about an hour west of Las Vegas. In Vegas, prostitution is illegal but quite common. But Pahrump is in Nye County where it's quite legally common. There are about twenty-five brothels in Nye County but none of them did business like the Kitty Kat. It was the cat's meow. The girls there were prostitutes, sure, but they weren't the typical low budget sex workers groveling for a buck or two (at least that's what I wanted to believe). They weren't like the Lot Lizards next door who patrolled truck stops, or the streetwalkers who made their money in the back seats of Buicks. No, I wanted to believe the girls at the Kitty Kat were high class, the upper crust of hookers. Now, even assuming that were true, which it wasn't, I'm not sure it really mattered. You can doll up prostitution all you want but it's still prostitution whether you do your business in a suite at the Four Seasons or in a pop-up camp trailer.

Crock parked in front and entered the place like he owned it, and I was right behind him. The reception area looked like the parlor in Gunsmoke that I used to watch with my dad on Sunday nights. I was just a little girl at the time and thought

Miss Kitty was pretty. I didn't realize back then that she was probably a retired hooker who'd become a madam.

The Kitty Kat was dimly lit and the windows were covered with heavy drapes. There were red velour sofas and lamps with tasseled shades. In the corner was a bar. Of course there was a bar—everywhere I worked there was a bar. There was also an ATM machine which was also fairly standard at the places I worked. The brothel was deserted early on a Thursday morning.

While we waited for the owner, I moseyed over to the bar where a stack of laminated menus was displayed. I scanned one of them too see the smorgasbord of offerings, and what a smorgasbord it was! There was the "Half & Half," the "Hot & Cold Oral," the "Hot French Oil Massage With Happy Ending," and the "Dominatrix Play Session." No prices were listed. This was so outrageous I didn't know if I wanted to laugh, or cry.

The owner came out looking nothing like I thought he should. He was in his mid-fifties and wore a suit and tie, like he'd just stepped out of an IBM board meeting. He was cleanly shaven and his hair was cropped short with silvering at the temples. He was handsome and well-mannered. I don't know exactly what I was expecting, but not this. He looked like Richard Gere in *An Officer and a Gentleman* and it sort of threw me for a loop.

"This is the girl I told you about. Kate, this is Gil."

"It's very nice to meet you, Kate." He gave me a polite handshake. Now, it's not like I expected him to grope me, but still. To the extent that he was checking me out, he did so expertly without me noticing because that is the sort of thing we women notice because we're not blind. So, yeah, I'm sure he checked me out and I wouldn't have expected anything less given the job I was applying for. Typing skills? Who needs 'em. Science or math strengths? Why bother.

"Crock told me about you but I had no idea you would be so beautiful. Thank you for showing some interest in our establishment."

Ah, The Establishment. Like it was a bank. I worried that he was too smooth. That always makes me leery because people like that are usually fake, or they're hiding something. I probably would have felt more comfortable if he didn't beat around the bush—if he'd just come right out and said, "Welcome to our little whorehouse. Wanna jump right in and get acquainted with the Hot and Cold Oral?"

"Let me show you around," he said. "And please feel free to ask any questions you might have."

Gil led us through the Gunsmoke lobby. From the outside, the place looked rundown but it was actually fairly plush inside, especially with the help of the dimmer switch. Of course, I presumed the customers weren't there for the décor. I doubt the typical John obsessed over the charmeuse silk on the love seat. And you'd probably never hear them gush over the wallpaper. Oh my gosh, is that from the Ralph Lauren fall collection?

"Um, I'm not sure I'm interested in, you know, actually working here. Crock said maybe I could just stay here for a little bit to see what I think."

Gil looked at Crock who pretended to be occupied with something on his shoe. "Well," Gil stalled, "we don't ordinarily offer free room and board to our girls unless they're working." He looked at Crock again who was now suddenly fascinated with his imitation gold-leaf wristwatch. "But if you'd like to stay for a day or two we might be able to work something out.

Here, let me show you some of the rooms." Another irritated glance at Crock.

The rooms were small with queen-sized beds and little dressers. I had no earthly clue what might have been in the dresser drawers but I doubt there were many Bibles. The walls were decorated with cheap art and made to feel homey. I thought this homey-ness was a bit odd because I assumed the customers were there to *escape* the feel of home. Why not up the ante and hang a photo of the missus and kids next to a Home Sweet Home embroidery?

Gil then led us to a separate hallway where the four "Theme Rooms" were located, all of which promoted super fun themes. These rooms cost extra and I'm here to tell you, they must have been worth every penny. The first was called the Arabian Nights room. I could only imagine riding in on a camel wearing only a veil and high heels. The room boasted a Jacuzzi next to the bed that was surrounded by sheer fabric to match the veil. It looked to me like a perfectly good place to escape a swarm of mosquitoes.

I'm sure the Wild West room was popular, too. The bed was surrounded by what I can only assume was meant to be a corral. The wood was old and dry and looked like you'd have to be careful or you'd get a sliver. There were two branding irons in the corner of the room (for decoration only, I hoped) and some rusty spurs. An old wagon wheel leaned against the far wall and a lasso hung from a hook next to a John Wayne poster. Boy, that oughta get you in the mood, huh? Everything you'd need to inspire a good ol' western romp, except maybe a cow pie on the worn shag carpet.

The Count Drag-u-la room must've been popular with the vampire and drag queen folks. Apparently, the Kitty Kat couldn't afford separate rooms for every fetish so they had to combine a few. Crossdressers with vampire fetishes must've been overcome with passion in this sucker. It was filled with life-sized mannequins dressed like Liberace and Cher.

The last room Gil showed us was the dark and dungeony Pleasure and Pain room. The bed was surrounded by the gray iron bars of a jail cell where a large metal ring with keys was stuck in the lock of the door. There was a wooden rack in the corner of the cell with readymade handcuffs fastened about six feet above the floor. I'm not kidding. A variety of whips and chains hung from the bars of the cell and a black-leather female cat suit hung on a hanger next to the bed. A pair of thigh-high black boots was draped over the foot of the bed.

I suppose I can wrap my head around the value of a mild fetish, even though I don't believe I had any, at least not any that would raise an eyebrow. Kinky lingerie? Sure. Role-playing? Perhaps. But being spanked? Navel eroticism? The thrill of being peed on? Seriously, what was it with some people?

Crock walked over to the handcuffs and started fiddling with them while I was taking all this in. "So, if I wanted to work here, when would I start?" I couldn't believe I'd even asked the question, especially after the tour. I mean, this was hardly the Louvre. In a way, it was so ridiculous to me that it somehow seemed less wicked, less serious. I can't explain it. Don't get me wrong, I had no doubt this was full-bodied prostitution but it was just so . . . *pathetic*, almost to the point of bordering on harmless. Of course, I knew it was anything but harmless, especially for the poor girls who sold their flesh there.

"You could start as soon as you fill out the paperwork and we get your medical clearance."

"Medical clearance?"

"Yes, all our girls undergo a thorough medical exam before they're allowed to engage any of the men. They're re-checked once a month to be sure they're healthy. We stress the health of our employees."

Well, my goodness, what a relief! Call the Better Business Bureau! Employer of the Year!

"Actually," he said, "you wouldn't technically be an employee—you'd be an independent contractor, so we don't offer health insurance or other benefits, other than the cost of the check-ups. Any medical concerns?"

"Um, no, not that I know of."

"Well, then we could probably have you on line within a day or two."

"And what would I get paid?"

"Maybe you saw our menu when you came in. We don't list the prices on it because we're not allowed to. The girls can only quote prices once the customer is back in the room with them. What you charge them is completely up to you. Like I said, you're an independent contractor. You pay the house fifty percent of whatever you get and you keep the rest. We'll give you some general guidelines about the charges we recommend but, as I said, it's really up to you."

"So, if I worked here, could I live here, too? I don't have a car at the moment."

"Sure. About half the girls live here on the premises. You'd be responsible for the house's fifty percent, plus a small fee for room and board. You might need to share a bathroom with one of the other girls but we haven't had any problems with that over the years." Yeah, right, I thought. I've shared bathrooms with girls before.

"Would I have to use my real name?"

"Only on the medical forms. We know the girls are concerned about confidentiality and we respect that. You can also get your mail here, but most of the girls choose to get a post office box, for obvious reasons."

"Can I stay here for a few days before I decide?"

"I suppose," he said with another sideways glance at Crock. "I hope you'll decide to work with us but you'll need to get your own place within a couple days if you, you know, decide this isn't for you."

I walked out to the parking lot with Crock. Ten years earlier I would have been mortified to be seen in the parking lot of a brothel with another man, even by strangers, and even if my presence there had been completely innocent and coincidental. But any mortification had gradually eroded like so much of me, my shield of righteousness waning to the point that it was nearly extinct.

"So, what did you think?" he asked. "Want me to take you back to Vegas, or do you wanna stay here?"

I was torn, I really was. I was being asked if I was going to be a prostitute. Unimaginable. How could I be torn? This should not have been a tough question. But still it was.

"Tell me the truth, Crock. Do you think I should do this? Maybe if I only stayed for a month or two I could save enough to buy a car. I'd be harder to find, too, and I'd have enough to pay off Spanos in case he found me."

Crock opened his car door.

"That's up to you, Kate."

It was hot and windy and dust blew up from the gravel parking lot. This was the moment, right there in that dry and dusty parking lot in Pahrump, Nevada with little dust devils swirling.

"You can always quit if it doesn't work out and I'd take you back at Sugar & Spice once this whole deal with Spanos blows over."

"Yeah, you're probably right," I said.

I wanted to hug him. I wanted to tell him how sorry I was for the loss of his wife and his beautiful little girls. It had always been about me but now I knew a tiny bit of Crock's backstory and it was heartbreaking. I'd judged him for the business he ran and now I was embarrassed for myself because of that misjudgment. Crock was a good man—a decent man who happened to run a strip club but had compassion for the down and out. There was Lucinda, and skinny Wayne, and me. I'm sure there were many others, too.

We stood in the parking lot with my inner conflict raging. I knew Crock had to get back on the road but he didn't rush me. There was the revelation about Crock's wife and daughters swirling in my head, competing for space with the realization that I was at the threshold of a final line to cross. And of course there was the absence of my husband who had deserted me and the uncertainty of my life's trajectory which appeared to be pointing due south.

I wanted Crock to tell me not to do it. I wanted him to order me back into his car. I wanted him to say I wasn't that kind of girl—that I was a good and decent girl from southern Utah who got temporarily mixed up in something she hadn't planned, something she couldn't control. Instead, he pulled two things from his wallet: his business card and a one-hundred-dollar bill.

"I'm a phone call away. Understand?" He leaned over and kissed me on the forehead and then bent into the Lincoln and closed the door. I watched him drive away, his tires kicking up the dust. I then turned around and walked back to the Kitty Kat, opened the door, and stepped inside.

36

KATHERINE

THE ECONOMY WAS IN THE PITS and Vaughn decided to scale back on the overhead, so the office in Cedar City had to go. Besides, Vaughn was closing in on retirement and wanted Keith back in St. George to run the whole shebang.

"I'm not moving," cried Jenna. "It's not fair! What about all my friends? I'll *die* if we move!" It was a dramatic speech.

"Honey, it'll be all right," I said.

"No it won't! You don't know! And you don't even care!"

Jacob's theatrics were just as impressive. He'd become a big deal since the water balloon bombardment. That's what shellacking the faculty will do. Here he was, about to start tenth grade as the most popular kid in school, and now we were *moving?* Had we lost our freaking minds? Trisha Dalton, the head cheerleader, had even said hi to him at the mall!

My mom was thrilled we were moving back. She'd been "down in the dumps" according to my dad who was on cloud nine after the county commissioner election and couldn't understand why my mom spent so much time in her room. "Jackie," he'd say, "you've been moping in bed far too long. You don't need to get hooked on all those pills. You just need to get up and get moving."

I told my dad the pills were for depression and that this was more than simple disinterest but he couldn't accept the fact that his wife had mental health issues, as if it reflected poorly on him somehow. She'd also occasionally dropped the ball on getting his dinner to him on time, and there were days she didn't do the dishes.

"She doesn't need a shrink and all that fancy talk. I've tried to tell her all she needs is a good hobby, but she won't listen. She just mopes around and takes those pills."

Keith and I sold our home in Cedar City and bought a place a few blocks from my parent's house. Want to guess who our real estate agent was? Renaldo. I felt butterflies when Keith recommended we hire him. This time Renaldo made his intentions perfectly clear when he came by to look at our home and all the fancy upgrades we'd made, like installing a few window shades and a brand new garage door opener. After all, how else was I supposed to interpret this: "Want to meet me Friday afternoon at a home I have listed in Santa Clara? I've got the key and no one will be there." I knew he didn't want to show me the upgraded appliances or the roomy linen closet. I hesitated then heard myself say, "Yeah, that'd be fun."

I decided not to eat anything for two days so I would be skinnier and did some updated grooming in places no one could see. Then there was the question of what to wear. Do I go with the button-up top or a tighter fitting pullover that might be a bit sexier? And I decided my bra collection was too functional. I needed a lingerie upgrade, stat. And, wait, I wore garments and there was no way I could wear those. They were asexual with a capital A so I needed a sexier pair of panties, too. The hypocrisy was startling. Excuse me for a moment Renaldo while I change out of my sacred underwear that is supposed to remind me of the covenants I made to Keith and the church.

I lay in bed that Thursday night and couldn't sleep. Here was my husband—naïve, trusting, good—and Renaldo was asking me to cheat on him (to say nothing of his own wife). I looked over at Keith who was splayed out on his back contentedly snoring, his mouth wide open like a fish on ice at the market. My guess is he was dreaming about the upcoming Raiders season opener or perhaps an order of new pipe sleeves for the plumbing supply store. Would I have rather spent Friday afternoon at the house for sale with Renaldo or Keith? Renaldo, for sure, and I'll admit that. Who wouldn't? He was drop dead handsome, and his body? Wow. But beyond that, Keith was the better man. The much better man, and I realized meeting up with Renaldo was wrong on every level. So, yes, of course I wanted to, but there was no way I could ever actually do such a thing. All that dieting would be for not because Keith wouldn't have noticed if I gained or lost ten pounds.

I called Renaldo the next morning to say I remembered I had an appointment that afternoon and couldn't make it. Sorta chickened out, right? I should have just been honest and told him that it was wrong and I couldn't do it. Then I thought about sending an anonymous note to his wife because I'd sure like to know if my husband was inviting attractive women to vacant homes for sale. But, wow, how hypocritical would *that* have been? Here I was practically egging him on, grooming my private areas and experimenting with sexy lingerie, then calling him out to his wife? And doing so anonymously because I would have been too ashamed to admit that I was the other woman? Pathetic.

I decided to banish all thoughts of Renaldo, or at least try to, because if I was having this much guilt and despair when we hadn't even touched each other, how bad would it have been if we ever did? Then I had to make an excuse to Keith for why I couldn't make it to the home closing (because Renaldo might be there) and we moved back to St. George.

A few days before moving, Keith found the bag from Nordstrom with my sexy new bra and panties that still had the tags on them. What's this? he asked. Oh that? I hemmed and hawed and then he became distracted by a sport's story on the news about some quarterback who was injured.

The kids got over the move quickly, especially when guilt forced me to splurge on the pricey Lucky jeans Jacob had to have. I also allowed Jenna to manipulate me into a shopping spree at Abercrombie & Fitch, even though it bugged me that their teenage models hardly even *wore* clothes. The kids were enrolled in their new school for fall classes and the complaining petered out.

Then Jenna started her period. She'd been an emotional wreck leading up to it. "Gol, what's gotten in to Jenna?" Keith asked. "She's so touchy all of a sudden." Fortunately, she started at home and not in her pre-algebra class like Amanda Ticknor. To this day, whenever I think about poor Amanda, I think of that day. It's what she became known for—the girl who bled all over her white jeans and grossed everybody out.

Because we were now living in the same neighborhood as my parents, we were also in the same ward, or church congregation. One redeeming thing about the move for Jenna, aside from the Abercrombie spree, was that all the cool kids at Snow Canyon Middle School were in our ward, including Justin Hill who apparently was the cutest of them all.

The first Sunday of every month was "Testimony Meeting" at our church. That's a monthly church service where the membership is invited to stand up in the congregation and testify about their belief. It's not a mandatory thing. In fact, most ward members just sit there and try to stay awake, but there are always a few who stand up to testify about how much they believe. Most of them are sincere but I swear others just take the opportunity to brag about their travel plans, or a spiritual experience they'd had, whether it was inspiring to the rest of us or not. A traveling microphone circulates through the pews for those who get the urge to stand and speak up.

Anyway, we'd been living in our new home for about a month, school was underway, and the kids were adjusting. That first Sunday in October was Testimony Meeting at our church. The meeting started but no one stood. Brother Hansen, a regular stander upper, finally broke the ice with a nice little ditty about why he believed. Then there was a lull when no one else stood to testify. When this happens, everyone looks down at their lap, or shows a sudden interest in the hymn book so as not to get the evil eye from their wife or the bishop about why they were sitting on their duffs when they ought to be testifying.

It was uncomfortably quiet—everyone hoping someone else would be brave enough to break the silence. That's when my sister, twelve-year-old Kylie, stood up in the middle of the congregation and waited for the portable mic to be handed down the pew to her.

There was a general murmur of encouragement. Fellow church members smiled at my parents for having raised such a special daughter. How sweet, they thought. Kylie stood for several awkward seconds, looking at all the people staring at her. She removed her thick glasses and wiped them on her dress, then put them back on to prolong her moment.

"I'm Kylie and, um, we moved here. This is Karolyn's dress." Her voice was loud and nasally. "I love Jesus and I miss my old house. Um, my Sunday school teacher gave us treats." The audience members smiled. "And, um, I know the church is true all the time." More smiles. How special but, okay, Kylie, it's time to wrap it up. Unfortunately, she wasn't finished.

"My mom sleeps in the day because she's sad and my dad he gets mad at her for being sad all the time."

I shot a look at my parents a few pews away. This was bad. Kylie was standing at the very end of the row; Kimberly, Kristy, Korbin, Kelly, and Karolyn sat between her and my parents.

"But, um, she takes these one pills so she won't be sad but my dad said they're stupid pills and they don't work good."

My dad was frantically motioning for Kimberly or Kristy to take the microphone away, but Kylie held the mic in a fervid grip and would have none of it.

"I like my new school. I go with Jenna. I'm her aunt. And now I'm old, just like Jenna, because I had my period just like her. She had a big period. It's gross. I don't like having a period too much."

Jenna was sitting next to me with a bewildered look on her face—a dawning look of realization that her whole life was being destroyed in real time right in front of Justin Hill and all the other popular kids at her new school. Several boys her age were sitting together, elbowing each other and trying not to burst out laughing. This was the funniest thing that had ever happened in church. No doubt this story would circulate throughout the entire student body the next morning before the principal could finish making his announcements over the school intercom. Jenna would become the next Amanda Ticknor. I was sick to my stomach.

My dad finally stood and scooted sideways down the row as fast as he could, banging the knees of my younger siblings as he went. He took the microphone from Kylie and handed it to the young man who was responsible for passing it on. Kylie looked confused because she'd only done what Jesus wanted.

It might have been slightly less traumatic if another person had immediately stood to explain why the church was so true. But no one did. The silence was thick and every second felt like a full semester. Jenna looked up at me with a pleading look as if to say, "Please, Mom, do something, anything." But I didn't know what to do.

Finally, an old man on the fourth row stood. He was a Regular Testifier who usually anchored the monthly testimony meeting. He was mostly deaf and probably hadn't heard the dramatic details of my mom's depression and my daughter's period. He described a road trip he and his wife had recently taken to the Carlsbad Caverns. This had nothing to do with Jesus, or the church, but he liked to ramble and his poor wife probably never listened to him. He wrapped up his travelogue with the inspirational message that they'd traveled safely with no hiccups, other than a low tire near Flagstaff, so God had been watching out for them. This was indeed faith promoting, but most people had tuned him out (they'd already heard about the road trip) because they were still digesting Kylie's little exposé.

Jenna bolted to the car the millisecond she heard "Amen" on the closing prayer, convinced as she was that everyone would see her as a human tampon from that time forth. I hurried out behind her and unlocked the car door so she could hide.

"I hate her! I hate her! I hate her!" She was sobbing uncontrollably.

I said nothing. What good would it have done to say that Kylie hadn't meant it, or that Jenna shouldn't hate her, or that it wasn't a big deal?

"Why did she have to say that?" Jenna begged.

"Oh, Jenna, I'm so sorry. Kylie doesn't understand. She just wants to be like you. She worships you."

"Well, I hate her and I never want to see her again!"

Just then Kylie came over to the car. She was smiling in her new dress and felt proud of her speech, oblivious to the mortification in its wake.

"Roll down the window, Jenna. I want to tell you something."

Jenna stared straight ahead. Kylie walked around to the other side of the car where I sat.

"Kafrun, roll down the window."

I did.

"Did you hear my talk?"

"Yes, Kylie, we did," I said.

"Can I have a ride home with you guys? I want to sit by Jenna."

I was in a bad mood following Kylie's revelation about Jenna and my mom. But mostly it was because of Halloween. I loved it as a kid, of course, but hated it as a mom. I'd like to believe this didn't make me a bad mother, or even an unhappy human being. But the expectations! I'm not a big planner, however that year I'd pledged to be a better mom and slaved away on a Luigi costume for Josh. The day before Halloween he tells me it's too itchy and he wants to be He-Man instead. I told him he was going to be Luigi whether it itched or not. Well, guess who won that fight? The net result was that he left the house with nude-colored pantyhose pulled down over his head. To be honest, he looked like a penis.

A neighbor a few doors down was a recent convert to the church who'd just moved to St. George from a small town in southern France. Evidently, the French don't do Halloween like we do because when the kids rang his doorbell and held out their pillow cases half-filled with candy, this man, who spoke limited English, reached into each pillow case and took a piece of their candy. I was such an immature mother that I told Josh this neighbor wouldn't have done that if he'd gone as Luigi.

37

KATE

MY ROOM AT THE KITTY KAT was small and all the way in the back. It had been one room divided in two. I'd been told a girl named Cinnamon had the other one. The two rooms shared a tiny bathroom. One of those faux-marble showers was wedged into the corner of the bathroom with a shard of soap and razor in the tray. I figured Cinnamon had to be small to fit into a shower like that.

I opened the mirror cabinet above the sink and saw it was crammed with orange pill bottles. I took one out and read the label. Percocet. I put it back and picked up another one. Lortab. Then another. Oxy.

"What the fuck you lookin' at?"

"Oh, hi," I said as I put the bottle back on the shelf and closed the cabinet. "Gil told me I'd be sharing this bathroom and I was just looking for some space to put my things."

"Just keep your hands off that shit. I need it. Back pain."

"Are you Cinnamon?"

"You some detective? Who else would I be?"

I was in no mood to deal with this girl. And that's what she was—she couldn't have been over twenty. She was tall and thin with cropped reddish hair and a spray of freckles across her nose. She was generally hip-less and from behind she reminded me of a matchstick. But when you saw her from the front or the sides you could not escape her huge, taut breasts. In profile, she looked like the letter P. For the life of me, I don't know how the plastic surgeon crammed them in there. They were sturdy and presumably rock hard. They wouldn't jiggle on a bet. I suppose you could pop them with a pin resulting in a geyser of saline squirting you in the eye, but they wouldn't jiggle.

"I'm Kate. I just got here and Gil said I could stay a few days in this other room."

"That cocksucker's such an FPS. Last thing we need is more girls around here. I'm lucky to turn two tricks all day."

I had no idea what an FPS was and decided not to ask. "Well, I'm not even sure I'll be working here. I'm still deciding."

"Deciding what?"

"I haven't done this before."

"Sure you haven't. I could put that shit on a fucking T-shirt."

"No, really."

"Whatever," and then she mumbled something about a GDG, whatever that was.

"Hey," I said, "I'm trying to be nice. We're sharing this bathroom, so quit being such a bitch about it. Okay?"

"Fine. Just keep your hands off my back pills."

I came to learn many things about my new bathroom mate. She never sat still but didn't use her inexhaustible supply of energy to clean. Succinctly stated, Cinnamon was a slob. I even found evidence of dried boogers on a hand towel in the bathroom. She also listened to country music, the twangy kind, and I've never liked that. And, finally, there was her potty mouth. There are times when a perfectly used swear word hits its mark but Cinnamon overdid it. She had the unique ability to use the word "fuck" as a verb, noun, pronoun, adjective, adverb, and probably a dangling participle, whatever those are. A typical sentence might sound like this: The dick fuck who hired me yesterday was so fucking fucked that I couldn't fucking believe it when he didn't even leave me a fucking tip.

There was a small kitchen and dining room in the back of the brothel. Dinner that first night was served to the girls by the fat, lecherous cook who ogled the new meat (that'd be me) and the other girls, too. Candy, who was accustomed to men ogling said, "Fuck off, Larry," without even looking up from her plate of spaghetti. "And quit looking at my tits while you're at it."

"Yeah," said Fantasee whose tits weren't worth ogling over but who had a humongous rear end, the kind that pivots with each step. The kind you could serve tea on.

"What you staring at?" Candy said to me even though I was hardly even looking at her.

"Nothing."

"Well, knock it off."

"All of this is rather inappropriate," said a girl named Evelyn. "Let's show our new friend proper decorum."

"Please," said Candy, "not another one of your lectures."

"Perhaps we should ask our new guest to tell us a little about herself." Turning to me, she said: "I apologize for our impropriety." Then she crossed herself.

I didn't respond. I'll admit Evelyn left me a bit off balance.

Here I was eating spaghetti in a brothel with the Lecherous Cook and a room full of sex workers, one of whom looked like a prim librarian and wore a neckless with a cross. It also threw me off that her name was Evelyn, a name that belonged on the lapel of a woman working behind the makeup counter at Macy's.

"You bitches seen that guy who come in today?" asked Fantasee.

"The fat one with the cowboy hat?" asked Candy. "Yeah, I saw him."

"Went and give me a fat $200 tip. Had hisself the smallest pecker in Nevada. Hardly swolled up at all. Course I tol' him he don't need to put on no raincoat jus' this once bees he's so handsome and bees he's some special kinda doctah o' lawyah o' somethin'."

"Motherfuckers never wanna use 'em," said Cinnamon. "Bunch a SLF's."

"Please, Cinnamon, your language," said Evelyn. "It's vulgar and offensive."

"Course, I 'nspected it first bees due for my checkup and can't be off no line. Got me a car payment and Jermaine he be suckin' me dry as one a dem goddamned bones. He don't care about nuthin' 'cept his precious truck. Gotta get hisself new wheels bees the ones he got ain't shiny enough and gotta get hisself a big ol' engine. Good Lord, is all I hear about."

"But I thought they were required to wear condoms," I interrupted.

The other girls looked at me like I was from Mars.

"Not if they pay some extra they don't."

"Gil says we gonna be godawful busy on account of there's a big ol' rodeo in Vegas this weekend. Gonna have us lots of them cowboys in town."

"Yeah, and I'm off the fuckin' line," said Cinnamon.

"Profanity shows a poor vocabulary and lack of imagination."

"Oh, go fuck yourself, Evelyn."

"You prove my point," said Evelyn with a weary nod of her head and then crossed herself again for good measure.

"Whatever," said Cinnamon with a dramatic eye roll. "You bitches gonna fuckin' take big money from me. WAPO. Cause ya know they'd all pick me. They're all SFB."

"Cuz your tits 're so big," said Candy. "I ain't walkin' around with no bowlin' balls on this sweet little thing. No sir."

"Why are you off line?" I asked Cinnamon.

"Cuz I'm havin' my fuckin' period, why else?" She looked at the other girls and rolled her eyes. "Fuck, Kathy, you got a fuckin' lot to learn, girl."

"It's actually Kate."

"Yeah, whatever."

Other than Evelyn, these girls at the Kitty Kat didn't strike me as classy, upgraded prostitutes. I'd never heard the F word so much in my life. And the makeup? I'm talking an abundance of the stuff. Maybe it was because of the language, or the makeup, but I thought I was so much different than they were. And by different I mean better. I wasn't a common hooker. Oh no, not me. I was only there because of the unique situation with Victor Spanos, that's all. As if I'd be in the Mormon Tabernacle Choir if not for him.

I called Crock the next morning. "Have you heard from Ricky?"

"No. Why would he call me?"

"I told him before he took off that I'd probably crash at your place for a few days. I figured he might try to reach me there."

"Well, he hasn't. Sorry, Kate."

I read so much frustration and disgust in Crock's reply. Frustration that I was still asking about Ricky, and disgust that I appeared to give a shit about him after all he'd put me through. And that meant something coming from Crock because I believed he really *did* care about me. Certainly more than Ricky ever did.

Gil gave me the name of the doctor I was supposed to see because he knew nothing, and I mean nothing, would zap the profits of the establishment like an ugly epidemic of crabs. He said I could borrow his car and the visit would be paid for. Evelyn was sitting in the reception area reading a novel written by a Russian author whose name I could never pronounce. She must have been eavesdropping when I was getting ready to leave because she told me it was free medical care, "which is invaluable in this chaotic economic environment."

The medical exam was fairly routine with an emphasis on my genital "skill set," as if it was noteworthy to go pro in my field. First they took a blood test. I hate those things because I have small veins and they end up poking me about ten times. Then the doctor felt my abdomen and did a pap. He told me to watch for STD's, insist on condoms, and come back in a month. That's about it. I was now free to legally sell myself for profit in Nye County, Nevada. And how cool was *that?*

Gil was in the front parlor area when I returned. As always, he was dressed in a conservative suit and tie. I can't imagine he dressed that way to impress the truck drivers and traveling sales reps who'd slink in. In fact, I'd yet to see a suit and tie at any of the places I worked in Vegas, except maybe on the old man who was with the girl I kicked that night at Sugar & Spice with my high heel—the old man who was probably going broke because of all the plastic surgery bills and trips to Zales. And I'm positive that was the only ascot I'd ever seen.

"You all checked out?" Gil asked.

"Yeah, I guess."

"Good. There's a big national rodeo coming to Vegas tomorrow and we could use you."

I think back to all those moments over the past fifteen years, moments when I had to choose. It wasn't one big jump but rather a series of hops. You don't go from Sunday school to a brothel in one tidy leap. I think of the story of the frog in the pot of water—you know the one where the water gradually gets hotter and hotter and before the frog knows it, he's cooked, through and through.

You probably look at me now and gasp. *But how could she! She knows better!* And I suppose you'd be right, but who do you think these girls are? Do you think we came out of the chute this way? Do you think this is what we dreamed about as kids?

I am Katherine Coombs from St. George, Utah. I was a little white girl from a middle class family who played with dolls and did dress up. I went to church and bore my testimony. I was the Homecoming Queen in high school with a good GPA and was voted Most Likely To Succeed, not Most Likely To Become A Prostitute.

It seemed as if my younger life had all been rehearsed, choreographed from generations of faithful, devout, rule-keeping relatives. I could deviate from the script but to do so would have been . . . well, it would have been an unexpected disappointment. There were times when my back was to the wall and I didn't think I had an option other than the one I chose. In fact, sometimes it felt like I hadn't chosen it at all—that it had "just happened" and it hadn't been my doing. But of course it had. No one put a gun to my head. No one forced me to work at Sugar & Spice, or Lil' Secrets, or the Kitty Kat.

If I could start over, do you honestly think I'd be sitting in some dingy brothel in Pahrump, Nevada trying to decide if I would cross that final line? No way. And neither would Cinnamon, Candy, Fantasee, Evelyn, or any of the others. But I felt stuck. This is who I'd become.

I'd already decided by default that I wouldn't *not* do it—which is almost the same thing as saying I would. You might not see the difference because it's pretty subtle, but it felt better to ease into the choice a little bit at a time.

I heard myself say to Gil, "Yeah, I guess I'll try it for a few days and see how it goes."

"All right, good. You've seen the menu. Look it over again. Like I said, there are no set prices, and don't quote anything until you're back in your room."

"So what's the Half & Half?"

"That's our most popular. Give them a blow job and sex." It sounded odd to hear this impeccably dressed gentleman with manicured nails speak so crassly. It felt like he should have blushingly said I would be performing fellatio and sexual intercourse. "I know some of the girls don't make them wear a condom because they'll usually get a bigger tip that way. But you should insist on them."

"What if they won't? What if a guy gets too rough, or won't listen to me?"

"There's a buzzer on the inside of the door, like a doorbell. I'll show it to you. There's another one by the bed. You get in trouble, you ring it. We've got people who will help you."

"So what should I charge them for the Half & Half?" This was the most ridiculous conversation of conversations. I mean, think about it. Here I was asking my employer how much to charge a complete stranger for the Half & Half. It was so pathetic it was actually funny, but not in a fun way.

"We've got some girls who'll only charge $250 and some who'll charge $500 or $600. If I were you, I'd charge $750."

"And how long do I have to give them?"

"Half hour, give or take."

"So, like, how does it work? Do we just rotate or something?"

"No, our customers choose. Joanne—she's the one you met in front—she'll let you know when to come out for the lineup. You'll line up with the other girls and the customer will select one of you. You want to be nice to Joanne or she won't call you out as often. Some of the girls give her a little something, maybe five percent."

"I just wait in the back until she calls me?"

"Yes, or you can hang out up front if you prefer. I don't like it when the girls do that but I wouldn't mind if you did. Just remember, no quoting prices until you've given them a tour.

That simply means you take the customer back to your room to negotiate. Most of the men already know the drill because we have a lot of repeat customers. Don't worry about it. I'm sure you'll do fine."

I obviously needed to go by another name. I couldn't be Kate or Katherine, not while working there. Other than Evelyn, all the women lied about their names. At least I assume Evelyn was her given name because who would choose that for a hooker name? The men lied about their names, too. And that was just the tip of the iceberg on all the lying going around. I decided to go by Trixie because I didn't have much time to deliberate. Yeah, Trixie, about the most cliché hooker name of all time.

That night, three men walked into the bar. It sounds like the start of a joke, doesn't it? These men wore cowboy hats and tight Wranglers with large shiny belt buckles. You could tell they weren't real cowboys who rode horses and roped calves. Their Wranglers were pressed with a crisp crease and there was no mud or manure on them. There were no sweat stains on their hats either and their pickup trucks had never been off the pavement. These were drugstore cowboys who'd preened in front of a mirror with their polished boots and their pearl-snap shirts, hoping for that authentic cowboy costume. Personally, I thought it was laughable. But that's just the opinion of a girl who worked at the Kitty Kat.

Joanne, who was a pleasant looking sixty-year-old, asked these imitation buckaroos if they'd like to see some of the girls. "Well, ma'am, we sure as shootin' would!" So Joanne walked into the back hallway and knocked on the girls' doors.

"Got customers," she announced.

Six of us came out of our rooms and walked to an area near the bar where we *literally* stood in a lineup wearing short shorts and sleeveless tops. It was humiliating. No, it was worse than that. Much worse. Remember I mentioned visiting my cousins up in Enterprise and going to my uncle's cattle auction when I was in the third grade? That's what I felt like—a side of beef at auction. And the worst thing about it, aside from the obvious worse things, is that I *wanted* them to pick me.

The tallest one pointed at me. When he did, his two buddies cracked, "Shee-it, Dale! That's who I was gonna pick, you ol' rascal." It felt like I got stabbed when I heard his name.

"You shoulda been quicker, Lar."

"Oh, you'll be plenty quick all right, Dale, you ol' son-of-a-gun!" and they laughed.

"Well, lemme see here," said the second one. "I'll take the short one there. No, not her, the other one," he said pointing at Desiree. I felt bad for Misty who'd been publicly rejected—like being the last one picked when choosing sides for volleyball in P.E. After the third one picked Fantasee I heard him whisper to his buddies, "Take a look at the ass on that one, will ya!"

I led Dale, aka Tex, back to my homey little room and sat on the bed while he stood by the door, nervously twirling the new cowboy hat in his hands. He was actually more nervous than I was which made me braver for some reason.

"So, what's this here gonna cost me?"

"It depends on what you want. Did you see the list of services?"

"Yeah, but I just sorta looked it over real quick like."

I was in it for the money, and only the money. Why else would I be sitting in that pathetic room? For fun? For the décor? I'd sold out, but I wouldn't sell out for peanuts. I told the nervous fake-cowboy that I'd give him the best blow job money could buy for three hundred dollars. "You want to have sex with me, that'll be another five hundred."

I saw his surprise, so I stood and began to unbutton my shirt. Tex was transfixed. I left my shirt unbuttoned but didn't take it off. He could see that I wasn't wearing a bra. He remained mute, so I undid the top button on my short jeans.

"So what'll it be, cowboy?" I almost laughed at how absurd this was. I felt like I was acting in a sappy B-rated western. And I was surprised that I was as comfortable as I was. Now, I wasn't actually *comfortable* comfortable mind you, like you think of being in your jammies and slippers with a cup of hot cocoa. I was just more comfortable than I thought I'd be. Besides, I didn't need to concentrate on the actual task at hand because it's not a complicated one. Even a dog can do it without any training whatsoever.

"Let's see then, altogether I'd be lookin' at, whaddya say, eight hundred in all? That there's pretty steep."

"Best eight hundred you'll ever spend." I took a step closer to him and reached for his belt buckle. "Do we have a deal?" I figured he hadn't driven all the way to Pahrump to have a Jack and Coke. And I knew there was a bulge in his back pocket, too.

He swallowed dryly and said, "Yeah, I guess."

"Then come over here, cowboy, and let's have some fun."

I unbuckled his belt and unzipped his zipper. I was surprised by how big he was. But even though he had a lean, chiseled body and a man-sized six-shooter, I didn't share his level of excitement. At all. But I pretended to. Oh, I was well practiced at pretending. This was a one-shot deal without any intimacy because, let's be honest, this wasn't a man I would share a silver anniversary with.

Tex was quick on the draw. He almost lost it when I rolled the condom down his barrel. Twenty minutes later we were both dressed. "That was fun," I said. "You were amazing." Hey, I figured if he was paying $800 for a grand total of twenty minutes it wouldn't kill me to butter him up a little with a white lie. That was the least of my sins. "I hope you'll come back and see me again."

"I think I wanna take you home," he said. Yeah, like that was going to happen. Hey Honey, let me introduce you to the hooker I met in Pahrump. Mind if she stays with us and the kids for a while? Maybe set up shop in the guest room?

"Can't do that," I said. "But you can come back and see me whenever you want."

"I think I'll do that, by golly."

"So," I said when he didn't make a move for his wallet, "that'll be eight hundred."

He pulled out his wallet and counted out $700. "Sure you can't cut me a piece a slack seems we were only at it such a short time?"

"I could, but then I'd have to tell your friends why I had to reduce the price."

"Okay, then. But I ain't got any left for a tip."

"You can tip me next time if you'd like."

I was leading him back to the bar in less than thirty minutes with eight hundred dollars in the front pocket of my daisy dukes. One of his buddies, the one who'd been with Fantasee, was already at the bar. I gave my cowpoke a peck on his cheek that smelled of aftershave and nothing like an actual ranch. As

I turned to walk back to my room, I overheard him say, "Geez, Lar, I went and gave her the goddamned ride of her life."

I went back to my room and washed my face. I was about to turn on the shower when Cinnamon barged into the bathroom, again without even knocking.

"So how much?" she asked.

"Five hundred." I'm not sure why I lied, other than I was a chronic liar. I just figured Cinnamon would be mad if the new girl made too much.

"Yeah, I gotta raise my fuckin' prices," she said. "I could easy get five hundred, but the last fucker didn't have enough money, so I just gave him a fuckin' BBBJ for a couple hundred. I did a CBJ for about half that earlier that day because it's been so fuckin' slow."

"A BBBJ?" Was this a new kind of sandwich?

"It's a fuckin' bare back blow job—you know, without a fuckin' rubber. He was so fuckin' cheap I had to talk him up from a CBJ—that's a covered blow job. I think the fuckin' economy's down or something. Had me a guy the other day alls he wanted was a Russian. I only charged him two hundred for that. Course I had to throw in a goddamned R & T before he'd fuckin' leave."

"A Russian?"

"Yeah, guy just wanted to tit fuck me. But he couldn't cum so I had to give him a fuckin' Rub & Tug. Course, he gave me a fifty-dollar tip for the R & T."

My new roommate was really something and I remained in awe of here comprehensive use of the F word. I also knew I'd have to brush up on my acronyms if I wanted to keep up with her. I'll start practicing here by using my own acronym: IN-

AGS. It's Never A Good Sign when your roommate takes fifteen minutes to shower and uses all your shampoo, and It's Never A Good Sign when she flushes the toilet only every other time.

"You takin' a fuckin' shower?" asked Cinnamon. And INAGS when your roomie cannot compose a complete sentence without at least one F word.

"Yeah, I was going to."

"Suit yourself, but it's still pretty fuckin' early."

"You think there'll be more? Tonight?"

"Probably."

And there were. I did two Half & Half's plus a Hot & Cold Oral before the night was over, all without taking a shower. Yes, without taking a shower. That isn't an articulated sin, per se, but it probably ought to be. I sat on the bed and counted my money; nineteen hundred dollars in cold hard cash. I got up and walked into the bathroom and locked the door. I stood at the sink and looked at myself in the mirror for a long, long time.

What had become of me? How many lines had I crossed to get to this point—to this point where I was staring back into the face of a prostitute?

38

KATHERINE

MY DAD COMPLETELY FLIPPED OUT when my sister, Kristy, announced she was pregnant. She was twenty-one and didn't have a husband. Not good. I figured he'd blame me for setting the standard, which is odd because Kristy's boyfriend didn't know me from Adam. And I highly doubt Kristy was thinking about *me* when they did the dirty deed in the back seat of his souped-up Mustang.

My mom was dealing with her own issues and didn't need the shame of another daughter's revved up hormones. So she retreated to her room and pretended it hadn't happened. But my dad, oh brother, was he ever steamed. Kristy told me he mentioned my name more than once in the sermons she got. I wasn't particularly flattered (or appreciative) of being the object lesson in his lectures. And speaking of the lecture circuit, I could never understand the wisdom in ripping her a new one when the deed had already been done.

I might be a total hypocrite because I would've been pretty upset if Jenna sprang that on me, too. "You're *pregnant? But how?*" as if it'd never happened before. I wonder if I could have mustered the maturity to treat her like I wished I'd been treated by my own parents. I'd like to think I would handle it better but you never know on these things. Sometimes there's an overreaction because you've been there and don't want them to suffer your same dire fate.

So, there was another shotgun wedding in the Coombs clan to retroactively atone for the sinning. My dad gave Kristy a $1,500 allowance. He'd given me $1,300 and must've found a soft spot to account for inflation. I thought it was unfair that he'd given my other sister, Kimberly, three times that much when she'd married as a virgin. Or at least that's what she claimed and I have no reason to dispute it. I told my dad how I thought it was unfair to be so inequitable. "When you're a parent," he'd said, "you can do what you want in these situations." Well, I was a parent and I thought it was wrong.

Sadly, Kristy miscarried before she could spend any of that handsome wad on fruit punch and a medley of chocolate éclairs. Everyone felt terrible about the miscarriage, including my dad. I know I make him out to be a sanctimonious jerk sometimes, but he was just doing the best he could with all of us. It couldn't have been easy. However, as long as Kristy was determined to miscarry, I'm sure he would've preferred that she do it *before* the big public announcement of another Coombs girl doing the naughty outside the holy bonds of matrimony.

Kristy's boyfriend was relieved. And who could blame him? When Kristy told him they still ought to get married, he'd simply asked, "But, why?"

"Because we love each other, that's why."

"Can't we just go back to the way things were?"

Well, apparently, he got his way and they went back to the way things were, to those happy, carefree pre-pregnancy days. That's when all the lectures began anew about not buying the cow when you're getting the milk for free. My parents had an entire repertoire of clever little analogies designed to trump the God-given desire to do it. But Kristy didn't listen; she just kept doling out free milk. She wasn't stupid though; she knew the milk wasn't free. It came at a cost. And the cost was her self-esteem because she knew her boyfriend would never actually pay for it. If she'd given him an ultimatum, he would've just gone and drank from another girl's jug.

My mom wanted me to talk some sense into her. "I don't know why she gets so defensive," my mom said. "We only want what's best for her. You need to talk to her because she'll listen to you."

My heart-to-heart with Kristy happened a few weeks later.

"I know it might not be any of my business, but—"

"It's not."

"I know, but—"

"Let's just say we had the talk, okay?" Kristy said. "I know they put you up to it."

"They're just concerned about you, that's all," I said.

"Well, they don't need to be. I'm fine. Geez, they act like we're the only unmarried couple in the world having sex. Come on, Katherine, that's ridiculous. I'm twenty-one-years-old. I'm older than they were."

"But try to see if from their perspective."

"And what, exactly, is that perspective?"

"They believe pre-marital sex is wrong," I said. "And you're going to hate me for preaching, but so do I."

"No hypocrisy there. Takes one to know one."

"And I regret it, Kristy. I do."

"What's the big deal? It's not like I'm sleeping around. Gol, you guys make it seem like I'm some kind of nymphomaniac."

"No we don't. But we think you'd be happier if you did what's right."

"What's right. Got it."

"We just want to remind you what the commandments say."

"Omigosh, you're right! I'd totally forgotten all about the commandments! Mom and dad forgot to remind me."

"Come on, Kristy. They're just doing their best."

"You know," said Kristy, "even as a little kid I remember having doubts about God and all that business. Remember we had the whole blessing thing after Kylie was born? Remember how dad promised her that she'd be healed? It might sound funny, but when everybody was closing their eyes and praying hard for Kylie, I opened mine and peeked around the room. And when she didn't get better, I thought it was my fault. It's dumb, I know, but I felt guilty about it."

"I'm sorry. Obviously, it wasn't your fault."

"Oh, I know that now. But back then I wasn't so sure."

"God made Kylie the way she is," I said. "There's nothing you could've done about that."

"Then what was the point of the blessing? Why bother if God was going to do whatever He was going to do anyway?"

"God will help us if we let Him. He'll answer our prayers if we ask sincerely."

"So," Kristy said, "I don't want to be mean here, but weren't you sincere when you prayed for Keith's arm? Or for Kylie? Or how about this—I bet you prayed your guts out when you and Keith were having sex before you got married—when you were late on your period. I bet you've never prayed so freaking hard in your life."

She was right about that. I'd prayed hard for each of those things. But even though none of my prayers seemed to make a difference, I still believed. I still do. I'm sure God in His infinite wisdom had a broader perspective than I did at the time.

"God blessed me with that baby who's now the light of my life," I said.

"And what about my baby, Katherine? Did God command the miscarriage, or am I just less worthy than you?"

I'd begun to think a lot about my own daughters. There were many times when I'd felt trapped in my role as full-time homemaker and I didn't know how to explain that to my daughters. I didn't want to suggest to them that motherhood isn't a beautiful thing, because it is. If that's what they really wanted, then sure, but I didn't want them to believe that marriage and breeding children was their only option.

My mom and grandma had followed the patriarchal script as textbook-style martyrs for motherhood. Did they complain or regret it? I don't think so, but maybe they did, silently though lest they be condemned for not having a good attitude about it. But I wanted more for my daughters. I wanted them to maintain their individual identity and be who they wanted to be without my judgment or guilt. I hoped they'd be mothers but if their whole lives were wrapped into that role they might feel trapped, too.

39

KATE

SO, I HEARD MY LITTLE SISTER had a miscarriage and I felt terrible for her.

"Mom told me about your miscarriage," I said to Kristy over the phone. "I'm so sorry. I wish there was something I could do."

"Thanks. I'm doing better. It's just that I can't quit thinking about the way they scraped her out. That was supposed to be my little girl."

I guess Kristy had the inside scoop that the fetus had been a girl. How she knew this was a mystery to me.

"So how does your boyfriend feel about it?" I asked.

"I think he's relieved."

"So are you guys still getting married?"

"I don't think so, at least not for now."

"How were mom and dad about the whole thing?"

"What do you think? They were pretty upset when they found out I was pregnant, especially dad. But then they both felt bad when I lost her, too."

Kristy didn't know that I once thought I'd been pregnant out of wedlock, too. But she did know that I'd become the black sheep of the family because everyone knew that. I'd like to think that made me more approachable. Kristy might have appreciated the trailblazing I'd done, veering off the mandatory beaten path, thrashing through the weeds of nonconformity with a cigarette in one hand and a cocktail in the other. It took some pressure off her. But, believe me, I didn't swell with pride over the fabulous example I'd set. I mean, look at me. If Kristy knew even half the truth about her big sister, I highly doubt she would've committed to our wicked little solidarity pact. The Bad Coombs Sisters. I think she wanted to act all bad, all defiant, but Kristy's badness was only a little pushback to our cultural convention; it wasn't the wholesale, dirty rotten kind of bad.

I'd been at the Kitty Kat for three weeks when I called Crock again. "Are you sure Ricky hasn't tried to call?"

"Positive."

"He has my car. He doesn't even know where I am."

"He'll show up soon."

"But why isn't he trying to find me?"

"Maybe he is," Crock said to make me feel better. "I'll keep looking for his call and let you know as soon as I hear anything."

"Could you do me a huge favor? Could you swing by my apartment to see if it looks like he's been there? Maybe check for messages? 32B. I left a key on top of the vending machine at the bottom of the stairs."

"Sure. I gotta go to Home Center out that way anyway. Goddamned neon sign went out on me again."

Crock called me an hour later to report that the apartment looked exactly as it had the day he picked me up. Nothing had been cleaned and all Ricky's stuff was still there. There were only two messages: one from my mom and the other from Kristy. Nothing from Ricky. I figured I'd give it another two weeks and then find a way to get back to Vegas to haul my stuff away so I wouldn't have the ongoing rent.

In the meantime, I was making a bundle at the Kitty Kat. Try $11,000 in the first three weeks, and that's after paying the house and tipping Joanne. I don't know why it took so long, but a woman from the medical clinic finally called to report the results of my initial blood test. By the sound of her voice she was middle-aged.

"Did you know that you are pregnant?" she asked me.

"Excuse me?"

"Yes, the test results confirmed that you are pregnant."

"But I'm on the pill."

"The pill is not one-hundred percent effective, as you may know."

I looked for somewhere to sit. I was *pregnant?* So much had happened in the past month—the Spanos quasi-rape, the iron, Ricky's escape, the brothel—that I hadn't even remembered I was a few days late. My feelings were mixed. I'd say the blend was five percent okay with it and ninety-five percent horrified. The baby would most likely be Ricky's but, then again, it might have been Spanos's. Either way, this was bad. If I'd had my druthers it would have been Ricky's, of course, because at least he was handsome. I was strong, but the thought of carrying Spanos's child was more than I could reasonably bear.

I decided to get an abortion. This was not a casual decision I made out of convenience. This was not a form of birth control. The fetus had done nothing wrong, even if it might have been biologically related to Victor Spanos. Sure, it might grow up to be bald, hairy, and disgusting, but for now it was as innocent as any other fetus. And yet.

I've talked about the Sin Next to Murder, but pre-marital sex, as wicked as it was, took a back seat to murder. And abortion was murder, at least according to my parents and church. I had sinned, a lot, over the past several years, sins that would ultimately put me on the cusp of hell. But an abortion? That would be the camel's final straw that would send me to the everlasting furnace in record time. And yet.

I believed in a just and compassionate God. He knew my story. He knew all about Ricky and Victor, too. The men in my life, even those I didn't know, like politicians and preachers, had told me what I could and could not do with my body. I believed their reasoning wasn't wrong, per se, even though it bugged me that they had so much to say on the matter, because I believed abortion was a sin. But was it an irredeemable one? And who should have the final say anyway? I chose to believe there was no win-win solution here. It could be a lose-win, or a win-lose, or even a lose-lose, but I couldn't see a win-win no matter how hard I tried. I chose to end the pregnancy.

Somehow Evelyn found out about my abortion and had plenty to say about it. She was a born again Christian and believed I had killed another human being. I didn't want to get into with her because many people believe as she did, including my parents. As I said, I also believed it was wrong but didn't believe she had the right to judge me.

"You do realize, do you not, that voluntarily terminating a pregnancy is tantamount to murder."

Um, no. And since when is it your business.

"Our Lord and Savior Jesus Christ has been rather explicit," she continued as she crossed herself. Evelyn crossed herself all the time like she had a nervous tic. I can see doing it when expressing gratitude or making an urgent plea to get to heaven, but she did it following routine statements. "I hope it's not too hot today," she'd say with an obligatory cross. Honestly, once she'd get going you might be tempted to confuse the obsessive crossing with Tourette syndrome.

"Then I'll leave it to him," I said.

"You should come to Bible study with me to acquaint yourself with His word."

She didn't realize I could have gone toe to toe with her on the Bible but I didn't want to engage her on the merits of my decision to end my pregnancy despite that all-too-famous line in the Bible: "Don't get an abortion, or else Jesus will hate you."

"Suit yourself," she said with another crossing. "Now, if you'll please excuse me, I have an engagement with a customer."

And off she went to know the customer in the Biblical fashion she was so familiar with. I used to think Evelyn was kind, and I suppose she was on some level, but arrogant people who impose their obsessively kind judgment and guilt were starting to annoy me.

I also decided to end my lease on the trashed apartment back in Vegas. This decision presumably met with Evelyn's approval. Fantasee's boyfriend owned a pickup truck and he agreed to let me borrow it for the day. Fantasee was suspicious of this generosity, however, because she assumed Jermaine must have misbehaved and was compensating by showing his nice side. I don't believe she confused his charity with him flirting with me because I had a comparatively smallish butt.

Fantasee agreed to help me move out my stuff. I was reassured she'd be with me for the day because Spanos and his goon squad wouldn't have wanted to tangle with her. Honestly, I'd put Fantasee up against just about anybody. I wore jeans, sensible sneakers, and a T-shirt that day and Fantasee wore a tight skirt and heels. We loaded up my stuff and left whatever belonged to Ricky in the apartment. I figured the landlord could throw it out. As we were getting ready to leave, I saw Fantasee pull Ricky's toothbrush from the stand and swish it around in the toilet before replacing it in the toothbrush stand. I'd be leery of making her mad if I were Jermaine.

On the way out to the truck with the final load, I saw Fantasee give Reginald Johnson a few dollars. She did so without fanfare and without saying anything to me. So, yes, she was a prostitute but I'd take her as a decent human being over ninety percent of the self-righteous crowd who publicly declare their charity for credit.

I'd seen a pawn shop a few doors down from the Kitty Kat and decided to pawn my wedding ring. It wasn't so much that I was strapped for cash as it was a symbolic thing. The guy at EZ Pawn said he'd give me $30 for it, providing ample evidence that Ricky had gone all out. I took the money. I wouldn't have dreamed in a million years that I'd find myself in a pawn shop in Pahrump, Nevada hocking my wedding ring for the price of two Pearl Jam CD's. Perhaps another gushing young bride could have a second-hand dream. I just hoped the ring wasn't jinxed, for her sake.

A week later I started where I'd left off. I worked every day, even on Sundays which was another no-no on my evangelical rap sheet. It wouldn't have headed the list but I'd been taught that we weren't supposed to work on the Sabbath Day because that was the Lord's special day of rest and we were supposed to follow His lead. The church doesn't specially list what is considered to be "work" and what isn't. So there are gray areas, even in our church which is quite specific when it comes to identifying sin. Some people are required to work, like firemen and nurses, but I'm confident that having sex with strangers for money wouldn't qualify as exempted work.

There were truckers, athletes, businessmen, and retirees. Each was a different price depending on my mood and how rich they looked. Here's a fun tip for you: Don't act all rich when you go to see a hooker. Once you've negotiated the price you can brag all you want about how rich you are because I'm here to tell you she'll really care about your embellished life. I know I did.

I always made the customer wear a condom and I never gave it away for free, or even a steep charitable discount. Except once.

A boy came to the brothel after I'd been there about a month. He was gawky and still had zits. He picked me. Not to brag, because who would brag about such a thing, but they usually picked me. Well, me or another girl named Naomi who had caramel-colored skin and was one of the most beautiful creatures I'd ever seen. But Naomi didn't last long at the Kitty Kat. She ran off to Spain with a guy named Gideon who must have been extraordinarily rich or extremely witty because I'd seen him hanging around the Kitty Kat from time to time and he was nothing to write home about.

"So what's your name?" I asked this boy when we were back in my room.

"Todd."

"How old are you anyway?"

"Nineteen," he said, but I had my doubts.

"So, Todd, have you ever done this before?"

"No, ma'am."

"Do you know how much it costs?"

"No, ma'am. But I have eighty dollars."

He was well groomed and his button-up shirt was smartly tucked in around his small waist. He wore a baseball cap and I could tell he'd shaved his head. He was nervous, but not in an excited way. In fact, he didn't seem excited at all, more like determined to go through with it because it was something that needed to be done.

"Sorry to burst your bubble, Todd, but I charge a lot more than eighty dollars."

"I'm sorry, ma'am, but that's all I got. I took the bus here."

"You took the bus?"

"Yes, ma'am, I took the bus from Henderson."

"Have you ever been with a woman before?"

"No ma'am."

"You've never had sex?"

"No ma'am."

"Maybe you could come back when you have more money."

"Couldn't we just do it for the eighty? I don't think I can come back."

"Why not?"

"I have leukemia."

I never made love to my johns—I had sex with them. I did it exclusively for the money and thought most of my customers were simply pathetic. Not so much this kid. Yes, it was as desperate and joyless as any act within the hallowed halls of the Kitty Kat but it was different—it was sincere and purposeful. He fumbled and fussed in his duty and when it was over he reached into his pocket and pulled out four crumpled twenty-dollar bills. I thought about giving them back to him, but I didn't want to wound his pride. Such a saint, huh? I could've starred in the role of "Whore with a heart of gold."

"Thank you, ma'am" was all he said.

I watched him walk down the street to the bus stop for the hour and a half bus ride back to Henderson. I really hope that kid survived, but if he didn't, I hope it was worth it.

They weren't always polite and well groomed. Far from it. Usually they were fat and their breath smelled like cheap liquor, or worse. Most of them treated me like a whore, because that's what I was. They'd bargained for my flesh and felt entitled to it.

It almost always disgusted me; not so much the act, but the fraud I'd become in pretending to enjoy it with the fat, the lecherous, the smelly, the conceited, and the pathetic. There was the self-loathing for actually encouraging them to get on top of me. I'd fight the feeling of nausea, but at least that nauseous feeling reassured me that I was still alive—that I still had a piece of my soul, because there was no apathy, I can tell you that.

I was never suicidal but there were times when I'd close my eyes and try to temporarily die inside. In fact, I don't know any girls who took their own life exclusively because they were sex workers. I did know a few who OD'd though, and I presume prostitution may have had something to do with that. It's complicated though and I don't know how to untangle it because emotionally healthy girls don't usually become prostitutes in the first place.

I remember a church youth activity where we all went to the desert in western Utah to hunt for geodes. It was fun and came with an object lesson to boot. They told us that geodes might be ugly on the outside but when you crack them open you discover how beautiful they are inside. The point was that exterior, superficial beauty is only skin deep; it's what's inside that's important. Well, it turns out I might have been the anti-geode, pretty on the outside and ugly on the inside where it mattered most.

Maybe I have oversold how universally awful it was because sometimes it wasn't so bad, especially if the customer was attractive. After all, I like sex and sex is sex when you get right down to it. It's not like having an earache. I also had a few steady customers I'd come to enjoy. Not "enjoy" as in wanting to have a relationship with them, but "enjoy" as in being with them wasn't unenjoyable. I had one guy who'd come in about once a month to simply talk. He never wanted anything else, which was fine with me, but I thought it was crazy that someone would pay $500 an hour just to chat. I told him he could talk to a therapist for a lot less money but he was content to pay me to reminisce about his childhood mother issues, his job, and his marriage. Sometimes the way he talked to me about his marriage felt like a deeper betrayal than having sex with me would have been, but I'm no therapist.

But back to the regular grind. I'd been working for a few months when a man who called himself John came in. By the way, I doubt John was his real name, which is understandable. And there was something ironic about this john calling himself John. But here's a fun fact that should cause all the John's out there to rest a bit easier: We don't rat you out. It's not codified in a legal treatise anywhere but it's part of the unwritten prostitute code.

Anyway, this John John guy was short and very wide. He tried to hide it under an XXL Hawaiian shirt which fooled no one. He agreed to pay the freight and stood naked before me like a gelatinous sumo wrestler with bad BO. Normally it wasn't a problem for my customers to get an erection, but not this guy. I could hardly even see it, hidden as it was under his apron of fat and bushel of pubes that'd never been trimmed. I'd read somewhere that a man loses an inch of length with every thirty pounds of fat he gains. You do the math. All I could see was the tip. It looked like a mushroom cap, or maybe a small pink egg in the straw of an Easter basket.

John John arrogantly assumed it was my job to find it and straighten it out. For $800 I suppose I owed it a try. I held my breath and tackled the job with enough experience to make it hard and barely long enough to do the trick. Then the smelly fatso lay on top of me for the worst two minutes of my life. He strutted out, waddled, actually, like he'd really rocked my world—like it'd been an injustice that *I* hadn't paid *him*.

This customer was memorable, but not outside the standard deviation. The vast majority of my johns were unattractive. When I first started, there was a middle-aged man with huge bags under his eyes, sagging there like a set of forlorn testicles. I felt terrible for judging him and his testicle eyes, for who among us would like to walk around with those bags? My feelings toward the man changed to pity and I had to wonder if that's why he and many other unattractive men are forced to pay for it in the first place.

I'd earned enough to put aside $18,000 in a rainy-day fund. I'd use that money to pay Ricky's debt to Victor Spanos if it ever came to that. To be clear, I was doing this for my own protection and not for Ricky. I also bought a car. Speaking of Ricky, I figured it was time to accept the truth—that after stealing my love and my trust, as worthless as they must have seemed to him, he'd discarded me as easily as if he'd taken off a dirty shirt.

I went for my monthly medical exam on a Friday. I sat in the waiting area for thirty minutes and then again in a small exam room for another thirty. I think they do that on purpose—switch you to a new room to make it feel like you're making progress. I was bored and picked up a *Time* magazine. There was an article on the newly appointed Supreme Court Justice Clarence Thomas and how his senate confirmation fight shined a light on sexual harassment in the work force. That was rich, I thought, as I sat in the clinic waiting for my monthly STD work exam.

The same doctor I'd seen before asked me if I'd had any symptoms of pelvic pain, itchiness, or anything like that. The answer was no because I was a stickler for condoms. He asked me to get in the stirrups which is always such a treat. He held one hand on my tummy and examined me with the other hand. Again, always such a treat. It seemed like his exam lasted longer than it normally does and I looked at his face. There was no expression.

"I feel some fullness off to the left side of your uterus and something on your left ovary. It could be nothing, but I'd like to run a few tests."

I know people hear things like that when they aren't expecting it and it freaks them out, because nobody expects it. They always think it'll be someone else and, fortunately, it usually is.

"You feel something?" I asked. "What does that mean?"

"I feel a small mass," he said as he removed his surgical glove with a snap and tossed it into a garbage can next to the stirrups. "Again, it may be nothing so I don't want to alarm you, but I think I'll have you undergo an ultrasound and a blood test."

"Am I going to have the tests now? Like, is this an emergency?"

"No, but I'd like to take a blood test—a CA-125—and let's get an ultrasound of your pelvis. We can schedule that today."

Like I knew what a CA-125 was. All I wanted to know was whether or not I was a goner. "A CA . . . ?"

"CA-125. It's a blood test with a marker for ovarian cancer."

He saw the look on my face.

"I'm not finding anything else on your exam that concerns me. However, I want to run the blood test to assess the risk of cancer, or otherwise rule it out. You aren't having any bloating or pelvic pain?"

"No, I don't think so." I swear I suddenly felt a case of bloating and pelvic pain that very moment, bloating and pain so severe I wanted to double over with it, even though it was all in my head. Or was it? See, that's the thing.

He told me to come back on Monday for the results of the blood test.

"We can't know until then?"

He said it takes time to complete the lab work and they wouldn't know for a few days. "Even if it's a small cancer on your ovary, we can remove and treat it fairly easily because we've caught it so early."

"So, is there anything I should or shouldn't do between now and then?"

"You should be able to continue working," he said, "but if you begin to experience any pelvic pain through penetration, I recommend you stop immediately."

I felt like a total slut. I hadn't meant to ask if I could go on *having sex with customers*. That's not what I'd meant at all. But he knew what I did for a living.

I got dressed and drove back to the Kitty Kat in a daze. And where in the hell was my husband?

I didn't open my purse (that's what Cinnamon called her vagina—her purse) the rest of the week even though there was a medical convention in Vegas that week and the girls figured we'd be busy. Gil tried to talk me into taking a few shifts but there was simply no way I could allow a strange man to probe my cancerous ovaries. Any man or inanimate object for that matter. What if it ruptured or something?

I spent all weekend rehearsing how I'd break it to my parents and who would speak at my funeral. You know how your mind goes to all the worst places? Well, mine was going wild with worst-case scenarios. How soon before I went bald? How bad would the nausea be? How would I pay for the medical expenses? It was a long weekend, I'll just say that.

I returned for my doctor's appointment first thing Monday. I was even a few minutes early which is simply ridiculous because you always have to wait. I sat there, anxious, afraid, and increasingly annoyed by my doctor who I saw casually chatting up a nurse like he had all the time in the world while the rest of us in the waiting room tried to find interest in the out-of-date magazines and a crummy fish tank with a few bored fish swimming around a sunken pirate ship and treasure chest. I was finally led to the exam room when, after another ten-minute wait, a new doctor appeared.

"Hi, I'm Dr. Wetzel. I specialize in gynecological diseases."

Now they had a specialist on the case. This was not good.

"I've looked over your lab results," he began. "The CA-125 is mildly elevated. That was the blood test we ran to look for cancer antigens in your ovaries. I think we're dealing with some cancer here." Just like that I was dealing with some cancer. "The ultrasound confirms a mass on your left ovary of approximately four centimeters. It has some complexity to it given its size." And now I was dealing with some cancer that was complex and sizable.

"So . . . like . . . what does that mean? Am I going to die?"

"No, no, no. We've caught this very early and you should be fine. But I recommend you have it removed as soon as possible. I can put you on my schedule for next week."

While I had him cornered, I would've also liked to know how soon I'd go bald from the chemo.

"The procedure is fairly simple. I'll be able to do it right here in the surgical center. We'll do what we call a laparoscopy, or a keyhole surgery, where we go in with a small scope through your navel. I'm afraid we'll have to remove your entire left ovary to biopsy it because we can't biopsy it while it's still in your abdomen."

"Why not?"

"The contaminated cells have the potential to spill into surrounding abdominal tissues if the tumor is probed too thoroughly. So we'll remove it first before we biopsy it. Once we have a comprehensive biopsy we'll know much more, but I'm confident you'll be fine."

"How long will I be laid up from the surgery?"

"You may not feel like working for three or four days. Then you should feel fine. The incision is a small one at your navel that will only require a few stitches."

"So, like, will I need chemotherapy and all that?"

"No, no. This is a simple procedure at this point. I think you'll be fine. We'll be as non-invasive as possible and just remove the left ovary. That way you may still be able to have children if you choose to do so."

The surgery was scheduled for Friday of that week and the doctor wanted to do it in Vegas. This left me five more days to worry about the tumor leaking. I hardly dared move and the thought of anyone, or anything, probing anywhere *near* the area was unthinkable. I accidently dropped my keys and hardly dared bend down to pick them up for fear I'd squish the tumor and send the cancerous cells squirting in all directions. My posture was never so good. I even sat on the toilet gingerly.

I called Crock and told him I had some "female issues" that needed tending to. He asked no follow up questions which was typical because I've found that any mention of "female issues" sorta shuts down the convo with most men. Crock told me there'd still been no word from Ricky.

Then I called my mom.

"Hi, it's me."

"Oh, hi, Sweetheart! It's so good to hear from you. How are you?"

"Well, Mom, I'm . . . I think I might be real sick."

"What? You're sick? My goodness, is it the flu? I know it's been going around here. It seems like everybody in the ward has it. Just drink lots of fluids."

"It's not that, Mom. I have cancer."

I'll admit it was a bit melodramatic to say it without any preamble—like, for example, that it was technically cancer but it wasn't going to kill me or anything, or that I wouldn't even be hospitalized or need chemo. But it was still the truth; I did have cancer. I wasn't proud of it, the cancer bit, but there was a certain martyrdom in it. Why, I don't know.

There was silence on the line at first. "No, Katherine, no. Please, no," and she turned her head from the receiver and yelled, "Dale! Hurry and pick up the phone! It's Katherine. It's our Katherine."

"Mom, it's going to be okay. The doctors say I'll be fine and I won't even be—"

I heard my dad pick up. "Katherine? What's the matter?" I could tell he was worried, even though he had yet to be given the dramatic news.

"She has cancer!" my mom hysterically blurted into the other receiver from the bedroom where she spent most of her time those days. I was mildly annoyed that she had unfairly stolen my news.

"Dad, I'll be okay. I just have a small tumor on one of my ovaries. But the doctor says they can remove it and I should be fine. They're doing the surgery on Friday. It's an out-patient procedure and I'll only be out of work for a few days."

"How did you know?" my mom asked. "Are you having pain down there?"

"No, I haven't had any problems at all. But I just had a physical and they did a blood test and that's how they found it. They said they caught it so early that it hasn't spread."

"Can Richard take time off work to take care of you?" my dad asked.

Yeah, right. Everything about that question was absurd. If my dad had only known the truth—that the loyal and upstanding Ricky Waters who'd bought me a fake diamond ring for our drive-thru wedding had now disappeared on me and didn't have a job to miss in any event.

"Or maybe we can come down there for the surgery," my mom said. "We could bring you back to recuperate here in St. George."

"Let me figure that out with Ricky and I'll let you know."

They had just been told their daughter had cancer and I didn't have the nerve to drop another bombshell on them—that my beloved husband had abandoned me to escape a beating from a loan shark—the same one I tried to kill with a clothes iron in partial repayment for having basically raped me after I'd quasi-volunteered to have sex with him.

They wanted to know, again, "word for word" what the doctor had said. Then my dad asked if I'd made arrangements with the restaurant to get the time off.

"Yeah, I told them I'd miss next week and they were good about it."

"I think you need a priesthood blessing. I could come down there to administer one, or maybe you could just talk to your local bishop about it."

"I might ask him," I said.

I told Gil next. "That's too bad," he said, "but I'm sure you'll be okay and it doesn't sound like working is going to make it any worse. But, of course, it's totally up to you."

Gee, Gil, thanks for that. Like I was going to keep working with a ticking timebomb inside my womb ready to explode. Gil did agree to drive me to Vegas though, which was very generous of him to do. The plan was for him to drop me off at the surgical clinic there and have my mom pick me up and drive back home with her to St. George for a few days.

I called my mom again the next day. "You said you might be able to come down Friday for the surgery. Ricky has an important business trip he can't get out of and he won't be in town. I told him maybe I could drive back with you to St. George and recuperate there for a few days."

"Of course."

I'm sure my dad flipped out when he heard my husband was too busy to take care of his cancer-stricken wife. I wouldn't have blamed him. I was pretty upset about it myself.

The surgical procedure was successful. They removed my left ovary and didn't find a trace of cancer anywhere else. This was great news, obviously.

My mom had driven down for the surgery with Kimberly and Kristy. I'm glad they didn't get a chance to look at the intake form to see where I worked. The Kitty Kat? What's the Kitty Kat? I was still groggy when they wheeled me out to the car. I slept most of the two-hour drive to St. George where they put me up in my old bedroom. It had since been commandeered by Kelly who'd kept my Donny and Marie poster on the wall above my bed. I had a crush on both of them growing up. Everybody in the church did. I remember thinking that if Donny and Marie were members of our church then it must be the truest one.

My dad tried to bite his tongue about the whole Ricky thing but getting my dad to hold his tongue was, like, impossible. After two days without even so much as a phone call from my beloved husband to check on his dying wife, my dad had finally had enough.

"What's going on with Richard? He hasn't even called. I want the truth, dammit."

I don't know what was more shocking; Ricky not calling, or my dad swearing. I'd only heard him utter a few swear words in my life, and they were never the bad ones. And I'd *never* heard him take the Lord's name in vain. He'd rob a bank in broad daylight without a mask before he did that. Anyway, I knew the gig was up—there was no way to keep this blatant lie afloat. It was time to tell them the truth, dammit.

"Well, Mom and Dad, the truth is we're separated. I didn't tell you guys because I didn't want you to be worried."

"Oh, Katherine," my mom said, "I'm so sorry."

"So, what, he can't even make a phone call?" asked my dad.

"We haven't spoken in about a month. He doesn't even know I had the surgery. I'm sure he would have been concerned had he known."

"Well, that is completely unacceptable." I think my dad felt like swearing again but he didn't want to push it. Once a decade was about his limit.

"Katherine," my mom said, "I know you like your job down there but couldn't you find a good waitressing job up here in St. George? If you're thinking about, you know, getting a . . . you know, ending things, then maybe it's time you came back home."

Her discomfort with saying the word "divorce" tells you everything you need to know about how The Big D is thought of in St. George. We tend to stay in unhappy marriages rather than bail on them because we belong to the true church and need to show how happy we are. Divorce isn't forbidden but it is frowned upon because it's a buzz kill for the Chosen People. I remember when my Uncle Irv and Aunt Beverly got divorced because he'd left the church. Maybe there was more to it than that, because there usually is, but that was the big wedge. Anyway, I overheard another aunt comment on the difficult situation. "It's not right," she said. "Look at Newell and me. We've been unhappy in our marriage for 25 years but you don't see us going and getting divorced."

I told my mom that I really liked it in Vegas and that I'd made a lot of good friends there. I also told her I make more money waitressing there than I could in St. George, which is quite true by the way—about the only true statement I'd made to my parents in years.

Later that night I heard them discussing my marriage. I was on my hands and knees again with my head bent to the floor vent. My dad was brushing his teeth and had plenty to say. "I just can't believe that this so-called *husband* of hers would let his wife go through this whole ordeal alone." Spit. "For all he knows it could have been very serious." Spit. "He probably gave it to her in the first place."

"Gave her what?" my mom asked from their adjoining bedroom where I pictured her in bed reading a church magazine.

"The cancer. I wouldn't put it past him."

Ricky was a real gem, and I'd grown weary of apologizing for him, but I highly doubt he passed me ovarian cancer.

The next day I took a shuttle back to Vegas. "I'll be fine, Mom. Really. You heard what the doctor told me yesterday on the phone. The pathology report is good and I don't even need to follow-up with him. I'll go back in six months so they can check it just to be on the safe side. But, seriously, I'm fine."

"Promise me you'll see him again in six months," my mom said. "I don't care what he says. Cancer is cancer. Aunt Jean had it in her liver and it came right back. I don't trust some of these doctors as far as I can throw them."

40

KATHERINE

WE'D PARKED THE SPECIAL K in the corner of the backyard after the accident where it'd been banished—not merely unused, but forsaken. None of the kids had even *asked* to go boating. The gray canvas cover had turned nearly white from the sun and a tire on the trailer was flat. I wanted to sell the danged thing and Vaughn knew a guy who wanted to buy it but it was Keith who put the kibosh on the sale. He said selling the boat wouldn't make us forget the accident. And he was probably right.

"Whaddya say we take The Special K out for a spin tomorrow," Keith said. "We could all go down to Sand Hollow. The weather is supposed to be perfect."

The kids perked right up. Had The Special K served its full sentence? Was it finally out on parole? "Yeah, Dad. Let's go!"

I asked Keith if he was sure about this. "Sure I'm sure. You gotta get back on the horse. Besides, I can still drive," he said and raised his right arm and left stump into the air for the kids' benefit. "Look, Ma, no hands!" Typical Keith.

"Come on, Mom. Pleeeeease! Dad says it's okay."

"We'll see," I said, which the kids naturally took as a firm yes because I hadn't technically said no.

Eight-year-old Nathan took off at a dead sprint. "We're going on the boat tomorrow! Dad said!"

"Does Kylie have to go," asked Jenna. "Because I'm not going if she is."

I didn't want to fight with her. "Let's just make it our family this time."

We had a wonderful time on the lake, but I had a stomach ache. I soldiered through it like I always did because I never felt I had the luxury of taking a sick day. I couldn't bear the thought of what the house would look like when I emerged from the bedroom.

"Why don't you take a couple ibuprofens and get into bed," Keith said. "I'll get the kids down."

"I hate taking pills. I don't want to get addicted."

"Katherine, it's ibuprofen."

"What, are you a doctor now? You just never know with all these pills."

The next day was Sunday and I stood by the bedroom closet door modeling a dress for church while Keith was propped up in our bed reading the Sunday sports section.

"Does this look better with or without the belt?"

"Uh, with," said Keith.

"Keith! You're not even looking."

"Yeah I was."

I went with the belt. I was getting ready to teach Jenna's Sunday school class of fourteen-year old's and I didn't want to look like a frumpy mom. I told myself it was because I didn't want to embarrass Jenna, and that was part of it, but I also had pride. I wasn't elderly, you know.

It'd been two years since Kylie had publicly announced the arrival of Jenna's period. I'm sure most people had forgotten but Jenna knew the teenage boys hadn't, and never would. And now, adding further insult to injury, she was stuck with me as her Sunday school teacher, telling her and her teenage girlfriends that they were "going through some changes," as if they hadn't noticed. Yes, it was now official—I had become the new Sister Harding from seventeen years earlier reminding these girls that pre-marital sex was about the worst thing they could do—you know, the sin next to murder. No hypocrisy there. I'm sure Jenna was mortified. The girls in the class probably wondered if I even knew what I was talking about. "Eww, do you think Sister Murphy still does it?" "I mean, *maybe?*"

Keith taught the twelve-year-old boys in Sunday school and didn't cram as much of the Bible into them as their parents would've liked. In fact, he avoided reading the scriptures because he said they were boring. No argument there. Anyone who says the scriptures are exciting and fun to read is probably too self-righteous to be good friends with. The scriptures weren't like a small paperback pamphlet either—one you could fit in your pocket for some light reading—because the church had combined the Bible and Book of Mormon into one volume, so it was really something to lug around. Keith had always insisted this voluminous gobbledygook was overkill and all you needed was The Golden Rule. I agreed with him on that, too, but did so privately because I didn't want to be found guilty of criticizing the freaking *scriptures.*

Keith infused his sermons to the kids with stories of his amputation and they ate it up. I'd overheard him embellish about how he'd come to within an inch of death but prayer had saved the day. He called it his "stump speech" and it was all very inspiring. He was also a big fan of pranks, so he'd usually weave one or two of them into his lessons. He said if Jesus had told His stories with pranks instead of parables it might have turned out differently for Him. Yeah, maybe, but Keith really had to stretch to put a religious spin on some of those pranks. Take, for example, the time he'd accidentally driven off the road into the barrow pit and tipped his car over. True story. Other cars had stopped on the side of the road by the time he'd crawled out of his car and trudged up the small incline toward the pavement. He didn't have a scratch on him but then looked down at his missing arm and started screaming, like it'd been ripped off in the crash and might still be in the car. One lady about passed out on the side of the road. He insisted that story was Sunday school material because he claimed to have been thinking about Jesus before he'd dozed off and left the roadway.

I took my belt off as soon as I came home from church that day because I still felt bloated. I put on my favorite jeans which were tight around the waist. I hadn't been getting much sleep those days and was tired. I felt like an old lady lately because I'd been getting up about four times a night to pee. I was constipated, too. I didn't tell Keith any of this because I knew they were female problems and the only thing he knew about female anatomy was what he could feel in the dark. Besides, I hated to complain about a little constipation when Keith had been through so much.

That night Keith was frisky. What else was new, right? I loved him like crazy but I'm sorry to say he wasn't the sexiest man alive, standing there in his one-piece Mormon underwear like a lumberjack with a pot gut. I should talk. I wasn't very sexy either. I felt fat and did laundry for six kids all day. Bring it on!

The pain I felt with intercourse that night was sharp and sudden. It felt like Keith had sprouted a carving knife. Something was terribly wrong.

41

KATE

IT TOOK RICKY, my committed husband, nearly two years to contact me. He'd really taken the marriage vow to heart. I'd long since given up on him, of course, so it caught me off guard when he showed up at the Kitty Kat. I have no idea how he tracked me down. Or maybe he hadn't been trying to track me down at all. Maybe he just stumbled upon me working there when he came to select a girl from a lineup.

We sat at the bar, just Ricky and me, while I listened to his sob story about how rough it'd been, and how much he'd missed me. Yeah, right. He would've called me earlier but he didn't want to expose me to danger. Uh-huh.

"Let's go back to your room so we can have more privacy," he said. "I feel stupid just sitting here at the bar."

"Sure," I said and led him back to my room and closed the door.

"So, what did you want?" I asked once we'd settled in.

"What do you mean?"

"Well, what do you want? You've seen the menu."

"You mean, like what kind of sex?" he asked.

"Yeah."

Ricky smiled that charming way of his. He was relieved I'd taken him back, and so quickly!

"How about the works?" he said with an easy grin, the one that used to get me every time.

"You want the Half & Half?"

"Sounds great," he said, and sat down on the bed next to me—starting to get that lovin' feeling just like the good old days.

"Hold on," I said. "That'll be $800."

"What? Are you serious?" he asked, stuck in that halfway smiling face with his head cocked back a little. You know the face—the one where the person is hedging their bet.

"Very."

"But we're married for God's sake."

"Normally I collect at the end. But with you, Ricky, I'll need the money up front." I wasn't mad. In fact, I felt no emotion at all toward him. Unless you call pure apathy an emotion.

He stared back at me for a moment, and then smiled. "Right. That's good. You had me there for a second." He stood and began taking his shirt off.

"I'm serious. You pay me the $800 in cash right now or I'll call for help. And, Ricky, you don't want me to do that."

"You're serious."

I just stared back at him.

"I come back to make things right and you treat me like some fucking *customer?* Like some loser who comes to a hooker to get laid?"

"Come on, Ricky," I said calmly. "Of course I'd never have sex with you. The only reason I told you I'd do it for $800 was because I knew you didn't have it. If you would've given it to me, I would've thrown it back in your face. So, no, I am not treating you like a customer. I'd actually have sex with a customer."

"I had to hide from Spanos because we busted up his face. I didn't have a choice. Then I took a big risk coming back to you, and now you treat me like a piece of shit?"

"But, Ricky, hold on for a second. You *are* a piece of shit. And, for the record, *we* didn't bust up his face, I did. If I recall, you were halfway out the door when I did it."

"I'm not going to stand here and listen to this shit!"

"So, what, you're just going to take off again in my car? Is that it? You're a pathetic coward, Ricky."

"This coming from a whore."

"A whore who won't even sleep with you for money. How's that for pathetic, Ricky? You've even been rejected by a prostitute."

For a brief moment I thought he might actually hit me. But then I realized he was too much of a coward to do that. When he slammed the door, I sat back on the bed and started to cry. At first, I cried for my lost marriage. Then I cried for everything else including the wreck of my life and the loss of my faith. I suppose it was partially a cry of penance, but I wasn't just crying for me. I was also crying for Kylie's chromosomal irregularity and for my younger brother, Kelly, who was born into a culture that was destined, determined even, to be unforgiving of his sexual orientation. I cried for my mom and her life of servitude. I cried for my lost innocence and for the futility of my so-called "industry." And I cried for Crock and his tragically lost family. I cried for everyone except for Ricky and Victor. I hated them.

I finally drifted off to sleep and was awakened an hour later by a knock on my door.

"Got customers."

I'd kept the promise I'd made with my mom, following up every six months with the doctor. Not a whiff of cancer anywhere.

My goal had been to put fifty thousand dollars in the sock and call it quits. At a thousand bucks a day what'd be so hard about that, right? After two years, the sock had only forty-three thousand dollars in it. There should've been more but drugs, booze, clothes, and God knows what else took its toll. Even so, it was still a lot more than Candy, Fantasee, and Cinnamon had, combined.

It was good money for sure, great money even, but there was no glamour in my job. Duh. No girl grows up dreaming about becoming a prostitute. Barbie the nurse. Barbie the model. Barbie the flight attendant. Barbie the hairdresser. Even Barbie the homemaker. But Barbie the prostitute? The only perk was all the free time. It won't surprise you to learn that business was rarely brisk during the mid-morning hours, or even the early afternoons for that matter. We didn't need to obsess over a time clock either. On the other hand, being with a fat truck driver who smells like tires and thinks he's better than you turns you into a clock watcher pretty quick.

Business was slow one afternoon so we all went to a movie down the street. Evelyn didn't go with us because she had recently run off with another born again Christian she'd come to know in the biblical sense while seeking the rapture in the Arabian Nights room. The movie we saw was that new *Pretty Woman* movie with Julia Roberts. We all sort of snickered, especially at the ending. Prostitutes don't get whisked away to the Kentucky Derby by handsome millionaires. They just don't. And would you like to guess how many luxurious bubble baths we'd taken with a bottle of Dom Perignon and crystal flute nearby? There wasn't even a bathtub in the brothel, and certainly no ice buckets brimming with champagne.

We made quite a foursome walking back to the Kitty Kat from the movie about a gorgeous prostitute with the dream life. The whole hooker vibe was in our walk (let's see you try balancing on five-inch heels). We wore clothes that were three sizes too small, especially Candy. We didn't look like a foursome of church ladies on our way to choir practice, I'll just say that. Church ladies don't show that kind of cleavage or wear that much makeup, and their hemlines tend to reach their knees.

"How come I never seen nobody in my room looks like that fella?" asked Fantasee. "All rich and handsome."

"I've never seen it either," said Cinnamon, "and I get all the fuckin' good ones."

We were the veterans at the Kitty Kat. Candy and Fantasee had been there for nine years and had nowhere else to go. You'd have to fumigate them out. The rest of the girls had come and gone like a routine case of vaginitis. There'd been fat ones and skinny ones. There'd been brunettes, afros, and fake blonds. These were the girls who'd never made Homecoming Queen—

never been tiara-wearing royalty in the back seat of their uncle's convertible as they drove down St. George Boulevard in their small-town parade—the ones where little girls lined the sides of the road and gazed at them with worship, dreaming about the day they might be waving from the back seat of the convertible, too. Instead, these girls were the ones who smoked cigarettes behind the gym, swore, and sassed their parents, if they even had them, that is. Some were foster kids who'd been passed around, fending off abuse. Then there was me, the small-town Homecoming Queen from a loving family who hadn't smoked, sworn, or sassed her parents a single time.

I'd come to love some of these women almost like sisters. And you can say what you will, but I had a lot of personal growth working there. Personal growth, you say? At a brothel? Well, it's true. My childhood world had been so sheltered and so *small.* Take my relationship with Fantasee, for example. I had never even met a black person face to face until high school, and then it was only one person. His name was Jamal and his family had moved to lilywhite St. George for God knows what reason. I had carried my racism without shame or embarrassment, mostly because I wasn't even aware of it. Maybe that's why I was so surprised to learn that Jamal was an honor roll student. This is an embarrassing admission, I know. Who would have dreamed that now one of my closest friends was an African American hooker who'd dropped out of high school and had never met her father?

I had never examined whether any of my inherited childhood beliefs were wrong, or right for that matter, but now I had come to spot my racism when it'd bubble to the surface. I had become a functioning racist by default, too lazy or indifferent to actually do anything about it. Until I met Fantasee. And now when someone makes an ignorant racial remark I'll think of her and call them out. "Geez," they'll say, "what's suddenly gotten into *her?*"

Later that night after the movie, I was sitting alone in the parlor area with my third glass of wine which I'd generously glugged into my glass. I swirled it in the glass as if it'd been an expensive bottle of cognac that needed to breathe instead of an eight-dollar bottle of sauvignon blanc with a convenient screw top. I saw the glow of Cinnamon's cigarette out the window as she leaned against the railing and tried not to pick the polish off her nails. What was she thinking about, I wondered? Maybe the guy who'd come in several times asking for her—the guy who'd hinted that he was rich and might one day swoop in and whisk her away to a velvet life in the suburbs. If so, she'd been forced to conveniently overlook the dent in his finger from where the wedding ring had been an hour earlier, or the fact that he drove a faded minivan with bald tires and probably had four kids waiting for him at home.

These girls had no future as far as I could see. You can imagine that a prostitute's shelf life is relatively short and there's no 401k waiting for you at the finish line when you're used up. No trophy, no plaque, and no gold watch either. There wouldn't even be a sheet cake in the office breakroom. *Good luck with your retirement Trixie!* And then what? How do you doctor up *that* resume? How do you explain the suspicious gap of honest employment over the past fifteen years? I suppose you could come up with some vague creative mumbo jumbo, but what do you say in the job interview when the prospective employer is perusing that very resume and asks you to elaborate on your career in the "customer service" industry? You either lie through your teeth or you hem and haw.

As I watched Cinnamon out the window, reflecting on the life of a prostitute with an expiring shelf life, Candy came out and sat on the velour sofa across from me. It was quiet and there were no customers so late at night. She was a beer drinker which seemed fitting to me and she set her bottle on the coffee table. We were both in a contemplative mood as we silently watched the sweat roll down the bottle.

"I hated that movie," she said.

I took another sip of wine. "Me too."

She started to cry. Girls rarely cried there. We were tough, or at least we acted like it. Instead of revealing ourselves and exposing our vulnerabilities, we made crude jokes about what we did and pretended to be apathetic about it. But the pretense was a sham because there was an infection deep down, an infection that was so tender it hurt to touch it. So we didn't—we didn't go anywhere near it, at least not in front of others.

I got up and sat next to her, putting my arm around her husky bare shoulders. She leaned her head into me. Candy was a girl who probably hadn't received a single vote for Homecoming Queen—never walked out to midfield at halftime in her prom dress and sash. She probably didn't even have a dress, or a field, or a homecoming. It wouldn't have surprised me if she hadn't made a single appearance in her high school yearbook. I'll bet she had hopelessly dreaded Valentine's Day, too, at once both envious and resigned, a girl who probably sat alone in her bedroom with a picture of David Cassidy on the wall, littering her diary with lamentations.

"You're going to be okay, Candy."

"Look at me," she said. "They pick me because I'm a fetish." I'd never heard her speak before without crudeness or stereotype. She was smarter than I thought. "I don't understand you, Kate. You don't need to be here. You're smart and pretty. You have options. But what are mine?"

"You're better than you think, Candy."

"Who's ever going to want me? Huh? I'm damaged goods. Even if I was prettier, I'd still be messed up on the inside." She wasn't trying to be melodramatic, searching for an insincere compliment from me. She was only speaking her simple truth. "I don't even remember when I was just regular unhappy."

I was damaged goods, too. The compounding rate of shame and humiliation made me feel unworthy of any good man. A good relationship with anyone for that matter, except with someone like Candy who knew the truth about my soul's condition.

Our little band of hookers was fairly harmonious even though the only thing we had in common was the fact that we worked in the same "industry" and had issues because of it (and a collection of pre-existing issues to partially explain those issues). But a girl named Breezy was different than most of us there. She was tall, sickly thin, and abrasive. Her bony chest and large implants didn't jive with the rest of her body and the tracks in her arms provided a wealth of frightening evidence that she was using. Her strung-out look may have also resulted from her diet of potato chips and Mountain Dew. And, finally, she wore glasses. You tell me; ever seen a prostitute with glasses? Me neither.

Breezy moved in down the hall and I assumed she was like anyone else—that she'd try to fit in. But we learned early on that she was a screamer. She was so loud we could hear it from our rooms. She was like the Pee'er at Lil' Secrets only louder. Was this meant to inspire John John—all this verge of orgasm nonsense? Or could it possibly have been real? If so, she needed to be separated from the rest of civilized humanity.

It was not uncommon for other johns to be startled, bolting upright when they'd hear Breezy's screams from another room. Was someone being assaulted? Was there a knife-wielding killer on the loose in the brothel? I overheard one of her dazed customers complain that it was distracting. But he'd said it with pride because he'd been the one to send her to such heights. And sometimes Breezy's johns must have felt obliged to produce unnecessary noises themselves—grunts, growls, and yes's! Gil told Breezy to knock it off, that he couldn't run a reputable whorehouse with all that distraction. "But I can't help it when I come," she said. "Then don't come," he said.

Breezy had endured a hard life, but nothing new there—brothels aren't stocked with long lines of nobility. Having a madam is about as close to aristocracy as we got. We didn't know her real name. Nothing new there either because no one knew anyone's real name. The IRS must've pulled its hair out trying to track down all the Bambi's, Butterfly's, Sparkle's, Bunny's, and Cherry's. But Breezy was more elusive than most. She bragged about all the top-of-the-line brothels she'd worked at, like we should care. And she was always dropping names of famous people she'd slept with. None of us had heard of these so-called famous people. You ever heard of some guy named Bruce Fleming who's supposed to be a famous singer? Me neither. The one famous person we *had* heard of was simply preposterous, because there's no way Clint Eastwood hired Breezy. No way. She wasn't even that cute, although I could never figure out some men's tastes. Gil hired her because he hired just about anybody who'd give a decent R & T.

So Breezy was already on the hot seat with the screaming when Cinnamon claimed someone had stolen some of her pain pills. Breezy told her I'd stolen them—that she'd seen me leave our bathroom with an orange pill bottle. This was a total lie, and I went off. I think I was more defensive than most people might've been because I needed to have at least *some* moral rudder. I was a prostitute, liar, and borderline alcoholic but, dammit, I wasn't a thief. Besides, there were a thousand orange pill bottles within the hallowed walls of the Kitty Kat so that was flimsy circumstantial evidence to begin with.

"Think about it, Cinnamon. Why would I suddenly start stealing your Percocet?"

"I got me a fuckin' eyewitness."

"Oh yeah? And who's that?"

"Breezy."

"*Breezy?* You've got to be kidding. She's a drug addict. Have you seen the stuff she takes? I'll bet it was her, because I swear to God it wasn't me."

My accusation fueled more bad feelings at the Kitty Kat. It all came to a head when Breezy wanted to use the Arabian Nights room. Apparently, the guy who'd picked Breezy from the lineup thought he was Lawrence of Arabia and needed an immediate fix with a skinny, strung-out drug addict in a see-through burka. Unfortunately, Fantasee was already in there with Sinbad the Sailor. (Fantasee was always in one of the theme rooms—her ample rear-end must have inspired it for some reason.) So, Breezy, who had to be high on something, started pounding on the door.

"Get the fuck outta there! It's my turn."

Fantasee came out wearing only a veil and stilettos. Say what you want, but it didn't look right. Arabs don't have butts like that.

"I ain't got to put up with no more a dat shit!" Fantasee screamed and slapped Breezy in the face so hard it left a welt. Lawrence of Arabia, who was standing next to Breezy in the hallway, took one look at Fantasee in that veil and decided he wanted her instead. He told Breezy he'd changed his mind and would wait until Fantasee finished with Sinbad. Well, Breezy screeched that she was going to sue for discrimination because it was pure racism (Breezy was white). Then she went and trashed Fantasee's room.

I thought Fantasee was going to kill her, I really did. But all she said was, "Dat ain't Christian what she done, the goddamned bitch."

Gil called Breezy into his office to fire her. We all crowded around the door to eavesdrop.

"I can't use you anymore," we heard him say. "You're completely out of control and I'm trying to run a legitimate business here."

"But that's not fair!" Breezy yelled. "They blame me for everything!"

"Clean out your stuff. I want you gone within the hour."

The door flew open before we had a chance to clear out.

"Fuck you!" she screamed.

Despite Fantasee's noble Christian attitude, she'd about had enough of Breezy's antics and started chasing her. Breezy took off running with Fantasee hot on her tail, hips thundering. "Dats right you afrait lil' bitch!" Breezy escaped to the parking lot where she started calling out Fantasee who stood just inside the doorway, winded, with her hands on her knees. The poor thing had simply run out of gas, and it's a good thing because you don't want to see a naked woman in stilettos and veil running through a gravel parking lot in broad daylight. Or maybe you do, but it wouldn't be right.

A week later I was up in the front. I'd just escorted an insurance salesman with a gaudy wedding ring from my room. I sat at the bar and ordered a double. It was always a double. Joanne came over and sat next to me.

We all liked Joanne because she didn't judge us. She'd started working at the Kitty Kat years earlier after her husband died. I'll bet she'd been a pretty woman back then, but now she was matronly. If you saw her at Walmart, you'd never guess she was the madam at a brothel. She looked more like an aging, chain-smoking hairstylist who spent her days rolling gray thinning hair onto rods.

"Everything okay, Kate? You look tired."

"I don't know how long I can do this."

"You can stop now. Gil would pretend he can't live without you but this place will survive. Course, I'd miss you. You're the only one around here with a brain in her head."

"Thanks."

"You've got some money saved up. Take it and get out of this place before it takes everything you've got. You don't want to be like me when you're sixty; working for peanuts in a dump like this."

I'd thought the same thing a million times but it had become the well-worn pattern of my life. Just then the front door opened behind us and Joanne got up to welcome the customer. I finished my drink in a gulp, then twisted around on the bar stool. A man stood just inside the door and removed his sunglasses. He had a receding hairline but was otherwise fit and well dressed. He took a few steps toward the bar once his eyes adjusted to the dim light of the parlor.

"Keith? *Keith Murphy?* Is that you?"

42

KATHERINE

LIKE I SAID, it felt like Keith had grown a carving knife. The pain down there was sharp. Keith made me promise to go in.

"Yeah, I think I will. I haven't had my annual for about three years anyway. I don't like them." And, honestly, what woman does? Oh goodie, it's time for my annual! Keith had been on the stirrups one time for a grand total of about twenty minutes so he ought to know. That's why I'd put it off for about two and a half years. Okay, maybe three.

"What do you think it is?" he asked.

"It's probably nothing. I must have a bladder infection or something."

I'd only said that to make Keith feel better because that's what we moms do half the time—focus on making our husbands and kids happy. But I've always been a big believer in intuition and I could feel it kicking in. Something was not right.

I couldn't sleep that night. I kept thinking of all the things it might be and eventually concluded it had to be cancer and I would most likely die. No, I definitely was going to die. That's what happens in the middle of the night when it's dark and you can't sleep and your mind goes to the worst place. Your headache becomes a cut and dried case of advanced brain cancer and your tummy ache becomes stage-four stomach cancer. When the sun comes up, you realize it'd just been a headache, or a tummy ache, and there'd been no need to feel sorry for yourself as you lay there in the dark planning your entire funeral.

That next morning I still felt bloated. I got the kids off to school and then called Dr. Voss, my OBGYN who had delivered the last four of my kids. I'd been surprised by how young and handsome he was when he'd first walked into the exam room twelve years earlier. He looked like one of those soap opera doctors—the ones that are almost *too* handsome. I immediately regretted not having done my hair and I'll freely admit I did more primping for my next appointment. Keith had said he wanted to go with me to that second appointment all those years ago but I really didn't want him to. I'd told myself it wasn't because I was going to flirt with the freaking doctor. I mean, come on, it's hardly the time to get all sexy when you're draped and having idle chit-chat about the weather while the doc pretends he didn't just stick an ice-cold prong up your vagina.

Keith could never admit another man was handsome. Me, I would gladly acknowledge how attractive another woman was. It didn't mean I was a lesbian, it simply meant I wasn't blind. But I knew Keith would balk at Dr. McDreamy putting anything near my vajayjay. And I was right.

"Gol," Keith had said as we were driving out of the parking lot, "that doctor guy looked like he was about twenty."

"Yeah, he looks really young."

"You think he's handsome?"

"He's okay," I said. "I've never really noticed, but, yeah, he's a pretty good-looking guy I guess."

"I'd hate to go to a guy like that if I were a woman," he'd said. "I'd want someone with more experience." Yeah, right. If his doctor looked like Christie Brinkley, he'd make his own hangnails to justify an appointment. Oops, just stubbed my toe. Time for another checkup!

Dr. Voss had a cancellation so I was able to get right in. I wasn't too worried but my mind did wander to all the worst-case scenarios. Fortunately, no one in my family had cancer and I knew I was just being overly melodramatic.

I lay on the exam table while he poked my stomach. It hurt, and I winced. He frowned.

"Any constipation?"

"Yeah, a little, I guess."

"How about frequent urination?"

"Yeah, I've been going four or five times a night lately for some reason."

I looked to see if he frowned. He didn't, which I took to be a good sign.

"Any nausea?"

"No," I was happy to report. "Tell me I'm not pregnant," I said with a nervous laugh.

"There's some fullness off to the left side of your uterus. Is that tender?"

"Yeah, that's pretty sore."

I usually hold my breath for the pelvic exam part, hoping they'll cut it short. But this time I wanted him to make sure he felt everything he needed to, even if it hurt.

"Katherine, I'm feeling a mass on your left ovary. I want to get an ultrasound right away. I'm also going to run a blood test. Let's get those done today."

"A mass?"

"I don't want to alarm you, but I'm concerned we might be dealing with a fairly large tumor that has some complexity to it."

"A tumor? You mean as in cancer?"

"Let's get the ultrasound and then we'll know a lot more. But, yes, it could be a cancerous lesion and that's why we'll run a CA-125—a blood test, to look for that."

"To look for what?"

"For ovarian cancer."

I don't remember driving home. I don't remember making dinner or what I talked to my kids about that afternoon. I waited until they were in bed before I broke the news to Keith.

"So, like, what does that mean?" he asked.

"He isn't sure but I'm supposed to go back the day after tomorrow to find out the test results."

"But it might not be cancer, right? I mean, he didn't specifically say you had it, did he?"

"No, but I could tell he's worried."

Two days later we were early for the appointment. Keith went with me even though he had to cancel a meeting with his largest supplier. Dr. Voss came in holding my chart and sat on the rolling stool in the small exam room, a fetus growth-rate chart hanging on the wall next to the scales I always hated to get on.

"Katherine," he said as he rolled up next to us. "I'm sorry to tell you that the ultrasound found a large complex tumor on your left ovary." Pause to let it sink in, which it did, and didn't. "There is also a collection of fluid in your abdomen which we call ascites. Unfortunately, we also found nodules on your liver and other tumors in your abdomen. The primary tumor on your ovary measures twelve to thirteen centimeters—it's a substantial tumor. The blood test suggests advanced ovarian cancer."

I didn't say anything and neither did Keith because this wasn't really happening, and you don't talk much in a dream. Keith reached over and took my hand.

"The symptoms of ovarian cancer are vague and that's why it's so difficult to diagnose. Women don't complain because they often feel no symptoms, so it has usually grown and spread to other organs by the time we find it." He set my chart on the desk and took my free hand in both of his. "I'm so sorry. I promise we'll do everything we can to treat it as aggressively as possible."

"So . . . could she die from this?"

"We're going to remove as much of it as we can. We'll likely have to remove your ovaries, uterus, fallopian tubes, and any other tumors we find. I'm going to refer you to a gynecological surgeon who specializes in oncology. He's excellent and I have a lot of confidence in him. Once he's removed as much of the tissue as he can, you'll undergo chemotherapy."

"So, is she going—" Keith couldn't finish, and I couldn't even begin.

"Once the surgeon gets in there, he'll have a better idea as to the cancer's stage and grade."

"What does that mean?" Keith asked. As for me, I was speechless.

"The stage refers mostly to the size of the tumor. I think we're looking at a Stage III cancer, and we'll know the grade as soon as the doctor removes it."

"Is that bad?"

"Most ovarian cancers are Stage III by the time we finally find them. Obviously, we never want to find any cancer, but Stage III is an advanced stage."

"You said something about the grade," Keith said.

"The grade refers to how aggressive, or angry, the cells are. We won't know that until after the tumor cells are sent to pathology."

The surgeon I was referred to had the bedside manner of a cinder block. Wouldn't you think they'd show some compassion and not make you feel like an idiot for asking a simple question or two? Not this guy. Of course, he could have been the Boston Strangler for all I cared as long as he was a good surgeon. It's not like I was going to invite him over for game night. I wanted him to suck out all the tumors that weren't supposed to be there, not play Scattegories over potato chips and a bowl of peanut M&M's.

They opened me up from stem to stern. There went my reproductive organs, the lymph nodes in my abdomen, parts of my liver, bladder, and bowel. My tissue was sent to pathology.

The next day the surgeon marched into my hospital room where I was recovering as if he had somewhere more important to be. He wore a lab coat and bow tie. Maybe it's just me, but bow tie wearers seem a bit full of themselves and I'm a bit leery of them. The tie was askew on his throat like a twisted propeller. I was still a bit groggy from the surgery but this guy was all business.

"It appears she has Grade III cancer cells," he said to Keith, as if I was still under general anesthesia.

"Grade III out of how many?" Keith asked.

"Grade III is the highest and most aggressive cellular activity. I'm sorry."

Just then Dr. Voss came into my hospital room. He took my chart from the bow tie guy, reviewed it, and then sat on the bed next to me and took my hand. He looked me square in the eye.

"Katherine, we are going to fight this."

He didn't flinch. He only looked away briefly to communicate the same look to Keith. I knew he cared about me and he'd see it through to the end, one way or the other.

My awful news spread through town like Grade III cancer cells. Prayers were said all over the place on my behalf. The Relief Society (that's the name of the women's service organization in our church) sprang into action and delivered more tuna-noodle casseroles and trays of enchiladas than our family could ever eat, even if we all lived to the Second Coming. But no one had much of an appetite.

My kids were so darling. It broke my heart. My parents were a mess, too. I think my dad was confused. He'd prayed so hard and had never missed a day of church and now his oldest daughter, the one with six kids, was battling for her life with a disease she didn't deserve. Then again, who deserves to get cancer? I guess you could say someone who smokes and gets lung cancer has no one to blame but themselves, but even they don't deserve it. Okay, fine, maybe Ted Bundy should get it. But he didn't. I did.

My mom, who had begun to climb out of her depression, fell back into it with a thud. But it was my kids. My kids and Kylie. I know little Kylie prayed for hours at a time, and her faith was as pure as it gets without any cynicism or doubt. She promised God everything she could think of, even things she couldn't possibly deliver on, if He would only fix me. But my reproductive system had betrayed me again.

43

KATE

"WHAT ARE YOU DOING HERE?" Keith Murphy asked me.

"What are *you* doing here?"

"Uh, just lookin' around, I guess."

"This is really embarrassing, isn't it."

"No kidding. You've probably heard it a hundred times, but I've never been to one of these before," he said.

"Make that a thousand."

"So, really, what are you doing here?" he asked. "Do you *work* here?"

"Afraid so. See? I told you it was embarrassing."

"I won't tell if you won't," he said and laughed.

"Yeah, that might not go over too well back home."

Keith looked surprisingly good, better than he ever had, actually. He was thin and his teeth were straight with no gaps. Probably veneers because you can't get the real ones to go that straight, or that white. I noticed no ring on his left hand.

"So, tell me Keith Murphy, what have you been up to the past, what, nineteen years?"

"Geez, it's a pretty long story and I don't want to bore you."

"Try me."

"Well, after you went away to college, I kept working for my dad's plumbing supply store. Then I got married to Becky Fulton. Remember her from Snow Canyon? Anyway, Becky's dad owned a convenience store and I started working there and took it over when he died. It worked out I guess but then I had some problems and lost it. In fact, I lost pretty much everything about six or seven years ago but now I'm back on my feet and things are going pretty well."

"Kids?"

"No, we never got around to it. We kept finding excuses and it just never happened. So it's just me and my dog."

"And Mrs. Murphy?"

"We divorced about ten years ago. My fault."

"Why do you say that?"

"I started drinking a few years into the marriage and never stopped. My second marriage ended for the same reason. I was an alcoholic. I'm still an alcoholic, even though I've been sober for five years now. Anyway, I lost everything."

"I'm sorry to hear that."

"Hey, life's good now. So what about you? Ever get married?"

"Yeah," I said. "I got married a few years ago but I'm separated. My lifestyle isn't the best one for a marriage."

"I bet not," Keith said and laughed. "Any kids?"

"Nope. Same as you. I just never got around to it." I pulled at my halter top to make it cover more, even though it could only do so much. "You still living in St. George?"

"Yeah, I just bought a convenience store—the Quik Mart over there in Santa Clara."

We talked at the bar for two hours. Joanne knew I was in the middle of a private conversation and ushered the johns to another room for the lineups, such was the tenure I had. Keith told me about his long road to recovery. He drank and dabbled in drugs. Then he drank and dabbled some more. Before long, he was a full-time drinker and dabbler. He tried to explain that there are people who drink and then there are drinkers, and it's the drinkers who have a problem. I tried to see the distinction. I knew plenty of alcoholics but, luckily, I wasn't one of them. Honest—I really wasn't. I drank like a fish, but could stop. Keith, who hadn't had a drink in five years, couldn't. And that's the distinction I suppose right there. Not fair, I know.

"It's weird how things work out," I said.

He dropped his head and shook it. "No kidding. Who would've bet we'd be sitting in a place like this talking about rehab? Long way from high school, huh?"

It is obvious that I would never have made that bet. Not in a million years. I didn't even know what brothels and alcoholism were when I was in high school. I mean, I'd *heard* of both of them just like I'd heard of nuclear physics and dwarfism but they were so foreign to me that I didn't comprehend the possibilities of my involvement in either of them.

"Remember when I thought I was pregnant?"

"Oh yeah," he said. "Scared the hell out of me. Sorry I was such a jerk about it."

"That's okay," I said. "But we dodged the bullet, didn't we? My parents would have freaked out."

"Mine too."

"My mom told me your dad had a heart attack a few years ago. It's Vaughn, right? Is he okay?"

"Yeah, he's fine. You didn't know him very well but he's really something. My first wife was Mormon and he gave her a pretty hard time about it. About drove her nuts."

"Are you still in the church then?"

"Oh, no," he said. "I left a long time ago. It was just never my thing. You?"

I smiled and looked around the brothel.

"Yeah, I guess not," he said.

"Do you ever wonder what would've happened if I'd been pregnant or if we'd stayed together after high school?" I asked.

"Actually, I do. I also think about what would've happened if you hadn't gone to school in Vegas. Pretty crazy. Everything probably would've been different."

"Yeah, I'd probably be a housewife with six kids by now." I chuckled at the thought and so did he because, honestly, six kids? Um, I don't think so. I then took a moment to look around the glitzy Gunsmoke parlor. "But that probably would've been better than what happened."

"You know," he said, "I don't think I ever got over you. I tried to call you a few times but then I got married and all that. I don't know, maybe it's that first love thing."

It was starting to get a little weird. "Well," I said, "you didn't come all this way to talk to an old girlfriend all night."

"Yeah, I guess not, but I'm glad I did. And you don't need to worry, I know it'd be too awkward to, you know . . ."

"I've had more awkward," I said. "Trust me."

He stood. "Well, I better get back on the road. It's a two-hour drive."

I stood too and we hugged. I don't remember the last time I gave a man a hug. I had sex with them, sure, but it would've been weird to hug them. Too intimate.

"It was good to see you, Keith. Really."

"It was good to see you, too. But I guess I better . . ."

"Yeah, I know. Long drive."

He reached over and put his hand on my arm. "If I came back next week could we maybe go out to dinner or something?"

"Sure, I'd like that."

A date? An actual real live date? "Hey, you know where to find me."

44

RICKY

I WAS TIRED OF RUNNING from Spanos. We should've killed the motherfucker in that motel room two years ago when we had the chance because he totally deserved it. It's like that question about whether you would've killed Hitler when he was a kid, knowing what you know now. I always came down on the side of yes—yes I would have shot the sonofabitch right between the eyes at close range. Now, I'm not saying Victor Spanos was like Hitler—Hitler had better hair. Those hair plugs were a joke.

Obviously, I couldn't live in Vegas with the wannabe Godfather and his goons out there looking for me. The last thing I wanted was to wake up and find some goddamned horse's head in my bed. And as long as I had to disappear, I figured I might as well go to a warm beach with a bunch of bikinis. I thought about calling Kate but I knew she'd survive just fine without me. Kate was always a fighter. I mean, look what she did to Spanos. I figured I would've heard something if Spanos had gotten to her, or if she had finished the job with him.

I know Kate was mad at me for leaving the way I did but part of it was for her own good. Besides, this was a two-way street and I didn't see her hiring a private detective to find me either. I knew she'd land on her feet anyway and I was right. But I'll admit I was a little surprised to run into her at the Kitty Kat because I had no idea she worked there. I assumed that she was still in Vegas, or that maybe she'd gone home to Utah. So imagine my surprise when I go in for a little female companionship and find her there. She still looked damned good and I'm sure she's making a killing.

I had nothing against Kate, other than the way she treated me like shit when I found her working there at the Kitty Kat. I could have been upset that my wife had become a fucking prostitute but I kept my mouth shut, at least until she pulled that shit about charging me to have sex. Kate was beautiful with a killer body and we hit it off pretty well, especially at first. But I felt like I'd been roped into marrying her. You'd have to know her family. Bunch of right-wing religious fanatics. My God, they wouldn't even drink coffee. She kept telling me her parents would never forgive her for "living in sin" and we had to make it legit, like this was the Dark Ages or something. So I ended up marrying her to get her and her family off my back. I'm sure the whole family hates me now.

After I left Vegas, I wound up in Venice Beach where I planned to lay low for a while—wait for Spanos to cool down, you know. But then I met some girl who let me move in with her. She was quite a bit younger than I was but I didn't see a problem with it. It's not like we were going to get married or anything. Why would I want to get married again?

The girl's condo in Venice Beach was amazing with a bunch of fancy art and shit but she got on my nerves pretty quick. She was a trust funder who thought she was special and strutted around like she was some kind of self-made millionaire when she hadn't earned a goddamned penny in her life. Special my ass. At least Kate had a job—admittedly not the most impressive job in town, but at least it was something. Then this girl springs it on me that she'd gone off the pill because she wanted to have a baby. I needed to get the hell out of there.

I really wanted to get back to the Vegas scene but knew I had to clean up the mess with Spanos first. He was still out there and I knew he wasn't going to forget the whole thing and let bygones be bygones. I got this spoiled girlfriend to loan me $30,000 which was enough to pay Spanos the $4,500 I owed him (like I "owed" it), plus another twenty-five grand for shits and giggles. I had no intention of repaying this trust-funder girl. Why should I feel guilty about taking a few bucks from her when she hadn't earned it? Let her bribe someone else to help raise her kid.

I still had Spanos's number so I held my breath and called him.

"Victor? It's me, Ricky Waters."

"What the fuck you want?"

"I've finally got the money and want to make it right between us. I would've had it sooner but Kate, you remember the girl I was with? Anyway, she took off with my money. So it's taken me a little longer to pay you back."

"Where are you?"

"California."

"Where in California?"

"Up north, near San Francisco," I lied. "Listen, if I pay you, we're good?"

"Fuckin' bitch busted up my nose pretty bad."

"Trust me, I know. She's psycho."

I could picture him on the other end of the line with a big gut and messed-up nose. He was probably wearing a complimentary bathrobe from the closet of some gaudy hotel room with metallic wallpaper, sucking down a Johnnie Walker from the mini bar at nine o'clock in the morning.

"How much money you got?"

"I have the $4,500 in cash."

"Well, Waters, that ain't gonna cut it now, is it. I've gotta have ten grand. Interest."

"Come on, Vic. I called you because I wanted to make it right."

"Yeah, ten grand oughta do it."

I finally agreed to pay the ugly sonofabitch ten grand, then splurged on a new cocktail dress for my soon-to-be-ex-girlfriend which got me another five grand from her trust fund. Spanos and I agreed to meet the following day at my old haunt off the strip. I rented a car for a one-way trip from LA to Vegas. My so-called girlfriend was having one of her "me days" and didn't even know I'd gone. I knew she'd be devastated, but she'd eventually move on. I left her a note on the kitchen counter so she wouldn't have to worry about me and then drove six hours straight to the restaurant, that is if you could call the Lucky Traveler a restaurant. I don't know why I'd spent so much time there because the vibe was all wrong—just a bunch of losers who were too fucking stupid to figure the odds.

Spanos was waiting for me at a table near the back. No goon squad or baseball bat, thank God.

I slid into the seat across from him. "Listen," I said, "about the whole injury thing, I meant to—"

"Shut up, Waters. Just give me the money."

I couldn't take my eyes off his nose. It looked like a boy scout had taken his dull pocket knife to it. It had a big gouge taken out of it and was totally bent out of shape. One nostril was twice the size of the other one. Kate would be happy to know she'd really done a number on it.

"Looks real good, don't it?" Spanos asked.

"What?"

"My nose, dumbass. This thing on my face you've been starin' at."

"It looks okay. I hardly even noticed it."

"Right. Now shut the fuck up while I tell you the deal."

"What deal? I just paid you the ten grand. I can't pay any more."

"And you won't need to, on one condition."

"Bullshit, Vic. We're done. No more conditions."

"I said we *might* be done. See, I'm gonna need another five grand on top of this. For medical expenses. Either that, or you tell me where she is so I can get it from her."

"Where who is?" Of course, I knew exactly who "who" was.

"Your ex. The one who hit me with the goddamned iron, you shit for brains."

"How am I supposed to know where she is? We're separated."

Victor stared at me. It was hard not to look at his nose which looked like a large, partially chewed cashew with pores in it. I hated him and wanted him dead, but I will say this: I felt sorry for that nose of his. He looked like a freak.

"Where is she?"

"I'm not sure. But I think I heard someone say they saw her in Pahrump about a year ago. Over at that Kitty Kat place."

"Would that someone have been you?"

"I can't remember where I heard it. That's all I know. I haven't heard from her in a couple years."

Spanos looked at me hard. I tried to focus on his forehead but that nose of his was like a fuckin' eye magnet. He then lifted his drink and looked at me again over the top of his glass. Then, for what must have been the first time in his sorry life, he lowered the glass without having taken a swig. I guess this little act was supposed to tell me he was seriously contemplating my fate which, to some degree, I suppose he was.

"We're done, Waters. Now get the fuck out of my life."

I walked out of the Lucky Traveler a free man. I knew I'd sold out Kate for five thousand dollars. Actually, this was the second time I'd sold her out for five grand, if you count the sleeping with Spanos thing, which she did voluntarily, by the way. Was I a jerk? Maybe. But don't forget how she'd treated me like a piece of shit when we'd reconnected at the Kitty Kat. Eight hundred dollars to have sex with her my ass. Here's a news flash, Kate: We were married, okay? Here she was making all that money and she'd held out on me, so I figured she had enough money from her whoring to pay Spanos's medical bills. Besides, she'd been the one who'd taken the iron to his face in the first place, not me. All he wanted was the money to reimburse the medical expenses and she could afford it.

45

KATE

I WAS SURPRISED when Keith Murphy called me a few days after we'd awkwardly, and I do mean awkwardly, reconnected. I knew he liked me but, come on, I was a freaking prostitute. Prostitutes don't date real men. They don't really date at all. Maybe he thought his alcoholism and two failed marriages evened the score. But, yeah, I'm pretty sure a prostitute trumps all that, and then some.

Keith had turned his life around—back to making a respectable living, whatever that means. Society had determined long ago that the way I made money was *dis*respectable even though I never cheated anyone, never twisted anyone's arm, never gave my customers anything they didn't want, not even a mild STD. And then you have the so-called respectable jobs where people cheat each other to get ahead, or make enormous profit off other people's suffering. Where's the respectability in that? All I know is that Keith's living must have been respectable enough to allow him to drive out to Pahrump once a week to blow money on me. He didn't blow it on a BBBJ either. He blew it on flowers and clothes that actually fit me.

No one had ever bought me flowers before, not a single time, unless you count the time Ricky used my sock money to buy me that bouquet of red roses for sleeping with Victor Spanos. Oh, and I'd been given a carnation wrist corsage for the junior prom from a pimply boy named Ernest which lasted about ten minutes until I reached for a stick of gum in my purse and ruined it.

At least our biggest warts were on the table. Keith had gone shopping at a brothel where I was For Sale, which has got to tell you something about the tit for tat. Other uncomfortable disclosures would be small by comparison. It was reassuring to know that if pizza gave me gas, or if I couldn't back into a parking spot in one try, Keith might not automatically leave me. I wanted to lay it all out there from the get-go—no secrets. I probably wouldn't lead out with the pizza thing, but I didn't want to invest in something that was destined to fail from the start.

"You don't want to date me, Keith."

"Why not?"

"Why not? Look where I work."

"I already know that."

"And I probably don't want kids."

"Okay. Who said anything about kids?"

"I drink too much, and I'm probably addicted to pain pills."

"Keep going."

"My family has practically disowned me."

"Okay."

"All my friends are in the business. In fact, I'm not sure I have many friends left who aren't."

"Uh-huh."

He just sat there like I was listing my favorite date movies. Nothing seemed to bother him. I probably could have copped to being a serial killer. It's quite possible that my halter top had something to do with it, but I believed Keith really did like me. The real me.

"And none of that scares you?" I asked.

"Not really."

"Okay, then how about this: Just about everything about me is fake. My hair, my eyelashes, my boobs—they're all fake."

"I sorta knew that already."

"They say I snore."

"Got it."

"I'm terrible with money."

"Me too."

"I had a cancer scare a few years ago."

"I'm sorry. Are you okay?"

"I am now but you never know with cancer."

"Okay."

"Did I mention I'm a prostitute?"

"Yeah, that came up."

I listed all the things he'd eventually find out about me that weren't pretty because I couldn't bear the thought of my *real* self being rejected. It was bad enough when someone rejected who they only thought I was.

I think it was easier for Keith to expose all his warts because he'd had so much practice in AA. That's about all they do in those meetings, at least according to the movies I've seen—they sit around in a circle on folding metal chairs in a church basement holding Styrofoam cups of black coffee and lay it all on the line, one after the other. They might even get extra credit the more they spill their guts for all I know. My name is Keith Murphy and I'm an alcoholic. He knew what it meant to be down and out.

It was a Saturday morning when Gil knocked on my door. I was a bit annoyed because I'd been up until 2:00 a.m. and had hoped to sleep in.

"Kate," he said, "there's a message from Crock. Said he wants you to call him right away."

"Did he say what it's about?"

"No, but you can use the phone in my office."

I threw on some clothes and went to Gil's windowless office which was cluttered with files and papers and I wondered why it took so much paperwork to run a brothel. Law office I could see, but a brothel? There was nothing on the walls, not a single photo or memento. I didn't expect to see a plaque from the Chamber of Commerce, but I figured there ought to be *something*. Then I wondered what my office would be filled with if I ever had one. I didn't have any plaques either and even if I did, I doubt *Best Hooker Vegas Metro Area 1994* would impress a whole lot of people.

"Crock here."

"Hi, it's Kate. Gil said you were trying to reach me."

"Seen the *Sun* this morning?"

"No," I said. "I don't read the newspaper, especially this early in the morning."

"It's noon. Anyway, go get it. You're not going to believe it."

"Believe what? What's going on?"

"It's Victor Spanos. There's a big article in the *Sun*. They found him out behind those old warehouses next to the Frontier. Apparently, he pissed off some of his mob buddies. They say he'd been shot, execution style. They even cut off his dick and shoved it in his mouth."

"Don't mess with me, Crock. This isn't funny." I was shaking and nearly collapsed into Gil's desk chair. "Are you being serious?"

"Dead serious. Looks like he owed the wrong guys."

"I can't believe it. Do you have any idea who would've done it?"

"How the hell would I know? They said it was mob related and that's all I know. I'm surprised it took this long, to be perfectly honest. Such a prick."

"Yeah, he was a pig."

"Anyway, I figured you'd be happy to hear the low-life scumbag finally got what he had coming."

Happy? More like thrilled, and I hope you won't judge me for that because I'm just being honest. I walked across the street to the Circle K and bought a newspaper from the vending machine out front. I'll admit there might have been the tiniest spring in my step. I put the paper under my arm and walked back to my room at the Kitty Kat, then sat on my bed and opened it. There it was on the first page, big as life:

MURDER NEAR THE STRIP

Investigation >> Mob Ties Likely for Victim of Execution Style Killing

By Lucas Dugdale

Las Vegas, NV >> June 2, 1996. A gruesome murder was discovered early this morning near the Frontier Hotel and Casino west of Las Vegas Boulevard. The body of Victor Leslie Spanos was found by authorities near a dumpster following an anonymous tip. It is believed the murder took place sometime after midnight on Tuesday. Spanos, who was long thought to be connected to money laundering and loan shark related business interests, appeared to be the victim of an execution style slaying. Detectives within the Clark County Sheriff's Department released a formal statement indicating Spanos had been shot in the head. Portions of his body were mutilated. The investigation is ongoing, but the scene was described as gruesome.

I set the newspaper down. I couldn't believe it, but it was true—Spanos was really dead. *Halle-fucking-lujah.* I doubted a single person mourned for him, not even his fifth wife. I felt no guilt for being satisfied that he'd been murdered. In fact, I was glad to see it'd been painful, too, instead of the Good Lord allowing him to topple over on the twelfth tee from a heart attack. Sorry, but that's the way I felt. I was even happy that he'd been saddled with a middle name like Leslie his whole life.

I thought of Ricky. Obviously, he'd heard by now. For all I knew, maybe he'd done it, but I highly doubted it because Ricky was a coward. I wondered if he'd contact me now that the coast was clear. Maybe now he'd dare crawl out from under his rock.

Speaking of Ricky, I'd been tempted to blame him for the mess of my life. If not for him, I probably wouldn't have been a prostitute. When I'd get tired of blaming Ricky, I'd blame Victor, because it was Victor who had run me out of town and straight into the loving arms of the Kitty Kat. Or even Deborah who'd introduced me to the adult entertainment business in the first place. But the choices had all been mine.

I walked out to the bar. It was only one o'clock in the afternoon but I thought a drink was in order. I grabbed the bottle of wine by its throat and glugged it into a glass.

"Drinking so early?" Joanne asked.

"I'm celebrating."

"What's the big occasion?"

"I'm celebrating because some scum bucket was murdered."

"Whoa, Kate, that doesn't sound like you."

"I know. But this guy was the reason I'm here, Jo. I was running from him and wound up at this place."

"So, now that he's gone?"

"I don't know." And I really didn't. The default was to stay put, hang on to what I'd been accustomed to. But there was an element of cowardice in that, too. It might not have been Ricky-level cowardice, but fear of the unknown kept me there. The devil you know.

Joanne came over and sat next to me. She said nothing at first and I could tell she was composing whatever she was about to say, to make it more potent.

"Kate, what are you doing here?"

I didn't answer, just stared down at my mid-morning six-ounce pour. I'm not even sure she expected a response from me—it was more like a statement.

"Remember that life you couldn't wait to get away from? Maybe it's time to take another look at it."

A few months after I'd first begun working at Lil' Secrets, I met a guy whose name was John. Of course it was. Anyway, the guy threw money around like he worked in the mint. He asked for me and I pranced around his lap in my G string. When the song was over, he said he'd run out of cash and didn't have enough for a tip. Yeah, some big spender, I thought.

"I wanted to give you a tip but I'm out of cash."

"That's okay," I'd said, just to be nice, because it really wasn't okay, especially since I'd practically worn out the fabric of his khaki's. And did he not see the ATM in the corner?

"Here's the number of my stock broker." He handed me a slip of paper with *Will Mitchell, Smith Barney* scribbled on it along with a phone number. "I own a company that's going public and I'd like to give you a few shares of stock."

"Okay." Stocks schmocks. I'd never owned a share of stock in my life and going public sounded like something I'd do if I wanted to confess.

"It'll take me a couple of days to arrange for the shares to be transferred, so give him a week. Then you can call him to confirm it."

"That sounds good, thanks," I said as I scanned the crowd for my next customer, and hopefully one who left an actual tip.

I'd found the piece of paper in a pair of my cut-off jeans about two weeks later and called the broker at Smith Barney.

"My name is Kate Coombs. A guy was going to give me—"

"Yes, Ms. Coombs. John called me a week or two ago and asked that I transfer one hundred shares of Triton Micro to an account for you. That's ready to go. I just need a little information to set up an account in your name."

"So, like, how much is that worth?"

"We don't know at this point, but hopefully the shares will sell for ten dollars."

"So, this is only worth ten dollars?"

"No, excuse me," he said. "We hope each share will be worth ten dollars, and you have one hundred shares."

I did the math in my head. "So that'd be a thousand dollars?" Okay, I admit, I'm not Einstein when it comes to math.

"Correct."

"Can I have it now?"

"I'm sorry but these are restricted shares."

"What does that mean?" I knew it was too good to be true. There's always a catch.

"These shares cannot be sold for at least three years because they were transferred to you by the owner of the company."

"Then can I have the thousand dollars in three years?"

"I don't know what the shares will be worth at that time."

"So, what, I'm supposed to call you in three years then?"

"Yes, please do. You have my number. Say, while I've got you on the line Ms. Coombs, may I ask who handles your investment portfolio?"

"I don't have one."

That had been six years earlier and I'd completely forgotten about it. Then I saw something on TV about the stock market and it triggered my memory. I figured it wasn't worth anything by then but I might as well find out. I scrounged around and finally found the Smith Barney guy's name and number in a folder where I kept my birth certificate, social security card, and an expired library card from Washington County, Utah.

"This is Will Mitchell."

"Yes, this is Kate Coombs. We talked about six years ago. Someone transferred some stock to my name and I was just checking to see whatever happened with that."

"I'm sorry; you said your name was . . .?"

"Kate Coombs. It might be under Katherine."

"Okay, let me take a look."

I was sitting on the side of my bed, filing my nails. That's what I do when I'm on the phone. I could hear his breathing so I knew he hadn't hung up on me. "I'm not finding it. Can you spell your last name?" Yep, wild goose chase all right. I brushed the nail dust from my jeans.

"Oh, wait, here it is, Ms. Coombs. I show you still have an open account with one hundred and twenty shares of Triton Micro. It looks like I tried to call you a few times to see if you wanted to reinvest the dividends but I couldn't reach you, so the dividends were automatically used to buy more shares. I'm glad you called."

I thought I only had one hundred shares but I kept my big mouth shut. "Can I sell them yet?"

"Yes, you can sell as many as you'd like."

"Well, yeah, I'd like to get that thousand dollars out now if I can."

"So you'd like to sell one thousand dollars of the stock?"

"Yes." Yippee-ki-yay! This might be legit after all.

"We can certainly do that," the broker said. "Would you like me to wire the funds to an account, or just send a check?"

"Can you just mail it to me?"

"Certainly, I'll just need a current address."

I gave him my PO Box number in Pahrump.

"So, will you close my account now?"

"Well, no, unless you want us to direct your holdings to another account."

"But I thought you were going to mail it to me."

"Yes, I understand you'd like me to mail you one thousand dollars, but I'm referring to the balance of your account. Would you prefer to leave it in Triton stock?"

Hold it, I thought. "You mean I have more in there after I take out the thousand?"

"Yes, it looks like that would leave you with a balance of approximately fifty-one thousand."

"*Dollars?* I'd still have fifty-one thousand dollars?"

"Yes. The share price had a nice run-up. We're still recommending the stock, but there are others."

"Can I have the whole fifty thousand now?"

"If you'd like, but you might consider reinvesting some of it."

"Well, could I have, like, forty thousand now and keep the rest in there?"

"Certainly. If you like the technology sector, we recommend a company called Amazon. It's still relatively small, so there is some risk, but we think it may have some upside."

Did I like the technology sector? I didn't even know what the freaking technology sector was. "Okay," I said. "Sure, let's do that."

I couldn't believe it. Forty thousand dollars for doing nothing (well, there had been the lap dance). Plus, I still had all the money in my sock, Spanos was dead, and I was dating Keith Murphy. And, on top of all that, I still had over ten-thousand dollars of stock in some little company called Amazon, or a company in the Amazon, or whatever.

46

KATHERINE

THEY ONLY GAVE ME a few weeks to recover from the surgery before they started zapping me with the chemo. I felt like crap.

"Do you think you'll get remarried?" I asked Keith as we were getting ready for bed.

"Don't even say that. We're going to beat this thing."

"I can't imagine what you must be thinking," I said. "Raising six kids on your own."

"You'll probably outlive me. Besides, many hands make light work," he said as he tapped his toothbrush on the edge of the sink and then raised his stump and right hand like he was leading an orchestra.

This made me laugh. But then it made me cry. Any woman would be lucky to have him. There were times earlier in my marriage when I'd had my doubts about him but he'd proved me wrong. Dead wrong. I remembered how nervous I'd been to leave him alone with little Jacob after Emily drowned and now I might be leaving him alone to parent all six of our kids, with one arm, and I couldn't imagine leaving them with a better man.

The kids took the news in stride, if in stride meant they cried themselves to sleep for weeks. I think it hit Jenna the hardest. I'm no shrink, but she'd begun to pull away from me and now the guilt caused her to be clingy, even at her age. Jacob was angry at the world and all Josh cared about was whether this meant we'd have to cancel our trip to Disneyland that summer.

I'd always had good hair but now it was coming out in clumps. I wanted to get it over with so I shaved my head and wore a bandana. This was about the ninth different hairstyle I'd had since we got married. And I'd rank it dead last, right below my crimping stage. When I felt well enough to go out, like to the grocery store, strangers would see the bandana with nothing underneath and give me the "Aww, she has cancer, the poor thing" look.

I was propped up in bed going through a photo album a few days after I'd shaved the last few clinging wisps of my hair. I heard the kids laughing and then Keith came waltzing in with the kids surrounding him like a moat. There was a sheet over his head. The kids pulled the sheet off and there he stood in his out-of-style jeans, braided belt, tucked-in golf shirt, and white socks. Oh, and he was bald—Bic-shaved bald. He'd done it with the kids' help as a sign of solidarity. I laughed, then cried and cried.

I'd been trading on my looks for as long as I could remember and my looks had served me well. But now they were nearly gone, vanishing by the day from chemo and all the rest. I think it's more distressing to have been beautiful and then lose it than if you'd never been beautiful in the first place because so much of your identity is tied up in being attractive. When a pretty woman gains weight, or has a breakout of zits, or gets old, she probably suffers more than a less physically attractive woman might under the same circumstances. Call me vain but I think I'm right about that. Katherine Coombs, you know, the pretty one? Well, not anymore.

Of course, when the chips are *really* down your looks don't matter so much. Everyone knows this, or at least they claim to. You realize, perhaps too late, that the people who really love you don't care about how pretty you might have been. And then you realize all that trouble you went to—the battle to hide the graying, the diets, the Botox, and all the waxing and exfoliating—may have been painful overkill. People don't care what you look like as much as you think. They just don't. Most people are so busy obsessing about their own weight and skin to notice yours anyway. Besides, they'd probably like you more with crow's feet, twenty extra pounds, and the gray.

I didn't have much energy but I still tried to keep the house up. I'd set the table and then consider resetting it with matching silverware and plates. Do I bother, or don't I? I was reminded of the time my grandma dropped a quarter on the driveway. I detected an inner turmoil and debate raging in her mind over whether or not it was worth it to bend all the way down to pick it up. She regarded the coin for a moment or two before walking away with a slight huff, presumably concluding her threshold for bending down was higher than twenty-five cents. At any other time in my life I would have gladly picked up the quarter but I concluded my new threshold for insisting on matching silverware was too high.

Vaughn postponed his retirement so Keith could spend more time with me and the kids, and Dottie, bless her heart, took the kids for hours at a time. She told me that Vaughn was a mess. "He's even been praying for you," she'd said. "He probably wouldn't admit it, but he has. We all have."

I'd sit in those comfy recliners during chemo treatments along with the other patients as the poison dripped into our veins. One voluntary drip after another. An older woman knitting. A teenage boy playing with his Rubik's cube. A middle-aged man holding the hand of another middle-aged man as he reclined in the chair with a blanket over his legs. A college-aged girl propped up reading a John Steinbeck novel. None of us deserved it, but I honestly thought my death would be the most devastating of all because of my six kids.

When chemo ended, I'd go home and vomit. I'd had pretty bad morning sickness during my pregnancies so I was used to all the vomiting, but life was being created then and now it was being destroyed. It hurt to puke, too, because my entire torso had been cut in half with a power saw and my abdomen had a bunch of staples in it. It was even worse than the time I developed a wicked cough after tripping over a lawn sprinkler and bruising my ribs.

I wondered about the future as I sat in those recliners. Not my own future, for there wasn't much left to it, but for my kids and grandchildren—grandchildren I would never get to meet. I wondered what future generations would think if they saw us lined up in the recliners being voluntarily poisoned to within an inch of our lives. I imagined them saying: Wait, they poisoned people to *cure* them? How barbaric.

As long as I'm whining, I might as well complain about my nose. I lost the little hairs in there, too, so it was constantly running. It was red and sore from all the wiping.

Even though they said my odds of being alive after five years were only in the five percent range, I thought I'd make it. I really did. All the others in those recliners probably thought they'd be in the lucky five-percent group, too. Maybe it's human nature to think that way—an irrational belief that we are somehow immune to death. We all know we are going to die at some remote time but we generally don't obsess about it. Until we are given the short term sentence, that is. Then it gets real.

I'd always seen myself growing old, having the grandkids over, and eventually moving to one of those homes where they play bingo and serve dinner at four-thirty. The doctors said it helped that I was young, but the cancer had spread. It was Grade III. Oh, trust me, I'd become an expert on grades and stages.

"What do you think the timeline would be?" Keith asked the doctor.

"Again, we don't know. But the probability, based on similarly situated patients, is in the one to two-year range."

It seemed like everybody had a cancer story and felt entitled, or perhaps obligated, to tell me all about it. "When my Uncle Burt was diagnosed with his cancer—I think it was in his throat or something—why, they said he might die but he's still hanging in there and it's been nearly four years now." My whole life had become consumed with mutating cells—mine and it seemed like everyone else's too. I don't mean to be rude, but why would they think I cared about their aunt in Florida and her skin cancer? Or their colleague at work and his prostate biopsy?

So many pep talks. You're a fighter! You'll beat this thing! They meant well, of course, but they made it sound like I was in a brawl that I could actually win. These mutinous cells were on an unwitting suicide mission, intent on killing the host (that'd be me) and destroying themselves in the process. Didn't these cells know they were signing their own death warrant? Didn't they know they couldn't survive without me? I would have loved to talk some sense into them, to remind them that their plot would surely backfire, but you can't reason with a tumor cell, you just can't.

I kept thinking about all the what ifs. What if I'd gone in for my annual sooner? What if I'd caught it earlier? What if this and what if that? Like it was going to make a bit of difference now. My mom was one of those "Everything happens for the best" types. But I think she was wrong because everything does not happen for the best, and the deep purple bags under her eyes proved it. Her eyes were sad. Her posture was sad. Her cheeks were sad. Even her chin was sad. If it were possible that her elbows and knees could register sadness, I bet they would have.

I prayed more than I ever had in my whole life. I'd always been taught that faith could move mountains, and I believed it. But if that were true, then why couldn't faith get my wayward cells to shape up and behave? Surely that'd be a heckuva lot easier than scooting Pine Mountain around. I hadn't lost my faith. In fact, I doubled down. It wasn't a death-bed kind of thing either because I had believed with all my heart for thirty-eight years. But when I'd gently question the impact of faith and prayer, all I'd get was the party line: God moves in mysterious ways.

Boy, you can say that again.

47

KATE

KEITH FINALLY WORE ME DOWN. I'd run out of excuses now that I had the money from the Triton Micro stock and Victor Spanos was out of the picture.

Joanne was happy for me. Cinnamon, Fantasee, and Candy pretended to be happy for me, too. They'd make more money with me gone but they didn't want to see me escape when they were still stuck selling their bodies on the cheap. Misery tends to love company.

Cinnamon summed it up. "She got herself a real ANM this time." I will assume this was a positive endorsement but I cannot be certain because I'd quit trying to decode her acronyms years earlier. Honestly, I think she made them up on the fly.

The girls threw me a little going-away bash in the Wild West room. I was leaning against the corral that surrounded the bed, nibbling on a piece of sheet cake and trying to avoid a sliver from the corral when Joanne informed us a customer had come in. Fantasee was mad because she'd planned the party and wanted everyone there. But what really galled her was that the customer chose Candy instead of her and wanted to use the Wild West room to boot. "Ruinin' the whole goddamned party for Kate. It ain't right."

So we cleared out of the WWR and headed for the Arabian Nights room. Fifteen minutes later, Candy galloped into the party on a stick pony. All she wore was a holster with toy cap guns around her waist and a bandana around her neck. Her hips were so big and round that the cap guns on either side hung at a 45° angle.

"Couldn't take it any longer," Candy said, not the least bit self-conscious that she happened to be straddling a stick pony while standing buck naked in the middle of a birthday party. "The guy's tryin' to lasso me with the goddamned rope we got in there. Thinks he's John Fuckin' Wayne."

"So where is he?"

"He's still sittin' in there twirling the god-danged rope. Said I had to take a pee."

She grabbed a glazed donut and galloped back out. I wouldn't miss the place for a second, but I would miss my friends. After all, there aren't a lot of company breakrooms where you're trying to make small talk with your co-workers over a sheet cake and someone gallops in on a stick pony, buck naked.

The next day I drove to Las Vegas to pick up an old paycheck from Lil' Secrets. Most of our money had come from tips but we also earned $2.80 per hour and they'd been holding my check for a long time. I then went to the bank and withdrew $500 in cash. I drove to Sugar & Spice and sat in my car in the parking lot to reminisce. Sometimes I'll have these bouts of melancholy reflection and this was one of those times. I saw

Gulliver come out and drive away and then Crock came out to sweep the porch area. I ducked low in my seat. I realized I would probably never see him again and began to cry thinking about all that had happened to me—from my first audition there to my time at Lil' Secrets and then to the years at the Kitty Kat. I finally drug my sleeve across my eyes and pulled out of the parking lot to hit the road back to Pahrump, presumably for the last time. Before getting on the freeway though, I drove to the apartment I'd shared with Sandra and Deborah. He was still there on the corner as I hoped he'd be.

"Miss Kate," Reginald said. "Ain't you a sight for sore eyes."

"I'm leaving Nevada in a few days and wanted to see you before I leave."

"You come all this way just to see me?"

"Of course," I said. "And I wanted to give you a little something." I handed him the envelope with $500 in cash. "I wish I could do more."

He opened the envelope and began to cry. I leaned down and kissed him on the forehead, then got in my car and drove back to Pahrump.

Keith drove down to Pahrump a few days later in his pickup and we loaded it with my possessions. The truck was overkill—my things would've fit snugly into the back seat of a VW. After I said my goodbyes, I asked Keith if he wouldn't mind stopping by my old apartment in Vegas because I wanted to say a final goodbye. The spot where Reginald had been every day for as long as I'd lived there was now empty. I got out of the car and walked to the corner that had already been swept clean. There was no evidence that he'd ever been there.

"Everything okay?" Keith asked when I got back in the car.

"I hope so."

"Want to go in or anything?"

"No, we can go. I just wanted to see someone before I left but he's not here."

I've thought a lot about Reginald since then. Did my modest charity help him, or did it kill him? Was he able to use the money for a down payment on an apartment or did he use it to finally OD? I suppose I'll never know.

Keith drove straight to the kennel to pick up his dog. He hadn't told me much about this dog other than he'd saved her from the needle several years earlier. I waited in the truck while Keith went in. I'm fairly lukewarm about dogs. Maybe I was stricken by Enos, our wiener dog and his variety of smells. He'd been a good family dog I suppose but I think we could have done better, maybe with a lab or golden retriever. I feel bad talking about the deceased this way because poor Enos couldn't help his shape or his odors.

A few minutes later Keith came back out with an ugly, scruffy little dog trotting behind him. The trot was awkward because she only had three legs and one good eye. Honestly, she looked like she'd survived the Battle of Gettysburg. Keith called her Triclops. Who couldn't love a guy with a one-eyed, three-legged dog?

Keith drove me to the lousy apartment I'd rented in Santa Clara, the quaint small town that borders St. George. The Villas at Santa Clara was an outrageous misnomer. It came with a treeless, balding yard with stains on the stucco walls from the dripping air conditioning units. My one-bedroom apartment had matted shag carpet, avocado appliances, and an asbestos ceiling with a large yellow pee stain in the corner. For the life of me, I don't know how it got there.

"You sure you don't want to move in with me?" he asked. "I've got plenty of room."

"I just want to settle into my own place and I don't want my family freaking out. Let's just see how this goes."

My parents were happy to have me back from Sin City but I think they were also relieved I lived over in Santa Clara where their neighbors wouldn't see much of me. I still didn't look like the farmer's wife, you know. I had left St. George nearly twenty years earlier as a sheltered, naïve teenager and had returned a different woman. I read somewhere that all the cells in our bodies are replaced with new ones about every ten years or so. So, when I say I returned to St. George a new woman, I mean it. My thoughts, ideas, attitudes, and beliefs had all changed. Nothing was the same about me. Not my skin, my hair, my brain, or my bones. I was literally a different person, inside and out.

While I had undoubtedly changed, I had discovered that change isn't always evolutionary, unless by evolution you mean *any* change. I'd like to think I'd taken an evolutionary step forward, a giant leap even, but my parents would have considered my evolution in the same way they considered Darwin's. They would have said my progress had regressed, that my evolution was backward and the new me was misguided, wicked even. My bubble had popped.

I was over at my parent's house for Sunday dinner where the entire clan had congregated. Kenny was there with his three kids and chaos reigned as it usually did at my parent's house. His wife, the mature-for-her-age one, gently tried to keep the kids away from me. It was fairly insulting but I understand.

"So, Katherine, what are you going to do for work?" my mom asked. "You've got a lot of good waitressing experience." My parents had never even contemplated the unthinkable notion that their daughter had been a prostitute. They wouldn't have believed me even if I'd told them, and even if my confession had come with live eyewitnesses and a positive lie detector test. And yet every prostitute is someone's child.

"I've decided to go to cosmetology school. There's a good one here in St. George and I want to open my own salon."

"Why, that's wonderful!" my mom said.

"Maybe you can hire me when it gets up and running," said Kimberly, who was now twenty-nine-years old, dead broke, and the mother of two small children who were running through the house with dripping popsicles. Kimberly had always assumed she'd be a homemaker her entire life and live it up on Easy Street, but the returned missionary she'd hastily married turned out to be gay. He was just as disappointed as she was to learn he preferred men. He'd tearfully confessed on their fifth wedding anniversary that he was in love with a man at his work. I know I shouldn't laugh, because it wasn't funny, but she's the one who got married in the temple to the perfect guy, a marriage that was blessed with everyone's enthusiastic stamp of approval. Of course, no one publicly acknowledged that he was gay, just that he and Kimberly weren't a good match. Ya think? Anyway, he'd moved to Salt Lake City and tried to be forgotten by the Coombs family.

The girls I went to cosmetology school with were young, mostly blond, naïve, conservative girls like I once was. They'd stand in front of their Styrofoam heads gossiping about boys and the other girls who'd called in sick as they practiced perming, teasing, and coloring. A nineteen-year-old girl was standing over her mannequin's head with strips of tinfoil sticking out everywhere. It looked like one of those old Sputnik satellites. "Some of us are driving down to Las Vegas this weekend," she said to me. "Wanna come? We're gonna lay out and maybe go to a show. Plus, they have this awesome water park. It's gonna be a blast!"

"Uh, no," I said. "I think I'll pass."

"You sure? I've heard Vegas is tons of fun."

When I graduated from cosmetology school, I spent fifteen thousand dollars to open my own salon in St. George where I specialized in acrylic nails. Luckily, I got started before the Asian Invasion. Don't get me wrong, I've got nothing against Asians, but I'm intrigued with their mani-pedi obsession.

"Your place is so lovely!" my mom said when she and my dad drove up in their ten-year-old minivan to see my new salon. "Look, Dale, she already has all the furniture and equipment!" She tried so hard to be supportive. Everything she said to me was followed by a robust exclamation point. "You're menu is ideal!" "And look at these perfect blue chairs for while they're waiting!" "And look at all the mirrors, Dale!" I gave her the first manicure of her life and she walked around for two days showing it off with her arms stuck out in front of her, hands and fingers pointing down like Frankenstein.

"I'm fond of the name, too!" she said. "It's catchy and short! Women will know right away that this is where they can get their nails done!"

"Well, I think it's highly inappropriate," my dad said as he impatiently sat in a perfect blue chair waiting for my mom's manicure. "It's too suggestive."

"What on earth, Dale? Why would you say such a thing? Don't listen to him, Katherine. And I just love how you've drawn the sign! It looks like it was written with red nail polish!"

It pleased me that prudes like my dad might blush over the salon's name. Customers who might have been turned off by the name *Get Nailed* could go a block down the street to *Nail Knowledge* and speak their English slowly.

I knew Keith was crazy about me, but there was a sticking point.

"Kate, I can't be with someone who drinks."

"I understand."

"I just wanted to be honest about it. I hope you know I don't judge you, but I just can't be around that ever again."

I decided to stop drinking. Cold turkey. I make it sound so easy, don't I? I missed the good buzz every now and then, I really did, but I'll tell you the toughest thing was giving up the smoking. I'd go a few weeks, then sneak one and feel guilty about it. It tasted so good, I doubted I'd ever be able to quit. And since I had one, I figured I might as well have a few more. After sucking five cigarettes in one night, I was ready to renew my Cigarette Fast. But a week later I went to an AA meeting with Keith and when we came out there were some guys leaning against the wall smoking. I just had to have another one. But after throwing my phone into my purse and punching the steering wheel about ten times, I finally quit for good.

I'd been back in St. George for about six months when Keith proposed. I'd sat facing him at the El Chihuahua restaurant on a bench seat covered in clear plastic when he popped the question. Well, he sort of popped it. It was the "We ought to get married" sort of line that was designed to sweep me off my feet. Keith, for all his virtues, had never been a hopeless romantic. I was now two for two in the elaborate proposal department.

"Are you proposing?" I asked.

"Yeah."

I took a sip from the straw of my Diet Coke and looked down at the paper placemat. "I'm still married, remember? I never got a divorce."

"Can't you just call him? He has no reason to jerk you around. Not after all this time."

"You don't know Ricky. I'm not even sure how to find him."

"But you'll try?"

"Yes."

"So does that mean . . .?"

"Yeah, Keith, that's what it means. But let's not tell anyone until I figure out how to get divorced first."

And so it was that Mrs. Ricky Waters became engaged to her old high school flame Keith Murphy.

It didn't take long for me to track down Ricky. Now that Victor Spanos was dead, Ricky was back to his old self—working the tables and the women of Vegas. I'd often wondered how many times he'd cheated on me—how many times he'd used that You're-the-most-beautiful-woman-I've-ever-seen line that he'd used on me. Probably a lot.

"Ricky, it's me. Kate."

"Whoa, I didn't expect to hear from you. I tried to call you a few months after Spanos got murdered, but you'd left. Where are you anyway?"

"I moved back to St. George."

"Really? That little hick town? You all right?"

"I'm fine. Thanks for your concern."

"By the way, I've forgiven you for the way you treated me at that dump in Pahrump. We ought to get together again sometime."

"Actually, Ricky, I never want to see you again. But it's awfully big of you to forgive me."

He was quiet on the phone. I think I'd thrown him for a loop because most women give Ricky what he wants. "Then why are you calling me?"

"I want a divorce and was hoping you won't make it difficult."

"Oh, so now you want a favor from me?"

"Ricky, we aren't married. You know that. You took off and left me four years ago. I want to get my life back and I can't do that if we're still technically married."

"Let me guess. You want to marry someone else but you can't as long as we're married."

"Yeah, actually that's part of it."

"That's classic, Kate. You want me to just sign it over to save you the time and money of lawyers and court and all that shit."

"If you'll just sign a waiver, we can both do this quick and cheap."

"Are you going to pay me alimony?"

"Come on, Ricky, don't jerk me around. Can I just send you something to sign?"

"Yeah, I'll sign it."

"Thanks," I said.

"For five grand."

"What? Don't do this Ricky. Don't be a jerk."

"I had to pay Spanos another five thousand just before he was murdered. It's the only way I could come back to Vegas and get my life back. He said it was for all the medical bills."

"That was your debt, Ricky, not mine. I paid most of it anyway."

"I'm not going to fight about it, Kate. Send me five grand and I'll sign it. Otherwise, you can go fuck yourself. If I'm not mistaken, that's the last thing you told me to do out there in Pahrump."

"Let me be crystal clear, Ricky. Hell will freeze over before I give you another penny. Did you hear me? Not another penny."

"No?"

"You're pathetic, Ricky. Pathetic."

"It's funny hearing that from a hooker."

"Go to hell, Ricky."

"So, you're sending the check?"

"Not a fucking dime. I'd rather pay it to my lawyer. And I'll forewarn him that you'll probably run and hide from him, too."

He was furious, hurling insults which only grazed me, darting around me like a school of fish. He was mid-rant when I hung up.

It cost me two thousand dollars in legal fees to finally get my legal freedom from Ricky Waters. It would have been more but Ricky didn't have enough money to hire a lawyer. It was the best two grand I ever spent.

You can always reflect on the what ifs in life. Everyone does it. You know, the whole "If I'd only known then what I know now" bit. One thing is quite clear, however; I never would have allowed myself to fall for Ricky in the first place. I would have run from him as fast as I could. Most divorced couples could say the same thing but they'd probably begrudgingly admit there had been at least *some* good that came from their marriage—perhaps a child, for example. And yet, when I look back on my relationship with Ricky, the only happy time that comes to mind is our initial courtship when Ricky deceptively revved up his charm offensive.

We were in Keith's seldom-used kitchen when he announced he had a big surprise for me. He wrapped a dish towel around my eyes and led me by the elbow through his living room and out the front door to his porch. The screen door slammed behind us.

"I wanted to buy something to celebrate our engagement," he said as he untied the dish towel. "I hope you like it."

It was parked in the driveway with a large bow on the side.

"A boat?"

"Yeah, you like it? It's a Sea Ray and it'd be perfect for water skiing and just cruising around. We can take it to Sand Hollow whenever we want."

"Thanks, I really like it." And just like that, our engagement started off without the blunt honesty I'd promised myself. I could have been more truthful if there'd been a new Mustang in the driveway.

48

KEITH & KATHERINE

THEY STOPPED KATHERINE'S CHEMO because it wasn't doing any good. Seems modern science couldn't fix it, we prayed because there was the feeling that we should do *something* rather than just sit back and watch her waste away. Our kids honestly believed she'd get better if they prayed because we'd always taught them that God knows when people are sick and He'll step in if you ask Him, so why *wouldn't* they believe? They had pure faith too, without an ounce of cynicism or disbelief. That ought to be enough, right? I mean, what more could God expect from them? Unfortunately, I'd come to see that faith and reason are frequently out of rhythm. After all, if faith and prayers worked as well as advertised, everyone would quickly get better and no one would die. But we kept praying despite the dismal track record. It beat doing nothing.

This was mostly about Katherine, of course, but there were symptoms we all had to endure, and they were everywhere. I wallowed in self-pity because this hit close to home, bulls-eye close. Anyone who has been in my position could probably relate. I felt so helpless. And here's a very small thing on top of everything else that I didn't dare mention to Katherine (and I'm slightly embarrassed to mention now), but I got the worst sunburn of my life on my shaved scalp.

Katherine was no longer in control of her body. Then again, who really has control of their body? No one tells their heart to keep beating. No one tells their cells exactly what they're supposed to be doing. Do you even know what a proton looks like, or what it does? So why did her cells misfire and not mine? And who told them how to fire in the first place? If God was really in control of every cell and lymph node why did He allow hers to go haywire? Heck, for all I know, maybe He's the one who issued the order. But why in the world would a loving God do that? I knew this was a lousy time to start questioning my faith, and I only did it sparingly, but as Katherine's weight sunk below one hundred pounds my faith occasionally misfired, too.

Katherine insisted on keeping up the house and I don't know how she did it. A wave of nausea would hit while she was helping with algebra homework, or between loads of laundry. She'd bend over in pain and the kids would look at me with a horrified look, like I should *do* something. Was she going to die right in front of them at that very moment?

I kept praying non-stop but there was a subtle change to my pleas, one I hoped was less pestering of God and therefore more likely to be considered. I switched from begging Him to cure her to humbly asking for the strength to cope. I hoped there was nothing unreasonably selfish in that sort of plea—no groveling which might have come across as off-putting to God. And all the while I tried not to be angry at Him because I still held out hope that He might help me and I didn't want to upset Him. But it was hard to express a great deal of thanks because what good was God if He wouldn't help with this, of all things?

I found Katherine in our room, sitting up in bed, writing letters to each of our kids. The pages were crinkled messes from her tears. I couldn't bear to read them. Here I was, the one-armed father of six kids who'd barely graduated from high school. I had to fight the feeling that Katherine's death would somehow be partially my fault—a personal punishment for one or more of my failures. But I'd tried my best. Katherine was Katherine—gorgeous, smart, capable, and funny. This incredible woman had married *me*—frumpy and balding me. I wasn't smart, or sexy, or rich. I wasn't very handy around the house either. Heck, I couldn't even pound a nail in the wall to hang a picture with one hand or thread a marshmallow on a s'mores stick, much less a needle. But I know how much she loved me. And I swear to God I loved her more than any guy has ever loved a woman.

It was late August and hot. Hospice workers told us it wouldn't be long before she passed. Passed to what, and to where? I hoped she'd pass straight to heaven because that's where she belonged. But I didn't *know*, because who can really know these things? Who has ever been to heaven to file a report about the place?

Katherine couldn't have weighed more than eighty pounds and she was only taking a sip or two of water. The kids walked around the house in a daze. They looked at me like I should rescue the situation, like I should know what to do. But their look also registered the dawning realization that their mom was actually going to die and I couldn't fix it, that nobody could. Not even God, apparently.

I couldn't be mad at Katherine, of course, because this is not something she wanted. It wasn't something she chose. She was dying out of order and leaving me behind to comfort our kids. That's the way *she* looked at me—a look that said she was counting on me. Exactly how was I supposed to do that when all I wanted to do was throw myself down on the floor and sob? But I couldn't. I needed to be strong for my kids. They watched me. They needed me. This was impossible for them but at least they still had their dad. So I was there and only in private did I cry so hard I thought I'd never stop. My thirty-eight-year-old wife was dying and I was complaining about how bad it was for me. Well, it was. It was awful.

Visitors tip-toed in to say their last goodbyes and then backed away to whisper to others in the room. They whispered things like "How's she doing?" and "How're you holding up?" They said we were in their prayers. They said to call them if I needed anything. It's just what you say. Thoughts and prayers when there is nothing else to offer, nothing that will actually fix it.

Some of Katherine's old high school friends came by. They faked being upbeat as they reminisced about the good old days. Janet told her she'd report back on their twenty-year high school reunion the following week and Sandra shot her a look because we knew Katherine probably wouldn't make it until then.

My dad fell apart. Yeah, my dad. All his life he'd played this gruff role of his. My father-in-law, Dale, was the same way. And my poor mother-in-law, Jackie, was inconsolable. All she'd say was that she was sorry she wasn't more help.

Maybe it's in bad taste that I tell you about Dale and Jackie's final moments with their daughter because there's probably nothing more private than that. Jackie was unable to speak. She sat on the edge of the hospital bed they'd wheeled into our house a month earlier. Her whole body shook. I'd never seen Dale cry but he was sobbing too, loudly and without shame. We'd both given her healing blessings but they hadn't seemed to help. And now he insisted it'd been God's will all along, that this was the proper order of things despite the hardship and despair, because he had nothing else to hold on to.

Katherine's youngest sister, Kylie, rotated between smiles and tears. She'd never seen someone die, none of us had. Our family poodle had died ten years earlier and we'd consoled the kids by promising them that Gretchen was in heaven and we'd see her again. Are you sure? they'd asked. Of course, we're sure. I'd winced a bit when I'd made the promise about Gretchen because, come on, how could I know we'd see our dog again in heaven? Did dogs even go there? And if so, how would we find her up there among the billions of dead dogs. She hadn't even been buried with her collar. Then we got a new dog and the kids tended to forget. I was now promising them the same thing about their mom. But this time I forced myself to know it *had* to be true. It just had to.

I knelt down by the side of the hospital bed now parked in our living room next to the IV drip, the sofa and coffee table having been shoved to the corner. A few of our kids hovered nearby and the others who couldn't bear it spied on us from a distance. I lifted her upper body with my right arm and pulled her close. She opened her eyes because she knew it was me. She didn't say a thing; just stared at me. I knew what she was thinking though. She was thinking about her loss, and my loss, and the kids' loss. She was willing me to be there for our kids. She was begging me to be the humongous father figure in their lives, so big that maybe I could somehow compensate for her absence. I tried to communicate the look that she needed to see from me. There was no deceit in the look either, just broken-hearted resolve.

I laid her back down and stroked her head with my only hand. She closed her eyes for the final time.

I tried to feel her the moment she died. Was she still in the room? Was she watching us, aware of us, trying to talk to us? I could lie and say I felt her hand on my shoulder, or heard her whisper encouragement, but I didn't. Her body was still there, but it wasn't Katherine. The shrunken body looked about the same but Katherine was suddenly and permanently gone.

It was Monday afternoon, September 3rd. Labor Day.

49

KATE

KEITH LOVED THE BOAT. Actually, I think he was in love with it, which is much worse. I put my foot down when he started talking about getting married on it. I didn't need the Ritz, and just about anything would be better than the *Si, Como No*, but bobbing out in the middle of Sand Hollow reservoir with an orange life-jacket over my dress?

I didn't even know why we had to get married. Most people in our town got married to have sex, but that seemed like a pretty stupid reason to me. Geez, if that were so compelling I'd have about two thousand husbands by now. But Keith really wanted to so, si, como no.

We held the glitzy affair in Keith's backyard. He mowed the lawn and bought a gazebo from Home Depot that he'd hauled over in his truck and plopped into the corner of the yard next to the fence. We said our I Do's surrounded by the smell of freshly cut plywood and redwood stain. A string of Christmas lights hung around the patio, plugged in next to the grill and propane tank. It was pretty fancy.

I'd thought about inviting some old friends like Cinnamon, Fantasee, and Candy, but then envisioned them strutting up in their tight miniskirts and war paint, their five-inch heels aerating the back lawn. Cinnamon would've demanded to know where the GDB was, and because this was a dry wedding we didn't have a goddamned bar. My little brothers would've been in hog heaven with their tongues hanging out and their hands stuffed into their front pockets, but my parents would have been stupefied. *What on earth . . .?*

A week later, Keith insisted we go to our twenty-year high school reunion as newly minted husband and wife. You can probably imagine how *that* went.

"Katherine? Katherine Coombs? Is that you? Omigosh! It's me, Sandra!" A matronly woman stood before me with a name tag stuck to the lapel of her blue polyester pantsuit. The name tag read "Sandra Webb Young." There is no way I would have recognized her without the name tag. No way. Her hair was graying and the tight curls were cropped short like fleece around her plump face. Her breasts were still huge, even more so. I remember in high school how jealous I'd been because they'd practically popped the buttons of her pep club uniform, but no ordinary bra could hold them now—they would've popped the straps off a straitjacket.

"Sandra! Hi!" I said. "You look great!" and then I felt like a complete idiot for publicly broadcasting such an obvious fib.

"Thanks, you too. I've gained a little weight, but that's what five kids'll do!"

I saw Keith out of the corner of my eye hanging out with other proud ex-football players as they embellished their career highlights at Dixie High, reliving their lives in past tense. They looked like they'd all peaked in high school and had now pretty much thrown in the towel, except Keith who, I must say, looked quite handsome.

"So, what've you been up to?" Sandra asked.

"Oh, you know, just doing my thing."

"Janet said she saw you in Las Vegas on her way to a game show a few years back. She said you were working at a casino."

"Yeah, I just came back a little over a year ago."

"And did I hear right that you just got married to Keith Murphy?" She looked around for him. "Oh, there he is. Omigosh, do you remember our talks when you two were dating? Can you believe it's been *twenty years?*" She moved in for a second hug which felt good. She turned to a huddle of others. "Look you guys! It's Katherine Coombs!"

So there we were—the prostitute and the alcoholic who'd reconnected at a brothel.

I also saw the girl who'd become a quad our senior year when the cheerleader dropped her on her head. She had been so athletic, so pretty, so full of energy and life. But in an instant it had all changed. Now she was small and shrunken in her electric-powered wheelchair. She wore comfortable sweat pants and an orange beanie on her head. When I say the sweats were comfortable, I am projecting a bit because she probably couldn't feel if they were comfortable or not. Everyone knew her and her tragic story, of course they did, but I noticed not many people approached her. That included me. Maybe it was because I didn't know what to say and it was awkward so I avoided her. It occurred to me that I was like this quadriplegic in a small way because I had changed tribes and many of my ex-classmates avoided me, too.

I'm glad I went though. I saw so many ex-classmates I hadn't seen since high school and would probably never see again. There was Danny Martin, a boy I dated a few times who had blossomed into a heavyset produce manager at Safeway, and his plump wife. Her withering look dared me to give it another go with her husband. And there was Mike Sorensen who no one remembered from high school but had become a smashing success in the new world of computer gizmos. No one had given him the time of day until he got rich and now he was the toast of the town, hopping from cluster to cluster to be admired for his good fortune. But Adolph Mortensen *wasn't* there and I presume it may have had something to do with his name. The kids in high school alternately teased and feared him. His parents must have been either incredibly insensitive or just plain cruel to saddle him with a name like Adolph.

I'm sure there were plenty of whispers about Katherine Coombs that night. I no longer looked and dressed like they did, the vast majority of whom had morphed into their parents and remained devout in the faith. My appearance alone was compelling evidence that I'd lost my testimony in the true church, which was a lot to whisper about right there. "How about that dress she wore, huh?" "I'm with you; I thought it was totally inappropriate." "And did you see the way she practically shoved her breasts into my husband Blaine? I hardly even knew what to *say* to her." There were probably a few rumors that I had bulimia, too.

So, yeah, they'd probably judged me about as much as I judged them. I'd been weighing people on my scale for as long as I can remember but now I'd become tired of all the ranking, all the judging. She's too obnoxious. He's too fat. She's too skinny. He's too this, and she's too that. I assume these former friends and classmates wanted to step on my scale about as much as I wanted to step on theirs.

And here's something else I'm tired of. I'm tired of trying so hard to be pretty, and thin, and attractive to everyone else. I'm tired of having poison injected into my forehead and painfully removing every single solitary hair from my body. I'm tired of dieting to the point of misery, nibbling on salads and celery instead of the carrot cake. I'm also tired of outsourcing my beliefs to others and fearing my parent's judgment. I'm done with people trying to tame me and guilting me into believing their shit. I'm as tired of my own cage as I am of criticizing everyone else's. I'm finally ready to call a truce.

Monday, September 3rd was Labor Day and the weather was perfect. Keith insisted we all go boating that afternoon. We invited Karolyn and Kylie to join us. Karolyn had become a stunning twenty-three-year-old who was *still* frightfully unwilling to settle down as a homemaker. There remained subtle leftovers from her childhood speech impediment: "I'd love to go but can we thop by Thears on the way? I need to return a thirt I bought there."

Kylie wore a yellow one-piece swimming suit that was at least two sizes too small and didn't flatter her plump seventeen-year-old frame. She sat in the front of the boat, holding onto her large floppy hat with one hand and raising a stick with an orange plastic flag atop it whenever anyone was in the water.

"Anybody else wanna go for a spin?" Keith asked. "Last chance before we head home."

"Why don't you go, Keith," I said. "I can drive."

"Yeah, you go!" Kylie yelled too loudly.

"Come on, Keith," said Karolyn. "Thow us your thuff."

"Yeah, show us your stuff. It's not that hard," said Kylie, who'd never once been in the water to my knowledge.

"All right, you asked for it," said Keith. He pulled on a wet life jacket and complained about the cold. He took the orange ski rope from under the seat, tied the end to the back of the boat, and tossed the tangled slack into the water. He picked up the slalom ski and threw it into the water next to the floating rope where it landed with a splat. "Okay, here goes nothing," he said and dove into the cold water.

"Take out the slack nice and slow!" he yelled up to me.

When the rope was fairly taut, Keith yelled "Hit it!" and I thrust the throttle down with my right hand. The boat fought Keith's drag but finally pulled him out of the water. He teetered at first and then regained his balance long enough to release one hand from the rope's handle to wave at us. We all laughed when he wiped out and everyone in the boat told me I should turn around to get him, something that had never occurred to me.

I made a wide arc and swung back around. "Wanna go again?" I hollered over the noise of the engine and the lapping water.

"Lean back a little more," said Karolyn. "And keep your arms thraighter."

"Yeah, lean back," said Kylie.

"All right, I'll give it another shot."

I pulled the boat around to where I thought the rope was fairly straight in the water. Keith was busy untangling a loop of rope a few feet in front of him. I didn't realize at the time that the rope was looped around his left arm just under the surface of the water. I put the boat in gear, just enough to keep the slack to a minimum.

I was looking forward when I thought I heard Keith yell "Hit it!" I put my hand on the throttle and was about to slam it forward.

"Wait, Kafrun! Don't go!" It was Kylie who had turned around with her flag held high in the air. "Keef said, 'Hold it,' so you can't go yet."

I turned around to see Keith still fussing with a knot in the rope. He finally unwound it and the rope floated free in front of him.

"Okay," he yelled. "Hit it!"

50

KEITH & KATHERINE

WE HELD THE FUNERAL at our church three days after Labor Day. The chapel filled up first and then they had to remove the portable wall that separates the chapel from the gymnasium. It was packed, too—hundreds of people holding funeral programs and wads of Kleenex. A banquet table was set at the door to the chapel which Kimberly had stocked with Katherine memorabilia. There were photos from our wedding and one with Jenna on Katherine's shoulders from a hike we took years ago. There were others of Katherine standing next to Bob Barker and all of us on the Special K. There was also her Homecoming Queen sash and the misshapen afghan she'd crocheted for me.

The photo of Katherine on the front of the program was my favorite picture of her. I'd taken it years earlier when she'd been on her hands and knees in the living room, carrying two kids on her back while a third one was trying to climb on. She was looking up at the camera, head slightly cocked. The look on her face was priceless. It was the look that said *What on earth have we done, Keith? But it doesn't get better than this, does it?* It's the look I'll cherish and never forget.

My oldest daughter, Jenna, was openly sobbing. I wanted to comfort her, but how? Tell her mom was coming back? Tell her it would be okay when she knew it wouldn't? Katherine's youngest sister, Kylie, had been sitting a few pews away but got up and wedged herself next to us. She put her arm around Jenna and reminded her that Kafrun was up in heaven, so she didn't need to cry.

The speakers all promised that we'd see Katherine again. They said it with such conviction, like, duh, of course we would. They promised that if we hung in there until we were also dead then we'd all be reunited in heaven. This promise was a stretch. How many dead people had they talked to? Had they been given a special VIP tour of the place? I wanted to believe it too, of course I did. In fact, I wanted to believe it so much that I demanded that it *must* be true. And maybe that was enough.

I wish that Katherine could have been there to hear the amazing things they said about her. She deserved at least that. Then again, maybe she was. At least that's the way I've always thought it would be, or at least the way it ought to be—looking down on my own funeral at all the weepers telling each other how amazing I'd been. In Katherine's case it would have all been true.

I lined up with my sons to carry their mom's casket. They wore hand-me-down suits that didn't quite fit and their shoes were scuffed. I thought of Katherine looking down at us and bawling her eyes out as she watched her sons carrying her casket. She probably would've said, "For crying out loud, Keith, would it have killed you to make sure their shoes were shined?" But, really, do you think anybody cared one iota about their shoes?

After the funeral service, we loaded the casket into the hearse and drove slowly to the cemetery on the other end of town. The line for Katherine was led by two policemen on their motorcycles and stretched three and a half blocks. For a simple woman like Katherine, it was the finest escort I'd ever seen. I wish she could've seen that, too.

We stood in the hot St. George sun surrounding the casket that sat next to the hole partially covered by a piece of green Astroturf. One by one, we removed our corsages and placed them on top of the casket. After one more prayer, the friends and neighbors drifted away until there was no one left but me and my kids. We couldn't leave. It was inconceivable that we would leave Katherine there. I saw the cemetery worker check his watch out of the corner of my eye. I gathered up my numb and devastated kids and we walked down the slope of lawn to Katherine's minivan, clinging to each other like a rugby scrum. We piled into the minivan without the usual fights about who would sit where. I noticed no one sat in the front seat as we slowly pulled away.

I don't have much to be proud of in my life except for Katherine and my kids. I pretty much won at life despite my average looks, intelligence, and below-average education. I won at life because of Katherine. I try not to be bitter that the best thing in my life was now gone. I try not to be jealous of anyone who still has someone, but it's hard. When Katherine died I lost most of me—all the good stuff, all the happiness and joy. People think that I'm okay now, that I'm getting over it. But I'm not. I remember what it was like to be normal, so I do an impression of that for others. When Katherine was dying, I tried to be brave for her, you know, put a face on and try to be positive. But then I'd break down and she would have to comfort me. I couldn't even give her that, for even when she was dying she was still on duty. She was still on duty looking after me.

Time heals all wounds, or so they say. It's been a few years now and I've yet to see evidence of it. I suppose it's better than it was, in those first two years when it was all I could think about. I can go three or four hours at a time now before it hits me: Katherine is really dead. But I go on, for Katherine and for my kids. I will put on the face and do my impression. It's all I can do.

51

JENNA

I WAS UPSET WITH MY DAD when he first started dating. I didn't care that it'd been over a year since my mom died of cancer. I know my dad wasn't being disloyal to mom or anything, but it still bugged me.

"I'm sorry, Jenna," he'd said to me. "But mom is gone."

"You don't think I know that? Go on dates if you have to but just don't act all excited about it. It's embarrassing." In truth, my dad hadn't acted overly excited about it at all. The women in his ward tried to line him up with every single woman in the church, making it their mission to get him remarried. They thought they were doing him a favor and perhaps they weren't completely wrong. There was one woman in particular who was as lonely as my dad and encouraged the relationship. My dad basically went along with it.

"I will always love mom," he said, "but I'm lonely and want to find some happiness with a partner like I did with mom."

"Gol, she isn't even that pretty. Mom was way prettier. And I hate her kids." I know that was a mean thing to say, about her not being pretty and all, but it was true. Course, my dad was no knockout either. It was also true that her kids were total nerds.

Everyone always said I looked just like my mom and sometimes I'd catch my dad looking at me with this look—like he'd seen my mom in me for a split second. Then he'd smile and I knew why, but even his smile was sad.

So, yeah, I gave my dad a rough time over dating. But it's not like he was gaga over who I was dating either. This guy was popular and everything—the captain of the football team and all that. My dad said that was overrated. In fact, he told me he'd been the captain of his high school football team too, which was hard to believe. My dad a jock? Course, maybe he was because my mom was drop dead in high school—I'd seen their yearbook. There's no way she would have gone out with him based only on looks. I know I'm being hard on my dad here, but you should've seen my mom in high school.

I know they had to get married and I'm not quite sure how to feel about it. I hope they really loved each other back then and didn't get married only because they had to. Don't get me wrong, I'm happy to be alive, but I'm sure they went through hell when my mom got pregnant. You'd have to know my Grandpa Coombs. I bet he scared the bejesus out of my poor dad back then. I still think he's scary and he's, like, seventy now.

All I saw growing up was how much my dad worshiped my mom. You could just tell. I hope my mom always knew that about him. I wish she could have seen him raising us, too. She would have loved him even more, but I bet she would've rolled her eyes at how lousy he was with our hair.

I was still living at home on my twenty-first birthday (please don't think I was a loser). I'd been out that night and got home late. When I walked into my bedroom, I saw a red envelope resting on my pillow. It was a birthday card. *Jenna* was written on the envelope in my mom's almost extinct handwriting. It jolted me at first. I sat on the bed and stared at my mom's writing, then opened the envelope.

Dearest Jenna,
I asked Dad to leave you this birthday card on your 21st birthday. I am so sorry I couldn't be with you today but I promise I'm there in spirit. Just close your eyes and think of me. I'm there.

Did you know that you are my favorite person in the entire world? What a lucky mom I was to have you. I am so sorry I had to leave you. I've had moments of self-pity but I wouldn't have traded my life for all the money in the world because I had you.
I love you forever and always.
Mom

My dad must've heard me crying because the next thing I knew he was sitting next to me on the bed and we sobbed together, his stump resting on my shoulder. My dad. If there was a more amazing dad than him, I'd like to know who he was. He was there for everything. I'd see him walking the sidelines at all my soccer games with his empty sleeve swinging at his side. I didn't give him enough credit for going to every single Back to School and Parent Teachers by himself. And he made sure we were all there in church on Sundays, lousy braids and all. I probably ought to cut him some slack because it must be hard to do hair with one hand. He was a bawl baby, too. It was embarrassing when we were ready to go to a school dance and there'd be my dad, standing in the kitchen bawling with a dish towel covering his face. Nope, there is no one on earth I love more than my dad.

I went through a bunch of boyfriends, comparing all of them to him. None stacked up. They were cuter and wore clothes that weren't nearly as dorky, but my dad made me feel like I was the coolest girl in the world. Right before she died, my mom told me to hold out for someone like my dad. "You may not realize it now," she'd said, "but your dad is the most amazing man on earth."

I finally found someone who comes close. We got married about a year ago, right after my twenty-third birthday. My dad walked me down the aisle, sobbing the whole way, and then sat by himself on the front row next to where my mom was supposed to be. I know he would have given his other arm too if my mom could've been there with him for just that one night. He told me he pictured her in the dress she would've fussed about for months. She would have bought it one size too small and then gone on one of her crazy diets for three weeks.

I think about my mom every single day. We would have hashed out the details of my wedding for hours at a time, a wedding my dad paid for with who knows what without saying a thing. She would have bawled her eyes out over how handsome my brothers were in their tuxes, and my dance with the one-armed hero of my life.

My mom and I would have poured over my wedding album and all the photos. But the photo that would've made her the happiest isn't in a photo album. It's sitting on the nightstand next to my bed. I'm standing in my wedding dress with a smile. My smile is nearly as big as the one on the face of the chubby twenty-three-year old with coke-bottle glasses and small teeth standing next to me. My arm is wrapped around Kylie, my radiant Maid of Honor.

Made in the USA
Monee, IL
25 April 2023

32418806R00308